W9-BSF-449

The Nibelungenlied

Translated and with
an Introduction and Notes by
D. G. Mowatt

DOVER PUBLICATIONS, INC.
Mineola, New York

Published in Canada by General Publishing Company, Ltd., 30 Lesmill Road, Don Mills, Toronto, Ontario.

Bibliographical Note

This Dover edition, first published in 2001, is an unabridged reprint of the translation by D. G. Mowatt, originally published by J. M. Dent & Sons Ltd., London, in 1962.

Library of Congress Cataloging-in-Publication Data

Nibelungenlied. English.
  The Nibelungenlied / translated and with an introduction and notes by D.G. Mowatt.
    p. cm.
  ISBN 0-486-41414-0 (pbk.)
    1. Mowatt, D. G. II. Title.

PT1579.A3 A6 2001
831'.21—dc21

00-049418

Manufactured in the United States of America
Dover Publications, Inc., 31 East 2nd Street, Mineola, N.Y. 11501

INTRODUCTION

THE *Nibelungenlied* has on occasion been compared to the *Iliad*. The fact that Germans have been impelled to make, and foreigners disposed to deride, such a comparison, is revealing in itself, for it shows the veneration both works have suffered. Assessment of their literary merit has been geographically conditioned, with Homer belonging to western civilization as a whole, and the *Nibelungenlied* for the most part only to Germany. But in both cases scholars have painstakingly erected a barrier between heritage and inheritors. The occasional whiff of vanished glory that came over has been made to serve the literary and political establishment. The interesting circumstance that both works deal with events and customs that must have appeared exotic, if not bizarre, to their authors, is not emphasized. The suggestion that the virtues of our Achaean or Germanic ancestors could have been held up to bardic ridicule is discouraged. And yet they obviously are. Agamemnon, as Robert Graves points out in the introduction to his recent translation, *The Anger of Achilles* (Cassell, 1959), is completely out of his depth throughout most of the *Iliad*. What poet, after all, would wish to identify himself with a bloodthirsty, conceited and obstinate king, who is not successful even by his own standards, and eventually comes to a sticky end? And the career of King Gunther in the *Nibelungenlied* is no more exemplary. Like Agamemnon, he is killed in ignominious circumstances, by a woman. Admittedly she is only his sister. But his wife shows little respect for his kingly person either: she removes him from their conjugal bed on the first night, and hangs him on a convenient nail till morning. It seems that the whole concept of royal infallibility was at least questionable in the eyes of these two poets.

The *Nibelungenlied* goes further in this direction than Homer, and the efforts of its scholarly guardians not to notice the fact have been correspondingly stronger. Unfortunately, the increase in narrative detachment seems to have involved a deterioration in traditional clichés, so that the recitals of bloody deeds and barbaric splendours are even more perfunctory in the

Nibelungenlied than in the *Iliad*. Stripped of its irony, the *Nibelungenlied* is tedious in the extreme, and can only be taken seriously by someone in desperate need of a heroic past. The blond Germanic beast marching bravely towards his fate is not to everyone's taste. Nor, for that matter, is the hidebound medieval court, obsessed with power and protocol. As long as these two elements were kept isolated, and regarded with bovine earnestness, the *Nibelungenlied* was guaranteed a cool reception by most people, and in most ages. It was offered, and rejected, as a work extolling two self-contradictory orthodoxies, neither of which is very interesting in itself. Luckily, however, orthodoxies are seldom sacred in literature and the *Nibelungenlied* is no exception to this rule. Positions are certainly taken up in the work, but they clash, sometimes comically, sometimes tragically, and very little is left of any of them at the end (cf. stanzas 2377–8). The particular pretensions chosen for undermining were historically conditioned. Instead of Trafalgar, the sanctity of the home and the royal family, for instance, they had their heroic past, the sanctity of woman and an ideal of courtly behaviour. Instead of the hydrogen bomb, or sex, they had mythical figures like Sifrid and Brünnhilde on which to focus their hopes and fears.

Much work has been devoted to finding out something about the author, and the literary tradition in which he worked. (This mass of research is entertainingly reviewed, with original contributions, by Fr. Panzer, *Das Nibelungenlied* (Stuttgart, 1955). There is also an exhaustive account in English, *The Study of the Nibelungenlied*, by Mary Thorp (Oxford, 1940). The yield is meagre: he was an unknown poet, probably of knightly (i.e. unexceptionable) status, writing at the turn of the twelfth and thirteenth centuries. He was probably Austrian, and may have worked for a certain Bishop of Passau. He must have known earlier versions of parts (perhaps the whole) of the material he was using, because variations on the same characters and situations are found scattered throughout Scandinavian and German literature. Any attempt to achieve greater precision on this score must be speculative. All the Scandinavian sources are later than the *Nibelungenlied*, although parts of them must be based on much earlier material. (Panzer even argues that one of them was directly influenced by the *Nibelungenlied*). In Germany there is the *Hildebrandslied* (written down at Fulda in the ninth century), which treats the story of Dietrich, Hildebrand and his son in archaic and highly idiosyncratic language. It is possible that the *Nibelungenlied* poet was familiar with a version of this poem, but if so he made no use of it. The Walther story referred to by Hildebrand in stanza 2344 is similarly unexploited, apart from this one mention.

The truth is there are no immediate sources; and those who need something to compare with the finished product have been reduced to reconstructing earlier versions for themselves. The process is circular, and the result unverifiable. Heusler's edifice (*Nibelungensage und Nibelungenlied*; Dortmund, 1922, second edition) was admired for a while, but is now generally regarded as oversimplified. It seems reasonably certain that there were in existence a number of short episodic lays clustering round such figures as Sifrid, Brünnhilde, Dietrich, Hagen and Kriemhilde; and perhaps an extended narrative treating the downfall of the Burgundians. Nothing is established for these works beyond the bare probability of their existence.

The ultimate sources of the *Nibelungenlied* are much easier to discern. They are: legend (from a heroic past in the fourth to sixth centuries), chivalry (an orthodoxy from the twelfth and thirteenth centuries) and myth. The wars and great migrations following the advent of the Huns in eastern Europe threw up legendary heroes like Theoderic (Dietrich) of Verona, Hildebrand, Hagen and Gundaharius (Gunther), King of the Burgundians. Some of these men actually existed, as Theoderic, who ruled over Italy from 493 to 526, and Gundaharius, whose kingdom by the Rhine was in fact destroyed by the Huns (though not under Attila) in 435. Others, like Hildebrand, are just prototypes of the Germanic fighting hero. These figures carry their legendary past with them, and their social unit is the family or tribe, As might be expected from their origins, there is often something of the landless knight or exile about them, especially when heroic exploits are involved. But the details of their dress, speech, eating and courting habits, public rituals and, in the case of Rüdeger at least, of their moral preoccupations, are taken from medieval courtly society. These details constitute the second, or chivalric, element. The third, or mythological, element is embodied in figures like Sifrid, Brünnhilde and Alberich the dwarf, who stand out as belonging to no society at all, as being in some way subhuman or superhuman.

So much for the ingredients. The mixture seems to have gone down well, to judge from the number of manuscripts which have survived, and it is not difficult to see why. Past greatness, present pretensions and the possibility of rejuvenation (or destruction) from outside—this is a combination which must exercise a perpetual fascination for all self-conscious societies. It is true that an expansive community may believe for short periods that sophistication is an irreversible process; but recent history has shown how easily the most complex network of relationships can be reduced to primitive posturing, given the right circumstances. And this is exactly what happens in the *Nibelungenlied*, where a highly developed society reverts under strain.

We are shown, first of all, the court at Worms. It is presided over by the brothers Gunther, Gernot and Giselher, and actually run by Hagen. Everyone knows his place, and there are set procedures for every situation. They are, on the whole, a tedious and complacent company. Their sister Kriemhilde is outwardly an exemplary Burgundian lady, but she shows signs of being self-willed about her emotional life (stanza 17), and has an ominous future foretold for her (stanza 14).

The court at Santen is much the same. As at Worms, the homogeneity extends to the names Sigebert and Sigelinde, but their son Sifrid is even more of a misfit than Gunther's sister. Not only is his name wrong (just as Kriemhilde refuses to alliterate with her brothers), but he has a rather unorthodox past. As we later learn from Hagen, he is invulnerable, has slain a dragon and owns a magic treasure.

The court at Isenstein, by contrast, is dominated by a single remarkable woman, determined to rely on her own strength until the right man arrives. Her demands are quite simple: he must be the best (i.e. the strongest and bravest) man available. This is not perhaps so very different from the standard applied at Worms, where the king is by definition endowed with both these qualities. But the really anti-social thing about Brünnhilde is that she insists on putting royal pretensions to the test, and killing all the mighty monarchs who fail. She is a challenge to people like Gunther to justify their title. Of course Gunther himself is no fool, and would never dream of exposing himself to such a blast of reality; but the arrival of Sifrid opens up new possibilities. Here, suddenly, is a man who equates kingship with conquest (stanzas 108 ff.), just like Brünnhilde, and who is eminently capable of meeting the challenge. Moreover he wants to marry Gunther's sister, and is prepared to go to any lengths to do so. Presented with this happy circumstance, it is an easy matter for the practised diplomat to manipulate Sifrid into satisfying all Brünnhilde's demands incognito, leaving all the credit, and the tangible prize, to Gunther. There is the rather intimate question of the bed, but after that has been solved and hushed up the glory of Burgundy seems assured.

The thing which destroys the foundations, if not at first the complacency of Worms, is the tension between inflated appearance and mean reality. The qualities in Sifrid and Brünnhilde that eventually uncover this tension are precisely those which the Burgundians have tried to use for their own aggrandizement. Brünnhilde is too honest and uncompromising to accept the official version of Sifrid's status, and once again she insists on putting appearances to the test. The quarrel between the two queens and the ritual murder of Sifrid are the result. Sifrid's own crime is simply to behave in character. He is quite willing to let the Burgundians use his strength, but he makes no attempt to disguise his superiority. He is quite blandly indifferent to all the jealousies, rules and compromises which hold the society together. He is not interested in money (stanzas 558, 694–5), status (stanza 386), face-saving ceremony (stanzas 748–9) or political etiquette (stanzas 314–15). And, worst of all, he seems to have forgotten all about the sanctity of women as soon as he married Kriemhilde (stanzas 858, 894). Such innocence is in itself provocative. His one vulnerable spot is known only to Kriemhilde, and she, like a good Burgundian, betrays it to Hagen.

With Sifrid dead, and his treasure hastily dumped in the Rhine, it is left to Kriemhilde and Hagen to fight it out. In the process, the whole way of life at Burgundy is inexorably deflated and destroyed. The last magnificent tournament ends in a brutal killing; the elaborate political speeches are reduced to childish defiance; the subtly interlocking loyalties and prohibitions to blind tribal solidarity; the splendid feasting and drinking to the final macabre meal of blood, with corpses for benches. The mighty king is trussed up, and slaughtered by his sister. The crown of courtly womanhood is carved up by Dietrich's retainer.

Loyalty and good faith, made for security, are turned to destruction, so that allegiance to either side is the equivalent of a death sentence. Neutrality, on the other hand, is impossible, as even Dietrich discovers. He does, it is true, survive, but stripped of all the relationships which he and Hildebrand had built up round themselves (stanza 2319). Rüdeger, a much weaker and more dependent character, is pathetically caught in a dilemma of his own making. His hospitality and his readiness to oblige a lady, both excellent social qualities, have tied him equally to the Burgundians and to Kriemhilde. Obsessive generosity, designed to win lifelong friends, provides the instrument of his death. The bonds that once held society together now destroy it. At Etzel's court everyone is an exile.

1962   D. G. MOWATT

A NOTE TO THE TRANSLATION

THE STYLE of the work is not as uniform as might be expected. The narration is generally factual and economical, with occasional flashes of irony. The dialogue is by turns formal (even pompous), laconic, racy and brutal. Most of these variations are functional, and no attempt has been made to smooth them out in translation. The highly conventional and repetitious descriptions of court ceremony presented a rather more difficult problem which has not been satisfactorily solved. Their tedium (which is noticeable even in the original) is also functional, in that an edifice must be built up before it can be broken down. Perhaps the poet is rather too thorough in this respect, but if he had been less so the final 'feast and tournament' would lose much of its force. Similarly with the stock adjectives and appellations, which have been kept as far as, or farther than, the English language would stand. The occasional shock, when their use is blatantly inappropriate, is perhaps worth waiting for (e.g. 'lovable', stanza 425).

The text used is that of Bartsch-de Boor (*Deutsche Klassiker des Mittelalters*, F. A. Brockhaus, Wiesbaden, 1956). Free or unorthodox renderings are explained in the notes at the end.

Stanza numbers are given at the head of each page, and include every stanza, or part of a stanza, found on that page. Stanza divisions within paragraphs are shown by spaces. Every paragraph begins a new stanza.

In the notes (pages 219–25) the first number is that of the stanza, the second that of the line in the original text.

SELECT BIBLIOGRAPHY

Apart from those mentioned in the Introduction, the following German books have been found useful for students:

A. Sources: H. Hempel, *Euphorion 50* (1956), pp. 113–19. (A review of recent research.) G. Weber, *Nibelungenlied* (Sammlung Metzler, Stuttgart, 1961).

B. Interpretation: B. Mergell, *Euphorion 45* (1950), pp. 305 ff., 'Nibelungenlied und höfischer Roman'. B. Nagel, *Zur Interpretation und Wertung des Nibelungenliedes* (Heidelberg, 1954). W. J. Schröder, *Das Nibelungenlied. Versuch einer Deutung* (Max Niemeyer Verlag, Halle/Saale, 1954). (A reprint of an article in *PBB.* 76.) Schröder's views are discussed by B. Nagel in *ZfdPh.* 75, (1956), pp. 57–73.

Work in English is rare. Apart from M. Thorp's book (see Introduction, p. vi), the following articles may be of interest:

D. G. Mowatt, *German Life and Letters*, vol. xiv (1961), pp. 257–70, 'Studies towards an Interpretation of the Nibelungenlied'. (This article also reviews briefly some recent German interpretations.) Arnold H. Price, *Monatshefte*, vol. li (1959), pp. 341–50, 'Characterisation in the Nibelungenlied'. Hugh Sacker, *German Life and Letters*, vol. xiv (1961), pp. 271–81, 'On Irony and Symbolism in the Nibelungenlied: two preliminary notes'. (This article provides a basis for some of the attitudes taken in my Introduction.)

D. G. Mowatt and H. Sacker, *The Nibelungenlied, an Interpretative Commentary* (UTP, 1967).

ACKNOWLEDGMENTS

I should like to thank Brian and Peggy Rowley for reading through the manuscript and offering many helpful suggestions; but most of all I am indebted to Hugh Sacker, who insisted on many changes at an early stage, and since then has been tireless in the pursuit of howlers and infelicities.

CONTENTS

CONTENTS

THE NIBELUNGENLIED

AVENTIURE 1

THE OLD stories tell us of great heroes, joy and misery, feast and lament, and the clash of brave warriors. All this you may hear now, if you will.

There lived in Burgundy a young girl of great nobility, and beauty unparalleled in any country, and her name was Kriemhilde. Later she grew into a beautiful woman, and caused the death of many a knight.   She seemed made for loving; many a brave knight would have had her if he could, and no one was her enemy. She was unbelievably beautiful, and her qualities were such as any woman could desire.   She grew up in the care of three noble, mighty kings; Gunther and Gernot, renowned in arms, and young Giselher, a rare warrior. The lady was their sister, and the princes were entrusted with her upbringing.

These lords were of ancient and noble birth, endowed with incredible strength and bravery, open-handed, peerless knights. Burgundy was their country, and terrible were the deeds they later performed in Attila's lands.   They lived in might and glory at Worms by the Rhine. Many proud knights owed them service, and followed them loyally to the end, only to die miserably through the hatred of two noble ladies.

Their mother was Lady Uote, a mighty queen; their father's name was Dankrât, a man of great courage, who heaped honour on himself as a young man, and left them his inheritance when he died.

As I have said, the three kings were of outstanding bravery, and under them served the best knights that were ever known; strong and valiant they were, and always eager for a fight.   There was Hagen of Tronege, and his brother Dankwart the Bold, Ortwin of Metz, the two Margraves Gere and Eckewart, and Volker of Alzei, whose courage never

I

failed.   Rümold the cook, a rare warrior; Sindold and Hunold, who maintained the honour * of the court. All these lords were vassals of the three Kings; and there were many more besides, but I cannot give you their names.   Dankwart was marshal, * while his nephew Ortwin of Metz was steward; * Sindold, a rare warrior, was cup-bearer; * Hunold was treasurer. * The honour of the court was safe in their hands.

Indeed, no one could tell you the whole story of this court: of its power and wide dominion, its lofty eminence and the chivalrous ideals which the lords there cheerfully followed throughout their lives.

It was against this lofty background that Kriemhilde had a dream. She thought she trained * a falcon, strong, beautiful and wild, only to see it torn to pieces before her eyes by two eagles, and this, she felt, was the most terrible thing in the world that could have happened to her.   She told the dream to her mother Uote, but the best interpretation she could give of it was this: 'The falcon you train is a noble man, and unless God protects him you will soon lose him.'

'What is this about a man, dear mother? I want nothing to do with knights and their love. I want to stay beautiful as I am until I die, and never experience the love of men or the misery it brings.'

'Be careful what you say,' replied her mother. 'If you are ever to know true happiness, it will have to be through a man's love, and if God gives you a good knight for a husband one day, you'll make a beautiful woman yet.'

'No, my lady,' she answered. 'It's no use saying that to me. You can see often enough, with woman after woman, how the happiness of love turns to pain in the end. If I avoid both, I can't go wrong.'

Kriemhilde had decided to deny herself the experience of loving altogether. And indeed the good girl lived through many happy days without ever meeting anyone who aroused her desire. But the day came, nevertheless, when she was gloriously married to a very brave knight.   This was the same falcon of her dream, that her mother had prophesied she would find. And what a revenge she took on her nearest relatives, who killed him afterwards! Many mothers lost their sons for the death of this one man.

AVENTIURE 2

CONCERNING SIFRID

At about the same time a young and noble prince was growing up in the Netherlands. His father's name was Sigemund, his mother's Sigelinde, and they lived in a mighty city on the lower Rhine called Santen.

Sifrid was the name of this brave, good warrior. He proved his strength and courage in many different lands, and a bold company of warriors it was that he eventually discovered in Burgundy.   At his best and in his youth, many wonders were told of Sifrid; how he showed promise of great honour to come, and how beautiful he was to look at. Later in life he was loved * by the finest ladies in the land.   Much care was spent in his upbringing, as was only right; and from his own resources he added virtue after virtue to himself. He showed himself lordly and commanding in all he undertook: a fitting heir to his father's kingdom.

When he was of an age to appear at court, he was such a success that many a lady and maiden hoped he would never want to leave, and the young lord was well aware of the good impression he made.   He was seldom allowed to ride out unattended; Sigemund and Sigelinde saw to it that he was beautifully dressed; and wise men, who knew what honour was, also had a hand in his upbringing. In this way he learnt how to win peoples and lands to himself.

When he was of a strength to bear arms, he showed that he had all the necessary qualities. He courted beautiful women with skill and discrimination, and they considered themselves honoured to make love to the brave Sifrid.   His father Sigemund accordingly announced to his people that he intended to stage a celebration, together with his close friends. The news was then carried into other kingdoms, and to all, stranger and friend alike, he gave a horse and fine clothes.   Wherever they found any noble youths who were suited by birth to become knights, they invited them home to join in the celebration, and later to take the sword with the young king.

The feast itself was fabulous. Sigemund and Sigelinde knew what honour was to be won with gifts, and great were the riches dispensed by their hand—so that strangers came flocking into their land in consequence.   There were four hundred candidates due to assume knightly dress together with Sifrid, and many beautiful maidens were busy sewing—willingly enough, as you can imagine. The gold braid on the proud young knights' clothes was richly inlaid with precious stones. All these details had to be attended to by the ladies, and in addition the host had seats made for the many brave men who would be there on a certain midsummer day to see his son knighted.

They went first to the cathedral, many rich youths and noble knights. The old and wise were obliged by tradition to wait on the young and foolish, just as they had been waited on in their time. They anticipated much happiness to come, and they enjoyed doing it.   After a Mass had been sung to the glory of God, there was much crowding and jostling among the people, as they were made knights according to established custom, and with such honour as is not likely to be seen again.

Then they ran off to where they found a crowd of horses ready saddled, and the tournament in Sigemund's court was so violent that the palace and the great hall resounded with the din. These irrepressible warriors certainly knew how to make a noise.   Young and old, you could hear their thrusts, as the air was filled with the crack of their lances; you could see the splinters flying from many a knight's hand in front of the palace. There was nothing half-hearted about this tournament.   And when the host asked them to break off, and the horses were led away, you could see many a stout shield-boss smashed and many a precious stone flung from its setting on to the grass. It was the shock of the charges that did this.

Now the guests were shown to their seats, and forgot their weariness in the great variety of choice foods and liberal helpings of the best wine imaginable. Stranger and friend alike, they were honourably served at that table.   And the travelling entertainers, who had been hard at it all day, many of them still had no thought of resting. They offered their service in proportion to the rich gifts they received there, and the whole of Sigemund's land was praised in song as a result.

Lord Sigemund then allowed young Sifrid to bestow fiefs, lands and castles, just as he himself had done on previous occasions; and Sifrid's hand was so liberal to those who had

4

taken the sword with him that they blessed the journey they had made into his lands.

The celebrations lasted seven days, and Sigelinde the mighty queen took care, in the traditional way, to dispense her red gold for her son's sake. In this way she made sure that the people loved him,   and afterwards you could not have found a single poor man among the travelling entertainers. Horses and clothes were handed out as if they all expected to die the next day. I doubt if any house ever showed greater generosity.

The celebrations broke up with praise and honour all round, and it was not long before the mighty lords were heard saying how much they would have liked the young king as their ruler. But Sifrid, this splendid man, was not interested.   As long as Sigemund and Sigelinde were still alive, their dear child had no desire to wear the crown. What he wanted, the brave and bold warrior, was to make himself master of all the power which he saw and feared in the lands about him.*

AVENTIURE 3

SIFRID COMES TO WORMS

Lord Sifrid was not generally troubled by emotions. But he heard tell of a beautiful maiden who lived in Burgundy, fashioned after any man's heart's desire; and this maiden was to give him much happiness and strife before long. Her outstanding beauty was known far and wide, and, as many a hero had discovered, the maiden had a regal disposition to match. The challenge attracted many guests into Gunther's land. But whoever the suitor, Kriemhilde never consciously admitted that she could want anyone at all as a lover. The man she eventually submitted to was still a stranger in a distant land.

When the child of Sigelinde turned his thoughts to serious courtship no other suitor had a chance. Beautiful women were his by right, and in due course the noble Kriemhilde was married to Sifrid the brave.

When they knew that he was set on true and constant love his relatives and many of his men advised him to pay court to some suitable lady of his choice. The bold Sifrid answered: 'In that case I will take Kriemhilde, the fair maiden of Burgundy, because of her outstanding beauty. I know well enough that the mightiest emperor alive, if he wanted a wife, would find it fitting to love this great queen.'

The news came to Sigemund's ears as he heard his people talking amongst themselves, and he was not at all pleased with his son's idea of courting the proud maid. Sigelinde too, the noble King's wife, heard of it, and was greatly concerned for her son's safety; she knew Gunther and his men too well. And so they tried to turn him away from his project.

But the brave Sifrid said: 'My dear father, I'd rather never enjoy the love of a noble lady if I cannot woo where my heart directs and happiness calls. And so far as that's concerned, nothing anyone says can make any difference.'

'Well,' said the King, 'since you're not to be dissuaded, I shall welcome your decision in all sincerity, and help you, as well

6

as I can, to achieve your desire. But you know King Gunther has a great number of proud men at his command. And Hagen the warrior is enough by himself—his pride and arrogance know no bounds; I'm very much afraid we may live to be sorry if we court this proud maid.'

'Why should that hold us back?' said Sifrid. 'I'll ask him nicely first, and if he refuses me anything, I'm brave enough to win it for myself. I could take his people and his country from him by force if necessary.'

But Sigemund answered: 'I don't like to hear you say that. If they knew on the Rhine that you had said it, you would never even dare to ride into the land. Gunther and Gernot—I know them of old. No one can win the maid by force.' Such was King Sigemund's verdict: 'So I have heard, and so I believe. All the same, if you need knights to go with you into the country, they shall be summoned immediately. Our friends won't fail us.'

'No,' said Sifrid however. 'It wasn't my idea that knights should have to follow me to the Rhine, or that we should raise an army of any sort to help me capture the magnificent maid. I can win her easily enough with my own hand. But I should like to take twelve * companions into Gunther's land, and that's one way * you can help me, my father Sigemund.' And at this the knights were given grey and striped furs for their clothes.

When his mother Sigelinde heard the news, she began to grieve for her dear son. She was afraid to lose him at the hand of Gunther's men, and the noble Queen wept bitterly.

But the Lord Sifrid went over to her, and spoke kindly to his mother: 'Lady, don't weep for my sake. You know I'm not afraid of any fighting man. Help me instead on this journey to Burgundy, so that my knights and I have clothes fit for proud heroes to wear with honour. If you do, I shall be deeply grateful.'

'Since you're so determined,' said Lady Sigelinde, 'then I'll help you on your journey, my only child. You and your companions shall have the best clothes that any knight ever wore, and as many as you need.'

Young Sifrid bowed to the Queen and said: 'I'm only taking twelve men with me on the journey. Fit them out with clothes, if you would. I'm eager to find out more about Kriemhilde.'

And so, night and day, fair ladies sat with never a moment's rest, until Sifrid's clothes were finished. Nothing could put him off his journey now. His father had Sifrid's knightly dress specially decorated for the departure from Sifrid's lands, and

7

gleaming breast-plates were got ready for the twelve, together with their stout helmets and their shields broad and fair.   As the time for their journey to Burgundy drew nearer, men and women began to wonder anxiously whether they would ever come home again. But the heroes ordered their weapons and clothes to be loaded on to mules.   Their horses were beautiful, their harness red with gold. You could not wish for more confident assurance than Sifrid and his men displayed. And then Sifrid asked formally for leave to ride to Burgundy.

The King and Queen sadly granted what he asked, and he comforted them gently: 'Don't weep for my sake; you need never be anxious about me.'   The knights were sad too, and many a maiden wept. Perhaps they knew in their hearts that it would end in the death of many of their friends. They had real cause to lament.

On the seventh morning after setting out, the brave men rode on to the shore at Worms. All their dress was of red gold, their harness beautifully made. They rode easily, the men of Sifrid the brave.   Their shields were new, broad and shining, their helmets fair, as Sifrid the brave rode to court in Gunther's land, Never was such splendid clothing seen on heroes before.   Their swords pointed down to their spurs. Their spears were sharp, and the one that Sifrid carried must have been a good eighteen inches broad, with a gruesome cutting edge.   They held the golden bridles in their hands; their horses' collars were of silk. And so they came to the land of Burgundy. All round them the people stared in amazement, and many of Gunther's men ran towards them.

The proud knights and their pages approached the strange lords, as was proper, and received them as guests in their master's land, relieving them of their horses and shields.   They made as if to lead the horses away to their stables, but Sifrid the brave quickly stopped them: 'Leave the horses where they are! My men and I will not be staying long, if I have anything to do with it.   If anyone knows, let him tell me where I can find the King, Gunther the mighty of Burgundy; that's what I want to hear.' One of the bystanders who knew answered:

'If it's the King you want to find, that's easily done. I saw him in that great hall over there, with his heroes. That's where you ought to go. You'll find plenty of proud men in his company.'

Meanwhile Gunther had heard the news that knights of great
beauty had arrived, wearing bright armour and lordly clothing.
No one in Burgundy knew who they were.   The King was
greatly puzzled to think where they might have come from,
these majestic knights in shining clothes, with such excellent
shields new and broad. He was displeased that no one could
tell him.

Then Ortwin of Metz, a brave and mighty man, gave this
answer to the King: 'Since we don't recognize them, you should
send someone to fetch my uncle Hagen. Let him see
them.   He knows all the kingdoms here, and foreign lands
as well; and if he knows these people he'll soon tell us.'   The
king asked for Hagen and his men to be brought, and soon he
was seen walking proudly with his knights towards the court.

He asked what the King wanted of him, and was told: 'There
are strange warriors in my house, whom no one here can name.
Have you ever seen them before? Tell me all about them,
Hagen.'

'I will,' said Hagen, and crossed over to the window. He let
his eye rest on the guests, and was favourably impressed with
their appearance and their dress, both of which were quite
strange to him in Burgundy.   He said that wherever these
knights may have come from to the Rhine, they had the air of
princes, or the messengers of princes. Their horses were fine,
their clothes excellent, and wherever they came from they
certainly showed no lack of confidence.   'In fact,' said
Hagen finally, 'I must say, although I've never seen Sifrid, even
so, I'm almost ready to believe, whatever the explanation, that
he is the proud knight down there.   He'll bring something
new to our country. This hero slew the two rich Nibelung
princes, Schilbung and Nibelung, with his own hand, and since
then he's done wonders with his strength.

'As the hero was riding alone and unaccompanied, he found
at the foot of a hill, so I'm told, the Nibelung treasure, and
many a brave man with it. They'd been strangers to him up to
then, but he soon got to know them.   The whole Nibelung
treasure had been carried out of the hollow mountain—and now
comes the miracle. Sifrid saw that the Nibelungs were going to
divide up the treasure, and this puzzled the hero.   He came
closer, so that he could see the heroes, and they him. One of
them said: "Here comes strong Sifrid, the hero from the
Netherlands," and that was the beginning of his strange

adventures with the Nibelungs.   Schilbung and Nibelung were pleased to see him, and by common consent they asked the noble young prince to divide the treasure for them. In fact they begged him to do it, he looked so magnificent, and he promised he would.   When he looked at the precious stones, he saw that there were so many that a hundred carts, we're told, couldn't carry them; and of red gold there was even more. All this was to be divided by brave Sifrid's hand.   As a payment they gave him the Nibelung sword, but they didn't have much reason to be grateful for the service he rendered them in return. For the good hero Sifrid was unable to complete the task, and they got angry.   They had among their friends twelve giants, brave and strong, but it made no difference. The angry hand of Sifrid killed the lot of them,   and with the good sword, which was called Balmung, he overpowered seven hundred knights from the land of the Nibelungs. Many young knights, in great fear of the sword and his bravery, handed over their lands and castles to him.   The two mighty kings he killed as well. After this he was in great danger from Alberich, who thought he'd be able to avenge his two masters on the spot, until he discovered Sifrid's great strength.   The dwarf, powerful as he was, could not overcome him. Like wild lions they both ran back into the mountain, and there he won the magic cloak from Alberich. From now on he, Sifrid, this fearsome man, was the lord of the treasure.   All those who had dared to fight were dead. Sifrid then ordered the Nibelungs to carry the treasure back where it had come from, and put Alberich the strong in charge of it.   The dwarf had to swear on oath to serve him as his master,* but by this time he was ready to do anything at all for him. And that', said Hagen of Tronege, 'is what he's done. No knight ever had such great strength.   And that's not all I know about him. This hero's hand slew a dragon. He bathed in its blood, and it made his skin horny, so that no weapon can cut it. This has been proved many times.   So we ought to receive the lord as well as possible, in order to avoid earning the young knight's hatred. As he's so brave and has accomplished so many wonders with his strength, it would be a good thing to have him as a friend.'

The mighty King answered: 'You may well be right. See how warrior-like he stands, eager for battle, he and his knights, the brave man. I think we should go down to meet him.'

'You can do that without any loss of honour,' said Hagen.

'He is of noble birth, the son of a mighty king. And to judge from the way he stands, it's no small matter, by God, that brings him here.'

The King of the land answered: 'Well then, let him be welcome. He's noble and brave, you tell me; he shall be treated accordingly in Burgundy.' And Lord Gunther went to meet Sifrid.

The host and his knights received the guests with perfect propriety. They greeted him so pleasantly that the majestic man bowed in return.

The King spoke at once: 'Noble Sifrid, I'm eager to know where you have come from into this land, and what you hope to achieve at Worms on the Rhine.' 'I won't make any secret of it,' said the guest to the King. 'In my father's country I was often told that the best knights any king ever had were to be found here at your court. That was just what I wanted to hear, and that's why I've come. I've heard also that you yourself are an acknowledged warrior, and that a braver king was never seen. All through the country people are saying this, and I won't give up now until I've found out for myself. I too am a knight, and entitled to wear a crown, but I want people to be able to say of me that I hold my people and my lands by right. For that I'm prepared to risk my reputation and my head. Since you're so brave, as they tell me, I'll take from you everything you have whether anyone likes it or not; your lands and your castles shall be subject to me.'

The King, no less than his men, was amazed to hear this recital of how Sifrid wished to take his lands from him. His warriors, as they listened, felt their anger rising.

'And how should I have deserved this?' said Gunther the warrior, 'that our inheritance, which my father administered long and honourably, should be taken from us by force? That would be a poor proof of our knightliness.'

But the brave man answered, 'I'm not to be put off. Either you bring peace to your lands by your own courage, or I shall rule them all. And you can have my inheritance—if you're strong enough to win it. Your inheritance and mine shall be set against each other, and whichever of us defeats the other shall take the lot, people and lands.' Hagen and Gernot at once rejected the offer.

Gernot said: 'We have no desire to take anyone's lands by force, nor that anyone should be killed by a hero's hand in such a cause. We have rich territories which are ours by right. No one has a better claim to them than we have.'

His friends stood there grimly, and among them Ortwin of Metz, who said: 'I don't like this soft answer at all. Sifrid the strong has challenged you without reason.   Even if you and your brothers were defenceless, and he had a whole king's army behind him, I should be happy to fight until he's forced to abandon this arrogant behaviour.'

This infuriated the hero from the Netherlands, and he said: 'How can you have the insolence to measure yourself against me? I am a mighty king. You are a king's vassal. Why, twelve of you would never be able to face me in battle!'

At that Ortwin of Metz shouted wildly for weapons—he was a true nephew of Hagen of Tronege, whose long silence, incidentally, had begun to worry the King. In the event it was Gernot who intervened, that gay and gallant knight.   He said to Ortwin: 'Restrain your anger. Lord Sifrid has done nothing to us that we can't settle with decorum, so as to keep him as a friend. And as I see it, this would be more to our credit in the long run.'

Then Hagen the strong spoke: 'All the same, your knights are sorry that he should have come to the Rhine in such a warlike mood. My masters, I'm sure, would never have provoked him like this.' *

Sifrid answered, the man of force: 'If my words disturb you, Lord Hagen, then I must show, with my own hand, that I mean to hold power in Burgundy.'

But again Gernot intervened. 'That I cannot allow,' he said, and forbade any of his warriors to indulge in haughty or provocative speech. And then, too, Sifrid thought of the beautiful maid.

'How should we bring ourselves to fight with you?' continued Gernot, 'when you think of the heroes who would have to die in the process; such a combat would be neither to our honour nor to your advantage.' And to this Sifrid, son of King Sigemund, answered: 'Why does Hagen hold back, or Ortwin for that matter? Why doesn't he want to fight? He's got enough friends here in Burgundy to support him!' But they had to remain silent, on Gernot's instructions.

'We make you welcome,' spoke the son of Uote; 'you and your companions who have come with you. We place ourselves willingly at your service, I and my relations.' And orders were given that Gunther's wine should be served to the guests.

Then the Lord of the land spoke: 'All that we have is yours if you wish it, to do with it what you will, as far as honour permits. Our men and our possessions we will share with you.' At this, Lord Sifrid began to relent a little.

Then the visitors' clothes were laid away, and lodgings, the best that could be found, were arranged for Sifrid's men. They were well looked after, and it was not long before the guest became a welcome sight among the Burgundians. He was heaped with honours for many days after, a thousand times more than I can tell you. It was his bravery, you may be certain, which had accomplished this; indeed, no one could see him and remain his enemy. The kings and their men were at great pains to entertain him; and whatever they undertook, he was always the best at it. In stone- or spear-throwing, no one could keep up with him, he was so strong.

Whenever the gay knights, in pursuit of chivalry, spent their leisure with the ladies, there the young hero from the Netherlands was always welcome. He had set his mind on knightly love.* He was ready and eager for everything. For he cherished a fair maiden in his heart, and was cherished in his turn by that lady, whom he had never yet seen, but who often spoke warmly of him in secret. Whenever the young people, knights and squires, disported themselves at court, Kriemhilde, the proud queen, seldom forgot to look through the window now. During those days this was all the amusement she asked for. If he had known that she who carried him in her heart was looking at him, he too would have asked for no other amusement. And if his eyes could have lighted on her, I know that he could have had no greater pleasure on this earth. Standing among the heroes at court, as people still do in their leisure hours, the son of Sigelinde cut such a lovely figure that many a woman was to lavish her ardent love on him in days to come. And he frequently thought: 'How may I come to see this noble maiden with my own eyes? She whom I love so ardently and so long is still a stranger to me; sad I must remain.'

Each time the mighty kings went on a tour of their lands their knights had to go off with them, and Sifrid had to leave as well, much to Kriemhilde's regret. He in his turn suffered much and often for love of her. In this way he stayed with the lords, a whole year it must have been, in Gunther's country, and in all that time he never once set eyes on the fair maiden who was to cause him such pleasure and pain in the future.

AVENTIURE 4

HE FIGHTS THE SAXONS

Disturbing news was on the way to Gunther's lands. Messengers had been sent on ahead by distant and unknown warriors who apparently were hostile to the Burgundians. Their news was received with distress.   I will tell you who had sent them: it was Liudeger of Saxony, a proud and mighty prince, and King Liudegast of Denmark. And a great company of proud strangers were coming with them.   Meanwhile the messengers sent on by his enemies had arrived in Gunther's lands. The strangers were asked what news they brought, and invited to present themselves to the King at court.

The King greeted them affably, saying 'Welcome! As yet I don't know who sent you; but no doubt you will tell us now.' At which they were in great fear of Gunther's ferocity.

'If it is your wish, O King, that we tell you the news we bring, then we shall no longer keep silent, but name our masters who sent us here. They are Liudeger and Liudegast, and they intend to invade your land.   You have incurred their anger; we understand, in fact, that both of these lords are your sworn enemies. They are preparing to bring an army to Worms by the Rhine. They have many knights to help them—of that you may be certain.   The invasion will take place within twelve weeks. Let it be seen without delay whether you have good friends to help you protect your lands and castles. Many of their helmets and shields will be hacked to pieces on this ground.   If, on the other hand, you wish to negotiate with them, you should make them an offer. In that case, the great host of your enemies will no longer ride against you, much suffering will be averted and many fair and happy knights will no longer need to perish.'

'Wait a little,' said the good King, 'until I've thought it over, and can tell you my decision. If I have any loyal vassals, I shan't keep this news from them. My friends will hear of this offence.'

Gunther the mighty was troubled. He kept the news secretly in his heart, and sent for Hagen and others of his men. He also asked that Gernot should be sought out hurriedly at the court.   They came, the best that could be found, and he said: 'I have bad news for you. They are threatening to invade us with a great army.' Gernot answered, that gay and gallant knight:

'We have swords to prevent that,' said Gernot. 'Only the doomed will die. Let them fall. I shall not neglect my honour on their account. Let us welcome our enemies!'

But Hagen of Tronege then spoke: 'I don't like the look of this. Liudeger and Liudegast are too confident. We can't raise an army in so short a time,' said the bold warrior. 'Why not pass it on to Sifrid?'

The messengers were accommodated in the town, and although they were his enemies, Gunther very properly asked for them to be well looked after until he should have found out which of his friends were willing to support him.

But all the same the King was much worried and distressed. And it happened that a certain carefree knight saw him brooding, and not knowing what had happened, he asked King Gunther to tell him if anything was wrong.

'I am amazed', said Sifrid, 'how different you are from the happy man we have known for so long.' And Gunther answered, that accomplished knight:

'You realize that I can't tell everyone the burden that I carry secretly in my heart. A heart's distress is disclosed only to true friends.' The colour ebbed and flowed in Sifrid's face.

He said to the King: 'I've never refused you anything. I can help you to throw off all your sorrow. If it's friends you're looking for, let me be one of them. You can trust me never to let you down.'

'May God reward you, Lord Sifrid, for what you have said. And if I never need to enlist your bravery, it gladdens me to learn how much affection you have for me. Before I live much longer you will be well repaid.   I'll tell why I am sad. Messengers from my enemies have arrived to announce their intention of invading my lands. Such a thing has never happened to us before.'

'That's nothing to worry about,' said Sifrid. 'Cheer up and do as I suggest. Let me win the honour and the advantage for you, and call on your warriors to help as well.   If your enemies were so strong that they had thirty thousand men at their disposal, I'd happily take them on with no more than a thousand. You can rely on me.' Then King Gunther said: 'For this I shall be for ever at your service.'

'Good. Then get me a thousand of your men, since I have none of my own followers here, except for twelve knights, and I'll protect your land. The hand of Sifrid will loyally serve you for ever.   Hagen can help us, and also Ortwin, Dankwart and Sindold, your faithful knights. And Volker, that brave man, shall ride with us. He can carry the standard; no one deserves the honour more.   And let the messengers ride home to their masters. Tell them we're coming out to meet them shortly, so that our towns and castles may be left in peace.' And the King ordered his relations and his men to be called to arms.

The messengers of Liudeger attended at court, glad indeed to be sent home. Gunther, the good King, offered them rich gifts and gave them safe escort, which raised their spirits considerably.

'Now tell my enemies', said Gunther, 'that they would be well advised to campaign nearer home. If, however, they are intent on invading me in my own lands, they can expect to learn the meaning of hardship, if my friends do not desert me.'

Rich gifts, of which Gunther had enough and to spare, were then handed to the messengers. Liudeger's men though they were, they dared not refuse them. Happily they took their leave and departed.   When they arrived in Denmark, and Liudegast heard the report they brought back from the Rhine, he was dismayed at the confident pride of the Burgundians.   For he was told that they had many a bold man, and they had seen a warrior standing amongst them who was called Sifrid, a hero from the Netherlands. Liudegast was much distressed, as he realized the significance of this news.

When the Danes heard what was said, they rushed to round up still more of their friends, until Lord Liudegast, from among his brave men, had acquired twenty thousand warriors for his campaign.   King Liudeger of Saxony also combed the land, until between them they had forty thousand and more who would ride with them to Burgundy. Meanwhile, King Gunther, at home, had also summoned his strength,   together with his relatives and his brothers' men, whom they meant to lead to war, and also Hagen's knights, for the heroes were in desperate need. Many warriors were to die before this was over.   They made ready for the march, appointing Volker to carry the standard, and Hagen of Tronege to take charge of the army as they rode away from Worms by the Rhine.　　With them rode Sindold and Hunold, well qualified to earn Gunther's gold; Hagen's brother Dankwart, and Ortwin also, honourable acquisitions to the campaign.

And Sifrid spoke: 'You stay here at home, Lord King, since your knights are willing to be led by me. Keep by the ladies, and hold up your head. Leave it to me to look after your honour and possessions for you.　　As for the people who were going to invade you at Worms by the Rhine, I'll take care of that: they won't get far from their homes. We'll ride them so close into their own country that their proud boasts will be turned to anxious fear.'

And so they left the Rhine and rode through Hessen towards Saxony, where the battle was later joined. They devastated the land with fire and plunder, so that the two princes were dismayed when they heard of it.　　They came to the frontier, and the non-combatants withdrew. Sifrid the strong asked: 'Who will stay here and guard our retainers?' (Never did the Saxons experience a more disastrous attack.)

They said: 'Let brave Dankwart take charge of the young ones; he is a bold warrior. Liudeger's men won't inflict many losses while he's here. Let him and Ortwin form the rearguard.'

'In that case', said Sifrid the warrior, 'I can ride ahead myself to keep watch for the enemy until I find out where their knights are posted.' They hurried to arm the beautiful Sigelinde's son.

When he was ready to leave, he entrusted the command of the troops to Hagen and brave Gernot; then he rode alone into Saxon territory, and many were the helmets that he hacked to pieces that day.

Encamped in open country he saw the great army which had set itself against him.* There must have been forty thousand or more of them. Sifrid was glad, and his spirits rose as he looked at them.

At the same time a Saxon knight, armed to the teeth, had come out to look for the enemy. Lord Sifrid and the brave Saxon fixed each other with a hostile stare.

I will tell you who it was who had come to keep watch. A shining shield of gold was in his hand; it was King Liudegast, guarding his army. The noble intruder galloped up to him, a most imposing sight.

But Lord Liudegast had also picked out his enemy, and both

17

spurred their horses forward. Strongly they lowered their lances over their shields, and the mighty king was soon in great difficulty.

They clashed, and their horses swept the two princes past each other as if they were leaves on the wind. Like good knights, they wheeled and drew their swords, two grimly determined men.

Then Lord Sifrid struck, so that the country all round resounded, and his hand brought a shower of glowing sparks from the helmet, as from a great fire. Each had found his equal in the other.

And Lord Liudegast struck him back, many a ferocious blow. Their bravery was vented on both their shields. As it happened, thirty of Liudegast's men had ridden out on patrol, but before they could help him Sifrid had won,   with three terrible wounds which he inflicted on the King, through his shining armour, which would have withstood them if anything could. The edge of his sword drew blood from the wounds, and King Liudegast was disconsolate.

He asked for his life to be spared, and offered his lands in exchange, saying that his name was Liudegast. At that moment his knights arrived, having seen clearly enough what had happened between the two look-outs.

Sifrid was just going to lead him away when he found himself attacked by thirty men. Then the hero's hand defended his rich prize with incredible blows. And this was not the end of the damage done by this most charming knight.   He slaughtered the thirty others with zest, leaving just one alive, who rode off and spread the news of what had happened there. And he carried the proof of his words on his bloody helmet.

The Danes were sad and grim when they heard that their Lord was captured. They told his brother, who raged in ungovernable anger at this personal affront.

Meanwhile Liudegast the warrior was, by Sifrid's strength, led away to Gunther's men. He was handed over to Hagen, who saw no reason to complain when told it was the King.

The Burgundians were ordered to raise up their standards. 'Come on then,' said Sifrid. 'There's plenty more to be done, if I don't get killed before the day is out. We'll give those women in Saxony something to worry about.   You heroes of the Rhine, listen to what I say. I can lead you right into the middle of Liudeger's army, and you'll see helmets hacked by great heroes. Before we leave them they'll know what misery is.'

At once Gernot and his men rushed for their horses, and Lord Volker waved the standard, the musician with strength in his arm, and rode in front of the army. The followers, in imposing array, were just as eager for battle— and yet they were no more than a thousand men and twelve knights. The dust flew up in clouds as they rode over the land, and from their ranks came the gleam of many magnificent shields.

Now the Saxons too had come with their armies, and with good sharp swords as I have since been told. These swords were dangerous cutting instruments in the hands of heroes, and they intended to defend their castles and lands against the intruders. The commanders led their troops forward; and Sifrid was there as well, with the men he had brought from the Netherlands. That day saw many a hand grow bloody in battle.

Sindold and Hunold, and Gernot as well, they slew in the fight many a hero, before he had a chance to learn what bravery he was up against. And many a noble woman was left to weep.

Volker and Hagen, and Ortwin as well, they doused in the fight many a bright helmet with flowing blood, those battle-bold men. And many a miracle was performed by Dankwart.

The Danes were not slow to prove themselves; and many a shield rang out as it clashed upon shield, or was struck again and again by sharp sword. The Saxons, brave in battle, did damage there and to spare.

And when the Burgundians crowded into the fight, they hacked many a gaping wound, until the blood ran down over the saddles. This was how the brave and good knights strove to accumulate honour. You could hear the keen weapons resounding in the heroes' hands as the Netherlanders drove into the grim ranks behind their lord. Like warriors they advanced with Sifrid. None of the Rhinelanders could follow him. You could see the stream of blood flowing through the bright helmets wherever his hand fell, until he came upon Liudeger at the head of his men. By now he had been right through the army and back again, three times, and Hagen had come up to help him fulfil himself in battle. Many good knights fell dead before them that day. When the strong Liudeger found Sifrid, and saw how he swung the good sword Balmung so high in his hand, and slew so many of his men, he flew into a savage rage. And then there was a great heaving and clashing of swords, as their followers drove against each other. The two

knights were spurred on to ever greater efforts, the ranks began
to fall back and much bitterness was let loose.

The Saxon ruler had learned with great distress that his
brother was made prisoner. He might have known well enough *
that the child of Sigelinde had done this; they had said it was
Gernot, but he soon discovered the truth.   Liudeger's blows
were so strong that Sifrid's horse staggered under him, but it
recovered, and brave Sifrid took on a terrible aspect in the
battle.   With Hagen supporting him, and also Gernot,
Dankwart and Volker, the Saxon dead lay thick. Sindold and
Hunold, and Ortwin the warrior also had large numbers to
their credit.   The great princes were still locked in combat.
And all the time spears were flashing over helmets, to find
their mark in some bright shield, most of which were red with
blood.   Many men were parted from their horses in the
fierce fighting; but Sifrid the brave and Liudeger charged at
one another, while shafts and sharp spears flew all round
them.   Shields sprang apart under Sifrid's blows, and the
hero from the Netherlands realized he was on the point of
winning the victory from the brave Saxons, weakened as they
were by wounds. Many were the bright coats of mail that
Dankwart tore apart.

And then the Lord Liudeger recognized a certain crown
painted on the shield in Sifrid's hand, and at once he knew that
this was the man of strength. The hero called aloud to his
friends:

'Break off the fight, all my men! I see the son of Sigemund
here. I have recognized Sifrid the strong. The devil himself must
have sent him here to Saxony.'

He ordered the standards to be lowered in the battle, and sued
for peace. This he was granted, but he had to go as a hostage
into Gunther's land, subdued by the hand of brave Sifrid.

It was universally agreed to abandon the fight, and they laid
down their helmets and broad shields, riddled with holes. It
would have been hard to find anything there that was not stained
with blood by a Burgundian hand.

The Burgundians had earned the right to take whatever
prisoners they chose, and after brave Gernot and Hagen had
ordered the wounded to be laid on stretchers, five hundred
stalwart men were led off captive to the Rhine.

The defeated Danes rode home; and the Saxons too were
downcast. Their achievements in battle were not likely to earn

20

them much in the way of praise; and they had their dead friends to mourn for.   Orders were given for the Burgundians' weapons to be transported back to the Rhine. Warrior Sifrid and his heroes had done good work; so good that * all Gunther's men had to admit it.   Lord Gernot sent word to Worms, telling his friends at home how well he and his men had succeeded. The brave men had indeed won honour.

The pages hurried on, for it was their job to make the announcements, and all sadness was swept away when those at home heard the glad news. Noble ladies plied them with questions   as to how the King's men had fared, and one messenger was sent to Kriemhilde, who received the news in great secrecy; she could not trust herself to hear it in public, for it concerned, among others, her heart's true love.*

When she saw the messenger coming to her room, Kriemhilde the fair spoke with great gentleness: 'Break your glad news and I will give you gold. Tell it truthfully, and you will enjoy my favour for ever.   How did my brother Gernot acquit himself in the battle, and my other friends? Are many of our men dead perhaps? And who fought the best? I must know that.' The messenger answered without hesitation: 'There were no cowards among us.   But there was no one who rode better, since you ask me, in peril and in battle, than our noble guest from the Netherlands. The hand of brave Sifrid worked many miracles on that field.   Whatever feats the knights all accomplished in battle, Dankwart and Hagen, and others of the King's men, however honourably they fought, it was nothing compared to Sifrid, child of King Sigemund.   Certainly they have many dead heroes to their credit, but of the fantastic feats that Sifrid performed when he rode to battle, I could never exhaust the tale. Great was the harm he inflicted on the women through their families.

'And many a lady's lover was left dead there. You could hear his blows ring out on helmets, so loud and strong that they fetched the blood spurting out of wounds. He is by every standard a brave and good knight.   And after him, in spite of the feats of Ortwin of Metz (everyone who came within reach of his sword was wounded or killed for the most part) it was your brother who wrought the greatest havoc   that can ever have been known in battle. You can't help admitting the truth about these outstanding men of ours; the proud Burgundians have shown by their actions that they know how to preserve their honour from every disgrace.   You could have seen saddle after saddle emptied by their hand, as the field rang with the clash of their bright swords. The warriors of the Rhine rode to such purpose that their enemies would have been glad to forgo the experience.   The brave men of Tronege caused great damage when the mass of the army rode out together. The hand of brave Hagen dispatched many to their deaths—I dare say they'll have plenty of tales to tell when they arrive in Burgundy.

'Sindold and Hunold, Gernot's men, and Rumold the brave, they have done enough to make Liudeger sorry for the rest of his life that he ever challenged your people on the Rhine.   But the most glorious fighting, first and last, on the whole battlefield, or anywhere for that matter, was performed by Sifrid's eager hand. He brings rich hostages to Gunther's court.   These he overcame with his courage, the splendid man, and even King Liudegast himself and his brother Liudeger of Saxony have suffered at his hand. Now listen to my news, proud and noble Queen: it was Sifrid who captured both of them. Never were so many hostages brought to this land as are now approaching the Rhine because of him.' Nothing could have pleased her more than this news.

'They are bringing into our country, unwounded, five hundred or more, and a good eighty on bloody stretchers badly wounded, my lady, and mostly the work of Sifrid's sword.   The men who proudly brought their challenge to the Rhine are now Gunther's prisoners. They are being joyfully escorted into our country.' As the news sank in, a bright colour unfolded on her cheek.

Her beautiful face was red as a rose when she heard that he was happily preserved from great peril, this splendid knight, young Sifrid. She rejoiced also, as was proper, that her own people had returned.

Then the fair maid said: 'I like your news. As a reward you shall have rich clothes and ten gold marks; I'll have them brought out to you.' No wonder people enjoy bringing news like this to powerful ladies.

He was given his reward, the gold and the clothes. And then many a beautiful maiden went to the window to keep watch on the road. There they saw a great crowd of men proudly riding into Burgundy.   Wounded and unwounded they came, and no need to hang their heads as their families welcomed them. The Lord of the land rode out happily to meet his guests, for his great sorrow had ended in rejoicing.   Friend and stranger, he received them well; what else could the mighty King do but thank them graciously who had come to his aid and won an honourable victory in battle?

Gunther asked for news of his own family, and who had been killed on the campaign. He learnt that he had lost only sixty men. These had to be mourned * as is still the custom when heroes die.   Those who were whole had brought back many a mangled shield and battered helmet to Gunther's land. The army dismounted before the king's hall, and the happy sound of joyful reunion was heard.   Then the knights were found shelter in the town, and the King asked that his guests should be well looked after. He saw that the wounded were cared for and made comfortable, thus showing his knightly qualities in his treatment of his enemies.

He said to Liudegast: 'Welcome! I've suffered great injuries through you, and now, if I'm not disappointed, I shall be repaid. May God reward my friends! They have given me great happiness.'

'You may well thank them,' answered Liudeger. 'No king ever won such noble hostages before; and in return for fair treatment we offer you great wealth, so that you may deal mercifully with your enemies.'

'I shall allow you both to go unguarded', he said, 'as long as my enemies remain here. I shall need pledges that none of them will leave my territory without permission.' Liudeger agreed, with a handshake.

They were conducted to their quarters and installed in comfort. The wounded were gently put to bed,* while those who were whole were given mead and good wine; and there was great happiness in the palace.   They were relieved of their battered shields, and large numbers of blood-stained saddles were hidden away to save the women's tears. Many a good knight had brought a weary body back from the war.

The King looked after his guests in great style, and his land was full of strangers and friends. He asked that the seriously wounded should be treated with special consideration, for their spirits were low.   Those skilled in medicine were offered rich reward, unlimited silver and shining gold, if they could restore the heroes after the perils of battle. On top of that, the King gave generous gifts to his guests.   Those who now wanted to ride home were asked to stay, as is usual with close friends, and the

King took counsel how he should reward his men. They had done his will with great honour.

Lord Gernot said: 'Let them go. But tell them to come back to a feast in six weeks' time. Most of the seriously wounded will have recovered by then.'

Sifrid from the Netherlands also asked for leave, and when King Gunther heard what he wanted, he begged him affectionately to prolong his stay; but nothing would have come of it if it had not been for his sister.

In any case Sifrid was too rich and powerful to accept any payment. It was true he had earned the affection of the King, and of those of the King's relations who had seen his feats of strength in the battle,   but it was for the sake of the beautiful lady, and in the hope of seeing her, that he decided to stay. And so it eventually turned out; he came to know the maiden just as he wished, and in due course he rode back joyfully to his father's kingdom.

The Lord of the land ordered chivalry to be practised night and day, and many a young warrior was eager to join in. In the meantime he had seats put up on the sands by Worms, in readiness for the guests he was expecting.   During this same period, while he was waiting for their arrival, the beautiful Kriemhilde had heard the news of how he intended to stage a feast for his dear friends; and at once the ladies were busy   with the clothes and headdresses which they were to wear. The great Uote had also been told of the proud knights who were expected; and many rich clothes were taken out of their wrappings.   To please her sons, she had clothes prepared, with which many a lady and maiden and many a young Burgundian warrior were to be adorned. For the strangers also she had magnificent clothes made ready.

AVENTIURE 5

SIFRID SEES KRIEMHILDE FOR THE FIRST TIME

Every day now you could see those who wanted to be at the feast riding towards the Rhine. Horses and magnificent clothes were offered to everyone who came to the country for love of the King.   There was accommodation at the feast for thirty-two princes, the noblest and the best, we are told, and the beautiful ladies were eager to excel each other in dressing for the occasion.   Young Giselher was particularly busy. He and Gernot, helped by their men, made sure of a friendly reception for strangers and friends, and greeted the warriors with all honour and respect.   Numberless saddles, red with gold, were ridden into the land; shields finely decorated and magnificent clothes were brought to the Rhine for the feast; and the wounded men's spirits began to rise.   Those who lay in bed and suffered from their wounds were forced to forget the bitterness of death. There was an end of mourning for the sick and wounded, and they rejoiced in anticipation of the festive days ahead,   when they would live under Gunther's hospitality. Bliss unmeasured and joy without restraint were experienced by all who took part, and great rejoicing was heard in all Gunther's lands.

And then, one Whitsunday morning, all the brave men who had come for the feast turned out in their finery; five thousand or more there must have been, and the entertainments began, rivalling each other in many places at once.   The Lord of the land was acute enough to know how deeply the hero from the Netherlands loved his sister, although as yet Sifrid had never seen this girl whose beauty was praised above all maidens.   And the warrior Ortwin said to the King: 'If you wish your feast to be crowned with the highest honours, you should bring out the delightful young ladies who live among us to the great honour of Burgundy.   What is a man's joy and delight, unless it stems from beautiful maidens and lovely women? Present your sister to your guests.' The suggestion was welcome to many a hero there.

25

'Gladly,' said the King, and all who heard it were pleased. He sent word to Lady Uote and her lovely daughter that they should come to court with their maids.

At this, fine clothes were fetched out of their trunks; and there in their wrappings were a multitude of precious garments, together with bracelets and braid, with which the beautiful girls proceeded to adorn themselves.

And many an inexperienced young knight began to wonder that day whether the ladies might find him attractive, thinking that this would mean more to him than a whole mighty kingdom, and eagerly looking forward to his first glimpse of these beautiful women.

Then the mighty King ordered his sister's retinue to go with her, sword in hand, a good hundred of his followers, his and her relations. These were the members of the Burgundian court.   Mighty Uote accompanied her, with a hundred or more beautiful ladies, richly dressed; and behind her daughter followed many a handsome girl.   They all appeared from one room, and a great crush of heroes ensued, all hoping to be lucky enough to see the noble maid if it were possible.

And now the lovely maid came forth as the dawn breaks through the clouds; and the man in whose heart she dwelt, and had dwelt for a long time now, was set free from care when he saw her standing so royally there.

Numberless precious stones shone from her dress; she glowed like a lovely rose. No one, even if he had wanted to, could have said that he had ever seen anything more beautiful on this earth.   As the bright moon stands out before the stars, and shines down so clearly through the clouds, just so she stood in front of many another excellent lady. The festive heroes' spirits rose at the sight.   Lordly chamberlains preceded her, but the excited knights were not to be restrained, and pushed forward to where they could see the lovely maid. Lord Sifrid felt joy and sorrow together.

He thought to himself: 'How could it ever be that I should win your love? A fond hope! And yet I would find it easier to die than to be separated from you.' And he went hot and cold at the thought.

He looked so lovable standing there, the child of Sigemund, that he might have been drawn on parchment by a master's cunning hand; and indeed, it was said of him that no more handsome hero was ever seen.

26

Those who accompanied the ladies ordered everyone to stand
back from their path, and great numbers of warriors obeyed the
command. Their hearts leapt up at the sight of all these ladies,
so fine and so well-bred.*

And then Lord Gernot of Burgundy spoke: 'Gunther, dear
brother! The knight who offered you his service so generously—
why not repay the compliment in front of all these knights? I
can't believe that anything but good would come of it.   Pre-
sent Sifrid to my sister, and let her greet him. It will work out
well for us. Let Sifrid be the first man ever to receive her greet-
ing, and so we shall have won this accomplished warrior to our
side.'

The King's men went to find the hero, and said to the knight
from the Netherlands: 'The King has granted permission for
you to appear at court. His sister is to greet you; you are
honoured.'

The lord was filled with joy at this. In his heart was pure
happiness at the thought of seeing the beautiful child of Uote.
And so she greeted him in accordance with her lovely nature.

When she saw him standing before her and felt his elation, her
face burned, and the fair maiden said: 'Welcome, Lord Sifrid,
most good and noble knight!' His heart rose at the greeting.

He bowed eagerly to her; she took him by the hand, and how
sweetly he walked with the lady! Lord and lady looked at each
other with love in their eyes, but naturally with great discretion
also.

It may be that a white hand was pressed affectionately in
heartfelt devotion; but if so I know nothing of it, although I can
scarcely believe that the opportunity was missed. She had
certainly lost no time in showing him her favour.   The near-
ness of summer and the approach of May could never have filled
his heart with greater joy than he experienced at that moment,
hand in hand with the lady he longed for as a lover.

Many a knight thought to himself: 'What wouldn't I give to
be in his shoes, side by side with her, or in bed with her for that
matter! I shouldn't need much persuading.' But Sifrid had
worked hard for his reward.*

The guests, from whatever land they came, all had eyes for
this pair alone, and Kriemhilde was allowed to kiss the splendid
man—for him an experience more delightful than any he had
ever known in all his travels.   The King of Denmark said at
once when he saw it: 'For the sake of this great honour, many a

27

man lies wounded by Sifrid's hand, as I have good cause
to remember. May God keep him out of my kingdom in
future!'   On all sides the court was ordered to stand back for
beautiful Kriemhilde, and so she went to church with many a
bold knight decorously following in her train. From now on,
Sifrid, this splendid man, was separated from her,   and she
entered the minster followed by many women. The Queen's
person was adorned to such effect that many a desire was
aroused which would never be fulfilled, and many a knight
singled her out to feast his eyes upon.

Sifrid could hardly wait till the singing was over. He thanked
his good fortune again and again, that she whom his heart had
chosen should show him such affection. That he loved the fair
lady in his turn goes without saying.   When she emerged
again from the minster, the bold knight, who was already out-
side, was invited to join her again. And it was only now that the
lovely maiden had a chance to thank him for the way he had
fought so gloriously ahead of her relations.

'May God reward you, Lord Sifrid,' said the beautiful girl.
'You seem to have earned the devotion and true loyalty of our
knights, to judge from what I hear them saying.' He looked at
Lady Kriemhilde with love in his eyes.   'I shall serve them
always,' said the warrior in his turn, 'and as long as I live, I shall
never rest without following their wishes. And all this is to win
your favour, my Lady Kriemhilde.'

Every day for the next twelve days, when the precious maiden
went to court before her friends, you could see the warrior at her
side. Such was her loving service to the knight.

And every day, in front of Gunther's hall, inside and out, you
could see a crowd of brave men shouting for joy and happiness.
Ortwin and Hagen worked miracles,   cheerfully and lavishly
supplying everybody's wants.* The guests soon got to know
these knights, and the reputation of Gunther's lands rose as a
result.   Those who had been lying wounded appeared again
on the streets, anxious to join in the entertainments, to throw a
lance or hold a shield with the rest. There were plenty ready to
help them.

When it came to the feast, their host fed them with the
very best food. He was determined to avoid all the various
pitfalls that beset a king, and was seen to approach his
guests amiably,   saying: 'Good knights, before you go,
accept these gifts from me. I should be sincerely indebted to you

if you could bring yourselves not to spurn my possessions. I want to share them with you, and I really mean this.' *

The Danes immediately answered: 'Before we ride home we would like a firm settlement. In fact, we can't go without one. After all, we've lost many close friends at the hands of your warriors.'

Liudegast was already healed of his wounds, and the ruler of Saxony had recovered after the battle, but a considerable number of dead were left behind in Burgundy. King Gunther, at this point, went to look for Sifrid.

He said to that warrior: 'Advise me what to do. Our enemies are eager to leave, and they want a firm settlement in respect of me and my men. Well, what do you think, warrior Sifrid? What would be the best thing to do?   I can tell you what they offer. They would be willing to give as much in gold as five hundred horses could carry if I let them go free.' But Sifrid the strong said: 'No, that would be quite wrong.   Just set them free and let them go, on condition that they never ride into your land with hostile intent again. Have the two lords give their word and their hand on it.'

'I'll follow your advice,' said Gunther, and with that they went and told his enemies that nobody wanted the gold they had offered. Their dear friends were pining for them back at home.

Shield after shield full of treasure was brought in, and Gunther shared it out liberally amongst his friends, five hundred marks a man, and some got even more. It was brave Gernot's idea.   When they were ready to go, they all went to take their leave. The guests were presented to Kriemhilde and to Queen Uote, who was also sitting there, and no warriors ever had a better leave-taking.   And so they rode away, leaving their lodgings empty behind them. But the proud king was still there at home, and his relations (a noble crowd of men), and they attended Kriemhilde every day.   Then the good hero Sifrid asked leave to go, since he was not confident of achieving what he wanted. But the King heard that he was thinking of leaving, and it was young Giselher who managed to dissuade him from the journey.

'Where are you off to, noble Sifrid? Be guided by me and stay here with the warriors, with King Gunther and his men. We have a lot of beautiful ladies here we should like you to see.'

And Sifrid the strong answered: 'Leave the horses where they are; I had intended to leave, but I've thought better of it. And carry the shields away again; I did want to go home, but Lord Giselher, in great good faith, has put that out of my mind.'

And so the brave man stayed behind to please his friends. Not that he would have been better off anywhere else, or in any other country, for he now saw the fair Kriemhilde every day.   It was her outstanding beauty which held him there. Entertainments of all kinds were offered, and he would have passed his time pleasantly in this way if he had not been so oppressed by love of her. This affliction never left him, and in due course the brave man came to a miserable end because of it.

AVENTIURE 6

GUNTHER GOES TO ICELAND IN SEARCH OF BRÜNNHILDE

Exciting * news reached the Rhine, and tales of many a fair maiden. The good King Gunther conceived the idea of winning one of them, and his spirits rose at the thought.   There was a Queen ruling across the sea, the like of whom was never seen. She was outstandingly beautiful and very strong, and for love she competed with bold warriors at spear-throwing.   She hurled the stone a great distance, and leapt far and wide after it. If anyone wanted the noble lady's love, his only chance was to beat her at these three games. If he failed in one, his head was forfeit.   The maiden had already won, time and time again. When this came to the ears of a handsome knight by the Rhine. he turned his mind to the beautiful woman—and many heroes later lost their loves.

The Ruler of the Rhine spoke: 'I will go down to the sea, away to Brünnhilde, whatever fate may befall me! For her love I will stake my life, and lose it if I cannot win her!' *

'I wouldn't advise that,' said Sifrid. 'Remember, this queen has such barbarous habits that anyone who courts her is risking a great deal. I honestly think you should give up the idea of this journey.'

'And my advice', said Hagen, 'is that you should ask Sifrid to share this heavy burden with you, since he apparently knows so much about Brünnhilde.'

'Will you help me, noble Sifrid, to win the lovely maid?' asked Gunther. 'If you do what I ask, and this lovely woman is brought to my bed, then I'll risk my life and my honour for your sake.'

And the son of Sigemund answered: 'Give me your sister, and I'll do it. Give me the fair queen Kriemhilde, and I ask for no other reward for my labours.'

'That I promise, Sifrid; give me your hand on it,' said Gunther. 'As soon as the fair Brünnhilde arrives in our land I'll

31

give you my sister in marriage; and may you live happily ever after with the fair one.'

The two proud knights took an oath on it, which only added to their labours before they brought the lady back to the Rhine at last. There was great trouble in store for these brave men.   Sifrid had to take his cloak of invisibility with him, which the brave hero had won, not without trouble, from a dwarf called Alberich. The brave and mighty knights prepared for the journey.   Whenever strong Sifrid put this cloak on he found power and to spare inside it; the strength of twelve men was added to his own, and he courted the proud maiden with skill and cunning.   And there was another property this cloak had: once inside it any man could do whatever he wanted without being seen, which was how he won Brünnhilde and brought great misfortune upon himself.

'Now tell me, warrior Sifrid, before my quest begins. Should we take any knights with us into Brünnhilde's lands, if we want to sail the sea without dishonour? Thirty thousand men can be raised immediately.'

'However many troops we were to take with us,' said Sifrid again, 'the Queen's behaviour is so barbarous that they would all have to die through her arrogance. I've got a better plan for you, brave and good knight that you are.   We'll go down to the Rhine as lone knights, and I'll give you the names of the company. There'll be four of us all told to go down to the sea and win the lady, whatever happens to us afterwards.   I shall be one of the party, you the second, for the third we'll have Hagen (we'll manage all right) and for the fourth Dankwart, that brave man. A thousand men won't stand up to us in battle.'

'I should rather like to know before we left (and I mean this),' said the King, 'what clothes we should wear in front of Brünnhilde so as to look our best. Gunther awaits your answer.' *

'The best clothes you ever saw are worn all the time in Brünnhilde's country, so we shall have to appear richly dressed in front of the lady if we don't want to be disgraced in the telling.'

The good warrior said then: 'Very well. I'll go myself to my dear mother, to see if I can persuade her to let her beautiful maidens help prepare clothes for us, which we can wear without dishonour before the haughty maid.'

Then Hagen of Tronege spoke in his lordly way: 'Why do you want to ask such services of your mother? Let your sister hear what you intend, and she'll put herself at your disposal for this royal visit.'

So Gunther sent a message to his sister, saying he wanted to see her, together with the warrior Sifrid. Before they arrived the fair lady decked herself out in all her finery; she was not at all averse to a visit from these brave men.

Now her retinue was also fittingly dressed, and as soon as the princes heard this, they both approached. She stood up from her seat, and went to receive the noble guest and her brother with due ceremony.

'Welcome to my brother and his friend. I should like to know what it is that brings you gentlemen to court,' said the maiden. 'Let me hear what you noble knights have in mind.'

King Gunther said: 'I'll tell you, lady. We must bear great hardship with confidence and fortitude, for we wish to pay court far away in foreign lands, and we need fine clothes for the journey.'

'Sit down then, my dear brother,' said the princess, 'and tell me properly who these ladies are that have attracted your love to other lands.' The lady took the two choice knights by the hand, and led them to where she had been sitting before, on rich couches you may be sure, wrought with excellent figures and encrusted with gold.* Their visit to the ladies could not but be enjoyable. Affectionate looks and kindly glances were there for both in plenty. He carried her in his heart, she loved him as life itself; and in time the fair Kriemhilde became strong Sifrid's wife.

Then the mighty King spoke: 'My dear sister, we could never hope to do this without your help. We wish to go courting in Brünnhilde's land, and we need to appear in lordly apparel before the ladies there.'

Then the maiden answered: 'My dear brother, whatever help you want from me in this, I'm more than ready to offer, believe me. Kriemhilde would hate to see anyone refuse you anything. But it's not right that you, noble knight, should ask me with such diffidence; you should rather order me in lordly fashion. Whatever it pleases you to require from me, I'm ready to perform it willingly,' said the delightful girl.

'Dear sister, we wish to have good clothing to wear, and your noble hand shall help to prepare it. Let your maids perform this task so that it looks well on us, for there's no turning back from this journey.'

And the maid said: 'Listen then. I have the silks myself; arrange for precious stones to be brought in to us on shields, and we will work the clothes.' Gunther and Sifrid agreed.

'Who are the others to be dressed for their appearance at court with you?' asked the Queen. He said: 'Four of us all told: Two of my men, Dankwart and Hagen, are coming to court with me.

'And I should like you to take careful note of what I say, lady: the four of us, for four days, will need three changes of clothing each; and it must be of such quality that we can leave Brünnhilde's land again without having disgraced ourselves.'

The lords, after a pleasant leave-taking, departed, and Queen Kriemhilde fetched thirty of her maidens, highly skilled in such work, from their room.   Rich silks of Zazamanc, as green as any grass, and of Araby, white as the snow, were now inlaid with precious stones, to make clothing of high quality. Kriemhilde, the proud maid, cut them out herself.   Fine linings made from the skins of exotic fishes, fit to impress the foreigners, were collected and covered with silk, ready to wear. Now listen to the fabulous details of this glorious apparel!   From the land of Morocco, and from Libya, the best silks that anyone of royal blood could find, of these they had enough and to spare. Kriemhilde left them in no doubt of her affection.   Once they had set their minds on this lofty quest, ermine skins were no longer good enough for them. Velvet, black as coal, must be laid on top, such as bold heroes would not be ashamed to wear at feasts today.   Countless glittering jewels set in Arabian gold! The ladies were by no means idle, and within seven weeks they had the clothing ready. At about the same time the good knights' weapons were waiting for them.

At the appropriate moment a stout little ship was eagerly launched on the Rhine, to carry them away down to the sea. The high-born maidens were weighed down from their labours.   Then the knights were informed that the fine clothes they were to wear were ready for them; everything, just as they had wanted, was finished, and they began to look forward to leaving the Rhine.   A messenger was sent to ask if the members of the party would like to inspect their new clothes, to see if they were too long or too short for the heroes. The fit was perfect, for which they thanked the ladies.   Everyone they paraded in front of had to admit that they had never seen anything better in their lives, and they looked forward to wearing their clothes at court. No one could recall better ones.

Not forgetting to express their deep gratitude, the heroes, well satisfied, begged leave to go, like the well-trained knights they were. And bright eyes were wet and dimmed with tears.

Kriemhilde said: 'My dear brother, there is still time to change your mind. You could stay here and court some other lady, indeed I wish you would, without putting your life in such danger. You can find just as noble a lady nearer home.'

I think they must have known in their hearts what was to happen. They wept in unison, whatever anyone said to comfort them. Their gold breastplates were tarnished with the tears which fell unceasingly down from their eyes.

She said: 'Lord Sifrid, I commend my dear brother to your loyalty and affection. See that nothing harms him in Brünnhilde's land.' The brave man promised, taking Lady Kriemhilde's hand.

And the mighty warrior said: 'If my life is spared, lady, you won't need to worry. I'll bring him back to you safe and sound, you can rely on that.' The fair maid inclined her head in thanks.

Their golden shields were carried down to the river bank, their clothes were brought to them, their horses were ordered to be led out and they were ready to leave. Fair ladies wept, and sweet young girls stood at their windows, while a strong wind strained at their ship's sail. The proud companions embarked on the Rhine, and King Gunther said: 'Who's going to be in charge?'

'I am,' said Sifrid. 'I can lead you there across the sea all right. I know the best sea-routes, good hero, believe me.' And they departed happily from Burgundy.

Sifrid, the powerful man, quickly took a pole and began to shove off from the bank. Gunther the brave himself took an oar, and the bold and worthy knights drew away from the land. They had choice food with them, and a good supply of the best wine that could be found on the Rhine; their horses were snugly installed and comfortable. The ship proceeded smoothly and there was nothing to distress them. Their tough mainsheet was stretched taut, and, with a good wind, they made twenty miles down towards the sea before nightfall. Their confident labours were to bring them great suffering before long. On the twelfth morning, we are told, the winds had carried them far away towards Isenstein, into Brünnhilde's territory. Sifrid was the only one among them to recognize this.

When King Gunther saw such a great number of castles and the broad lands stretching on every side, he burst out: 'Tell me, friend Sifrid, whose are these castles and this lordly land? Do you know?'

To which Sifrid answered: 'I know very well. They are Brünnhilde's people and Brünnhilde's land, and Isenstein the impregnable, just as I told you before. You'll be able to see many a fair lady there before the day is out.   And I'd advise you heroes to agree on your story. I think this would be a good thing in case we're invited to appear before Brünnhilde today, because we must be on our guard in front of the Queen.   When we see the lovely maid and her following, you heroes of renown * must all say the same thing: that Gunther is my lord and I'm one of his men; then all his hopes will be satisfied.'   (They were ready to promise what he demanded. Not one of them was too proud to say what he told them, which was just as well for them when King Gunther set eyes on Brünnhilde.)

'And I'm not undertaking this so much for your sake as for your sister, the beautiful maid. She is as dear to me as life itself, and I want to earn the right to make her my wife.'

AVENTIURE 7

GUNTHER WINS BRÜNNHILDE

Meanwhile the ship had approached the castle near enough for them to see large numbers of fair maidens standing high up in the windows. Gunther was disturbed to realize that he recognized none of them. He asked his companion Sifrid: 'Do you know anything about the maidens who are looking down at us across the water? Whatever their lord calls himself, they look very sure of themselves.'

Lord Sifrid answered: 'Take a quiet look at all of them, and then tell me which one you'd take if you had the power.' 'I'll do that,' said Gunther, that brave and bold warrior. 'Well, I can see one of them standing in that window, in snow-white raiment; she is so fair that my eyes have chosen her by her beautiful body. If I had the power I should make her my wife.'

'Your eyes have chosen rightly. That is the noble Brünnhilde for whom your heart, your mind and your spirit strive.' Everything about her seemed good to Gunther.

Then the Queen told her proud maids to come away from the window. They were not to stand there in full view of the strangers. They obeyed, and we have since learned what the ladies then did. They dressed themselves in finery, in preparation for the unknown guests, a habit which elegant women have always had. To satisfy their curiosity, they took up their positions by the slit windows, where they could still see the heroes. There were just the four of them arriving in the land. Brave Sifrid led a horse on to the shore, watched by the fine ladies through their windows, and King Gunther's opinion of himself rose considerably.

Sifrid held the bridle of his fine steed for him, trusty and handsome, great and strong, until he was in the saddle. Such was his service to King Gunther—a service which was quickly forgotten. Then Sifrid led his own horse from the ship. It was a new function for him, standing at a great hero's stirrup, and the beautiful proud ladies saw it all theough their windows. Both alike, the confident heroes, their horses matching the snow-white of their clothes, their well-wrought shields

37

shining in their hands, they were an imposing sight. From their jewelled saddles and delicate collars hung bells of red gold as they proudly paraded before Brünnhilde's halls. It was their own courage that brought them to the land like this. With fresh-cut spears and well-made swords reaching down to their spurs, a majestic sight, keen and broad, the brave men wore them, and all this Brünnhilde saw, the proud maid.

After them came Dankwart and Hagen, and we are told how these warriors' rich clothes were coal-black. Their shields were beautiful, great, strong and broad. They wore jewels from India which you could see proudly dancing on their clothes, and leaving their boat unguarded by the shore, the brave good heroes rode to the castle.

Eighty-six towers they saw inside, three spacious palaces and a wonderful hall of noble marble, green as grass, in which sat Brünnhilde with her household. The castle was opened and the gates thrown wide, and Brünnhilde's men ran out to receive the guests in their lady's land, some being instructed to relieve them of their horses and the shields from their hands. Then one of her treasurers spoke: 'You are to give us your swords and shining armour.' 'Not likely!' said Hagen of Tronege. 'We prefer to carry them ourselves.' At which Sifrid was at pains to explain the real situation to him.

'I should tell you that it's the custom in this town that no guest should carry arms. You'd better let them take them away.' Hagen, Gunther's man, obeyed with great reluctance.

The guests were served with drink and made comfortable. Great numbers of bold knights were to be seen walking about in princely clothing at the court. But all the same there were many glances cast at the brave strangers.

Then the news was brought to Brünnhilde that unknown knights in lordly clothing had come sailing across the water, at which the good fair maid began asking questions.

'Tell me,' said the Queen, 'who might these unknown knights be, who stand so gloriously in my castle? And for whose sake have the heroes travelled here?'

One of her following answered: 'Lady, I can truthfully say I have never seen any of them before, except that there is one among them who is very like Sifrid. You should receive him well. That is my loyal advice. The second of the companions is so admirable that he might well be a mighty king, if he had the power, and rule over princes and broad lands, if such was his inheritance. You can see him standing there majestically by the others.   The third companion is so fearsome (although handsome to look at, mighty Queen), that to judge by the swift glances he keeps darting about, I imagine he is a savage man at heart.   The youngest among them is so adorable! I can see him, the mighty warrior, standing so lovably there, with innocent grace and noble bearing. If anyone here had done him wrong we should all have reason to fear him.   However mild and controlled his manner, and however beautiful his body, he would be quite capable of bringing fine ladies to tears if he were moved to rage. He is so fashioned that he lacks no quality to make him a brave bold warrior.'

Then the Queen spoke: 'Bring me clothing. For if strong Sifrid has come to this land after my love, let him save himself if he can. I'm not so frightened of him that I shall let him take me as his wife.'

Brünnhilde the fair was quickly clothed, and many a fair maid, a hundred or more, went with her, richly attired and eager to see the guests.   Icelandic warriors accompanied them, Brünnhilde's knights, with swords in their hands, five hundred or more of them. The guests were disturbed at this, and the brave young heroes rose from their seats.

When the Queen saw Sifrid, what do you think she said? 'Welcome, Lord Sifrid, to this land. I should be glad to know what is the purpose of your journey.'

'You are indeed most gracious to me, my Lady Brünnhilde, magnificent princess, in that you greet me before this noble knight who stands in front of me, for he is my lord. I'd rather have dispensed with this honour.   He is a Rhinelander by birth: what more need I say? We have come here for your sake; he wants to win your love, whatever may happen to him in the process. You should think it over before it's too late, for my lord is not to be put off.   He is called Gunther, and is a great king. If he could gain your love he would ask for nothing more. After all, it was the handsome knight's own idea; he ordered me to come here; if I'd been in a position to refuse, I should gladly have stayed behind.'

She said: 'If he is your lord and you are his man, he must face me, if he dares, in the contests I lay upon him. If he masters me, he shall have me as his wife. But if I win, you will all lose your lives.'

Then Hagen of Tronege said: 'Lady, let's see these arduous

games of yours. They would have to be very hard indeed to make my lord Gunther admit defeat to you. It should hardly be beyond his powers to win such a beautiful maid.'

'He must throw the stone, then jump after it, and then compete with me at spear-throwing; and you needn't look so eager. You have every chance of losing your honour and your life before you leave. Think it over carefully,' said the lovable maid.

Sifrid the brave went up to the King, and asked him to reveal his entire unshakable purpose to the Queen; he need have no fear. 'I'll protect you from her with my trickery.'

So King Gunther said: 'Proud Queen, lay upon me what you will. I would go through that and more even, for the sake of your beauty. I would willingly lose my head if I cannot have you for my wife.'

When the Queen had heard his speech she showed a natural eagerness to start the games. She ordered them to fetch her the right clothes * for fighting—armour of red gold and a sturdy shield.   An undershirt, beautifully made of Libyan silk, and never yet pierced by a weapon in any battle, was placed on the maid. The borders shone with bright embroidery.

Meanwhile our knights were subjected to provocation and threats. Dankwart and Hagen were not at their ease. They were concerned for the fate of their King, and thought: 'This journey of ours is proving a mistake.'

Sifrid meanwhile, the splendid man, had slipped off to the ship without anyone noticing, and fetched the cloak which was hidden there. He drew it on quickly, and from then on he was in no danger of being recognized.   He hurried back and found a crowd of knights where the Queen was setting forth her fateful conditions. He came up secretly as part of his plan, and of all of those that were there, not one saw him.   The circle was drawn, and the games were due to begin in the sight of a great crowd of knights, more than seven hundred. They were armed, and it was these heroes' job to say who had won.

Now Brünnhilde had also arrived, armed as if she was about to fight all the kings in Christendom for their lands. For she wore over her silks a multitude of golden clasps, and her lovely figure was now proudly resplendent.   Her followers came, carrying in their hands a shield of red gold, great and broad, with buckles hard as steel. This was to be the lovely maid's protection in the games.   The lady's shield-strap was a costly band set with precious stones, green as grass, sparkling on all sides against the gold. It would need to be a brave man who inspired this lady's love.   The boss of the shield which the maid was to bear was a good two feet thick, we are told. It was enriched with steel and gold in abundance, so that four men, including her treasurer, could scarcely carry it.

When strong Hagen saw the shield being carried, the hero of Tronege grimly said: 'Look where you've brought us now, King Gunther. We shan't get out of this alive! The woman you've set your heart on is the devil's wife.'

But there is more to tell of her many articles of clothing. She wore a battle-tunic of silk from Azagouk, rich and costly; and many a noble gem shone from it and from the Queen.   Then they brought out for the lady a great heavy spear, very sharp, which she always used; it was strong and barbarous, long and broad, with a murderous cutting-edge.   Let me tell you about the fabulous weight of the spear. A good half a ton of metal had gone into its making, and three of Brünnhilde's men could hardly carry it between them. The high-born Gunther was extremely worried.

He thought to himself: 'What's the use? The devil out of hell wouldn't survive this. If I were safe and sound back in Burgundy she'd be in no danger from my love for a long time.'

Then brave Dankwart, Hagen's brother, spoke up: 'I heartily regret this whole courtship. We always used to call ourselves knights—and now look how we're going to die! Are we to perish here at the hands of women?   I wish I'd never come to this country. If only my brother Hagen had his sword in his hand, and I had mine, then all these men of Brünnhilde's might show a little less arrogance.   They'd have to behave differently then. And if I'd sworn a thousand oaths to keep the peace, this beautiful maid would have to die before I saw my dear lord lose his life.'

'We should leave this country as free men easily enough', said his brother Hagen, 'if we had the clothes we need for fighting, and our good swords. And this strong lady might show a little less confidence too.'

The noble maid heard what the warrior said, and looked over her shoulder with a smile on her lips: 'Since he thinks he's so brave, bring them their armour; put the knights' sharp weapons in their hands.'

When they received their swords on the maid's instructions,

the brave Dankwart blushed for joy. 'Now let them try what games they like,' said the bold man, 'they can't get Gunther now that we've got our weapons.'

Brünnhilde's strength became more apparent than ever; they brought out a heavy stone into the ring, huge and unwieldy, round and vast. Twelve bold brave heroes could hardly carry it.   This was the stone she always threw when she had cast the spear, and the distress of the Burgundians grew. 'My God,' said Hagen. 'What sort of bedfellow has the king picked himself? Why, she'd be better off betrothed to the devil in hell!'

She rolled up the sleeves on her white arms, and took the shield in her hand. She raised the spear, and the contest was about to begin. Gunther and Sifrid were afraid of Brünnhilde's hostility.   And indeed, if Sifrid had not come to his aid, she would have killed the King. He came up secretly and touched his hand, throwing Gunther into great confusion by this trick.

'What was that touching me?' thought the brave man. He looked round, but could see no one there. Then a voice said: 'It's me, Sifrid, your dear friend. You're not to be afraid of the Queen.   Hand your shield to me, and let me carry it, and listen carefully to what I say. You go through the actions and I'll do the work.' When Gunther realized who it was, he felt a great relief.

'Don't let anyone see what I'm doing, and say nothing about it to anyone, and the Queen will have very little chance of winning the renown she hopes for. Just look at her standing in front of you quite unperturbed!'

Then the glorious maid gave a mighty throw at the shield, new, great and broad, which the son of Sigelinde was holding in his hand. The sparks leapt from the steel as if blown by the wind.   The strong spear-blade burst right through the shield, and fire flickered from his chain mail. The two powerful men staggered back from the impact, and if it had not been for the magic cloak they would have lost their lives on the spot.

Blood gushed from the mouth of brave Sifrid, but the good hero quickly leapt forward again, and took up the spear which she had thrown through his shield. It was sent back to her by the strong Sifrid's hand.

He thought: 'I don't want to pierce the fair maid,' and turned the point of the spear backwards over his shoulder. He aimed with the shaft at her armour, and cast so that it resounded from his courageous hand.

42

Sparks showered from the mail as if driven by the wind. It was a hearty throw by the child of Sigemund, and for all her strength, she could not keep her feet at the shock. King Gunther could certainly never have done that.

Not that the fair Brünnhilde was slow to jump up again: 'Gunther, noble knight, I thank you for that throw.' She thought he had done it with his own power, but it was a far stronger man who had crept up on her.

She moved off quickly, her anger roused, and lifted up the stone, the good noble maid. She hurled it powerfully far off from her hand, and jumped after the throw, so that all her armour clanged about her.

The stone had fallen a good twenty yards away, and she bettered the throw with her jump, the sweet maid. Lord Sifrid went up to where the stone was lying; Gunther held it while Sifrid took care of the throwing.

Sifrid was brave, tall and very strong. He threw the stone farther, and jumped longer as well, and because of his special powers he was strong enough to carry King Gunther as he jumped.

The jump was made, the stone had fallen—and no one was to be seen but Gunther the warrior. Brünnhilde the fair was red with anger, and Sifrid had averted King Gunther's death.

When she saw the hero safe and sound at the other end of the circle, she raised her voice a little as she said to her followers: 'Come closer at once, you my family and my people! You are all to be subject to King Gunther.'

Then the bold ones laid down their weapons, and a great crowd of brave men prostrated themselves at the feet of King Gunther from Burgundy. They imagined he had brought off the contests by his own strength.

He greeted her charmingly, for he was a man of many accomplishments. And the admirable maid took him by the hand, thus surrendering to him the power in her land. Hagen, the bold brave warrior, rejoiced at this.

She asked the noble knight to go off with her into the spacious palace. Once this was done they were at pains to make up to the Burgundians for their previous lack of attention, so that Dankwart and Hagen had to forget their anger.

Sifrid the bold was no fool. He took his magic cloak back to its hiding-place, and then returned to where the ladies were sitting. He said to the King, with calculated cleverness:

'What are you waiting for, my Lord? When do you start the contests which the Queen has laid on you in such numbers? It's time you let us see what they're like.' The cunning fellow behaved as if he knew nothing.

Then the Queen said: 'How did it happen, Lord Sifrid, that you missed the games which Gunther has just won here by his own hand?' Hagen of Burgundy answered her.

He said: 'You had put us into some confusion, Lady; and the good hero Sifrid was standing by our ship when the Ruler of the Rhine beat you in the games. That's why he knows nothing about it,' said Gunther's man.

'This is good news indeed,' said Sifrid the warrior, 'that your pride has taken such a fall, and that there's someone alive who can master you. Now, noble maid, you shall follow us to the Rhine.'

But the fair creature said: 'I can't. My family and my people must be told first. It's not so easy, you must realize, for me to leave my country. My best friends must first be summoned.'

Then she sent messengers riding off in all directions. She summoned her friends and vassals, asking them to come to Isenstein without fail, and ordering rich and magnificent clothing to be given to them all.

Every day, from morning to night, they rode up in swarms to Brünnhilde's castle. 'Oh God! Look what we've done now!' said Hagen. 'We're mad to wait here for Brünnhilde's people. Now that they're arriving in force, there's no knowing what the Queen intends—what if she's so furious that she's plotting our deaths? This noble maid was born to get us into trouble.'

Then strong Sifrid said: 'I'll see to that. I'll make sure this thing you're so anxious about doesn't happen. I'll bring you help here, hand-picked warriors that you've never seen before.   Ask no questions. I'll go now, and God will have to look after your honour while I'm gone. I'll be back shortly, bringing you a thousand of the best warriors I could ever hope to find.'

'But don't be too long,' said the King. 'We are naturally reluctant to be without your help.' Sifrid replied: 'I shall come back to you in a very few days. Tell Brünnhilde you've sent me off somewhere.'

AVENTIURE 8

SIFRID FETCHES HIS MEN

Then Sifrid in his magic cloak went out through the gate to the shore, where he found a little boat. He boarded it secretly, the son of Sigemund, and it moved off as if the wind had caught it.   No oarsman was to be seen as the little boat sped along by Sifrid's power—and this was so great that they thought an exceptionally strong wind was blowing it along.* But no, it was Sifrid, the beautiful child of Sigelinde, who urged it forward.   By the next morning he had covered, with prodigious exertion, a hundred long miles if not more, and had reached that country called Nibelunge, where he kept this great treasure of his.

The carefree hero sailed alone until he came to a broad headland,* where he soon had the boat made fast. He came to a hill with a castle on top, and began to look for lodging in the manner of a weary traveller.   When he arrived at the gates he found them locked, for the people here, like people everywhere, were jealous of their honour. The visitor began to beat on the door, which was well guarded, for he discovered behind it   a monster, who looked after the castle with his weapons continually lying at his side. 'Who's that banging so loudly on the door?' said the monster, and Lord Sifrid outside disguised his voice.

He said: 'A knight. Now open up the door! If I stay out here, before the day is out I'm going to annoy some of these people who'd rather lie comfortably in their soft beds.' The doorkeeper was incensed at Sifrid's words.

By now the brave giant was already armed, with his helmet strapped on. The strong man quickly grabbed up his shield, hurled open the door, and flung himself with the utmost ferocity at Sifrid!

To think that this fellow was prepared to wake up so many a brave man! Blows came from his hand in swift succession, so that his lordly guest was at pains to protect himself. Then, when the door-keeper with his iron pole   sent the buckles on

his shield flying apart, the hero was really in trouble; he was
even in some fear of death from the door-keeper's mighty
blows. All in all, his master Sifrid was well pleased with this
performance.   They fought so hard that the whole castle
resounded, and the din was heard in the Hall of the Nibelungs.
At length Sifrid subdued the door-keeper, and bound him. The
story spread through all the land of the Nibelunge.

Deep in the mountain, brave Alberich, that wild dwarf, heard
the fierce struggle. He armed himself hurriedly and ran out to
where this noble guest had firmly bound the giant.   Alberich
was very fierce, and strong as well. Helmet and chain mail he
wore on his body, and in his hand he carried a heavy scourge of
gold. He rushed swiftly at Sifrid.   With the seven heavy
knouts which were fixed on the end he rained such furious blows
on the brave man's shield that the greater part of it was smashed
in his hand as he held it in front of him. The magnificent guest
began to fear for his life.   He threw his shattered shield away,
and thrust his long sword into its sheath. He had no desire to kill
his own treasurer, and characteristically, he restrained his
hand.*   Instead he attacked Alberich with his own strong
fingers, grabbed him by his grey and venerable beard, and
dragged him about so barbarously that he cried aloud. The
heavy hand of the young hero was painful indeed to Alberich.

The brave fellow called out: 'Spare me! If I could be bound
to anyone but that one knight that I swore to serve, I'd follow
you rather than die,' said the cunning man.

Sifrid now bound Alberich as he had previously done the
giant, and his strength was painful to bear. The dwarf then
asked: 'What is your name?' He answered: 'My name's Sifrid,
and I'm surprised you don't recognize me.'

'Thank goodness for that!' said Alberich the dwarf. 'Now
I've felt your heroic deeds at first hand, and I see that you have
a genuine right to be master of this land. I'll obey you in
everything if you spare my life.'

Then Lord Sifrid said: 'Go quickly and bring me a thousand
Nibelungs from among the best knights that we have; let them
meet me here.' But he told no one why he wanted this.

He untied the giant and Alberich, and Alberich ran straight off
to find the knights. In some trepidation he woke up the Nibe-
lungs and said: 'Come on, you heroes, you're wanted by
Sifrid.'   They leapt out of their beds, ready and willing. A
thousand bold knights dressed themselves and went to where

46

Sifrid was standing, and welcomed him warmly, suiting their actions to their words.   They lit many candles and offered him blended wine. He thanked them all for coming so promptly, and said: 'You're going away with me across the sea.' The good brave heroes expressed their readiness.   Some three thousand warriors had soon arrived, and he picked the best thousand from among them. These had their helmets and other equipment brought to them, for he intended to lead them into Brünnhilde's land.

He said: 'Good knights, I have something to say to you. As we'll be appearing before many lovely women at this court, you'll need to be richly attired. So dress yourselves up in fine clothing.'   Early in the morning they set off, and a bold set of companions it was that Sifrid had collected. They had good horses and magnificent clothes, and they made a great impression when they entered Brünnhilde's land.

The lovely young girls were standing at the battlements, and the Queen said: 'Does anyone know who they are, that I can see sailing this way, far out at sea? Their sails are of good quality, whiter than the snow.'

The King of the Rhineland answered: 'It's just my men, Lady. I had left them on the way, just near here; now I've sent for them, and they've arrived.' The lordly guests attracted much attention.

Then Sifrid could be seen standing at the prow of one of the ships, magnificently clothed, and many others with him. The Queen said: 'Tell me, Lord King, should I receive the guests, or deny them my greeting?'

He said: 'You should go to meet them in front of the palace. Leave them in no doubt that we are pleased to see them.' The Queen did as Gunther suggested, and as she greeted them she singled out Sifrid from the others.*

They were found lodgings for the night, and relieved of their armour. By now there were so many strangers in the country that the crowds were getting in each other's way, and the brave Burgundians were eager to go home.

The Queen said: 'I should be much indebted to anyone who could distribute my gold and silver, of which I have so much, to my guests and the King's.' Dankwart answered, brave Giselher's man.

'Most noble Queen, let me have the key. I'm confident that I can distribute it,' said the brave warrior, 'so that the blame for

47

any mistakes can fall on me alone.' And he proceeded to give a magnificent display of generosity.

When Hagen's brother had taken charge* of the key, he handed out so many rich gifts that if anyone needed a mark he was given enough for all the poor to live off happily for the rest of their lives.   And again and again, without bothering to count up, he gave away a good £100 at a time, and many went away richly attired who had never worn such gorgeous clothes before. When the Queen realized this she was not at all pleased.

And the proud lady said: 'My Lord King, I could do without your treasurer giving away my last clothes; he is literally throwing my gold away. I should be much indebted to anyone who stopped him.   He's giving so liberally, this warrior, he seems to think I'm celebrating my own funeral. I expect to need my money for some time yet; and in any case, I'm quite capable of squandering my father's inheritance on my own. Never was a Queen saddled with such a generous treasurer.'

Then Hagen of Tronege spoke: 'Lady, you can take it from me that the King of the Rhine has so much gold and clothing of his own to give away, that we don't need to take any of Brünnhilde's wardrobe with us.'

'No, for my own sake,' said the Queen, 'let me fill twenty travelling-boxes with gold and silks, so that I can distribute them with my own hand when we come across into Gunther's land.'   They packed the boxes for her with precious stones, but her own treasurers had to be there, since she was reluctant to trust Giselher's man with the task. At which Gunther and Hagen laughed.

Then the Queen said: 'Who shall I leave in charge of my lands? You and I must arrange that before we leave.' The noble King answered: 'Call on anyone you like, and we'll make him governor.'

The lady saw one of her most eminent relations by her (her mother's brother it was), and said to him: 'I now put you in charge of my castles and lands, until King Gunther shall come to sit in judgment here.'

Then she chose two thousand men from her household to go with her to Burgundy, together with the thousand knights from Nibelunge. They made ready for the journey, and could soon be seen riding down to the shore.   She took with her eighty-six women and at least a hundred maids, of great beauty. They had waited long enough, and were eager to go. But what weeping

48

there was among those left at home! She went from her own country with exemplary behaviour. She kissed her dear friends who were present, and with warm farewell they went down to the sea. Never again did the lady see her father's lands.

On the journey was heard music of all kinds, and plenty of varied entertainment was provided. A fair wind helped them on their way, and they joyfully left the land behind them. During the voyage she refused to sleep with her husband. This pleasure was saved until they should come, as they and the heroes eventually did with great joy, to his house, his castle at Worms and the celebration of his marriage.

AVENTIURE 9

SIFRID IS SENT AHEAD TO WORMS

They travelled for nine full days, and then Hagen of Tronege spoke: 'Listen. We're taking too long with our news for Worms by the Rhine. Your messengers should be in Burgundy by now.'

'You are right,' said King Gunther, 'and no one would be so suitable for such a journey as yourself, friend Hagen. Ride ahead into my land. No one could better tell the tale of our courtship.'

But Hagen answered: 'I don't make a good messenger. Leave me in charge of the valuables.* I'll stay aboard with the ladies, and look after their finery until we've brought them to Burgundy.   Ask Sifrid instead to take the message. He can carry it out with strength and courage. If he refuses to go, you should make an effort to be polite, and put the request in a friendly way, saying it's for the sake of Kriemhilde.'

He sent for the knight, who came as soon as they had found him, and said: 'Now that we are nearing home and my own lands, I ought to send messengers to my dear sister and my mother, announcing our approach to the Rhine.   I ask you to do this, Sifrid. Carry out my wishes, and I am always at your service,' said the good warrior. But good Sifrid raised objections, so that Gunther had to beg and implore him.   He said: 'Ride for my sake, and for Kriemhilde the fair maiden. Let me and the proud maid together deserve this of you.' Once he heard this, Sifrid was eager to go.

'Give me what messages you will, then; I'll deliver them all. I am ready to do this for the sake of that most beautiful maid. How could I deny her anything whom I hold in my heart? Whatever you ask for her sake shall be done.'

'Then tell my mother, Queen Uote, that we hold our heads high on our journey. Let my brothers know what we have achieved, and inform our friends of this as well.   From my beautiful sister you should conceal nothing.* Commend me and Brünnhilde to her service, and similarly with all the household and all my men. How brilliantly have I achieved that for which my heart ever yearned!   And tell Ortwin my dear nephew to

50

arrange accommodation at Worms by the Rhine, and to let the
rest of my relations know that Brünnhilde and I intend to put on
a magnificent feast.   And tell my sister, as soon as she hears
that I have landed she should spare no effort in providing a
reception for my beloved wife. In doing this, Kriemhilde will
earn my undying gratitude.'

Lord Sifrid then took his leave of Lady Brünnhilde, and all
her retinue in fitting terms, and rode to the Rhine. A better
messenger there could never have been in all the world.   He
rode to Worms with twenty-four knights. When the news spread
that he was coming without the King, all the household was
weighed down with sorrow. They feared that their lord had been
killed in Isenstein.   The horsemen dismounted, with a
confident air, and Giselher, the good young King, came up at
once with his brother Gernot. When he had looked in vain for
King Gunther, he lost no time in speaking.

'Welcome, Lord Sifrid. Tell me where you left the King, my
brother. I fear that Brünnhilde's strength may have taken him
from us. If so, this lofty aspiration of his will have done us great
harm.'

'You can forget that worry. My companion on the journey
commends himself to your service, and to that of his relations.
I left him in the best of health. It was he who sent me to you, to
be his messenger bringing news to your land.   And please
arrange as soon as possible for me to see the Queen and your
sister, somehow or other. I must let them hear the message
Gunther and Brünnhilde have given me. Both of them are doing
very well.'

Then young Giselher spoke: 'Go in and see her then. Your
news will make my sister very happy. She is terribly worried
about my brother. The maid will be pleased to see you; I
guarantee you that.'

Then Lord Sifrid spoke: 'It will be my pleasant duty to serve
her in any way I can. But who's going to announce my approach
to the ladies?' It was great Giselher who took the message.

Giselher the bold said to his mother and sister, when he found
them both together: 'Sifrid has come to see us, the hero from the
Netherlands. My brother Gunther has sent him here to the
Rhine.   He brings us news of the King. Allow him to
present himself, and he'll give us the news we've been waiting
for from Iceland.' The ladies were still full of anxiety.

They ran for their clothes and dressed. They asked Sifrid to

51

come to court, which he was willing enough to do, since he was eager to see them, and high-born Kriemhilde spoke to him affectionately:

'Welcome, Lord Sifrid, glorious knight. Where is my brother Gunther, the noble mighty King? I fear we may have lost him through Brünnhilde's strength. Alas, poor maid, that ever I was born!'

The brave knight answered: 'You beautiful ladies can stop weeping, and give me my reward as messenger! I left him safe and sound, I can assure you. He and his wife have sent me here with a message for you both.   He and his sweetheart offer you their devoted service, and intimate affection, most noble Queen. Now dry your eyes; they'll soon be here.' It was the most welcome news they had heard for a long time.

With her snow-white sleeve she wiped the tears from her eyes. She thanked the messenger for this news she had received, and in that moment her great grief and her weeping left her.   She asked the messenger to sit down, which he was not loath to do, and the lovely girl said: 'I should very much like to give you gold of mine in reward for this message, but you are too mighty a King for that. Instead I offer you my undying gratitude.'

'If I were the sole master over thirty lands', he said, 'I should still be pleased to accept a gift from your hand.' 'Let it be so then,' said the excellent maid, and she ordered her treasurers to fetch the messenger's reward.

She gave him twenty-four rings with precious stones, and the hero's character was such that he had no desire to keep it. He gave it away immediately to the first member of her household he found in the room.

Her mother then offered him her service in the most friendly way. 'I am to tell you', said the brave man, 'what Gunther wants you to do when he arrives at the Rhine. And if you do it, he says he'll always be indebted to you.   I heard him asking that you should welcome his eminent guests, and should do him the favour of riding to meet him on the shore outside Worms. And he earnestly hopes you will do this for him.'

Then the lovely lady said: 'I am ready and willing. I couldn't deny him any service that is within my power. It shall be done as a pleasant family duty.' And the colour deepened which happiness brought to her cheeks.

No royal messenger was ever better received. If she had dared to kiss him the lady would have done so. How sweetly he took his leave of the ladies! And the Burgundians did as Sifrid advised.   Sindold and Hunold and Rumold the warrior were kept busy putting up seats and accommodation on the shore in front of Worms. The masters of the King's household were seen hard at work.   Ortwin and Gere did not forget to send in all directions for their friends and relations, telling them of the celebration which was to take place at Worms, and all the fair maidens began to adorn themselves in preparation.   The palace and the walls were decorated throughout in honour of the guests; Gunther's hall was furnished to accommodate all the strangers, and so this great feast was joyfully begun.   From all directions the relations of the three kings came riding through the land. They had been called in so as to wait for the expected arrivals, and in the meantime great quantities of costly clothing were fetched from storage.

Then the news spread that Brünnhilde's people had ridden into sight, and there was bustle and confusion in the crowded land of Burgundy.* You could scarcely move for the throngs of brave warriors on every side.

And Kriemhilde the fair said: 'Now, those of my maids who want to be at the reception with me, look out your very best clothes from your trunks, so that we shall be praised and honoured by the guests.'

The knights were there as well, and ordered the magnificent saddles of pure red gold to be brought out, which the ladies at Worms by the Rhine were to ride. Better ladies' harness was never seen.   And the bright gold shining from the horses! And the numberless precious stones sparkling from the bridles! The golden footstools were brought out for the happy and excited ladies, and set down on shining silk.   Mounts for the noble maidens were ready at the court, as I have said. The delicate collars worn by their horses were of the best silks ever known.

Eighty-six ladies then appeared wearing their head-dress, and took their places with Kriemhilde, a beautiful sight in their shining clothes. Then came many an elegant Burgundian maiden, also well attired.   Fifty-four of them there were, the noblest that were to be found, their golden hair encircled with bright braid. Great pains had been taken to meet the king's wishes in advance.

They wore costly stuffs, the best that could be found, to confront the strange knights; and this array of good clothes was a fitting foil for their great beauty. He would have had a jaundiced eye who could have found fault with any one of them.*   Sable and ermine were in great demand; rings and bracelets were fitted over silken sleeves—but it would be impossible for anyone to exhaust the story of their preparations.   Noble coats of ferrandine were finished off with girdles rich and long, cunningly fashioned of Arabian silk. It was a happy time for all those noble maids.   No beautiful girl was going to miss the chance of showing herself off in her dress, and they all laced themselves up to the best possible advantage. It must have been the most charming royal household ever seen.

As soon as the lovely women had finished dressing, a great crowd of high-spirited knights, with shields and ashen lances in their hands, came up and offered to escort them.

AVENTIURE 10

BRÜNNHILDE IS RECEIVED AT WORMS

Across the Rhine they saw the numerous companies of the King and his guests approaching the bank, and many maidens led by the bridle. Those who were to receive them were all ready.   When the visitors from Iceland and Sifrid's Nibelungs had embarked in their ships, they rowed eagerly across to the near bank, where the King's family were waiting for them.   But first I must tell you how Uote, the mighty Queen, rode in person at the head of her ladies-in-waiting out of the town, providing an opportunity for knights and maids to make each other's acquaintance.

Duke Gere led Kriemhilde by the bridle, but only as far as the city gates. From then on, Sifrid had to perform this service. She was a beautiful girl, and he was well rewarded for it later.

Brave Ortwin rode with Lady Uote, and the other knights and maids followed in pairs. Never before, I could swear, were so many women seen together for such a magnificent reception.

All the way down to the ships the knights jousted for fair Kriemhilde as they were expected to do; after which the ladies were lifted down from their horses.

Now the King had come over, with many more important guests. And the strong shafts that were broken before the ladies! The clashing of shields as they came together! The loud ringing of rich shield-bosses as they jostled!   The lovely ladies stood at the quay, while Gunther came out of the ship with his guests, leading Brünnhilde by the hand. It would have been impossible to say which were the most dazzling, their shining jewels or their clothes.

Then Lady Kriemhilde very correctly went to meet Lady Brünnhilde and her followers. As they kissed you could see their white hands adjusting their virginal headgear. It was a form of courtesy.

And Kriemhilde the maid then spoke the appropriate words: 'Welcome to these our lands, and to me and my mother, and to all the loyal friends that we have!' The ladies inclined their

heads,   and embraced repeatedly where they stood. Such a
loving reception as the two ladies accorded the bride was never
seen before. Again and again Lady Uote and her daughter kissed
her sweet lips.

When Brünnhilde's women had all come ashore, every knight
took a fair lady by the hand, as the girls stood before Lady
Brünnhilde.   It was a long time before she had finished
greeting them, for there were many rosy lips to be kissed. And
still the two princesses stood side by side, a sight which gave
pleasure to many a glorious knight.   They looked carefully,
since they had it as yet only on hearsay that the two ladies were
the fairest ever seen; now they had to admit it was true. And
there was no hint of any deceptive art to be seen on them.   The
connoisseurs of ladies and loveliness praised Gunther's wife for
her beauty; the wise ones who looked closer said that one might
well prefer Kriemhilde to Brünnhilde.

Then maids and ladies came together in their finery, and you
could see all the countryside before Worms filled with rich
silken tents, large and small.   The King's household were
crowding in, and Brünnhilde and Kriemhilde were advised to
withdraw, with all the ladies, into the shade; the Burgundian
warriors would escort them.

By now all the guests had come up on horseback, and many a
powerful joust was taken on the shield. Dust rose from the field
as if all the land were smoking with fire. Heroes made their
names that day.   There were plenty of maidens to watch
what the knights were doing, and I should not be surprised if
Lord Sifrid did more than one turn before the tents, with a
thousand handsome Nibelungs behind him.

Then Hagen of Tronege came, acting on instructions from the
King, and gracefully broke off the tournament, so that the
beautiful young maidens should not become too dusty. The
guests obeyed, considerately enough.   And Lord Gernot
said: 'Leave the horses standing until it gets cooler; then we
shall joust for the beautiful ladies in front of the broad palace.
Be ready for the moment when the King decides to start.'

As the tournament was finished all over the field, the knights
went into the many lofty tents to take their ease with the ladies,
in the hope of great delight to come. There they whiled away the
time until it was decided to move on.   In the cool of the
approaching evening, when the sun had sunk lower, they felt
they had waited long enough, and a great crowd of men and

women made off for the town. There was hardly a fair lady there who was not lovingly regarded by some knight.

The high-spirited heroes jousted right up until the moment when the King dismounted before the palace. In characteristic service to the ladies, and following the custom of the country, they happily rode their clothes to shreds.

Then the mighty Queens were separated, as Lady Uote and her daughter withdrew to a spacious room with their following. A great and joyful noise resounded on all sides.   The benches were got ready, and the King went to take his place at table with the guests. Fair Brünnhilde stood at his side, King Gunther's great and powerful Queen.   There was a lavish array of benches and good broad tables heaped with food, and I am told that nobody went short out of all those proud guests who sat there with the King.

The host's cup-bearers brought round water in golden vessels. It would be no use for anyone to talk of better service at any royal feast—I would not believe him.   But before the Lord of the Rhine took water, Lord Sifrid reminded him of an obligation, a promise he had made before ever he set eyes on Brünnhilde in Iceland.   He said: 'You should remember that you swore you would give me your sister if Brünnhilde should ever enter this country. Well, where are the oaths now? After all, I played a strenuous part in your expedition.'

The King answered his guest: 'You were right to remind me, for my word is not to be broken in this. I will do everything in my power to help you achieve what you want.' Accordingly, Kriemhilde was summoned before the King.

As she came up to the hall with her beautiful maids, Giselher ran down to meet her, saying: 'Send these maids back; my sister is to appear alone before the King.'

And so they took her to where Gunther was sitting. Noble knights from many countries were standing in the great hall. Brünnhilde had meanwhile gone right up to the table and taken her place there.   Silence was requested and King Gunther said: 'My dear sister, honour my oath, and yourself in the process. I have promised you to a man. By taking him as your husband you may show how dutifully you respect my wishes.'

The noble maiden answered: 'My dear brother, you shouldn't ask favours of me. You know I shall always be whatever you want me to be, and do whatever you say. I will willingly promise myself to whatever man you choose for me, my Lord.'

Blushing under Kriemhilde's gaze, Sifrid pledged himself to her service. The two were then told to approach the circle together, and Kriemhilde was asked if she wanted this splendid man for her husband.

She showed some maidenly embarrassment, but as fortune and Sifrid's destiny would have it, she was not at all disposed to refuse him out of hand. Nor was the noble King of the Netherlands any less eager to take her as his wife.

After they had formally accepted each other, Sifrid's tender embrace was waiting for the lovely girl, and he kissed the beautiful Queen before all the heroes.

Then the company divided; and when they had taken their seats, Sifrid and Kriemhilde could be seen opposite Gunther. Their following was numerous. The Nibelungs were there at Sifrid's side.

But when the maiden Brünnhilde, who had sat down with the King, caught sight of Kriemhilde sitting next to Sifrid, she began to weep, so that the hot tears ran down her fair cheeks.

'What's the matter, my lady,' asked the Lord of the land. 'Why are your bright eyes clouded over? I should have thought you had some reason to be happy, now that you rule over my lands, my castles and many fine men.'

'I've more reason to weep,' the beautiful maiden answered. 'It's your sister I'm sorry for, sitting there next to one of your vassals. What else can I do but weep to see her ruined like this?'

But Gunther said: 'Don't say anything now. Some other time I'll tell you why I gave my sister to Sifrid. In any case, I see no reason why she shouldn't live happily with him all her life.'

'But it still saddens me to see such a waste of beauty and breeding. If I had anywhere to go, I'd leave you now, and never share your bed!—unless you tell me how Kriemhilde comes to be Sifrid's woman.'

Then the noble King said: 'Very well, I'll tell you. He has as many castles and broad lands as I have. He's a rich and powerful king, believe me—that's why I think he's a suitable match for my sister, rare and beautiful as she is.'

But no matter what the King said, she remained doubtful and depressed. At this point many knights hurried from the table to try their skill in combat. The noise was so great that the whole castle resounded. But their host began to be restive in the company of his guests.   He thought how much more comfortable it would be in bed with his beautiful wife, how much delight she was bound to afford him, and he began to look at Lady Brünnhilde with affectionate anticipation.   And so his guests were asked to cut short their chivalry, since the King wished to retire to bed with his wife. On the way out Kriemhilde and Brünnhilde came together at the head of the stairs—as yet there was no hatred between them.   The knights, the followers of the two Kings, went their separate ways; rich chamberlains brought them light, and it was noticeable how many warriors Sifrid had with him.

The two lords arrived at their respective beds and each thought how he would conquer his fair lady in love. And indeed, Sifrid's pleasure was as great as may be.   For when he lay with Kriemhilde and made love to the maiden as only he could, they were united once and for all. He would not have exchanged a thousand other women for her alone.   I shall say no more of what he did with the lady. Listen instead how Gunther, that accomplished warrior, lay with Brünnhilde. He had had many more comfortable nights with women.

His following, male and female, had left, and the door was quickly closed. Now was the time, he thought, when he should make love to the beautiful creature; unfortunately, he still had a long way to go before he could take possession of her.   When he saw her approach the bed in her white linen shift, the noble knight thought to himself: 'All that I have ever wished for, I have here before me.' And indeed, her beauty could not fail to please him.   His royal hand put out the lights one by one and the bold warrior went up to her. He lay down near to her— his excitement was great—and the hero took the lovely lady in his arms.   He was in a mood to make long and passionate love, if the noble lady had allowed it. But in fact she was so unfriendly that he was quite put off. Instead of the affection he expected, he found nothing but hostility.

She said: 'Noble knight, you'd better resign yourself. What you're hoping for is out of the question, I intend to remain a virgin (and you may as well recognize this) until I find out what's at the bottom of the match between Kriemhilde and Sifrid.'   Then Gunther got really annoyed with her.   He tried to take her by force, and succeeded in getting her clothes off, but at that moment the magnificent maiden got hold of her girdle, a stout band which she wore round her waist, and proceeded to give the King some real trouble.

To stop him disturbing her sleep any longer, she bound his

hands and feet together, carried him to a nail, and hung him up on the wall. She also forbade any further attempt at love-making—but in any case he was lucky to escape with his life, she was so strong.

The would-be lord and master began to implore: 'Untie me, most noble Queen! I see I shall never conquer you, fair lady, and I certainly won't lie so close to you again in a hurry.'

But she was not concerned with his plight, now that she had the bed comfortably to herself, and there on the wall he had to hang until the morning light shone through the windows. If he had ever boasted any strength, he gave no evidence of it now.

'Now tell me, Lord Gunther,' said the beautiful maiden, 'would it distress you at all if your servants were to find you tied up by a woman?' 'It certainly wouldn't do you any good if they did,' answered the bold knight, 'And I shouldn't get much honour from it either. Just for the sake of your own reputation, let me come back with you. Since my attentions are so unwelcome, I won't even touch your shift with my hand.'

At that she untied him, and as soon as she had set him on his feet again, he got back into bed with her. He lay down so far away from her that he hardly touched her beautiful garment, and she was well satisfied with this arrangement.

Their servants entered, bringing them great quantities of new clothes specially prepared for that morning. But although he wore his crown in honour of the day, and put a brave face on it, the Lord of the land was not happy.   According to custom and law, Gunther and Brünnhilde delayed no longer, but went to the minster, where Mass was being sung. Sifrid came there too, and many others besides,   and they all four received the blessing of the Church, after which they stood forth, crowned and happy for all to see.

Many young men, six hundred or more, were knighted in honour of the King. There was much rejoicing in Burgundy and the din of the lances was heard far and wide.   Beautiful maidens sat at the windows, gazing at the multitude of shining shields. But the King had withdrawn from his men, sad amid the general rejoicing.

His mood and Sifrid's were hardly the same, but the good-hearted knight knew well enough what was the matter. He went up to the King and asked him: 'How did you get on last night? I think perhaps you ought to tell me.'

The host then said to his guest: 'I've made a bad and shameful bargain: I've taken the devil into my house. When I thought to make love to her, she bound me roughly, carried me to a nail and hung me on the wall.   And there I had to hang until she let me down in the morning. A fine, comfortable night she had meanwhile! I make this complaint to you as a friend, and in confidence.' 'Well, I'm very sorry to hear this,' said Sifrid the strong,   'and if you have no objection, I can undertake to bring her so close to you tonight that she'll never keep you waiting for her love again.' After his trials and tribulations, Gunther was much cheered by this speech.

Sifrid went on: 'We'll find a solution for you. It seems that my experience last night was different from yours. I now love your sister Kriemhilde more than life itself. And Lady Brünnhilde must be yours before the night is out.   I'll come to your room secretly in my invisible cloak, so that no one will see through the trick. Send the attendants back to their quarters,   and when I put out the lights in the pages' hands you'll know that I'm in the room and ready to serve you. Either I tame your wife for you so that you can enjoy her tonight, or I lose my life in the attempt.'

'I shall be happy,' said the King, 'so long as you take no liberties with my dear lady. Apart from that, you can do what you like to her, and even if you were to kill her in the process, I think I should be able to overlook it. She's a terrifying woman.'

'I give you my word,' said Sifrid. 'I shan't make love to her. So far as I'm concerned, your beautiful sister comes before all the women I've ever seen.' And Gunther believed what Sifrid said.

But now the amusements were interrupted and a halt was called to the noisy tournament, while attendants asked everyone to make way for the ladies to proceed to the hall.   The court was cleared of people and horses, and a bishop led each of the ladies to table in front of the Kings. Many a fine man followed in their train.   The King sat there full of joyful anticipation, thinking of what Sifrid had promised him. The day seemed like a month to him and all his thoughts were of his lady's love.   He could hardly wait until the meal was over. Meanwhile Brünnhilde and Kriemhilde had been conducted to their places, preceded by a great crowd of bold knights.   Lord Sifrid sat lovingly by his beautiful wife, his happiness unblemished. Her fair, white hand was clasping his, when suddenly she realized he had vanished before her eyes, without her noticing exactly when.

Finding him gone like that, while she was still caressing him, the Queen turned to her retinue and said: 'I'm very puzzled as to where the King may have gone to. Who took his hand out of mine?'

But she did not pursue the subject. Sifrid had gone to where he found many servants carrying lights. He extinguished them in the pages' hands, and Gunther knew by this that it was Sifrid.   He knew also why he had come, and at once sent away the maids and ladies. When that was done the mighty King himself shut the door, quickly secured it with two great bolts,   and shaded the lights with the bedclothes. Then Sifrid the strong began his inevitable struggle with the beautiful maid, while the King stood by with mixed feelings.

Sifrid lay down close to the maiden, and she said: 'It's no use, Gunther, however much you want to. Remember what happened to you last time.' And indeed the bold Sifrid was not to have it all his own way.

But he said nothing, so that she should not recognize his voice. Gunther, although he could not see them, could tell by listening that there was nothing intimate between them. In fact things were far from restful in that bed.   For when Sifrid embraced the rare maid as if he were Gunther, the mighty King, she threw him out of bed on to a nearby bench, so that he caught his head a resounding crack on a stool.

Undismayed, he jumped up again, the brave man, and returned to the attack. But when he began to try and subdue her by force, he found plenty of trouble waiting for him. I doubt if any woman ever defended herself like this before or since.

When he refused to give up, the maiden herself sprang up. 'Take your hands off my nice white shift, you uncouth beast, or you'll regret it!' said the fair maid.   She took the great warrior in her arms, intending to tie him up, as she had the King, so that she might lie more peacefully in her bed. She was not prepared to allow him to touch her clothes with impunity.   His great strength and his mighty power were no use to him. She showed that she was stronger than the warrior by lifting him up —there was nothing he could do about it—and squashing him unceremoniously between a cupboard and the wall.

'Alas!' thought the knight. 'If I let this maiden kill me now, all women in time will come to think they have the right to ignore their husband's authority.'

At this point Gunther, who had been listening all the time,

began to fear for the man. But Sifrid was roused to anger by his humiliation. He resisted with unheard-of strength, and in desperation, tried once again to subdue Brünnhilde.

To Gunther it seemed a terribly long time before he succeeded. She gripped his hands so tightly that the blood spurted out from under his nails. This was more than the hero could stand, and he soon made the proud maiden give up her impossible demands.   While the King still listened, saying nothing, he forced her down on to the bed till she cried out. Now she was made to suffer in her turn from his strength.   As before, she felt at her side for her girdle, hoping to tie him up, but he fought her down so brutally that every bone in her body cracked. That was the end of the struggle; from now on she was Gunther's wife.

She said: 'Spare my life, noble King; I'll make up to you in full for what I've done to you. Never again will I reject your love-making. You've shown me that you know how to conquer a woman.'

But Sifrid, as if he were going to undress, got up, and left her lying, still a virgin. Without the noble Queen knowing, he drew a golden ring from her finger.

He also took her trusty girdle. I don't know why he did this— perhaps out of high spirits. At any rate he gave them to his wife and had cause to regret his action later. Then Gunther and the fair maid lay with one another.

He made love to her as only he could, and that was the end of her recalcitrance and her modesty. His attentions took the blood from her face, and her special powers left her in the course of the love-making.   She was now no stronger than any other woman, and he took possession of her fair body. If she had tried to resist now it would have been useless. And all this had been done to her by Gunther and his love.   How sweetly and submissively she surrendered and lay with him till daybreak! Lord Sifrid, meanwhile, had gone off again to be welcomed by another fair lady.

He avoided answering all the questions she had ready for him, and for a long time after that he kept her in ignorance of the gifts he had brought back with him. In fact, it was not until she was a Queen in his own country that he showed them to her—and what fateful gifts they turned out to be! *

Their host was in a much better mood the next morning, and their was rejoicing in all the land when he invited many nobles to

his court, and showed them his great generosity.   The cele-
bration lasted all of fourteen days, and throughout that time the
revelry never ceased. The magnificent entertainment that the
King put on was highly appreciated.*   The noble host's
relatives gave clothes and gold, horses and silver to many an
entertainer. The King had ordered this to be done in his honour,
and all those who came for gifts went away happy.   All the
clothes that Sifrid, Lord of the Netherlands, and his thousand
men had brought with them were given away, together with their
horses and saddles. And they had high standards in such
things.   Those who were waiting to leave for home thought
that the largesse would never finish. Never were guests better
cared for. And so the feast came to an end, just as warrior
Gunther had wished.

AVENTIURE 11

SIFRID GOES HOME WITH HIS WIFE

When the guests had all left the child of Sigemund said to his
followers: 'We must also get ready to go back to my country.'
And his wife was pleased when she heard it.

She said to her husband: 'When must we leave then? I'd
rather we weren't in too much of a hurry. My brothers have to
divide our lands before we go.' Sifrid was disturbed when he
realized what Kriemhilde intended.

The three Princes came to him, and said: 'We should like you
to know, Lord Sifrid, that we shall always be faithfully at your
service unto death itself.' He inclined his head at this good-
natured treatment.

'And in addition', said young Giselher, 'we must share with
you the lands and cities which are ours. And whatever proud
lands are subject to us, you and Kriemhilde shall have a liberal
share.'

When the son of Sigemund heard and saw what they wanted,
he said to the Princes: 'God give you lasting enjoyment of your
inheritance, and your subjects as well. But my dear wife can
very well do without   the share you want to give her. In my
country, where she's to be Queen, she can hardly help becoming
richer than anyone living, if I'm spared. In any other matter I
am yours to command.'

Then the Lady Kriemhilde said: 'But even if you renounce
my inheritance, Burgundian warriors are not so easily spurned.
A King might well be pleased to lead them back to his own land.
And in any case my dear brothers are supposed to share them
with me.'

And Lord Gernot said: 'Take your pick then. You'll find
plenty here willing to ride with you. We give you a thousand
men from our three thousand knights. Let them be your new
household.' Kriemhilde at once sent   after Hagen of Tronege
and Ortwin, to see whether they and their family would like to
belong to her. Hagen was incensed at this and said:
'Gunther is not entitled to make a present of us to anyone on

65

this earth!   You'll have to choose others from your household to follow you. You know the custom of the men of Tronege: we stay here at court with the Kings. We shall continue to serve those we have followed up to now.'

The matter was dropped; they made ready to leave. Lady Kriemhilde collected her high-born retinue about her, thirty-two maids and five hundred men. And Eckewart the Count went with Sifrid.   They all took their farewells, knights and retainers, maids and ladies, as was right and proper, and without more ado they kissed and parted. With joy in their hearts they put King Gunther's land behind them.   Their families went a great distance with them, and all through the King's lands there were sleeping quarters ready wherever they chose to rest. Messengers were hurriedly sent off to Sigemund.

When he and Sigelinde heard that their son was coming and also the child of Lady Uote, Kriemhilde the fair from Worms by the Rhine, no news could have been more welcome.   'How fortunate I am', said Sigemund, 'to have lived to see Kriemhilde the fair bear a crown in my lands, and my inheritance made the richer for it. My son, noble Sifrid, shall be King here in person.'

Then the Lady Sigelinde rewarded the messengers with many red velvets, silver and heavy gold. She was glad at the news she had received, and her household set to work to dress themselves fittingly.   They were told who else would be coming into the country with Sifrid, and they ordered seats to be set up immediately where he would pass as King before his people. Then King Sigemund's men rode out to meet him.   If anyone was ever better received than were those great heroes in Sigemund's lands, I never heard of it. Sigelinde the fair rode out to meet Kriemhilde with many fair ladies and a following of gay knights.

It was a day's ride before they saw the guests. Strangers and hosts shared the discomforts of the road until they arrived at a spacious castle. This was Santen, where they later ruled as King and Queen.   With laughter on their lips, Sigelinde and Sigemund kissed Kriemhilde joyfully again and again, and Sifrid as well. Their sadness was gone. The whole company was heartily welcome.   The guests were brought before Sigemund's hall, the fair maidens were lifted down from their horses, and the men flocked round, eager to serve them.   However great the fame of the feast they had had by the Rhine, even so, the heroes were now given far better clothes than they had ever worn in all their lives. Many fabulous tales could be told of their costliness.   And so they sat surrounded by the highest honours and material plenty. And you could see from the golden sleeves worn by their followers, and the inlaid pearls and precious stones, how Sigelinde the noble Queen was at pains to look after them.

Then Lord Sigemund spoke before his people: 'I make it known to all Sifrid's relations, that he shall wear my crown in the sight of these knights.' The Netherlanders were glad to hear it.   He entrusted him with his crown, his lands and the administration of the law. From that time on Sifrid ruled over all who came before him, and as far as his legal power extended, to such good purpose that the husband of fair Kriemhilde was much feared.

And so in high honour he lived, ruled and pronounced judgment, until, in the tenth year exactly, his beautiful lady was given a son, much to the satisfaction of the King's relatives.   They hurried to baptize him, and gave him the name of Gunther after his uncle. It was a name of which he need never be ashamed; if he took after his relative he would have little to complain of. After this, he was carefully and suitably trained.

At about the same time Lady Sigelinde died, leaving the fair child of Uote in sole power, as was only fitting for such a great Lady with lands under her. Great was the lament when death took her from them.

Meanwhile on the Rhine, we are told, Brünnhilde the fair had also borne a son in Burgundy to Gunther the mighty. And they called him Sifrid, in loving honour of that hero.   And how jealously they guarded him! High-born Gunther gave him tutors who were well qualified to educate him into a solid respectable man,* little realizing that a cruel fate would one day rob him of all his family!

News was continually coming from Sigemund's lands, saying what a glorious existence the knights were having all the time there. It was the same with Gunther and his excellent family.

By now Sifrid ruled over the land of the Nibelungs, the knights of Schilbung and their joint wealth. Never had any member of his family been more powerful, and the gallant hero's assurance fed on the fact.   The biggest treasure that any hero ever won, apart from those who had guarded it before, was now in the brave man's possession. He had won it in battle in front of a hill, with his own hands, and had slain many a knight to get it.   He had honours as much as any man could desire. And even if this had not been so, no one could justly have denied that the noble knight was one of the best who ever mounted a horse. Everyone feared his strength, and with very good reason.

AVENTIURE 12

GUNTHER INVITES SIFRID TO THE FEAST

But all the time Gunther's wife kept thinking: 'How can the Lady Kriemhilde give herself such airs? Isn't her husband Sifrid one of our vassals? It's a long time since he rendered us any service.' She brooded over this in secret. It depressed her that they kept away from her, and that she received so little attention * from Sifrid. She would have liked to know the reason for this. And so she tried to find out from the King if it might be possible to see Kriemhilde again. She asked him in private, but her lord's reaction to the idea was not enthusiastic.

'How could we get them here to our country?' said the mighty King. 'It would be quite impossible. They live too far away from us. I dare not ask them.' Brünnhilde answered him, with some cunning:

'However great and powerful a king's vassal might be, he would hardly refuse any of his lord's commands.' Gunther smiled at this. He had never considered any of his encounters with Sifrid as feudal obligations.

She went on: 'My dear lord and master, make it possible for my sake that Sifrid and your sister should come to this country so that we can see them here. Truly, nothing would give me greater pleasure. Your sister's gracious manner and her ingrained courtesy—how sweet it is to remember how we sat together when I first became your wife! Brave Sifrid may well love her without dishonour.' She kept on at him until the King said: 'There are no guests I would sooner see, as you must know. Desperate entreaties are unnecessary. I shall send messengers for both of them to come to us by the Rhine.'

Then the Queen said: 'In that case you must tell me when you intend to summon them, and how long it will be before our dear friends arrive in this country. You should also tell me who you intend to send.'

'Very well,' said the King, 'I shall dispatch thirty of my men.' He summoned them before him, and entrusted them with the mission to Sifrid's land, while Brünnhilde gave them fine clothes, much to their joy.

Then King Gunther said: 'You knights are to tell Sifrid the strong and my sister from me (and nothing that I say should be omitted) that no one loves them better in all the world.   Ask them both to come and visit us by the Rhine, and my wife and I will always be at their service. Before next summer, he and his men shall see many people here who accord him the highest honour.   And give my respects to King Sigemund, saying that I and my friends are eternally devoted to him. And tell my sister she should not fail to come and see her friends; no feast was ever more worthy of her.'

Brünnhilde and Uote, and the other ladies, all sent their respects to the lovely ladies and brave men in Sifrid's lands. The King's friends were consulted, and the messengers sent off.   They were well equipped for the journey. And when they had all received horse and clothes they left the country. They journeyed towards their destination with some haste, and the King was careful to grant them safe conduct.   Within three weeks they rode into the country and came to the castle of the Nibelungs to which they had been sent. By the time they found the warrior in Norway, the messengers' horses were tired out from the long journey.

Sifrid and Kriemhilde were both told that knights had arrived, wearing the sort of clothes that were fashionable in Burgundy at that time. Kriemhilde leapt up from the bed where she was resting,   and asked one of her maids to go to the window. She saw the brave Gere standing in the court, together with the companions who had been sent with him. How her sad heart rejoiced at the news!

She said to the King: 'Do you see them standing there, moving about the court with strong Gere? My brother Gunther has sent them down the Rhine to us.' Strong Sifrid answered: 'Let them be welcome.'

All the household ran to see them, and each had a kind word of welcome for the messengers. Lord Sigemund was particularly glad they had come.

Gere and his men were then found lodgings, and relieved of their horses. The messengers, who had been invited to present themselves at court, went to where Sifrid was sitting by Kriemhilde.   The host and his wife stood up at once and warmly received Gere from Burgundy and his companions, Gunther's men. They asked the mighty Gere to come and sit down.

'Allow me to deliver my message before we take our seats.

Let us travel-weary guests stand for a little while yet. We have news for you, entrusted to us by Gunther and Brünnhilde, whose affairs, incidentally, are prospering.   And also we have messages from Lady Uote, your mother; and young Giselher, and also Lord Gernot, and all your nearest relatives, these are the people who have sent us. They send you their respects from Gunther's land.'

'May God reward them!' said Sifrid. 'I have no doubt of their goodness and loyalty—they are our friends after all—and nor has their sister. Tell us, are our dear friends at home still in the best of spirits?   Or has anyone done my wife's family any hurt since we parted? Let me know, and I'll loyally stand by them until their enemies have reason to complain of my faithful service.'

Then the Margrave Gere, a very good knight, spoke: 'They rejoice in the confidence of their own excellence. They invite you to a feast by the Rhine, and you may be sure they would be delighted to see you.   And they ask my lady to come with you. They would like to see you when the winter has passed, before the beginning of summer.' And strong Sifrid said: 'I doubt if that would be possible.'

But Gere of Burgundy spoke again: 'Your mother Uote begs you, and Gunther and Giselher; you cannot refuse them. Every day I hear them lamenting that you are so far away.   And my Lady Brünnhilde and all her maidens rejoice in anticipation; if it were possible for them to see you once more, their contentment would be complete.' Kriemhilde the fair was gratified at this news.

Gere was her relation, and the host bade him be seated, ordering the guests to be served with drink without further delay. Sigemund had also come to see the messengers, and he spoke to the Burgundians as a friend: 'Welcome, you knights, you men of Gunther. Since my son married Kriemhilde we might have expected to see you more often in this land, if our friendship is worth anything to you.'

They said they would be glad to come whenever he liked, and their weariness was exchanged for joy. The messengers were asked to sit down and food was brought them. Sifrid made sure his guests had plenty.

They had to stay there a full nine days, until at last the bold knights began to protest against the delay in riding home to their own country. Meanwhile King Sifrid had sent for his friends.

He asked their advice about going to the Rhine. 'My friend Gunther has sent for me; he and his family are arranging a celebration. I should be very pleased to go if only he didn't live so far away.   And they're asking Kriemhilde to go with me. Tell me, my friends, how's she going to get there? If it were a matter of invading thirty countries for their sake, they'd find Sifrid willing enough to help.'

His knights answered: 'If you want to undertake the journey to this feast, we advise you to ride to the Rhine with a thousand knights. In this way your honour will be upheld in Burgundy.'

Then Sigemund, Lord of the Netherlands, spoke: 'If you're going to a feast, why keep it from me? I'll ride there with you, unless you despise my company. I can bring a hundred knights and increase your following.'

'Why, I should be very happy for you to ride with us, my dear father,' said brave Sifrid. 'Within twelve days I shall be leaving my lands.' All who asked were given horses and clothing.

Once the noble King had decided on the journey, the bold and trusty messengers were sent home again. He asked them to tell his wife's family by the Rhine that he would be extremely pleased to attend their feast.   Sifrid and Kriemhilde, so we are told, gave so generously to the messengers that their horses were unable to carry it all home. He was indeed a man of substance, they thought, as they happily led away their sturdy pack-mules.

Now Sifrid and Sigemund equipped their followers, while Count Eckewart immediately ordered to be gathered together the best women's clothes that could be found or obtained in all Sifrid's lands.   They set about preparing shields and saddles. The knights and ladies who were to leave with them were given whatever they needed. All their wants were supplied. Sifrid intended to bring a great array of imposing guests to his friends.   The messengers hurried on their journey, until Gere the warrior arrived in Burgundy, where he was warmly received. They dismounted in front of Gunther's palace.

Old and young came up to ask for news, as people often do. But the good knight said: 'You'll hear soon enough when I tell it to the King.' And he went up to Gunther with his companions.

The King leapt up from his seat for joy. Brünnhilde the fair thanked them for their prompt return, and Gunther addressed the messengers: 'And how is Sifrid, to whom I owe so much happiness?'

Brave Gere answered: 'He blushed for pleasure, and your sister as well. Never did a man send a more honest answer to his friends than Lord Sifrid and his father send to you.'

Then the noble King's wife said to the Margrave: 'Tell me, will Kriemhilde come? Is her beauty still matched by the good breeding for which she was so celebrated?' 'Certainly she will come,' said Gere the warrior.

Uote then asked the messengers to come straight over to her. It was easy to see from the way she put her questions that she was honestly concerned about Kriemhilde's health. He told her how he had found her, and that she would be with them shortly. Nor did they forget to tell the court of the gifts Sifrid had given them. The gold and the clothes were brought out and shown to the men of the three Kings, and the donors' liberality was noted with gratitude.

'Not that he needs to think twice about giving anything away,' said Hagen. 'He could never spend it all, even if he lived for ever. He took the treasure of the Nibelungs in his hand. I wonder if we shall ever see it in Burgundy!'

The whole household looked forward to their arrival with pleasure, and from morning to night the men of the three Kings were busy setting up great numbers of seats for the soldiers. Hunold the brave and Sindold the warrior were constantly occupied, overseeing the stewards and cup-bearers as they set up bench after bench. Ortwin helped them as well, and earned Gunther's gratitude. Rumold the chief cook ruled wisely over his subjects: his great kettles, his pots and pans, of which there seemed to be no end! And so they set about preparing the food for those who were coming to the country.

AVENTIURE 13

SIFRID BRINGS HIS WIFE TO THE FEAST

But let us now leave them busily preparing, and tell how Lady Kriemhilde and her maids travelled from the land of Nibelunge towards the Rhine. Never were horses so richly arrayed.*   With a long line of laden mules beside them,* Sifrid and the Queen and their friends rode on towards the joys they imagined were in store. Great suffering finally awaited them all.   Sifrid's child, Kriemhilde's son, had to be left at home. Their journey to court brought him misery enough, for the little lad never saw his father and mother again.   And Lord Sigemund, who rode away with them—if he had known what would happen later at the feast, and how terribly he would suffer through his friends, he would never have shown his face there.

Messengers were sent forward to announce their arrival, and a joyous crowd rode out to meet them; great numbers of Uote's friends and Gunther's men. The host began to fuss about his guests.

He went up to where Brünnhilde was sitting. 'You remember how my sister received you when you first entered my country? Well, I should like you to receive her as Sifrid's wife in the same style.' 'I will,' she said, 'and willingly. I have every reason to love her.'

Then the great King spoke: 'They're coming early in the morning. If you want to receive them, you'd better start straight away, so that they don't find us waiting in the castle. I've never expected such welcome guests.'

She then ordered her maids and ladies to look out at once the best clothes they could find to wear in front of the guests. It would be no exaggeration to say that they were eager to follow her instructions.

Gunther's men also hurried to pay their respects, and the host collected all his knights about him. Then the Queen rode proudly out, and the dear guests were greeted again and again. With what joy the Burgundians proclaimed them welcome!

It struck them that Lady Kriemhilde's earlier reception of Lady Brünnhilde in Burgundy suffered in comparison. Those who saw her for the first time now learnt the meaning of confident assurance.

By now Sifrid and his men had come up, and the heroes could be seen dashing about all over the field in boisterous * crowds. The dust and the commotion were something that nobody there could prevent.

When the Lord of the land caught sight of Sifrid and Sigemund, he said most charmingly: 'You are indeed welcome, to me and to all my friends. Your journey has given us great pleasure.'

'May God reward you,' said Sigemund, a man jealous of honour. 'Ever since my son Sifrid made you his friend, I have felt in my heart that I must meet you.' King Gunther answered: 'I'm glad it's happened.'

Sifrid was fittingly received with great honour. There was not a man there who wished him ill. Gernot and Giselher played their part with great decorum, and I doubt if guests had ever been treated with such consideration before.

Then the two Queens approached each other. Saddle after saddle was left empty as fair ladies were set down on the grass by heroes' hands, and those who liked waiting on the ladies found plenty to occupy them.   Then the two lovely women went up to each other, and it brought joy to the heart of many a knight to see how graciously each offered her greeting. A great crowd of warriors stood by with their partners.   The magnificent retinue took hands, and there followed a great deal of deep bowing and sweet kissing from the fair ladies. Gunther's and Sifrid's men rejoiced to see it.

They rode to the town without further delay. The host asked everyone to make it clear to his friends how welcome they were in Burgundy, and many a mighty joust was performed before the ladies.   Hagen of Tronege and Ortwin showed how powerful they were. Not a man dared to neglect their commands, and the service they rendered to their dear guests was considerable.   Shield after shield rang to the thrusting and clashing before the castle gate. The host and his guests stayed out there a long while before they went into the city, for the time passed quickly in such absorbing entertainment.

Joyfully they rode to the spacious palace, while on all sides could be seen numberless costly and beautifully fashioned draperies, hanging down from the fair ladies' saddles. Gunther's men followed.   Orders were immediately given to conduct the guests to their rooms. Several times Brünnhilde was seen looking at Lady Kriemhilde; she was certainly very beautiful, with her colour proudly shining against the gold.   The whole town of Worms was filled with the noise of her followers, and Gunther asked his marshal, Dankwart, to look after them. Accordingly he set about finding them quarters, with great care and consideration.

Then they were fed, inside and outside the castle. Never were guests from abroad better cared for, and their every wish was readily granted. The King was so rich that nobody there need be refused anything.   They were served as friends and without hostility, as their host sat down at table with his guests. Sifrid was asked to take up his old place of honour, and many splendid men went with him where he sat.   He must have had a good twelve hundred knights sitting round him at table, and it occurred to Brünnhilde that there could seldom have been a mightier vassal. But her affection for him was still so strong that she had no thought of murder as yet.

It happened one evening, when the King was seated, and the cup-bearers were approaching the tables, that a great number of rich clothes were drenched with wine.* Every service was performed with the utmost zeal,   as has long been the custom at feasts like this. Ladies and maids were pleasantly accommodated. Their host was ready to serve them, wherever they came from, and all were honoured with kindness and generosity.   When night had passed and the dawn came, the opened luggage revealed many a precious stone shining amongst costly stuffs. They were fingered by ladies' hands, and magnificent clothes were looked out to go with them.

Before it was fully light, a great crowd of knights and squires assembled in front of the hall, some time before an early Mass was due to be sung in honour of the King. Once more a great noise was heard, as young heroes jousted to earn the King's approval.   There was a succession of loud trumpet calls, and a great noise of drums and flutes, until the spacious town of Worms resounded. All round, high-spirited heroes sprang into the saddle,   and a great tournament began in the land, with many good warriors taking part. These sweet knights appeared behind their shields in all the confidence of youth.

The proud women and many fair maidens sat richly adorned

in the windows. They were entertained by many a brave man, and the host himself rode out with his friends.   And so the time passed quickly until they heard the bells ringing in the tower. Then their horses were brought to them, and the ladies rode off. Many brave men followed after the two noble Queens.   They dismounted on the grass before the cathedral. As yet Brünnhilde still felt affection for her guests, and they passed, crowned, into the lofty church. Her love was soon to be broken by great jealousy.

They left, after hearing Mass, and joyfully took their places at table amid great honours. Their happiness persisted unbroken until the eleventh day.

AVENTIURE 14

THE QUEENS ABUSE EACH OTHER

One afternoon before the time for vespers there was a great unrest * among the many knights at court. They had started a tournament in the hope of amusing themselves, and a crowd of men and women had run up to watch. The two mighty Queens were sitting together, and their thoughts were of two praiseworthy knights. Then the fair Kriemhilde said: 'I have a man who is fit to rule over all these kingdoms.' Lady Brünnhilde answered: 'What can you mean? If you and he were the only people in the world, he might well take over these lands. It hardly seems likely while Gunther is alive.'

But Kriemhilde went on: 'Just look at him standing there! See how gloriously he outshines the other knights, like the bright moon the stars! I have every reason to be happy.'

Then Lady Brünnhilde said: 'However impressive your husband may be, however good and beautiful, you must still rate him lower than warrior Gunther, your noble brother. You must surely allow that Gunther is greater than all other kings.'

Then Lady Kriemhilde answered: 'I think my husband's worth is enough to justify the praise I have given him. He has won great honour in many different ways. You can't deny, Brünnhilde, that he is Gunther's equal, at least.'

'I don't want you to think I'm just being malicious, Kriemhilde. I had reasons for saying what I did. They both said it in my hearing, when I first met them, and when the King took possession of my body and won my love with his knightly prowess. Sifrid himself said he was the King's vassal. And so, ever since I heard them say it, I've thought of Sifrid as my own property.' * And the fair Kriemhilde answered: 'That wouldn't be very nice for me, would it? What sort of achievement would it be for my noble brothers to have married me off to one of their vassals? So I would ask you in all friendship, Brünnhilde, to be so kind as to drop this claim, out of consideration for me.'

'I can't do that,' said the Queen. 'Would you want me to give

78

up all the knights who are bound to us in service, together with
this warrior?' Kriemhilde the fair began to lose her temper.

'I'm afraid you will have to give up all idea of getting him to
render you any services. He's worth more than my brother, the
noble man. You would have done better to have spared me the
necessity of listening to this from you.   And it still causes me
some surprise, since he is your property, and you have such
power over us both, that he's gone so long without paying you
any dues. These pretensions of yours are something I might
reasonably expect to do without.'

'You're getting above yourself,' said the King's wife. 'I'd
just like to see if they pay you as much homage as they do me.'
By now both the ladies were furious.

And Lady Kriemhilde said: 'You won't have long to wait.
Since you've claimed my husband as your property, the men of
both kings can see today whether I dare to enter the cathedral
before the Queen.   I'll show you today that I'm answerable
to no one, and that my husband is worth more than yours. This
is an insult I will not endure. By this evening you'll see how
your serving-maid   goes to court in Burgundy with her
knights behind her. I will be more honoured and respected than
any Queen who ever wore a crown until this day.' The great
hatred between the two ladies was now open.

And Brünnhilde spoke again: 'If you prefer not to be my
vassal, then you and your waiting-women must separate from
my household as we approach the cathedral.' 'We shall!'
answered Kriemhilde.

'Now dress yourselves, my maids,' said Sifrid's wife. 'Don't
let me down. Show them what rich clothes you have and
Brünnhilde will be glad to take back what she's said.'

They needed no persuading, but sought out costly clothing.
Meanwhile a great crowd of ladies and maidens, magnificently
attired, formed the noble Queen's retinue as she too approached,
similarly adorned,   with the forty-three maidens she had
brought to the Rhine. As these fair maidens, in shining silks of
Araby, came up to the cathedral, all Sifrid's men were waiting
for them outside the house.

The people were amazed, and wondered what had happened,
when they saw the Queens separated, and not walking together as
they had done up to now. Many a warrior was to suffer pain and
distress as a result.   Gunther's wife was already standing in
front of the church, and many knights were amusing themselves

with the fair ladies who attracted their attention, when Kriemhilde arrived with her numerous proud following. Whatever clothes had ever adorned young noble knights, they were nothing in comparison with her proud household. Her wealth was so great that thirty queens together could not have produced the display that Kriemhilde now presented. No one, however tempted, could claim to have seen such rich clothes ever worn before or since as her beautiful maids were wearing at that moment. And the only reason why Kriemhilde had done it was to humiliate Brünnhilde.

They came together in front of the great cathedral, and the Lady of the House, full of hate for Kriemhilde, rudely ordered her to stop: 'Do you think the King's wife should be preceded by a serving-maid?'

Then the fair Kriemhilde answered in a rage: 'It would have been better for you if you could have kept your mouth shut. You've brought this disgrace on yourself: how was a vassal's whore turned into a king's wife?'

'Who are you calling a whore?' said the King's wife. 'You!' said Kriemhilde. 'Your fair body was first used by Sifrid, my dear husband. Surely you know that it wasn't my brother who took your virginity from you? I wonder what you can have been thinking of; the trick was hardly worthy of you. Why did you let him seduce you, if he's only your vassal? I can't see that you have any reason for complaint.' 'Gunther shall certainly hear of this,' said Brünnhilde.

'What do I care? Your own arrogance has given you away. You have openly claimed me as your servant, and you may rest assured I shall never forgive this offence. I'm no longer prepared to keep your secrets.' *

Brünnhilde could only weep; and Kriemhilde, without further delay, led her following into the cathedral before the King's wife. Great hate was let loose, and bright eyes were dimmed with tears in consequence.

Brünnhilde was impatient for the service and the singing to end, for she was oppressed in body and mind. Many a good brave hero had to pay for this in time.

She went and stood with her ladies in front of the church, thinking: 'That shrew Kriemhilde will have to explain what she so blatantly accuses me of. If he's really boasted of this, Sifrid must die.'

And when the noble Kriemhilde came up with many brave

men, Brünnhilde said: 'Stop a minute. You said I was a whore;
now prove it. And I should warn you that your words have given
offence.'

Lady Kriemhilde said: 'You'd better let me pass. I can prove
it easily enough by the gold I wear on my hand. My lover
brought it back to me when he first lay with you.' Never had
Brünnhilde suffered so much.

She said: 'This precious gold was stolen from me, and has
been criminally concealed for a long time. Now I realize * who
took it.' Both the ladies were beside themselves by now.

And Kriemhilde answered: 'I will not be called a thief. If you
had any respect for your honour, you would never have said that.
I can prove I'm not lying with this girdle I wear round my
waist. My Sifrid was your lover.'

She wore the belt of precious stones and silk from Nineveh.
There was none other like it,* and when Lady Brünnhilde saw it
she wept. Gunther and all the men of Burgundy would have to
learn of this.

And the Queen said: 'Call the Lord of the Rhine here. I want
him to learn how his sister has insulted me. She says here, in
public, that I am Sifrid's mistress.'

The King came with his knights, and found his loved one
weeping. With great gentleness he said: 'Tell me, dear lady,
who has ill-treated you?' She said to the King: 'How could I not
be unhappy?   Your sister grudges me all my rightful
honours. I accuse her, before you, of saying that Sifrid her
husband has made me his whore.' King Gunther answered: 'It
was wrong of her to say that, if she did.'

'She's wearing my girdle that I lost, and my red gold. And if
you, the King, don't free me from this deep humiliation, I shall
wish I'd never been born. If you do, you will earn my undying
gratitude.'

And King Gunther said: 'Let him come before me, and if
he has boasted of this, he shall explain himself, or deny it, the
hero from the Netherlands.' Kriemhilde's lover was brought at
once.

When Lord Sifrid, who was ignorant of what had happened,
saw the distraught women, he said without hesitation: 'What
are these ladies weeping for, I should like to know; and why has
the King sent for me?'

King Gunther answered: 'My Lady Brünnhilde has told
me something here that has saddened me considerably; she

complains that you boast of being the first to enjoy her beautiful body, or so your wife Kriemhilde says.'

Then Sifrid the strong spoke: 'If she said that she'll be sorry for it before I've finished with her; and I'll prove to you my innocence by swearing in front of all your men, on my highest oath, that I said no such thing.'

The King of the Rhine answered: 'Prove it then. If you swear the oath you offered, here and now, I will absolve you from all suspicion of falseness.' The proud Burgundians were asked to form a circle.

Brave Sifrid raised his hand for the oath, and the mighty King said: 'I know your innocence so well, that I'll acquit you of the action that my sister has laid at your door.'

But Sifrid went on: 'I should be deeply sorry if my wife got away with this insult to Brünnhilde.' The gay knights exchanged glances.   'Women should be trained to keep their tongues in order. You stop yours and I'll stop mine. I'm heartily ashamed of her for this shocking behaviour.'

Many fair ladies parted company for what had been said. Brünnhilde's grief was so great that Gunther's men were full of pity; and when Hagen of Tronege approached his Lady   he asked her what it was that made her weep, and she told him what had happened. Without hesitation he promised never to rest until Kriemhilde's husband had paid the penalty for it.

Ortwin and Gernot joined the group as the heroes were plotting Sifrid's death. Giselher also came up, the son of Uote; and when he heard what they were saying he added, with his usual honesty: 'Good knights, why do you want to do that? Sifrid never deserved such hatred that he should die for it! We all know how easy it is for women to quarrel over nothing.'

But Hagen said: 'Are we to put up with this cuckoo in our midst? Good warriors like us are hardly likely to win honour that way. He's boasted of lying with my dear Lady, and I'd rather die than see him live after this.'

Now the King himself spoke: 'He has brought us nothing but wealth and honour. Let him live. What would be the good of my hating him now? He's always been loyal to us, and offered his services freely.'

Then the warrior Ortwin of Metz spoke: 'His great strength can't save him. Give me your permission, Lord, and I'll make him suffer.' And with that the heroes had sworn enmity to him, and without cause.

Nobody did anything about it, however, except that Hagen persistently worked on Gunther the warrior, suggesting that if Sifrid were out of the way, he would rule over many more kingdoms. The hero began to be uneasy.

The matter was left for the moment, and they watched the games instead. Lance after lance was broken before the wife of Sifrid at the entrance to the cathedral and right up to the hall. But many of Gunther's men were still far from happy.

The King spoke: 'Forget your murderous anger. He was born to give us honour and happiness. And in any case he's so fierce and strong, and of such unbelievable bravery, that no one would dare to face him if he once heard of it.'

'But he won't,' said Hagen. 'You need not do or say anything. You can trust me to arrange it secretly and effectively; he shall suffer for Brünnhilde's tears. He shall have Hagen as his sworn enemy for ever.'

Then Gunther said: 'How are you going to do it?' and Hagen answered: 'I'll tell you. We order messengers, men unknown to anyone here, to ride into the country and make a public declaration of war. Then you say, in front of the guests, that you and your men are going to war. As soon as he hears that, he'll promise to come with you to help. And so he loses his life. I'll find out what I need to know from Kriemhilde.'

The King made the fatal mistake of being guided by his vassal Hagen; and this choice band of knights fell to plotting the great treachery before anyone should find out. And so many a hero perished from a squabble between two ladies.

AVENTIURE 15

SIFRID IS BETRAYED

Four mornings later, thirty-two men were seen riding to court; and it was announced to mighty Gunther that war was declared upon him. From this lie grew the greatest grief that women had ever known. They obtained permission to enter the King's presence, and said they came from Liudeger, who had previously been subdued by Sifrid's hand, and brought as hostage to Gunther's country.

He greeted the messengers and invited them to be seated. But one of them spoke: 'Lord, let us stand until we have delivered our message to you. For you must know that many mothers' sons are your enemies. Your challengers are Liudegast and Liudeger, on whom you once inflicted bitter suffering. They intend to invade your land in force.' The King was at pains to be angry, when he heard this news.

The traitorous messengers were sent to find their own lodgings. How could Lord Sifrid, or anyone for that matter, protect himself from such a conspiracy? They themselves suffered for it in time. The King went to plot with his friends. Hagen of Tronege gave him no peace, for a large number of the King's men were still prepared to forget about it, and Hagen had no intention of giving up his plan.

One day Sifrid found them plotting, and the hero from the Netherlands asked: 'Why have the King and his men such long faces? If anyone has done them a wrong, I'll always help to avenge it.'

Lord Gunther answered: 'I have reason to be sad. Liudegast and Liudeger have declared war against me, and intend to ride openly into my lands.' 'Sifrid's hand', said the brave warrior, 'will always be eager to support you wherever your honour is threatened. I'll do the same to these knights as I did before; I'll turn their cities and lands into a wilderness before I give up. I pledge my life to that. You and your knights stay behind at home, and let me ride against them with the men I have. I'll show you how pleased I am to serve you, and your enemies will suffer at my hands; you can rely on me.'

'This is happy news,' said the King, as if he were seriously grateful for the help. In hollow mockery he bowed low, this faithless man, and Lord Sifrid said: 'You need not worry about anything.'

Then they equipped the troops for the journey, but only to convince Sifrid and his men. He himself ordered his Netherlanders to prepare themselves, and they looked out their warlike clothing.

Then strong Sifrid said: 'Sigemund, my father, you stay here. It won't be long, God willing, before we return to the Rhine. Stay here with the King, and don't fret.'

They fixed their insignia as if they were ready to leave, although the greater part of Gunther's men knew nothing of the real reason for these preparations. All they saw was the imposing number of followers with Sifrid.   They bound their helmets and breastplates on to the horses, and many a stalwart knight made ready to depart. At this moment, Hagen of Tronege sought out Kriemhilde, and asked to take leave of her, as they were about to set out for other lands.

'I am lucky', said Kriemhilde, 'to have been given a husband who can protect my dear friends as bravely as my Lord Sifrid does. It gives me confidence to know this.   Hagen, my dear friend, remember how I always served you willingly, and never bore you any ill will. Repay me for this by your treatment of my dear husband. He should not be held responsible for any offence I have done to Brünnhilde.   I've had time to regret it,' said the noble woman; 'and in any case he's thrashed me soundly for it. If I ever said anything to make her unhappy he has punished me well enough, the good brave hero.'

He said: 'You and Brünnhilde will be reconciled in due course. But tell me, dear Lady Kriemhilde, how can I serve you through Sifrid your husband? I should be glad to do so, for there is no one I would rather help.'

'I should have no fear of his losing his life in battle', said the noble woman, 'as long as his over-confidence doesn't carry him away. Apart from that, the good brave warrior would always be safe.'

'Lady,' said Hagen, 'if you have any idea that he may be wounded, you should tell me what I must do to prevent it. Riding or on foot, I'll never let him out of my sight.'

She said: 'You are of my family and I am of yours. I commend my sweet love to your loyalty; protect him well, my dear husband.' And then she revealed something to him which had been better left untold.　　She said: 'My man is brave and strong. When he slew the dragon by the mountain, you know he bathed in its blood, and ever since then the carefree knight has been safe from every weapon in battle.　　All the same, I'm worried when he stands there fighting, with spears flying from many heroes' hands; afraid of losing my dear husband. You'll never know how often and how much I suffer on account of Sifrid.　　My dear friend, I tell you in the confidence that you'll never break faith with me. You shall hear where my dear husband can be wounded, but in confidence, mind.　　When the dragon was killed and his hot blood poured out, and the good brave knight bathed in it, a broad lime leaf fell on his back between the shoulder-blades. In that spot he can be wounded, and that's why I'm so worried.'

Then Hagen of Tronege spoke: 'Sew a little patch on his clothes so that I know where to protect him when we are in the fighting.' Thinking to save the hero, she made certain of his death.

She said: 'I will secretly sew a cross of fine silk on his clothes. There let your hero's hand guard my husband when the battle rages, and when he confronts his enemies in the fight.'

'I will, my dear lady,' said Hagen. And in this moment, when Kriemhilde imagined she had been of some use to him, her husband was betrayed. Hagen took his leave and went away happy.

All the King's household were well satisfied. I doubt if any knight will ever equal the treachery that Hagen committed that day, when Kriemhilde put her trust in him.　　The next morning Lord Sifrid rode off happily with a thousand of his men. He thought he was avenging the offence to his friends. Hagen rode close enough behind to examine his clothes.　　When he saw the sign he sent off two of his men with fresh news: Gunther's land was to remain in peace, and Liudeger had sent them to tell the King.

Sifrid rode home with a bad grace. He felt he had done nothing whatever to avenge the offence of his friends, and indeed Gunther's men could hardly get him to turn back at all. He rode straight to the King, who started thanking him.

'May God reward you for your good intentions, Sifrid my

friend. I shall always be ready to serve you, as is only right and proper, for your willingness to do as I ask. I have greater faith in you than in any of my friends.   Now that we are spared this campaign, I intend to go hunting bear and wild boar over towards the Waskenwald, as I've often done before.' (This was the treacherous Hagen's idea.)   'All my guests shall be informed that we are riding early in the morning. Those who want to hunt with me should be ready. Those who would rather stay behind, however, and wait upon the ladies, are welcome to do so.'

Lord Sifrid answered, rather stiffly: 'If you're going hunting I should be pleased to come. Just let me have one beater and a few hounds, and I'll ride off into the forest.'

'Are you sure you only want one?' said the King immediately. 'If you like, I can let you have four. They know the forest well, and the paths that the animals frequent, and they won't lead you out of the way when you set up camp.'

Then the carefree knight rode to his wife, and Hagen lost no time in telling the King how he proposed to master this incomparable warrior. No man should take treachery to such lengths.

AVENTIURE 16

SIFRID IS KILLED

Gunther and Hagen, bold knights both, announced their treacherous hunting expedition in the forest. With their sharp spears they intended to hunt for boar, bears and bison. What could have been braver?   Sifrid rode with them, proud as ever, and they took plenty of food. Later he lost his life by a cold spring. King Gunther's wife Brünnhilde was behind it all.

But now the bold warrior went to Kriemhilde. His noble hunting habit and those of his companions had been packed, and they were ready to cross the Rhine. Kriemhilde was sadder than she had ever been.   He kissed his darling on the mouth. 'God grant that we may see each other safe and sound again. You'll have to pass the time with your trusted relatives, as I can't be at home with you.'

Then she thought of what she had disclosed to Hagen, and without daring to admit it now, she fell to cursing the day she was born. Lord Sifrid's wife burst into violent sobbing.   She said to the knight: 'Please don't go on this hunt. I had a dreadful dream last night: I dreamt you were chased across country by two wild boars, and the flowers turned red. No wonder I weep so bitterly.   I dread some plot or conspiracy, from someone who has been offended perhaps, and can vent his hate and enmity on us. I beg you, dear Lord, take my advice and stay behind.'

He said: 'My dear, I shan't be away long. I know of nobody here who hates me. I have the goodwill of all your family, which is only to be expected, considering what I've done for them.'

'No, no, Lord Sifrid, I'm honestly afraid you are going to your death. I had a dreadful dream last night; I dreamt that two mountains fell on top of you, and I never saw you again. I shall suffer most cruelly if you leave me now.'

He held the excellent woman in his arms, and comforted her sweetly with kisses. Then he took his leave and left abruptly— she never saw him alive again, I'm sorry to say.

So Gunther and his men, and many bold knights, rode away into the depths of the forest, in search of amusement. (Gernot and Giselher had stayed at home.)   A long line of horses crossed the Rhine ahead of them, carrying bread and wine, meat and fish for the hunters; and a host of other provisions so necessary to a king. The order was given to set up camp in front of the green forest, on a broad headland where the bold huntsmen were to do their hunting, close to the place where the game would break cover. Then the King was informed that Sifrid had meanwhile arrived as well. The huntsmen spread out to take up their positions in readiness, and strong Sifrid, the brave man, said: 'Which of you gallant heroes is going to lead us to the game in the forest?'

'I suggest we separate', said Hagen, 'before we begin to hunt. Then my lords and I can see who are the best hunters in the party. We'll share out all the men and hounds, and each of us can take whatever direction he pleases. In this way, the one who hunts the best will get the credit he deserves.' The huntsmen quickly scattered.

Lord Sifrid said: 'I don't want a pack of hounds; just one will do, as long as he's tasted blood recently enough to follow the animals' tracks through the wood. That's all we shall need to hunt with.'

Then an old huntsman picked them out a good hound, who soon led his master to where there was plenty of game. Anything that broke cover was hunted down by the men, as is still the way with good hunters today. Whatever the hound put up, Sifrid the brave, the hero from the Netherlands, slew it with his own hand. His horse galloped so hard that nothing escaped him, and he distinguished himself above all the others in the hunt. He was good at everything. He made the first kill himself: a strong young boar. And shortly afterwards he came across a savage lion. As soon as the hound chased it into the open, he shot it with his bow. It was a sharp arrow he had used, and the lion made no more than three leaps after feeling the shot. Sifrid's companions thanked him. After that he slew in quick succession a bison, an elk, four strong aurochsen and a fierce stag. His horse carried him so fast that nothing escaped him; neither deer nor hind had any chance of getting away.

The hound then unearthed a great boar. As it tried to escape, the master huntsman cut it off in full flight, so that the enraged animal charged straight at the brave hero. Kriemhilde's husband killed it with his sword. No other hunter could have done it so easily. When he had slain it, they called off the hound, and showed the Burgundians what a rich bag Sifrid had made.

But his huntsmen said: 'Lord Sifrid, if it's not asking too much, you might leave some of the animals for us. In one day you're going to empty hill and dale.' The bold brave warrior only grinned.

Then they heard shouting and crashing of men and dogs all round them. The noise was so great that hill and dale resounded. The huntsmen had let loose twenty-four packs of hounds.   Many of the animals were slaughtered, and some of the men still fancied their chance of winning the prize for hunting—their hopes were dashed, however, when strong Sifrid appeared at the camp-fire.   The hunt was over, except for one thing. The men returning to the camp-fire carried with them a great selection of skins and game in abundance. You should have seen how much they brought in to the King's kitchen!

Then the King ordered it to be announced to all these outstanding huntsmen that he wished to eat. They gave one loud blast on the horn to inform everyone that the noble King was back in camp.   Whereupon one of Sifrid's huntsmen said: 'Lord, I hear from the horn sounding that it's time for us to return to the camp. I'll answer.' At the same time, they blew a series of calls to summon their companions in.

And Lord Sifrid said: 'Yes, we'd better leave the wood as well.' He rode easily, and they hurried at his side. But the noise they made disturbed a fierce animal from its lair, a savage bear; and the warrior said over his shoulder: 'Now I'll provide some amusement for us campaigners.* Let the hound loose; I can see a bear. If he doesn't get away quickly, I'm afraid he'll have to come back to the camp with us.'

The hound was loosed, and the bear was away. Kriemhilde's husband tried to ride him down, but got caught in some rough country, and had to give up. The great animal thought for a moment that he was safe from the huntsman,   but the good proud knight leapt from his horse, and ran after it on foot. The animal was off its guard, and unable to escape. The hero grabbed it quickly, without suffering any hurt, and tied it up in a second.   It had no chance to scratch or bite the bold man. He bound it to his saddle, jumped straight up himself, and brought it to the camp-fire. The brave good knight did it for amusement, out of high spirits.

How proudly he rode to the camp! His spear was huge, strong and broad. His richly ornamented sword hung down to his spurs; he bore a handsome horn of red gold. I never heard of finer hunting clothes. He wore a jacket of black silk for all to see, and a costly hat of sable. And then the rich embroidery on his quiver! A panther skin was stretched over it for the fragrance; and he carried a bow which needed a winch to bend it—except when he did it himself. His outer coat was made entirely of otter skin, interlaced from top to bottom with other colours. And from the shining fur glittered countless golden spangles, as it hung down on either side of the brave master huntsman. And he bore Balmung, that broad and intricately fashioned weapon, which was so sharp that it never failed, whatever helmets it was brought down on, and its cutting edges stayed as keen as before. The proud hunter was well pleased with himself.

I will miss nothing out. His noble quiver was full of arrows with heads a foot or more across, and mounted in gold. No one lived long who was pierced by them! And so the noble knight rode off, in predatory splendour. When Gunther's men saw him coming, they ran out to meet him, and took his horse. He had a great strong bear in the saddle with him.

As he dismounted, he untied the bonds from its feet and muzzle. The hounds suddenly set up a great noise when they saw the bear, and the animal tried to escape into the wood, while the people around were thrown into confusion. Maddened by the noise, the bear blundered into the kitchen, and there were plenty of kitchen-boys ready to give up their places by the fire! Saucepans were overturned, burning brands were scattered everywhere. You should have seen the good food that they found lying in the ashes!

At this the lords and their men jumped up from their seats. The bear was angry by now, and the King ordered all the dogs to be let off the leash. The company would have been glad to see the end of the incident. Without waiting, the bolder ones pursued the bear with bows and stakes; but there were so many dogs around that no one could shoot. The hills on every side rang with their shouting. The bear was busy escaping from the dogs, and the only one who could follow him was Kriemhilde's husband. He ran him down, and killed him with his sword, after which the bear was carried back to the camp-fire. Those who were watching all said this must be a powerful man indeed. The proud huntsmen were invited to come to the various tables, and a great company of them took their seats on a pleasant meadow. You should have seen the rich foods which were served to the noble hunters! Apart from the absence of the cup-bearers who should have been bringing the wine, no heroes could ever have been better served. If it had not been for the perfidy of some among them, these knights would have been free from all disgrace.

Then Lord Sifrid said: 'Seeing that they're sending out so much food from the kitchen, I'm surprised the bearers don't bring us any wine. If the hunters aren't to be treated better than this, I'd rather not be one of the company. I should have thought I'd deserved more consideration.' The King answered deceitfully from the table where he was sitting: 'If we have failed in anything, we shall be glad to make it up to you. It's Hagen's fault; he seems determined to keep us thirsty.'

Hagen of Tronege said: 'My dear Lord, I thought the hunt was to be in the Spessart today, and I sent the wine there. But although we may go without drink this once, I'll make sure it never happens again.'

But Lord Sifrid answered: 'Curse the lot of them! They should have led out seven mules loaded with mead and wine for me. If they couldn't manage that, they should have set up camp nearer the Rhine.'

Then Hagen of Tronege said: 'You noble knights and bold, I know a cold spring near by. Forget your anger,* and let us go there.' The suggestion was to bring great distress on many a warrior.

Warrior Sifrid was in the grip of a great thirst, and was all the more eager to have the meal cleared away. He wanted to go to the spring at the foot of the mountains; but there was treachery in this suggestion of his fellow knights. The animals that Sifrid's hand had slain were ordered to be taken home in carts, and everyone who saw it was compelled to respect him greatly. But nothing remained of Hagen's faith to Sifrid. When they were about to leave for the spreading lime-tree, Hagen of Tronege said: 'I've often heard that no one can keep up with Kriemhilde's husband when he decides to hurry. I wish he'd give us a demonstration.'

The hero from the Netherlands, bold Sifrid, answered: 'You can put it to the test easily enough if you'll race me to the spring. When we get there, they can name the winner on the evidence of their own eyes.'

'All right, then, we'll put it to the test,' said Hagen the

warrior; and Sifrid added: 'I'll lie down in the grass at your feet.' Gunther was delighted to hear this. And the brave warrior went on: 'And in addition I'll carry all my hunting gear with me, spear and shield and clothing.' And he quickly tied on his sword and quiver. They stripped down, until each was standing there in his white shirt. Like two wild panthers they ran through the clover—and there was Sifrid, first at the spring. He excelled everyone at everything. Quickly he undid his sword, laid down his quiver, and leant his strong spear against a branch of the lime-tree. And there he stood, the proud stranger, where the spring gushed out.

Sifrid's qualities were of the highest order. He put down his shield by the flowing spring, and however great his thirst he would not drink before the King. He was miserably rewarded for this. The spring was cool, clear and fresh. Gunther bent down to the water, and when he had drunk he stood aside. Brave Sifrid would have liked to do the same.

But now he was made to pay for his restraint. Bow and sword were both removed from him by Hagen, who then leapt for the spear and looked for the sign on the brave man's clothes. As Lord Sifrid was drinking from the spring Hagen pierced him through the cross. His heart's blood spurted from the wound, and soaked Hagen's clothing where he stood. No hero ever took a falser step.

He left the spear sticking through Sifrid's heart, and took to flight in grimmer earnest than he had ever run from any man in the world, when Lord Sifrid felt the terrible wound.*

The Lord sprang up raging from the spring with a great length of shaft protruding from his heart. He looked for his bow or sword, and if he had found them Hagen would have been repaid according to his deserts. Finding no sword, the gravely wounded man had nothing but his shield. He snatched it up from the spring, and ran at Hagen. King Gunther's vassal was too slow to escape him. Mortally wounded as he was, he struck so strongly that the precious stones rained from the shield, and it flew apart. The proud guest would have taken his revenge if he could.

Hagen was felled by his strength, and the headland rang with the force of the blow. If Sifrid had had his sword to hand Hagen would never have escaped alive; such was the wounded man's rage, as you might expect. His colour drained away, and he could no longer stand. His body was robbed of all its strength, for the pallid hand of death was on his face. Before long he would be mourned by fair ladies everywhere.

And the husband of Kriemhilde fell among the flowers. The blood flowed freely from his wound, and he began to curse, as he must, those who had treacherously plotted his death.

'You vile cowards,' said the dying man; 'what have I done to earn death at your hands? I always kept faith with you; and this is how I am rewarded for it. You have brought dishonour on your house.   Their issue will bear the stigma for all time. You have gone too far in venting your anger on me. You shall bear the shame of it alone, shunned by all good knights.'

The knights all ran to where he lay, and many of them were sad at heart. Those who remembered their loyalties mourned the brave and carefree knight, as he had well deserved.

The King of the Burgundians joined in the lament, but the dying man said: 'There's no sense in a man bemoaning a wrong he's committed himself. He only brings insult on his own head, and would do better to keep silent.'

Then fierce Hagen said: 'I don't see why you have to lament in any case. All our sorrow and distress is ended by this deed. We won't find many who dare to face us now. For my part, I'm glad to have shaken off his authority.'

'It's easy to boast,' said Sifrid. 'If I'd realized what murderers you were at heart, I should have had no trouble in defending myself against you. But my greatest sorrow is for my wife Kriemhilde.   Would to God she had never borne me a son who must live to hear himself reproached for having murderers in his family. That is something I should fittingly lament if I could,' said Sifrid.

And the dying man pitifully went on: 'Noble King, if you still wish to keep faith with anyone in the world, take my dear loved one under your protection.   And let her know what a blessing it is to be your sister. Care for her faithfully, in the name of all kingly virtues. My father and my men will grow weary of waiting for my return. No lady was ever made to suffer more for her dear husband.'

The flowers all round were drenched with blood. He struggled for his life, but not for long, for the weapons of death are always too keen. The brave and carefree knight could say no more.

When the lords saw that the hero was dead, they laid him on a shield of red gold, and discussed how they could conceal the fact that Hagen had done it.   Many of them said: 'This is an evil day for us. Nothing of this must ever be told. You must all say that he went off alone to hunt, and was killed by bandits as he rode through the forest.' But Hagen of Tronege said: 'I'll carry him home. I'm not in the least worried if she does find out. She's caused Brünnhilde enough sorrow, and she can weep as much as she likes for all I care.'

AVENTIURE 17

SIFRID IS MOURNED AND BURIED

They waited for nightfall, and then crossed the Rhine. It had been the most ill-fated hunt ever undertaken by heroes. The children of kings wept for the wild animal they had killed; and many good warriors later paid for his death.

And now listen to a tale of great arrogance and frightful revenge. Hagen had them carry dead Sifrid of Nibelunge to Kriemhilde's room.   He ordered him to be laid quietly against the door, so that she should find him when she came out early next morning on her way to matins, which the Lady Kriemhilde never missed.

The bells rang in the cathedral as usual, and Kriemhilde the fair roused her numerous maids. She asked them to fetch her clothes and a light, and in the process one of the servants stumbled upon Sifrid.   He saw him red with blood, his clothing soaked, and had no idea it was his master. And so he carried the light into the room, the bearer of heavy news for Kriemhilde.   As she was getting ready with her maids to go to the cathedral, the servant cried out: 'Stop! A knight lies dead outside this room.' And Kriemhilde burst into wild lamentation.

Even before she knew for certain that it was her husband, she thought of Hagen's question, and remembered how he had offered to protect Sifrid. Then for the first time she knew the real meaning of sorrow, for his death cut her off from all happiness.   She sank to the ground without speaking, and lay there, fair and forlorn, for all to see. When she recovered, her grief knew no bounds, and she filled the room with her savage screams.

'Perhaps it's one of the strangers,' said her attendants; but the blood from her broken heart came pouring from her mouth, and she said: 'It is Sifrid, my dear husband. This is Hagen's work, and Brünnhilde was behind it.'

The lady ordered them to lead her to where the warrior was lying. With her own white hand she raised his fair head, and red with blood as it was she recognized him immediately. It was the

Hero from the Netherlands lying pitifully there.   'Oh, that I should suffer this!' cried the bountiful Queen in her distress. 'Your shield was never hacked by any sword; you lie murdered! If I knew who had done it, I should never rest until he was dead.'

All her attendants wailed and lamented with their dear lady, for they were sad at the loss of their noble master. Hagen had done his work thoroughly, and Brünnhilde's anger was avenged.

Then the stricken Queen said: 'Go quickly and rouse Sifrid's men. And tell Sigemund of my distress, so that he can join me in mourning for brave Sifrid.'

A messenger ran off to where Sifrid's Nibelungs were lying, and plunged them into misery with his sad news. Indeed, they were reluctant to believe it at first—until they heard the weeping.   The messenger quickly passed on to where the King, Lord Sigemund, was resting. He was not asleep; perhaps he knew he would never see his dear son alive again.

'Wake up, Lord Sigemund! I come from my Lady Kriemhilde. A wrong has been done her, the bitterest wrong she could ever know. You should join her lament; it concerns you closely.'

Sigemund sat up and said: 'What is this wrong that you say has been done to the fair Kriemhilde?' The messenger answered in tears: 'I can't conceal it from you. Brave Sifrid from the Netherlands has been killed.'

'You might have more consideration for me than to joke about such a terrible thing.' said Lord Sigemund. 'How can you go about telling people he's been killed? Nothing would ever console me for his death, as long as I live.'

'If you don't believe what I say, you can hear for yourself how Kriemhilde and all her attendants are mourning Sifrid's death.' At that Sigemund was taken aback, as he had every reason to be.

He leapt from his bed, with a hundred of his men. They snatched up their long sharp swords, and ran distractedly towards the source of the weeping and wailing. Brave Sifrid's thousand knights arrived at the same time.   When they heard the ladies so desperately lamenting, it occurred to some of them that they should have dressed with more care, but they were too demented with grief, and their hearts were weighed down with sorrow.

Then King Sigemund joined Kriemhilde, and said: 'Why did we ever come to this land? Who among such good friends could have murderously robbed me of my son, and you of your husband?'

'If only I could be sure!' said the noble woman. 'I should hate him with every part of me for the rest of my life. I should hunt him down till his friends wept because of me.'

Lord Sigemund took the Prince in his arms, and his friends' grief was so great that hall and palace were filled with the wailing, and the city of Worms echoed to their lament.

No one could comfort Sifrid's wife. They took the clothes from the fair corpse, washed his wounds and laid him on the bier. His men were distracted with grief.   And his knights from Nibelunge said: 'We shall never rest till we have avenged him. The man who did it must be in this town.' And all Sifrid's men ran for their weapons.

The splendid warriors assembled with their shields; eleven hundred knights, now led by their Lord Sigemund. He was eager to avenge his son's death, as was only to be expected.   But they had no idea who to attack, unless it was Gunther and his men, with whom Lord Sifrid had set out on the hunt. Kriemhilde was dismayed when she saw them up in arms.   For however deep her wretchedness, and however strong her need, she still dreaded the thought of the Nibelungs being killed by her brother's men; and she decided to prevent it. Out of the goodness of her heart she warned them, as friend to friend.

And she said, in the midst of her grief: 'My Lord Sigemund, what are you thinking of? Don't you know, or have you forgotten, how many brave men King Gunther has? It would be certain death for you to attack them now.'

But the fearless warriors had their helmets strapped on, and were firmly set on battle. The noble Queen ordered and implored them to give up, and was honestly distressed when they refused to be dissuaded.   She said: 'Lord Sigemund, leave it to a more suitable time, and you'll find me as eager as you to avenge my husband. If I once get proof of his guilt, he won't escape me.   But the Rhinelanders are too many, and too confident, for you to fight them now. They are easily thirty to one in numbers. Let God give them the reward they've deserved from us.   You stay here, and bear my sorrow with me; and when day breaks, you gentle warriors, help me to lay my dear husband to rest.' The knights answered: 'It shall be done.'

Neither I nor anyone else could do justice to the lament that now arose from the knights and ladies. The wailing was heard as far away as the town, and it brought the worthy citizens running out. They lamented with the guests, for their sorrow too was great. No one had told them of any crime Sifrid had committed, nor how he had lost his life. And the wives of the good townsmen wept together with the ladies. Smiths were ordered to make ready a coffin of silver and gold, big and strong, with bands of tough steel. Everyone was sad at heart.

When the night had passed, and day was announced, the noble lady had Sifrid, her dear husband, carried to the cathedral; and all his friends followed weeping. As they brought him to the church the bells rang out and sacred singing was heard on all sides. Then King Gunther with his men joined the lament, and fierce Hagen as well.

And Gunther said: 'Oh, my dear sister! How sad that you must suffer like this. If only we could have avoided this terrible bereavement. We shall never cease to lament for Sifrid. 'You can save yourself the trouble,' said the wretched woman. 'If it was really something you were sorry about, it would never have happened. You didn't think of me, I might remind you, when you were robbing me of my dear husband. I wish to God you had killed me instead!' said Kriemhilde.

They denied it repeatedly, until Kriemhilde said: 'If any of you are innocent, let them show it. Let them walk up to the bier in full view of us all. Then we'll soon know the truth.'

There is a miracle which can often still be seen: whenever a bloody murderer approaches his dead victim, the wounds bleed afresh, as they did in this case. They saw from this that the guilt was with Hagen. The wounds flowed as freely as they once had done, and the lamentations became even louder than before. But King Gunther said: 'I tell you, it was bandits who killed him. Hagen didn't do it.'

'I know those bandits only too well,' she said. 'May God yet avenge him through his friends! We know who did it; it was Gunther and Hagen.' The hope of battle flared up in Sifrid's warriors again.

But Kriemhilde said: 'Come and bear my affliction with me.' Then Gernot and young Giselher, her brothers, approached. These two now saw him dead for the first time, and joined their honest lament to that of the others. Silently they wept for Kriemhilde's husband. A Mass was to be sung, and men, women and children gathered in the cathedral. There were some among

them who were glad to be rid of Sifrid, but they wept for him
when he was dead, all the same.   Gernot and Giselher said:
'Dear sister, be comforted; you can't mourn his death for ever.
We'll do our best to make it up to you as long as we live.' But no
one in the world could give her any consolation.

His coffin was ready about midday, and they lifted him up
from the bier where he lay. The lady was still reluctant to let him
be buried, and the agony was prolonged for everyone.   They
wrapped him in costly stuffs, and wept without exception.
Uote, that noble Lady, and all her household, mourned the loss
of this great man from the bottom of their hearts.

When the people heard the singing in the cathedral, and knew
that he was laid in his coffin, they began crowding up with
offerings for the salvation of his soul. He was not without friends,
even among so many enemies.

Then poor Kriemhilde spoke to her treasurers: 'All those
who love me, and wish him well, must suffer hardship for my
sake. Let Sifrid's gold be distributed for the salvation of his
soul.'

The smallest child that was old enough to understand had to
attend the offering; and more than a hundred Masses were sung
that day before they buried him. Sifrid's friends were there in
force.

When the singing was over the people departed. And Kriem-
hilde said: 'You should not leave me to watch over this great
warrior alone tonight. All my happiness is contained in his
body.   Three days and nights I will let him lie, while I enjoy
my beloved man to the full. Perhaps it is God's will that death
should take me too; that would be a welcome end to Kriem-
hilde's wretchedness and misery.'

The citizens went back to their beds; priests and monks she
asked to stay behind, and all the dead hero's men to attend him.
Sour nights and comfortless days they had.   Many remained
without food or drink, and those who asked to eat were told that
they would be amply feasted by Lord Sigemund. The Nibelungs
now passed through an arduous time.   During these three
days, we are told, the greater part of the burden fell on those who
could sing. And the offerings that were brought! Poor men were
made rich there.   And those who would not accept the gifts
for themselves were told to bring the gold as an offering to Sifrid
from his own treasury. Now that his life was over, thousands of
marks were given for his soul.   She distributed the income

from her widely scattered lands to monasteries and good people wherever they could be found, and the destitute were showered with silver and clothing. She certainly behaved as if she loved him.

On the third day, when Mass was due, the great churchyard before the cathedral was full of weeping. They served him like a friend, when he was dead.   In the course of those four days, so we are told, something like thirty thousand marks or more were given to the poor for the sake of his soul. And this was all that was left of his great beauty and his achievements in life.   When the service and the hymns to God were over many of the people were torn by violent grief. They ordered him to be carried out of the cathedral to his grave; and those who were sorry to lose him could be seen weeping and wailing.

The people followed him crying aloud, and not a man or woman rejoiced. There was more singing, and a service was read at the grave; none but the best priests were assembled for his burial.

Before Sifrid's wife could bring herself to approach the grave, her loyal heart was torn with such grief that they had to sprinkle her repeatedly from a spring. Her discomposure was great and unrestrained.   It was a wonder that she ever recovered. She was joined in her lament by her ladies, and she said: 'You men of Sifrid, remember your loyalty, and do me this favour: Give me a little pleasure after my grief, and let me see his fair face once again.' She was so importunate in her extreme distress that they had no choice but to break open the handsome coffin.

Then they led the lady up to him. She raised his fair head with her white hand, and kissed the good and noble knight as he lay dead. Her bright eyes in their grief shed tears of blood.   The final parting was pitiful to behold. They had to carry her bodily away, this once proud woman, now helpless and insensible. The lovely creature nearly died of grief.

When they had buried the noble lord all those who had come with him from Nibelunge gave way to uncontrollable grief. Sigemund was inconsolable.   There were those who had taken nothing for three whole days, because of this great mourning. But their natural wants could not be so completely denied, and they survived their misery, as people generally do.

AVENTIURE 18

SIGEMUND GOES HOME

Kriemhilde's father-in-law sought her out, and said: 'We must go home. We feel we're no longer welcome by the Rhine. Kriemhilde, dear lady, come back to my country with us. Although treachery in this land has robbed us of your noble husband, I shouldn't want you to suffer for it. You can always be sure of affection from me; and I say this out of love for my son. And you can still have all the power that Sifrid, that bold warrior, lent you before. The country and the crown can be yours, and all Sifrid's men will serve you willingly.'

Then they told the troops to get ready to leave, and there was a great rushing for horses. They had no urge to stay with their powerful enemies, and ladies and maids were told to look out their clothes.

As King Sigemund was on the point of going, Kriemhilde's relatives begged her to stay behind with her mother. But the proud lady answered: 'Never! How could I ever bear to see the man again, who brought me such sorrow and loss?' And young Giselher said: 'My dear sister, loyalty demands that you stay here with your mother. As for those who have wronged and persecuted you, you don't need to accept anything from them. I've got enough wealth for both of us.' But she said to the knight: 'I'm afraid it's not possible. I should die of grief if I had to see Hagen again.'

'I still advise you, my dear sister, to stay with your brother Giselher. Surely I can make up to you for the death of your husband.' And she answered in her utter desolation: 'If only that were possible for Kriemhilde!'

When they heard young Giselher making his kind offer, Uote and Gernot joined their entreaties to his, and their loyal families as well. They asked her to stay; for, as they pointed out, she had no blood relations among Sifrid's men. 'They are all strangers to you,' said Gernot; 'and there's no one so strong that he won't have to die one day. Remember that, dear sister, and be comforted. Stay with your friends and, believe me, you'll never regret it.'

And so she promised Giselher to stay. Horses had been brought out for Sigemund's men, who were eager to ride away to Nibelunge, and all the knights' clothing was loaded on to mules.

Then Lord Sigemund went and stood by Kriemhilde, and said to the lady: 'Sifrid's men are waiting for you by their horses. Let's ride away at once. I've very little pleasure in the company of these Burgundians.'

But the Lady Kriemhilde answered: 'My friends, the faithful ones I still have left, advise me to stay here with them. I've no one of my own in Nibelunge.' Sigemund was sad when he discovered this about Kriemhilde.

He said: 'It's not true. You can wear the crown before all my family, and with power as real as you enjoyed before. There's no question of holding you responsible for Sifrid's death. And for the sake of your little child you should come back with us. You can't leave him to grow up an orphan. When your son is a man he will be a comfort to you. In the meantime there are plenty of good brave heroes waiting to serve you.'

She said: 'Lord Sigemund, you must see that I can't come. Whatever happens to me here I must stay with my family, who will mourn with me.' The good knights were uneasy when they heard this. They all said with one voice: 'In that case, we might as well say that our grief has only just begun. If you intend to stay here with our enemies, then we can look forward to the most anxious journey that heroes ever made.' 'You can go in God's name,' she said, 'and without anxiety. We'll give you safe conduct as far as Sigemund's country, and I'll see to it that nothing happens to you on the way. My dear little child I entrust to you knights. Be gentle with him.'

When they realized that she had no intention of leaving, all Sigemund's men wept. Wretchedly, and with rising irritation, Sigemund parted from Lady Kriemhilde.

'A curse on this feast!' said the proud King. 'Never again will a King and his household suffer such entertainment as we have suffered. We shall never set foot in Burgundy again!'

But Sifrid's men murmured aloud: 'They could still expect a visit from us, if we once found out for certain who killed our Lord. Whoever it is, they can count on plenty of powerful enemies among his relatives.'

Sigemund kissed Kriemhilde, and being finally convinced that she intended to stay, he said despondently: 'So we ride home unhappily to our country. My cares weigh more heavily on me than ever before.'

They rode out from Worms to the Rhine without escort, secure in the confidence that the brave Nibelungs could defend themselves if they were attacked by their enemies.   They took leave of no one. But Gernot and Giselher were seen to approach Sigemund amicably, and the brave, light-hearted heroes made it clear to him how much they regretted the loss he had suffered.   Prince Gernot addressed him formally: 'God in heaven knows I was never guilty of Sifrid's death, nor did I know of anyone here who was his declared enemy. I have every right to mourn for him.'   The boy Giselher, for his part, gave them safe escort, carefully conducting the anxious King and his knights out of the country, and then home to the Netherlands. When they got there, not a single happy man was to be found in all the household.

I cannot tell you the details of their journey. Back in Burgundy, Kriemhilde was heard constantly lamenting that no one could comfort her heart and spirit—except Giselher, who was kind and loyal.

The fair Brünnhilde was now firmly in the saddle. Kriemhilde's tears were nothing to her now that she had broken faith with her for good. But the time was coming when Kriemhilde would make her suffer deeply too.

AVENTIURE 19

THE TREASURE OF THE NIBELUNGS IS BROUGHT TO WORMS

Now that the noble Kriemhilde was widowed, the Count Eckewart and his men stayed with her, and served her constantly. He also helped her to mourn unceasingly for her lord.   They erected a wooden building for her, just by the cathedral. It was large and spacious, great and costly, and there she sat and sorrowed with her household. She liked being in the church, and went there regularly and devotedly.   She was seldom to be seen away from the place where they had buried her lover. Again and again she visited his grave, and with a sad heart asked God in his mercy to take pity on his soul. Again and again the warrior was mourned with faithful tears.   Uote and her household comforted her all the time, but her heart was so deeply scarred that no consolation that was offered could help her. She yearned for her loved one more   than any woman ever yearned before. And this was a sign of her noble qualities. She mourned as long as she lived, and eventually the wife of brave Sifrid took a brave revenge.

She stayed in retirement like this for more than three and a half years after the shock of her husband's death; and during the whole time she spoke not a single word to Gunther. Her enemy Hagen she refused even to see.

Then the hero from Tronege said: 'If you could manage to win your sister over, the gold of the Nibelungs would find its way into this country. You might acquire a large share of it, if only we were in the Queen's favour.'

Gunther answered: 'We could try it. My brothers visit her; we'll ask them to bring about a reconciliation, or to see if we can persuade her to look favourably on such an idea.' 'I doubt if we shall succeed,' said Hagen.

Then he told Ortwin and Margrave Gere to attend her at court. After that they fetched Gernot and the boy Giselher, who proceeded to sound her in a friendly way.

Brave Gernot of Burgundy spoke first: 'Lady, you've

mourned Sifrid's death too long. The King wants to prove to you before the law that he didn't kill him. And all the time we hear you weeping and wailing.'

She said: 'No one has accused him of it. It was Hagen's hand that killed him. When he found out from me where to wound him, how was I to know that he hated him? I could have prevented this,' said the Queen.   'If only it hadn't been me that betrayed him! Then I could abandon my grief, desolate as I am. But I shall never forgive those that did it.' The splendid knight Giselher then began to plead with her.   'Very well, I'll greet the King,' she agreed at last, and immediately he appeared before her with his closest friends. Hagen, however, was afraid to show himself; he was too well aware of his guilt and the hurt he had done her.

Now that she was prepared to bury her hatred of Gunther it would have looked better if he had been able to kiss her. He might have approached Kriemhilde less apprehensively if he had not conspired to wrong her.   No reconciliation among friends was ever accomplished with so many tears, for she still felt her loss deeply. She forgave them all, except for one man. No one but Hagen could have killed him.

It was not long after this before they prevailed on Lady Kriemhilde to fetch the great treasure from Nibelunge and bring it to the Rhine. It was her bridal gift, and it was only fair that she should have it.   Then Giselher and Gernot, on Kriemhilde's orders, rode out with eight thousand men to fetch it from its hiding-place, where the warrior Alberich guarded it with his closest friends.   When they saw the Rhinelanders coming for the treasure, brave Alberich said to his friend: 'We can't withhold the treasure from them, now that the noble Queen claims it as her bridal gift.   But we'd never have had to give it up if only the good magic cloak hadn't disappeared with Sifrid. Fair Kriemhilde's sweetheart always had it with him.*   Still, I'm afraid it's turned out badly for Sifrid that he ever took the cloak from us, and conquered all these lands.' With that, the treasurer went to get the keys.

Kriemhilde's men, and those of her family who had come, waited outside the mountain. The treasure was taken down to the sea, and loaded on to their ships, which were to bear it over the waves and up the Rhine.   Now listen to the tale of this fabulous treasure. It was as much as twelve baggage-carts could carry away from the mountain in four days and nights, and they

had to make three journeys a day to do it.   It was composed
entirely of gold and precious stones; and if everyone in the
world had drawn their pay from it its value would still have been
exactly the same. It was easy to understand why Hagen had
coveted it.   And lying amongst the other things was the
greatest marvel of all—a small golden wand. If anyone had
known how to use it he could have made himself master of every
man on the earth. Many of Alberich's people came away with
Gernot.   When Kriemhilde had taken over all the treasure,
and they came to store it in Gunther's land, treasure-halls and
towers were stuffed full. Never again was such fabulous wealth
recorded.   But even if there had been a thousand times as
much Kriemhilde would have preferred to stand empty-handed,
if only Lord Sifrid could have stood, alive and well, at her side.
No hero ever had a more loyal wife.

Now that she had the treasure, it attracted large numbers of
strange knights into the country. Naturally enough, for the
lady's hand dispensed gifts with a liberality that was never seen
again, and everyone said what an excellent Queen she
was.   The way she set about giving to rich and poor alike
made Hagen complain that if she lived much longer she would
have so many men in her service that their safety would be
threatened.

But King Gunther said: 'I've no control over her life or her
property. How am I to stop her doing what she likes with it? I
had enough difficulty winning her over. Don't let's start worry-
ing about who she gives her silver and gold to.'

Hagen said to the King: 'No enterprising man would leave
any of this treasure in a woman's hands. If she goes on giving it
away like this the bold Burgundians will be sorry one day.'

But King Gunther answered: 'I've sworn never to wrong her
again, and I intend to keep my oath. She is my sister, after all.'
And Hagen said: 'Let me be the guilty one then.'

And so, forgetting their several oaths, they took away the
potent property from the widow. When her brother Gernot
discovered that Hagen had taken charge of * all the keys, he was
angry,   and Lord Giselher said: 'Hagen has offended my
sister too much; I ought to prevent it. If he wasn't related
to me, he'd be in danger of his life.' Sifrid's wife wept
afresh,   and Lord Gernot said: 'Rather than be plagued with
this gold for ever, we ought to sink the lot in the Rhine. Then
no one will have it.' Kriemhilde plaintively went up to her

brother Giselher   and said: 'My dear brother, think of me. You're supposed to be the protector of me and my property.' And he answered: 'I shall be, as soon as we come back. At the moment we have to ride off somewhere.'   At which the King and his family left the country. The best in the land departed, leaving no one but Hagen, who, in his hatred of Kriemhilde, was only too willing to stay behind.

By the time that the mighty King had returned Hagen had taken every bit of the treasure, and sunk it in the Rhine at Loch. He had hoped to make use of it, but this was not to be.   The princes came back with all their men, and Kriemhilde began to lament her great loss to her maids and ladies. They were deeply sympathetic, and Giselher was most anxious to serve her faithfully in any way possible.   Everyone said: 'He acted wrongly'; but Hagen avoided the wrath of the princes until he had regained their favour, and they let him go unharmed. Kriemhilde's hatred of him, meanwhile, was more embittered than ever.   Before Hagen of Tronege hid the treasure in this way they had bound themselves with terrible oaths to keep its hiding-place secret as long as anyone of them was still alive; and from that time on neither they nor anyone else ever managed to use it.   Kriemhilde's grief broke out afresh for her husband's death, and for the final loss of all his property. And she lamented without ceasing until her dying day.

After Sifrid's death she grieved for thirteen years, we are told, and never once forgot it. She was faithful to him; few people would deny that.

AVENTIURE 20

KING ETZEL SENDS AN ENVOY TO KRIEMHILDE IN BURGUNDY

At about the time when Lady Helche died, and King Etzel was looking round for another wife, his friends suggested a certain proud widow in Burgundy, by name Lady Kriemhilde. Now that fair Helche was no longer alive, they said: 'If you want to win a noble woman, the highest and the best any King ever had, then take this lady; she was strong Sifrid's wife.'

And the mighty King said: 'Yes, but how—since I am a heathen, and unbaptized, and the lady is a Christian? She won't agree. It would need a miracle to bring that off.'

And the bold warriors answered: 'But she might easily do it for the sake of your great name and wealth. In any case, it's worth sounding the noble lady; she's a magnificent woman, and you should have no difficulty in loving her.'

Then the noble King said: 'Which of you knows the people and the country by the Rhine?' and good Rüdeger of Bechelaren spoke up: 'I've known the proud and noble Queen ever since I was a child. And Gunther and Gernot, and the third one who is called Giselher—none of them would ever lose an opportunity to show his quality, and win the highest honours, just as their fathers did before them.'

But King Etzel said again: 'Tell me then, my friend, if she is fit to wear the crown in my country. If she's as beautiful as they say, my dear friends should have no objection.'

'Her beauty may justifiably be compared to that of my dear Lady Helche, our great Queen. Indeed, there could be no more beautiful wife for a King in all the world. The man she accepts as her lover should be well content.'

He said: 'Then undertake this, Rüdeger, for love of me. And if I ever come to lie with Kriemhilde, I shall reward you as richly as ever I can, for you will have done my will in every sense of the word. You and your companions shall be made happy with gifts I order for you from my treasure-house. Horses and clothes, everything you need on this embassy is yours.'

To this Rüdeger, the rich Margrave, answered: 'It would be discreditable of me to ask for material reward from you. I shall be glad to go as your messenger to the Rhine, and will use my own wealth, which you have already given me.'

And the mighty King said: 'And when do you intend to leave in search of the lovely creature? May God preserve you and my lady, and uphold your honour on the journey; may fortune smile on me, and let her receive us favourably.'

And Rüdeger said: 'Before we leave the country, we must first get ready our weapons and clothing, so that we are not disgraced when we appear before the princes. I intend to lead five hundred of my best men to the Rhine.   And wherever we go in Burgundy, they'll all have to admit that no king ever sent such a large and well-equipped embassy to the country before.   But without wishing to put you off, mighty King, may I remind you that she once gave her noble love to Sifrid, the child of Sigemund, whom you've seen here at court. That was a man who truly deserved the honours he was given.'

And the King answered: 'Even if she was the knight's wife, that noble prince was of such rare quality that I have no reason to reject her on that account. In any case, I have chosen her for her great beauty.'

Then the Margrave said: 'In that case I can tell you that we shall set off in twenty-four days. I'll inform my dear wife Gotelinde that I'm going personally as your messenger to Kriemhilde.'

Rüdeger then sent off a messenger to Bechelaren, telling Gotelinde that he had been chosen to win a wife for the King. The Margravine was sad and yet elated at the news, and her thoughts dwelt lovingly on fair Helche.   Hearing the message depressed her, naturally enough, and she wept, wondering if her new mistress would be like the old. She grieved deeply when she thought of Helche.

Rüdeger rode from Hungary in seven days' time, leaving King Etzel happy and cheerful. Since their clothing was being prepared in Vienna, there was no need for him to delay his journey any longer.*   Gotelinde was waiting for him at Bechelaren, and his daughter, the young Margravine, was always happy when her father and his men came home. The beautiful girls were full of joyful anticipation.

As soon as all the equipment was loaded on to the mules, noble Rüdeger left Vienna for Bechelaren, taking care that nothing was stolen on the way.   When they arrived in the town, Rüdeger's first thought was for the comfort of his fellow travellers, and he arranged their accommodation with loving care. Mighty Gotelinde was overjoyed to see her husband back.   And so was her daughter, the young Margravine. She had never been so happy before, and as she looked at the Hunnish heroes she laughed for joy, and said: 'A warm welcome to my father and his men.' While the good knights were bowing eagerly to the young Margravine, and thanking her nicely, Gotelinde could see very well that Rüdeger had something on his mind.

And so that night as she lay close to him, she asked him lovingly where the King of the Huns was sending him. He said: 'I'll tell you gladly, Lady Gotelinde.   I'm sent to win a new wife for my lord, now that fair Helche is dead and gone. I'm riding to the Rhine to find Kriemhilde. She is to be the great Queen of the Huns now.'

'God grant that you are successful,' said Gotelinde. 'We have heard much good of her, and I hope she may compensate us in our old age for the loss of our lady. I think we should be pleased to see her wear the crown among the Huns.'

Then the Margrave said: 'My love, be gracious to the men who are riding off to the Rhine with me, and offer them presents. There's nothing like wealth for keeping up a man's spirits on a journey.'

She answered: 'Before you go, I'll give a fitting present to every knight who's prepared to accept it from me. And I won't forget your men either.' The Margrave said: 'You've made me very happy.'

And you should have seen the rich clothes, lined from top to bottom, that were brought out of her store! Rüdeger had carefully chosen those noble knights for the journey, and each of them was given whatever he needed.

On the morning of the seventh day, the lord and his knights rode out from Bechelaren. They came through the land of the Bavarians with such an array of weapons and equipment that they were hardly ever attacked by robbers on the way.   Within twelve days they came to the Rhine, and the report of their arrival spread quickly. The King and his men were told that foreign guests were on the way, and the host began asking   if anyone knew them, and if so, would he tell him who they were.

It was easy to see they were rich, by the way their mules were loaded down, and so they were found lodgings in the town at once.

When the strangers were accommodated, they were closely inspected. Everyone wondered where these knights could have come from, and the King sent for Hagen, to see if he knew anything about them.

The hero from Tronege said: 'I haven't seen them yet. But when we get a look at them in a moment, wherever they've ridden from, I can tell you it'll have to be a very long way if I don't recognize them at once.'

By now rooms had been reserved for the guests, and the richly dressed messenger rode towards the court with his companions. Their clothes were of excellent quality, and beautifully made.   And bold Hagen said: 'As far as I can tell—and it's a long time since I saw the noble lord—from the way they ride along, it might almost be Rüdeger, the brave and lofty warrior from the land of the Huns.'

'I can hardly believe', said the King at once, 'that he'd come here from Bechelaren!' But even as he was speaking, Hagen the brave caught sight of good Rüdeger.   He rushed off with his friends, and the onlookers saw a warm welcome extended to the five hundred Hunnish knights as they dismounted. No messengers had ever worn such magnificent clothing.

Then Hagen said in a loud voice: 'Welcome, in God's name, to these warriors: the Lord of Bechelaren and all his men.' This reception was an especial mark of respect for the bold Huns.   The nearest relatives of the King now went out to watch, while Ortwin of Metz said to Rüdeger: 'I can honestly say that we've never seen more welcome guests here.'

They thanked the various knights for their greeting, and went into the hall with their followers, where they found the King surrounded by brave men. The lord rose from his seat, as a gesture of exceptional courtesy,   and approached the messengers with the greatest decorum. The guest and his men were eagerly and fittingly received by Gunther and Gernot, and Gunther took good Rüdeger by the hand   and led him to the seat where he himself was sitting. Warmly and promptly the guests were helped to the best wine that the Rhine could offer.   Giselher and Gere, Dankwart and Volker had heard the glad news, and came to welcome the guests as they were presented to the King.

Then Hagen of Tronege spoke to his lord: 'These warriors of ours will always be in the Margrave's debt for the kindness he had shown us. Fair Gotelinde's husband should not go unrewarded for this.'

And King Gunther said: 'I can hardly wait to hear how Etzel and Helche are keeping. Tell me the news from the land of the Huns.' And the Margrave answered: 'I shall be glad to.'

Then he stood up with all his men, and addressed the King: 'With your permission, Prince, I shall now have great pleasure in revealing the message I bring.'

Gunther said: 'Any message entrusted to you, I am willing to hear without consulting my friends. You may deliver it now to me and my men, for I am confident that you seek nothing but honour here.' *

And this messenger of substance said: 'My great Overlord conveys to you on the Rhine, and to all the friends you have, his faithful service. Nor is my message in any way a breach of faith.   The noble King has asked you to join in lamenting his sad fate. His people are joyless, since my Lady Helche, the illustrious wife of my lord, is dead. Many a young girl has lost a mother in her.   And the land is desolate, now that these noble princes' daughters have no one to care for them loyally. Because of this, I fear the King will be slow indeed to shake off his cares.'

'May God reward him', said Gunther, 'for offering me and my friends his service so willingly. It has pleased me to hear this greeting from him, and my family and my men will be eager to serve him.'

Then the knight Gernot spoke up from among the Burgundians: 'The world will never cease to mourn the death of Helche the fair, for she was possessed of many excellent qualities.' Hagen supported him, and many another warrior.

But then Rüdeger, the noble messenger, spoke again: 'Since I have your permission, O King, I will deliver the rest of the message with which my dear Lord, in his misery after Helche's death, has entrusted me.   My Lord has been told that Sifrid is dead, and Kriemhilde is still without a husband. If this is so, and with your approval, he suggests she should wear the crown before Etzel's knights. Such is the message from my Lord.'

And the mighty King answered, with his usual correctness: 'She will hear my decision, if she is agreeable, and I will let you know within three days. What reason could I have for refusing Etzel before I have discovered her feelings in the matter?'

Meanwhile arrangements were made for the comfort of the guests, and they were so well attended that Rüdeger could hardly fail to realize he was among friends with Gunther's men. Hagen was only too ready to serve him, just as he had served him before.*

And so Rüdeger stayed until the third day. The King, very wisely, sent round for advice, to see if his family approved of Kriemhilde taking King Etzel as her husband.   They were all in favour, except Hagen, who said to Gunther the warrior: 'If you're sensible, you'll make sure that you never agree to this, even supposing she wanted to herself.'

'Why shouldn't I agree?' said Gunther. 'I can hardly be expected to grudge the Queen her happiness; she is my sister, after all. In fact, it's our responsibility to make sure that it does happen, if it's going to improve her position.'

But Hagen said again: 'It's no use saying that. If you knew as much about Etzel as I do, you'd see that your real troubles were only just beginning, if Kriemhilde ever loved Etzel as you've just said.'

'But why?' said Gunther. 'If she ever became his wife, I should take good care not to do anything to offend him, or to incur his hatred.' But again Hagen said: 'You'll never get me to agree to it.'

Gernot and Giselher were sent for, to see whether they approved of Kriemhilde giving her love to this great and powerful King. Hagen was still opposing it, but no one else.   Then Giselher the warrior of Burgundy said: 'It's about time, friend Hagen, that you remembered your obligations, and made up for the wrongs you've done her. It's not right that you should oppose anything that might improve her prospects.   You must realize you've done my sister so much harm that she'd be quite justified in bearing a grudge against you. No man ever robbed a lady of so much happiness.'

'I'm merely telling you what I know only too well. If she takes Etzel, she'll manage to cause us plenty of harm before she dies, somehow or other. Has it occurred to you that she'll have a great number of proud men in her service?'

Brave Gernot's answer to this speech from Hagen was: 'There's no reason why we should ever ride into Etzel's land while they're both alive. We should keep faith with her, and honour ourselves in the process.'

But Hagen said: 'No one can prove me wrong when I say that

the noble Kriemhilde, once she is wearing Helche's crown, will cause us harm, however she manages to do it. You knights would be better advised to drop the idea.'

Then Giselher, the son of fair Uote, grew angry, and said: 'We don't all have to be traitors. We ought to be glad to see her honoured. Whatever you say, Hagen, I at least shall serve her loyally.'

When Hagen heard this, he was annoyed. But Gernot and Giselher, the good proud knights, and Gunther, the illustrious King, agreed in the end to put nothing in Kriemhilde's way, if she accepted the offer. Then Prince Gere said: 'I will ask the lady to look favourably on Etzel. He has so many men who serve and fear him, that he may well be able to compensate her for all the wrongs she has suffered.'

And the bold knight went up to Kriemhilde, who received him kindly. Without any hesitation he said: 'You should greet me gladly, as a welcome messenger; a happy chance is soon to take away all your sorrow. One of the best men that ever honourably conquered a kingdom, or wore by right a crown, has sent here to win your love. And noble knights have been chosen to carry out the task. That is your brother's message.'

But the wretched woman answered: 'God forbid that you and all my friends should mock me, miserable as I am! What should a man who has known happiness with a good wife want with me?' And she refused to consider it. Then her brother Gernot and young Giselher came and begged her lovingly to be comforted. If only she would accept the King, they said, her position would really be improved.

But she had decided not to love any man, and no one could make her change her mind. Then the warriors said: 'Well, at least agree to see the messenger, even if you do nothing else.'

'I can't deny', said the noble woman, 'that I should be glad to see Rüdeger, for the sake of his many virtues. But if any other messenger had been sent, he would never have seen my face.' And she went on: 'Let him come to my room tomorrow, and I myself will leave him in no doubt of my intentions.' And her great grief broke out afresh.

Now the noble Rüdeger wished for nothing better than to see the proud Queen. He had enough confidence in his wisdom to know that, once this was achieved, she would not be able to resist his persuasion. Early next morning Rüdeger appeared at Mass with his fellow messengers, magnificently adorned in

preparation for their presentation to Kriemhilde.*   Kriem-
hilde meanwhile waited, proud but wretched, for the good and
noble messenger Rüdeger, and he found her in the same
clothes as she wore every day. Her household, in contrast, were
richly dressed.   She came to the door to meet him, and
received Etzel's vassal with great friendliness. He came in to
her with only eleven others, and Kriemhilde and her ladies
treated them with great respect; they had never been visited by
nobler messengers.   The lord and his men were invited to sit
down, while the two Margraves, good Eckewart and Gere, stood
in front of them. They noticed how everyone wore a sorrowful ex-
pression, out of consideration for the Lady of the House.   They
saw Kriemhilde, with a crowd of fair ladies sitting at her feet;
she was still racked with grief, and her clothes were wet with the
tears that bedewed her breast. This made a great impression on
the noble Margrave.

And the proud messenger said: 'Most noble Princess, give me
and my companions permission to stand before you and deliver
the message we have brought.'

'You have my permission,' said the Queen. 'I shall be pleased
to listen to whatever you have to say; you are a good messenger.'
But the others could hear the reluctance in her voice.

Then Rüdeger, the prince of Bechelaren, said: 'The proud
King Etzel offers you his deepest respects, my Lady, and has
sent many good knights into your country to ask for your
hand.   He offers you love in place of sorrow, out of the full-
ness of his heart. He wishes to be bound to you in constant
friendship, as he was to Lady Helche before, whom he dearly
loved. Indeed, his days are often clouded by longing for that
excellent and virtuous lady.'

Then the Queen answered: 'Margrave Rüdeger, no one who
knew my bitter pain would ask me to love a man again. As you
know, I lost one of the best that woman ever had.'

'How else can we chase away sorrow', said the brave man,
'but by practising love and friendship, and choosing a
fitting partner? Nothing is more sovereign against heartfelt
grief.   And if you can bring yourself to love my noble lord,
you will rule over twelve mighty kingdoms. And in addition, my
lord promises you thirty princedoms, all of which were subdued
by his own courageous hand.   And you shall be mistress over
the many trusty vassals who were bound to my Lady Helche,
and the many high-born ladies who used to serve her.   And

in addition,' said the brave warrior, 'my lord asked me to tell you that he will give you the highest powers that Helche ever achieved, if you are willing to sit crowned at the King's side. This power you shall wield before Etzel's men.'

Then the Queen said: 'How could I ever want to be a hero's wife? Death has already robbed me so miserably of one, that I shall know no happiness until I die.'

But the Huns went on: 'Great Queen, your life with Etzel would be so glorious that your bliss would never end if you once took this step. The mighty King has many choice warriors.   Helche's maids and yours would make one household together, and what knight would not be content in such surroundings? Be advised, Lady; it is honestly the best thing for you.'

She said, very correctly: 'Let the matter rest until tomorrow morning. Come back then, and I will give you my answer.' The brave good knights had no choice but to obey.   When they had all gone back to their lodgings, the noble lady sent for Giselher and her mother, and told them both that weeping, and nothing else, was her lot.   And her brother Giselher said: 'My sister: they tell me, and I've no reason to disbelieve it, that King Etzel will take away all your sorrow if you marry him. Whatever anyone else advises, I think it is the right thing for you to do.   He is the one to compensate you, if anyone can,' Giselher went on. 'From the Rhône to the Rhine, from the Elbe to the sea, no king is more powerful. You can be very happy that he has chosen you as his wife.'

She said: 'My dear brother, how can you give me such advice? I should do better to weep and lament for ever. How could I ever appear before the knights at court? What beauty I had, I have lost.'

Then Lady Uote spoke to her dear daughter: 'My child, do as your brothers advise. Be guided by your friends, and you will be happy. For so long now I have seen you bowed down with grief.'

And then Kriemhilde begged God to restore her to the position she had held when her husband was alive, when she had been able to give away gold, silver and clothing. But she was never to experience such happiness again.   She thought to herself: 'But if I, a Christian woman, gave myself to a heathen, I should be disgraced before the whole world. Even if he gave me every kingdom on earth, I could never do it.'

And so she left it for the moment, and brooded all night long in her bed. Her bright eyes were never once dry, until she went to matins in the morning.

The Kings had arrived in time for Mass, and began to work on their sister again. Their advice, as before, was that she should love * the King of the Huns, but not one of them could see any sign of a change in her mood.   Then they ordered Etzel's men to be fetched, who by now were impatient to go home with their acceptance or rejection, whichever it might be. Rüdeger came to court, and the heroes agreed amongst themselves   that they must find out the noble Gunther's final decision as soon as possible, since they had a long ride home ahead of them. Rüdeger was brought before Kriemhilde.

The knight asked her very pleasantly if she would let him know what message she wished him to take back to Etzel. I imagine he was greeted with blank refusal   and protestations that she would never love a man again. And he said: 'That would be a mistake. Why should you waste such beauty as yours? You can still marry a good man, without fear of disgrace.'

But all their pleading produced no effect, until Rüdeger spoke to the proud Queen in private, and promised he would himself compensate her for everything. At this, her great misery began to lift a little.   And he said to the Queen: 'Weep no more. Even if you had no one among the Huns but me, my loyal family and my vassals, any man who had wronged you would have to pay dearly for it.'

By now the lady's spirits were reviving, and she said: 'Swear to me on oath then, that whatever anyone does to me, you will be the first to avenge my wrong.' And the Margrave said: 'Lady, I am ready to do that.'

Then Rüdeger and all his men swore to serve her faithfully for ever, and the proud knights from Etzel's land pledged themselves never to refuse her any honourable request. Rüdeger gave her his hand in assurance.   And the faithful woman thought: 'Now that I have acquired so many friends, I can let people say what they like, wretched as I am. My dear husband's death may yet be avenged.'   And then she thought again: 'Since Etzel has so many knights, I can do anything I like once I have them under my command. And he's rich enough for me to have plenty to give away as well. My own property was stolen from me by that cursed Hagen.'   And she said to Rüdeger: 'If you could have told me that he was no longer a heathen, I should have been glad to follow him wherever he wanted, and to take him as my husband.' To which the Margrave answered: 'Don't let that stand in your way.   He has so many Christian knights in his household, that you'll never be troubled by it once you're with the King. And who knows, you might even persuade him to be baptized himself. For all these reasons, you can happily become King Etzel's wife.'

And then her brothers spoke again: 'Accept now, dear sister, and put away your anger.' And they coaxed the sorrowing woman until she promised in their presence to become Etzel's wife.

She said: 'I'll be guided by you, desolate Queen that I am; as soon as possible, when I've found friends to take me to his country, I'll go to the Huns.' And she offered them her hand on it, in front of the heroes.

Then the Margrave said: 'If you had only two men, I could supply the rest. But the next thing now is to escort you honourably across the Rhine. You shouldn't stay here any longer in Burgundy.   I have five hundred men as well as my family. They will serve you here, Lady, and do whatever you command at home. And I will do the same myself; may I have no cause for shame * whenever you remind me of my promise.   Now prepare yourself for the journey—you'll never regret taking Rüdeger's advice—and choose the maids you want to bring with you. Warn them they'll have to meet plenty of grand knights on the way!'

They still had the trappings they had used before, in Sifrid's time, so that the maids were in no danger of being disgraced when they rode out. And you should have seen the fine saddles that were provided for the fair ladies!   To judge from the quantity of garments they now had freshly made, in honour of the King they had heard so much about, you would have thought they had never worn fine clothes before.   For a good four and a half days they were busy looking out their clothes from store; and Kriemhilde opened her treasure-chests, intending to make all Rüdeger's men rich.   She still had some gold left from Nibelunge, which she had hoped to distribute among the Huns. There was more than a hundred horses could carry, and when Hagen heard what Kriemhilde was doing   he said: 'Since my Lady Kriemhilde is never going to forgive me, Sifrid's gold must remain here. Why should I leave so much wealth in the hands of my enemies? I know well enough what

Kriemhilde will do with this treasure.   If she took it away,
I 've no doubt it would be handed out and used against me. In
any case, they haven't got the horses to carry it. They can tell
Kriemhilde that Hagen has decided to keep it.'

When she heard this she was hurt and furious. The three
Kings were also told about it, and would have liked to prevent it
happening, but when noble Rüdeger saw that there was really
nothing they could do about it, he said with great cheerful-
ness: 'Mighty Queen, why lament the loss of this gold?
King Etzel will love you so much as soon as he sees you, that
he 'll give you more than you 'll ever be able to spend. I swear it,
Lady.'

And the Queen answered: 'Noble Rüdeger, no daughter of a
King ever knew such riches as Hagen has robbed me of.' Then
her brother Gernot came up to her treasure-house.

In the King's name he thrust the key in the door, and Kriem-
hilde's gold was handed out, thirty thousand marks or more. He
told the guests to take it, much to Gunther's delight.

Then Gotelinde's husband said: 'Even if my Lady Kriemhilde
were allowed to keep everything that was ever brought back
from Nibelunge, neither she nor I would ever touch it.   Tell
them to keep it. I don't want it. I brought so much of my own
with me, that we shall have all we need on the journey, and our
style of living on the way will be princely indeed.'

While this was going on, Kriemhilde's maids had already
filled twelve chests of the best gold that ever was. These, and a
great quantity of jewellery for the ladies on their journey, were
now carried away.   She was overawed * by the power of
fierce Hagen, but she still had about a thousand marks left over
from the funeral gifts, and these she now distributed for the
salvation of her husband's soul. Rüdeger was impressed by such
great loyalty.   Then the lady, still in mourning, said: 'Which
of my friends will choose exile for love of me, and ride with me
to the land of the Huns? Let them take my gold, and buy horses
and clothing.'

And Margrave Eckewart answered the Queen: 'I 've served
you faithfully ever since I was first taken into your household,
and I 'll stay with you and continue to do so for the rest of my
life.   And I 'll bring with me five hundred of my men, whom
I loyally hand over to your service. Nothing but death will part
us.' Kriemhilde inclined her head in thanks, for she had real
need of his offer.

Then the horses were led up, and they were ready to leave. A great weeping of friends arose, as Uote and her maids showed how they would miss Kriemhilde. She took with her a hundred maids of noble family, fittingly dressed, with their bright eyes streaming with tears. But much happiness was in store for her at Etzel's court later on.

Then Lord Giselher and Gernot came up with their men. They knew how to behave, and intended to escort their dear sister on her way. They must have been followed by a thousand splendid warriors. Bold Gere and Ortwin came as well; and Rumold the cook was not to be left out of it. They took care of the sleeping arrangements as far as the bank of the Danube. Gunther, on the other hand, just rode out a little way from the town. Before they left the Rhine they had sent on fast messengers to the land of the Huns, telling the King that Rüdeger had won the proud and noble Queen for him.

AVENTIURE 21

KRIEMHILDE GOES TO THE HUNS

We can let the messengers ride on, and tell you of the Queen's journey through the lands, and where Giselher and Gernot parted from her, after loyally discharging their obligations. They rode as far as Fergen on the Danube, and then asked the Queen's leave to return to the Rhine. They wept when they parted, as good friends are bound to do.

Bold Giselher said to his sister: 'If you ever need me, Lady, let me know, or if you are ever troubled in any way, and I will ride to Etzel's country to serve you.'

She kissed her relatives on the mouth, while the bold Burgundians parted amiably from Rüdeger's men. A great crowd of beautiful girls followed after the Queen,   a hundred and four all told, richly dressed in embroidered silks. Many broad shields went with them on their way, and as many splendid warriors turned back.* They hurried on through Bavaria, and the news of the speedy approach of a great crowd of unknown guests was brought to a certain monastery, standing where the Inn flows into the Danube.

A certain bishop ruled over the town at Passau, and his court and all the houses round about were emptied of people, as they hurried out towards Bavaria to meet the guests. And so it was that Bishop Pilgrim came upon Kriemhilde the fair.   The local knights were delighted to see so many beautiful girls coming along behind her, and cast many admiring glances in their direction before they set about finding comfortable lodgings for the company.   The bishop rode to Passau with his niece, and when the merchants of the town heard that Kriemhilde, the daughter of their Prince's sister, was coming, they received her gladly.   The bishop had hoped they would stay there, but Lord Eckewart said: 'We can't. We must travel on, down into Rüdeger's country, where many warriors are expecting us. They all know about our journey.'

Now Gotelinde the fair was one of those who knew about it, and she and her noble girls were busy getting ready. Rüdeger had sent word that he would like her to cheer the Queen by bringing out his knights to meet her, up as far as the Ense. And so the streets on all sides were full of bustling activity, as they set out towards the guests, riding and on foot. By now the Queen had come as far as Everdingen. There were plenty of people in Bavaria who could have inflicted serious damage on the guests if they had robbed them on the highway, as they habitually did. But the proud Margrave had given them no opportunity: he had brought a thousand knights and more with him. Gotelinde had now arrived as well, and many proud and noble knights with her. As they crossed the Traun on to the open country near Ense, they saw the tents and pavilions already standing in the field where the guests were to spend the night. This was Rüdeger's hospitality to his guests.

Fair Gotelinde rode out into the open, to the sound of tinkling harness on every side. The whole reception was beautifully conducted, and Rüdeger was well satisfied. A crowd of warriors surrounded them, and jousted gloriously in front of the girls; and the Queen, who was also watching, was happy to see these knights serving her. When Rüdeger's men joined the guests the splinters really began to fly. They rode like the good knights they were, and the ladies were well pleased with the spectacle provided for them.

When they had had enough of this, the men greeted each other warmly. Fair Gotelinde was conducted into the presence of Kriemhilde, and those who prided themselves on serving the ladies were much in demand. The Lord of Bechelaren rode up to his wife. The noble Margravine was relieved to see him return safe and sound from the Rhine, and her worries began to leave her. When she had received him, he invited her to dismount with her ladies-in-waiting, and a great crowd of nobles were kept busy helping them.

When Lady Kriemhilde saw the Margravine standing on the ground she would not ride any nearer, but tugged at the reins, and asked to be lifted down immediately from the saddle.

Then the bishop could be seen with Eckewart, leading his niece to Gotelinde. The crowds fell back, and the exiled * Queen kissed Gotelinde on the mouth. And Rüdeger's wife sweetly said: 'My dear Lady, I count myself lucky to have seen your fair person in this land with my own eyes. I could have wished for no happier experience at this time.'

'May God reward you, noble Gotelinde,' said Kriemhilde.

'And if I live, and the son of Botelung, you may yet have reason to rejoice that you ever saw me.' Neither of them knew of course what was destined to happen.

The maidens dismounted and approached one another decorously, and many new friendships were made as they sat on the grass with the knights who attended them.   It was mid-day, and the ladies were served with wine; after which the noble company moved over to the pavilions which stood ready for them, where they found everything had been arranged for their comfort.   They passed a peaceful night, and in the morning their hosts got ready to find more permanent quarters for their illustrious guests. Rüdeger had certainly provided for them well.   The windows stood open in the walls, and the castle of Bechelaren itself was flung wide for the welcome guests to ride in. Their noble host ordered them to be supplied with every comfort.

Rüdeger's daughter came with her retinue, and sweetly received the Queen. Her mother, the Margrave's wife, was there too, and all the maidens were affectionately greeted.   They took hands and went into the spacious palace, beautifully appointed, with the Danube flowing away beneath it. They sat in the open air, and enjoyed themselves greatly.   I cannot tell you what else they did there, but Kriemhilde's knights began to complain about the slow progress of their journey, and were reluctant to stay any longer. A great company of good warriors then rode from Bechelaren with them.

Rüdeger offered his loving service, and the Queen gave twelve red bracelets, and dresses as fine as any she had brought with her to Gotelinde's daughter.   She may have been robbed of the gold from Nibelunge, but she won the love of all who saw her by distributing from the modest wealth that she still had. Her host's retainers were heaped with gifts.

Lady Gotelinde returned the compliment so generously that there were very few among the strangers who were not wearing jewels or splendid clothes given them by her.   When they had eaten and were due to go, the Lady of the House offered her faithful service to Etzel's wife, and Kriemhilde embraced her young daughter many times.   The girl said to her: 'If you approve, I know that my dear father would like to send me to you in the land of the Huns.' And Kriemhilde saw how devoted she was.

The horses were now ready, and led out in front of the castle.

The noble Queen took leave of Rüdeger's wife and daughter, and the fair maidens all kissed and parted.   They never saw each other again. As they passed Mölk, golden vessels of wine were handed out to the guests, as a sign of welcome.

There was a landowner there called Astolt, who showed them the way into Austria, and down the Danube towards Mautern. It was there that the great Queen was so well attended later.

The bishop took an affectionate farewell of his niece, earnestly begging her to take care of herself, and to earn as much honour as Helche had done by her generosity. And indeed, she could hardly have won more honour than she eventually did among the Huns.   The guests were then brought to the Traisen, Rüdeger's men taking care of them until the Huns rode to meet them. From now on the Queen was honoured on a really great scale.

The King of the Huns had a mighty castle near the Traisen, known far and wide, and called Seisenmauer. Lady Helche had once resided there, and her excellent qualities were such as will probably never be seen again   unless it were in the person of Kriemhilde. She knew how to distribute wealth, so that after all her sorrow she might well live to experience the joy of being honoured in her turn by Etzel's men. And that is exactly what did happen when she came to live among them.   Etzel's dominion was so widely recognized that the bravest knights ever known, in Christendom or heathendom, were always to be found at his court; and they had all turned out with him.   Christian and heathen lived together there, and followed their separate beliefs; a thing which will hardly be seen again. And whatever their way of life, the King's generosity was enough to provide for them all.

AVENTIURE 22

KRIEMHILDE IS RECEIVED BY ETZEL

She stayed at Seissenmauer for four days, and all the time the clouds of dust never ceased rising, as if the streets were on fire. Meanwhile King Etzel's men were riding through Austria.

The King's sorrow was now giving way to pleasurable anticipation, for he had heard of Kriemhilde's magnificent progress through the land, and now he was hurrying to meet the fair lady. A great and splendid crowd of brave knights, Austrians and heathens from many lands, rode before him as he approached: Russians, Greeks, Poles and Wallachians came swiftly riding on, all following the customs of their different countries; and warriors from Kiev, and wild Petschnegs, continually practising their archery on birds as they flew past, and spanning their bows to breaking-point.

There is a place in Austria, by the Danube, that they call Tulne; and it was there that Kriemhilde encountered many strange customs she had never seen before. But to those who welcomed her she brought suffering in the end. A rich and happy retinue rode in front of King Etzel, courtly and carefree, twenty-four princes at least, proud and respected; and all burning to see their mistress. Duke Ramung from Wallachia came storming up with seven hundred men, like a swarm of birds. Then Prince Gibeche followed with his splendid troops. Hornboge the bold, with a good thousand men, left the King's side, and turned towards his lady. There was much clamour and vigorous jousting by the Hunnish tribes, according to the custom of their land. Then came bold Hawart from Denmark, and Iring the bold and true, and Irnfrid of Thuringia, a majestic figure. They and their twelve hundred men received Kriemhilde with every honour. Then came Bloedelin, Etzel's brother from the land of the Huns, with three thousand. Proudly he rode up to the Queen. And then at last came King Etzel and Lord Dietrich, with all his companions, a great crowd of renowned and noble knights, stalwart and reliable. It was a sight to raise even Kriemhilde's spirits.

Then Lord Rüdeger said to the Queen: 'Lady, the proud

King wishes to receive you here. Just kiss those I point out to you; as you know, you can't treat all Etzel's men alike.'

Then the proud Queen was lifted from her horse; whereupon Etzel at once dismounted, with all his brave men, and was seen to approach Kriemhilde joyfully.

Two great Princes, we are told, walked at Kriemhilde's side, and held her dress as King Etzel went towards her. She received the noble Prince affectionately, with a kiss.

She lifted her veil, and her beautiful face shone out from the gold of her hair. Lady Helche herself could not have been more fair, as many of the men admitted. The King's brother Bloedelin was standing close by,   and Rüdeger, the mighty Margrave, bade her kiss him and King Gibeche. Dietrich also was standing there, and Etzel's wife kissed twelve of the knights in all, and then went on to receive a great many more with the appropriate greeting.

All the while that Etzel stood by Kriemhilde, the youngsters, Christian and heathen, according to their several customs, were jousting, as they still would today.   Dietrich's men, like the good knights they were, broke many a lance; while the guests from Germany left their mark on many a shield.   To the din of splintering lances, the King waited till all his knights and guests had assembled, and then left with Kriemhilde.*

They could see standing near them a splendid array of tents. The whole field was full of pavilions where they could rest after their exertions, and into these the heroes now led their fair ladies,   while the Queen was similarly conducted to the place where she was to sit in luxury.* The Margrave had carefully seen to this himself, and the seat provided for Kriemhilde was commended by everyone, much to Etzel's pleasure.   What Etzel said on this occasion I have never been told; but her pale hand lay in his, and they sat lovingly there, while * Rüdeger made sure that the King took no liberties with Kriemhilde.

Then the tournament was broken off, and all the noisy activity came to a glorious conclusion. Etzel's men went to the pavilions, and were found lodgings over a wide area.   After a good night's rest they took to their horses again, and provided Etzel with fresh entertainment.

The King exhorted the Huns to do him credit, after which they rode from Tulne to the town of Vienna, where they found a great crowd of ladies, richly dressed, ready to receive King Etzel with every honour.   Everything they needed was provided; lodgings were hurriedly found for them, as their excitement rose in all the noise and bustle, and King Etzel's marriage feast began amid general rejoicing.*   They could not accommodate everyone in the town, and Rüdeger asked those who were not actually guests to find themselves lodging outside. And all the time, I doubt if   Lord Dietrich, in company with many other warriors, was ever missing from Kriemhilde's side. They were all prepared to work without resting, so that they could cheer and comfort the guests. Rüdeger and his friends were delighted.

It was Whitsun when the marriage was celebrated, and King Etzel lay with Kriemhilde in the town of Vienna. I doubt if she had ever had so many men to serve her under her first husband.   By her gifts she made herself known to those she never actually saw; and many of them said to the guests: 'We thought Lady Kriemhilde had no property of her own, and yet here she is performing miracles of liberality.'   The great feast lasted seventeen days, and if any King ever had a greater one, we never heard about it. Everyone present wore new clothes for the occasion.   I don't think Kriemhilde ever sat down with so many knights in the Netherlands, and I can well believe that Sifrid, rich as he was, never won to himself as many noble knights as she saw standing before Etzel.   Nor had anyone before, at his own marriage feast, given away so many costly clothes as were presented that day for Kriemhilde's sake.   Both their friends and the guests were determined to leave themselves no property at all. Whatever anyone asked for was given to him without hesitation. And many of the warriors gave away the clothes off their back, stripping themselves for generosity.

Kriemhilde thought how she had once ruled by the Rhine with her noble husband, and the tears came to her eyes: she, who had suffered so much, and was now held in such honour. But she concealed it carefully, and nobody saw.

And Dietrich easily surpassed all the others in liberality. Everything the son of Botelung had given him he now parted with. And Rüdeger's generosity was wonderful to behold.   Prince Bloedelin from Hungary ordered many of his coffers to be emptied of silver and gold, all of which was then given away. The King's warriors showed their appreciation.   Wärbel and Swemmel, the King's minstrels, must have earned at least a thousand marks each at the feast, where fair Kriemhilde sat crowned at Etzel's side.

On the morning of the eighteenth day they rode out of Vienna, with much jousting,* and so King Etzel came to the land of the Huns. They stayed overnight at old Heimburg, and their numbers were so great as they rode through the land that no one could count them. And all agreed that the ladies in Etzel's country were beautiful indeed. At Meisenberg they took to boats, and the water as far as you could see was so covered with horses and men that you would have thought it was dry land. The travel-weary ladies now had some peace and comfort. A large number of stout ships were lashed together, so that they should be in no danger from wave or water, and numberless tents were set up on the deck, just as if they were still on land.

At about this time, the news reached Etzelnburg, and the men and women inside the castle rejoiced. Helche's household were destined to see happy days with Kriemhilde.* A great crowd of noble maidens, still weighed down by the death of Helche, stood waiting. Seven princesses were there to greet Kriemhilde, the glory of Etzel's land. The maiden Herrat, Helche's niece, was still in charge of the household. She was a girl of the highest qualities, daughter of the noble King Nantwin, betrothed to Dietrich, and destined for many honours. She was cheered by the prospect of the guests' arrival, and the material preparations were on a grand scale. Who could describe to you the magnificence which awaited the King? The life they took up with the Queen among the Huns was never equalled anywhere.

The King rode from the quay with his wife, and the necessary introductions were given. When they knew her, they singled out Kriemhilde with an especial greeting; and what power she later wielded in Helche's place! They made their loyal service known to her, and the Queen distributed gold and clothing, silver and precious stones. All she had brought with her from the Rhine had to be given away. And then all the King's family were pledged to her service, and all his men. They had to serve Kriemhilde till her death, and were subject to a power that Lady Helche had never wielded. And so the court, and the country round about, was so rich in honour that every kind of entertainment was available any time anyone wanted it; so great was the King's love and the fortune of the Queen.

AVENTIURE 23

KRIEMHILDE SUCCEEDS IN BRINGING HER BROTHERS TO THE FEAST

They lived together, greatly honoured, for seven years; and then the Queen bore a son, which made King Etzel's happiness complete.   She insisted on having Etzel's child baptized, when the time came, in the Christian faith. It was called Ortlieb, and great was the rejoicing throughout Etzel's land.   The excellent qualities that Lady Helche had possessed were now assumed by Lady Kriemhilde, and practised for a long time. She was instructed in this * by Herrat, the poor girl who still grieved in secret for Helche.   Kricmhilde was known to everyone, near and far, and they all said and even believed that a better or more liberal Queen never ruled over any kingdom. This was her reputation among the Huns until the thirteenth year.

By now she had discovered that no one was likely to resist her (as is still very much the case with a prince's vassals and his wife), and had grown used to the sight of twelve Kings in continual attendance on her. She began to dwell on the many wrongs she had suffered at home.   She also thought of the honours which she had enjoyed in Nibelunge, and how Hagen, in killing Sifrid, had stripped her of them all. She began to wonder if he might ever be made to suffer at her hands for all this.   'I could do it, if I could get him into this country,' she thought; and then she dreamed of walking hand in hand with her brother Giselher, again and again, and kissing him as he lay gently sleeping. Their peace was soon to be shattered.

It must have been the devil who put it into Kriemhilde's mind to break her friendship with Gunther, after she had given him the kiss of reconciliation in Burgundy. And her dress was stained afresh by her hot tears.   Night and day she brooded on the way she had been forced, through no fault of her own, to love a heathen. It was Hagen and Gunther who had brought her to this.   The desire never left her, and she thought: 'I am powerful enough, and have property enough now to make my enemies suffer. Hagen of Tronege is the one I want.   My

heart is full of painful longing for my faithful brothers; and if I
could meet those who wronged me, my lover would soon be
avenged. I can hardly wait.' said Etzel's wife.

All the King's men, and her own knights, were devoted to her,
which was an advantage. Eckewart was in charge of the treasure,
which gave him an opportunity to win friends. In fact, there was
no one who could prevent her doing what she wanted.   And
she kept thinking: 'I'll ask the King,' so that he would give his
affectionate approval to her inviting her family and friends to the
land of the Huns. Nobody suspected the Queen's evil motives.

One night, as she lay with the King, and he had put his arms
round her, as he usually did when he wanted to make love
to the noble lady he adored, the proud woman thought of her
enemies,   and said to the King: 'My dear Lord, I wanted to
ask you if you would agree to showing me how much and how
deeply you love my relations, if you think I've deserved such a
favour.'

And the mighty King answered in all good faith: 'Believe
me, I wish for nothing but happiness and prosperity for those
knights; no man could have gained better friends in loving a
woman.'

And the Queen said: 'As you know, I have a great and noble
family; and it makes me sad that they visit me here so seldom.
"The exile" is what I hear the people calling me all the time.'

Then King Etzel said: 'My dear Lady, if I wasn't afraid they
would think the distance too great, I would invite into my
country whoever you wanted to see from the Rhine.' The lady
was overjoyed at his response.

She said: 'My Lord, if you want to show how much you love
me, send messengers to Worms by the Rhine, and tell my
friends what I have in mind. If you do this, we'll soon see many
great and noble knights in this land.'

He said: 'If you say so, it shall be done. You couldn't be more
eager to see your friends, the children of noble Uote, than I am.
I'm sorry they have been away from us so long.   If you like,
dear Lady, I had thought of sending my fiddlers to Burgundy,
to bring your friends.' And he ordered the good fiddlers to be
fetched at once.   They hurried to where the King and Queen
were sitting, and he told them both that they were chosen as
messengers to Burgundy. Then he ordered rich clothing to be
prepared for them.   Clothes for twenty-four knights were
made ready, and the King explained their mission to them, and

how they were to invite Gunther and his men. Lady Kriemhilde later spoke to them in private.

But first the mighty King said: 'I'll tell you what to do. Wish my friends happiness and all prosperity from me, and ask them if they would consider riding here to my country. No guests could be more welcome.   And if they want to please me at all, ask Kriemhilde's family to come this summer, without fail, to my feast. My wife's relations are a source of great joy to me.'

Then the fiddler, proud Swemmelin, said: 'And when is your feast to be, so that we can tell your friends by the Rhine?' King Etzel answered: 'On next midsummer's day.'

'We shall do as you command,' said Wärbelin; after which the Queen asked for the messengers to be conducted secretly into her apartment, where she could speak to them—with unpleasant consequences for many warriors later.

She said to the messengers: 'You can earn a rich reward if you do as I ask, and give them at home the message I entrust you with. I'll make you wealthy, and dress you in magnificent clothes.   Don't tell any of my friends on the Rhine, whoever they are, that you ever saw me sad or downcast here. Give the good brave heroes my compliments;   ask them to accept the King's offer, and make me happy again. If I were a knight, I'd go and see them sometimes myself; as it is, the Huns are beginning to think I have no family or friends.   And tell Gernot, my noble brother, that no one in all the world loves him better than I do; ask him to bring our closest friends to this country, to improve our standing here.   And remind Giselher that none of my suffering was his fault, and I should be glad to see him again. I should love to have him here, for his great loyalty.   And tell my mother what honours are heaped on me. And if Hagen of Tronege wants to stay behind, ask them who else could direct them through the different countries. He's known the way to the Huns ever since he was a child.'

The messengers had no idea of her motives in not wanting Hagen of Tronege to be left behind on the Rhine; but they had reason to regret it later, when they and many other warriors were hounded to a cruel death.   They had now been given their letters and message, and were made wealthy enough to travel in great style. Looking their best in costly clothing, they took leave of Etzel and his beautiful wife.

AVENTIURE 24

WÄRBEL AND SWEMMELIN SUCCESSFULLY DELIVER
THEIR LORD'S MESSAGE

When Etzel had sent off his messengers to the Rhine, the news
was quickly spread through his territories, as he summoned his
people to the feast. Many came who never returned alive. The
messengers left the land of the Huns, and headed for Burgundy.
They were sent to bring three noble Kings and their men to visit
Etzel, and they had no time to lose. They came riding up to
Bechelaren, where they were well looked after. Rüdeger and
Gotelinde sent their respects to the Rhine, and their dear
daughter sent hers as well. Etzel's men were not allowed to
leave without receiving gifts to lighten their journey; Rüdeger
asked them to tell Uote and her children that no Margrave was
more devoted to them. They also sent gifts and compliments
to Brünnhilde, with protestations of loyal constancy and willing
service. The messengers were anxious to press on once they had
heard the messages, and the Margravin asked God in heaven to
protect them.

Before they had left Bavaria behind them, Wärbel the bold
met the good Bishop Pilgrim. I was never told what message he
sent to his friends on the Rhine, but I know that he gave his red
gold to the messengers out of friendship, and said: If I ever see
my nephews here, I shall be well content. It's not often I manage
to visit them on the Rhine.' I cannot tell you what roads they
took to the Rhine; but no one robbed them of their silver and
gold, for fear of their lord's anger. The noble King's power
extended far and wide.

In twelve days Wärbel and Swemmelin came to the Rhine,
and to the country near Worms. The news was brought to the
King and his men, that messengers from abroad were approach-
ing, and Gunther began asking questions.

'Who will tell me', said the Lord of the Rhine, 'where these
strangers come from?' But there was no one who knew, until
Hagen of Tronege caught sight of them, and said to Gunther:

'Here's news, I must say! It's Etzel's fiddlers I can see. Your sister must have sent them to the Rhine, and we should welcome them for the sake of their lord.'

They had already ridden up in front of the palace, and never did a Prince's minstrels travel in greater splendour. The King's household at once received them, showing them to their quarters, and relieving them of their heavy clothing. Their travelling clothes were so costly and well made that they could have appeared in them before the King without disgrace. Instead, the messengers let it be known that they had no further use for them at court, and anyone who wanted them only needed to ask. As might have been expected, people were found who were glad to accept, and the clothes were sent to them. The guests then dressed far better than before, with the magnificence proper to royal messengers.

Then Etzel's men were allowed before the King. Everyone was glad to see it, and Hagen politely jumped up to receive the messengers affectionately, for which they thanked him. To find out what had happened he asked if Etzel and his men were in good health. The fiddler answered: 'The country was never more prosperous, nor the people happier; have no doubts on that score.'

The guests passed through the crowded palace until they reached their host, who received them with the friendly salutation appropriate to strangers to the kingdom. Wärbel found Gunther attended by many knights.

The King very correctly offered his greeting: 'Welcome to both of you Hunnish minstrels, and to your companions. Has Etzel the mighty sent you to Burgundy?'

They bowed to the King, and Wärbel said: 'My dear lord offers his love and service to you and Kriemhilde your sister. We are sent to you knights in the certainty of your good faith.'

And the mighty Prince said: 'I am glad to hear it. And what is the news from Etzel', asked the warrior, 'and from Kriemhilde my sister in the land of the Huns?' The fiddler answered: 'I am to tell you   that no two people ever prospered better than they do. I am to tell you this, and also that all their warriors, family and vassals alike, rejoiced to see us come on this journey.'

'My thanks for the service he offers me and my sister, and for the news that the King and his men are well and happy. It's a great relief to hear it.'

The two young Kings who now arrived had only just heard the news. Giselher was pleased to see the messengers for his sister's sake, and he spoke to them affectionately: 'You messengers should ride to the Rhine more often; you would always be welcome, and you would find friends here that you might be pleased to see yourselves. You would never come to any harm in this country.'

'We have no fear of any dishonour at your hands,' said Swemmelin. 'I haven't the skill to describe to you how lovingly Etzel sent you his message, or your noble sister, who now enjoys the highest honours.   The King's wife reminds you of your love and affection, your never-failing devotion to her. But first and foremost we are sent to the King, to see if you will agree to ride to Etzel's country.   Etzel the mighty has commanded us to ask you; and he told us to say to all of you, that even if you weren't eager to see your sister, he would still like to know what harm he has done you,   to make you stay away from him and his country. Even if his wife were a stranger to you, he would still like you to think it worth while to visit him. If this could be arranged, it would be a source of great happiness to him.'

Then King Gunther answered: 'Within seven days I will tell you what I have decided with my friends. Meanwhile, you should go to your lodgings, and rest in peace.'

But Wärbelin said: 'Would it be possible for us to see Lady Uote, the great Queen, before we settle in for the night?' Noble Giselher answered very politely:

'Nobody will stop you doing that. By appearing before her, you'll be doing exactly as she would wish. She wants to see you, for the sake of my sister, Lady Kriemhilde, and you're certain to be welcome.'

Giselher brought them to the lady, and she was glad to see the messengers from the land of the Huns. She greeted them lovably, for that was her nature, whereupon the good and courteous messengers told her their news.

'My Lady sends you her loyal service,' said Swemmelin, 'and assures you that she could think of no greater joy in all the world than to see you more often, if it were only possible.'

The Queen answered: 'Unfortunately it's not. However much I should like to see my dear daughter at every opportunity, I'm afraid the noble King's wife lives too far away. Instead, I can only wish her and Etzel everlasting happiness.   But before you go, you must tell me when you intend to come again. It's a long time since I saw such welcome messengers as you.' They promised to do this.

While the Huns now went to their lodgings, the King summoned his friends. Noble Gunther asked his men what they thought of the invitation, and they all began talking at once.   Those he most trusted all advised him to ride to Etzel's land, all except Hagen. He was bitterly against it, and he said secretly to the King: 'You're asking to be killed.   Surely you remember what we've done? Do you think we can ever trust Kriemhilde since I killed her husband with my own hand? How could we dare to ride into Etzel's land?'

The mighty King answered: 'But my sister put her anger away. Before she left, she wiped out everything we did to her with a loving kiss. You're the only one, Hagen, that she still thinks of as an enemy.'

'Don't fool yourself,' said Hagen, 'whatever these Hunnish messengers tell you. If you insist on seeing Kriemhilde, you'll probably lose your honour and your life. King Etzel's wife is hardly a forgiving woman, is she?'

Then Prince Gernot gave his opinion: 'Very well, you have every reason to fear for your life in the kingdom of the Huns; but it would be quite wrong for us to miss an opportunity of seeing our sister just because of that.'

And Prince Giselher added: 'Since you're so conscious of your guilt, friend Hagen, you'd better stay here and look after yourself, and let those who aren't afraid come with us to my sister.'

Hagen, the warrior from Tronege, was angry at this, and said: 'See if you can find anyone to take with you on your ride to court who would be less afraid than me! If you're determined to go, I'll have to prove it to you.'

Then Rumold, the warrior cook, said: 'You've plenty of everything here; you can order strangers and friends to be looked after, just as you wish. And I'm not aware that Hagen has ever sold you into slavery by his advice.   But if you're not prepared to follow him, then listen to Rumold, who loves and serves you loyally. Stay here, for my sake, and let King Etzel stay there with Kriemhilde.   What easier life could you imagine? You've nothing to fear from your enemies. You can dress in good clothes, drink the best wine and court beautiful women.   And you're fed with the best food that any King ever had. And even if that wasn't true, you still ought to stay for the sake of your beautiful wives, rather than risk your lives in this childish way.*   So I advise you to stay. Your lands are rich. It's easier for people to do their duty by you here than amongst the Huns. Who knows what's waiting for you over there? You should stay here, my Lords. That's Rumold's advice.'

'We're not staying,' said Gernot. 'Now that my sister and mighty Etzel have sent us this friendly invitation, why should we refuse? Anyone who doesn't want to come can stay here at home.'

Hagen answered: 'There's no need to take offence, whatever you're letting yourselves in for. My loyal and honest advice, if you want to survive, is that you should travel armed to the teeth when you go amongst the Huns.   If you're determined to go, send for the best men you have or can find, and I'll choose a thousand good knights from them. Then you'll be safe from the malice of Kriemhilde.'

'I'm quite prepared to do that,' said the King at once, and he sent messengers riding throughout his extensive dominions. Three thousand or more heroes were brought in, little realizing the fate that awaited them.

They rode happily into Gunther's land, and all those who were chosen to leave Burgundy were given horses and clothing. The King had no trouble in finding enough who were willing.   Then Hagen of Tronege told his brother Dankwart to bring eighty of their knights to the Rhine. They came armed and equipped like good knights into Gunther's land.   Then brave Volker, the noble minstrel, arrived with thirty of his men, equipped like kings; and told Gunther he was ready to visit the Huns.   I will tell you who this Volker was. He was a noble lord, and ruled over many good knights in Burgundy. They only called him minstrel because he could play the fiddle.   Hagen picked a thousand. He knew them all personally, and had seen what they could do in battle, or anywhere else. Their prowess and reliability were beyond dispute.

Meanwhile Kriemhilde's messengers were getting impatient, for they were in great fear of their master. Every day they asked permission to leave, but Hagen would not grant it; he had a plan.   He said to his lord: 'We must be careful not to let them leave more than seven days ahead of us. That will give them less time to conceal any hostile intentions which certain people might have.   In particular, Lady Kriemhilde will not be able to arrange for anyone to do us harm. And if she does intend anything like that it may turn out badly for her—we shall be taking quite a number of hand-picked men with us.'

Shields, saddles and all the equipment they needed to take to
Etzel's land were now ready,* and Kriemhilde's messengers
were summoned to Gunther's presence.   When they arrived,
Gernot said: 'The King intends to accept Etzel's invitation. We
shall be pleased to come to his feast, and to see our sister. You
may take it as settled.'   And King Gunther added: 'Can you
tell us when the feast will be, or when we are expected?' And
Swemmelin answered: 'It is fixed for next midsummer's day.'

The King then gave permission for them to see Brünnhilde, a
thing which they had not so far done. But Volker prevented
them, out of consideration for her.   'I'm afraid my Lady
Brünnhilde is not in the right mood for you to see her now,' said
the good knight. 'Wait until morning, and then you can see
her.' And when the time came, it was still impossible.

Then the mighty Prince, to show his affection for the mes-
sengers, and in accordance with his own nature, ordered his gold
to be carried in on broad shields. His own wealth was great, and
costly gifts were also supplied by his friends.   Giselher and
Gernot, Gere and Ortwin made it plain that they were equally
generous. They offered the messengers such rich gifts that they
dared not accept them for fear of their master.

And Wärbelin said to the King: 'Lord King, let your gifts
remain in this country. We cannot take them. My lord forbade
us to accept any gifts; and we really have no need of them.'

But the Lord of the Rhine was annoyed at their refusing
presents from such a mighty King, and in the end they had
to accept both gold and clothing, and carry it back to Etzel's
country.   They wanted to see Uote before they left, and
Giselher the bold brought the minstrels to his mother. The lady in-
formed them that she wished them nothing but honour.   Then
the Queen ordered the same minstrels to be given braids and
gold, for Kriemhilde's sake, whom she loved, and for Etzel as
well. This time they could receive them gladly, for they were
given in good faith.*

The messengers now took their leave of everyone, and joy-
fully departed. Gernot had his heroes escort them as far as
Swabia, to protect them from any hostile action.   After they
had parted company with this escort, Etzel's power ensured
them a safe passage wherever they went, and no one robbed
them of horses or clothing. They hurried as hard as they could
into Etzel's land.   They stopped to tell any friends they knew
of that the Burgundians were on their way from the Rhine, and

would arrive any moment in the land of the Huns. Bishop Pilgrim also heard the news. As they took the road past Bechelaren they were careful to tell Rüdeger, and Gotelinde the Margrave's wife. She was overjoyed at the prospect of seeing them. The minstrels were seen hurrying with their news to Gran, where they found Etzel waiting. They passed on all the compliments and protestations of service which were sent to him, and he blushed with pleasure.

When the Queen realized that her brothers were really coming to the country her spirits rose. She rewarded the minstrels liberally, earning more honour in the process. She said: 'Now tell me, Wärbel and Swemmelin, which of my family intend to be at the feast, out of all the dear friends we invited into our country? And tell me, what did Hagen say when he heard the news?'

'He joined the deliberations early one morning, and what he said was not pleasant to hear. When they promised to make the journey to our country fierce Hagen saw it as a promise of death. Your brothers, the three Kings, are all coming, full of pride and confidence. I can't tell exactly who else will come, but Volker the brave minstrel certainly promised to ride with them.'

'I'm not at all keen to see Volker here,' said the Queen, 'but I have a great affection for Hagen. He is a good hero, and the thought of seeing him here is like a tonic to me.'

Then the Queen went to see the King, and spoke to him lovingly: 'Are you pleased at the news, my dear Lord? Everything I ever hoped for will now come true.'

'Your wish is my pleasure,' said the King. 'I never looked forward to the arrival of my own family in my country with more joy. All my cares have vanished at the prospect of seeing your friends.'

Everywhere, in palace and hall, the King's officials were arranging accommodation for the eagerly awaited guests who were to destroy his happiness.

AVENTIURE 25

THE NIBELUNGS GO TO THE HUNS

Now we leave this scene of activity, and tell you of the proudest knights that ever rode majestically into a King's territory. Weapons and clothing were all that could be desired. The Warden of the Rhine had clothed his knights, a thousand and sixty we are told, and nine thousand retainers, ready for the feast. Those they left behind would one day weep at the memory. As the harness was carried through the court at Worms, an old Bishop of Speyer said to fair Uote: 'So our friends are going off to the feast; may God protect their honour there!'

Then noble Uote said to her sons: 'You should stay here, good heroes. I dreamt last night of terror and sadness, and of how all the birds in the land were dead.'

'Anyone who trusts in dreams', said Hagen, 'has lost his sense of honour.* The sooner my Lord takes leave of the ladies, the better I shall like it. We should be looking forward to this ride into Etzel's land. There'll be plenty of opportunity for heroes' hands to serve their Kings when we have to look on at Kriemhilde's celebrations.' Hagen was now in favour of the journey, however much he may have regretted it later.

He might still have spoken against it, if Gernot had not attacked him so roughly, reminding him of Sifrid, Lady Kriemhilde's husband, and saying: 'That's why Hagen wants to miss the great journey to Etzel's court.'

Hagen of Tronege answered: 'I never do anything out of fear. You can start whenever you give the order. I'll be glad to ride with you into Etzel's land.' And many were the shields and helmets he later hacked in pieces.

The men assembled, and their equipment was stacked in the waiting ships. The crossing lasted till evening, and they left their homes with every sign of happiness. When the tents and pavilions had been set up on the grass on the other side of the Rhine, the King asked his beautiful wife to stay with him one

more night, and make love to his majestic person.   Early in
the morning they awoke to trumpets and flutes, signalling their
departure. They set to, and those who had their loved ones in
their arms embraced them once again—soon to be separated for
ever in sorrow, by King Etzel's wife.

The sons of fair Uote had one vassal who was brave and loyal,
and as they began to leave, he secretly disclosed to the King
what was in his mind, saying: 'I am sad to see you making this
journey.'   This was Rumold, a hero if ever there was one. He
said: 'In whose hands are you going to leave your people and
your lands? A pity that no one can turn you knights from your
purpose! I never liked this news from Kriemhilde.'

'My lands and my little child I entrust to you. And attend the
ladies well. If you see anyone weeping, comfort them. That's
how I would wish it, and I'm sure we have nothing whatever to
fear from King Etzel's wife.'

Their horses were ready, and they took their leave in high
spirits, with many a loving kiss. The ladies remembered their
parting later, and wept.   The bold knights fetched their
horses, while the ladies stood sadly aside, thinking uneasily of the
long separation, and wondering what misery lay ahead.   The
brave Burgundians then set out, leaving great activity behind
them, and much weeping of men and women on either side of
the mountains. But they rode off joyfully, however sad their
people were.

The Nibelung warriors rode with them, a thousand men in
armour, leaving at home the fair ladies they would never see
again. Kriemhilde still smarted from Sifrid's wounds.   They
struck up through East Franconia, in the direction of the Main.
Hagen, who knew the way, was leading Gunther's men, and
Dankwart, the hero from Burgundy, was responsible for food
and equipment.   As they left Franconia, and approached
Swalefeld, you could pick out the Princes and their family by
their proud carriage, those heroes of renown. On the morning of
the twelfth day, the King arrived at the Danube.

Hagen of Tronege, the saviour of the Nibelungs, was riding
at the head. The brave warrior dismounted on the sand, and
quickly tied his horse to a tree.   The river was swollen, and
no ship was to be seen. The Nibelungs began to worry about
how they could cross such an expanse of water, and many of the
carefree knights got down off their horses.

'Lord of the Rhine,' said Hagen, 'there's trouble ahead of

you here. As you can see, the river is flooded, and the current is strong. I'm afraid we shall lose a lot of good men today.'

'Is it my fault, Hagen?' said the proud King. 'Remember your own worth, and stop trying to discourage us. Find a ford over the river for us, so that we can get our horses and equipment across.'

'I'm not so tired of life that I want to drown myself in this flood,' said Hagen. 'I still have plenty of men to kill in Etzel's country, and I'm looking forward to it.   Stay at the water's edge, you proud knights, while I go and find the ferrymen myself to take us over into Gelpfrat's territory.' And strong Hagen took up his good shield.   He was fully armed, with his bright helmet strapped on, shield in hand, and a sword slung over his armour with two grisly cutting edges.

As he looked up and down the river for the ferryman, he heard the sound of falling water in a pleasant pool, and pricked up his ears. The noise was made by certain wise women, who were bathing and refreshing themselves.   When he realized this, he crept softly towards them, but they moved away as soon as they saw him. While they mocked him from a safe distance, he stole their clothes; but this was all the harm he did to them.

Then one of the water-sprites, Hadeburg by name, said: 'Hagen, noble knight, if you give us back our clothes, we'll tell you what's in store for you on your journey to court.'   They were floating in front of him like birds on the water, and he knew from this that they were wise and trustworthy. He was disposed to believe whatever they said, and they told him what he wanted to know.   She said: 'You can ride on into Etzel's land. I can pledge my word, without hesitation, that no heroes ever travelled towards greater honours in any kingdom. You can believe me, for I speak the truth.'

Hagen's heart was cheered by this, and he lost no time in giving them back their clothes. Once they were clothed in their magic dress again, they told him the real truth about the journey into Etzel's land.   The other water-sprite, Sigelinde by name, now said: 'I warn you, Hagen, son of Aldrian. My sister lied to you, to get her clothes back. If you ever get to the Huns, you will find yourself betrayed.   You should turn back while there is still time. You brave heroes have been invited into Etzel's land to die. Every one of you who rides on, goes to his death.'

But Hagen answered: 'It's no use trying to fool me. How

could we all be going to die through anybody's hatred?' So they explained in more detail.   And one of them said: 'You can't do anything about it. We know that not a single one of you will live, except for the King's chaplain. He'll come home safely to Gunther's land.'

Brave Hagen answered grimly: 'You can hardly expect me to go back to my Lords with this story. Lead us across the water, wisest of women.'

She said: 'If you still insist on making this journey, you'll find the only ferryman in a house which stands high on the bank of the river.' Hagen ignored everything else he'd been told, but   one of them called after the angry knight: 'Wait a minute, Lord Hagen, you're in too much of a hurry. You still haven't heard how to get to the other side. The lord of this frontier land is called Else.   His brother is the warrior Gelpfrat, a lord in Bavaria. You will have great trouble in passing through his territory. You should be on your guard, and treat the ferryman very carefully as well.   He is very fierce, and he'll kill you, unless you make a point of getting him to trust you. Give him money if you want him to take you across. He is the guardian of this land, and faithful to Gelpfrat.   And if he's slow in coming, shout over the water that your name is Amelrich. (Amelrich was a good hero who left this country because of a feud.) The ferryman will come as soon as he hears that name.'

Hagen bowed stiffly to the ladies, and said no more. He climbed higher up the bank, and went along the river until he saw a house on the other side.   He began calling out across the water: 'Come and fetch me, ferryman, and I'll pay you with a golden ring! Believe me, my business is urgent.'   Now the ferryman was too rich and powerful to want to serve anyone, and he was not used to accepting payment. Even his servants were proud. And so Hagen was left standing on this side of the river.

He shouted with all his force, till the words rolled back and forth across the water (he was a great strong man): 'Come and fetch me! I am Amelrich, Else's man, who escaped from this land because of a feud.'   At the same time he held up his sword high in the air, to show him the ring of bright shining gold, so that he would take him across to Gelpfrat's land. The proud ferryman took up the oars himself.

Now as it happened, this same pilot was recently married. As we know, material greed leads to a bad end, and he was eager to earn Hagen's red gold. His reward was a cruel death by the warrior's sword.

The ferryman pulled quickly across to the bank. When he saw no sign of Amelrich he was full of rage; and seeing Hagen, he said fiercely to the hero: 'Your name may well be Amelrich, but you're certainly not the one I expected to see. He was my brother. Since you've made a fool of me, you'll have to stay on this side.'

'No, by God,' said Hagen, 'I'm a foreign knight, and have soldiers under my protection. I shall be sincerely grateful if you accept my payment in a spirit of friendship, and take me across.'

But the ferryman said: 'No, it's impossible. My masters have enemies, and I never bring strangers into this land. If you value your life, you'd better get out on the bank, quick.'

'Don't make me do that,' said Hagen. 'I'm sad enough as it is. Take my good gold in friendship, and ferry us over, a thousand horses and men.' But the fierce ferryman answered: 'Never!'

Then he snatched up a strong oar, great and broad, and dealt Hagen a blow he could have done without, forcing him on to his knees in the bottom of the boat. This was certainly the fiercest ferryman the Troneger had ever encountered.   And he still hadn't finished provoking the haughty stranger. He hit Hagen over the head so hard that the oar broke. He was a strong man, Else's ferryman, and he was soon to suffer for it.   Without more ado, Hagen grimly drew his sword, cut off his head and threw it into the river. The proud Burgundians soon learnt what had happened.

To Hagen's annoyance the ship had drifted downstream while he was killing the pilot, and it cost him a lot of effort before he could get it back into position. Then he pulled with powerful strokes,   and so fast that the strong oar broke off in his hand. He was eager to get back to the knights on the bank, but it was the only oar in the boat, so he promptly tied it up   with a thin shield-strap, and made for a wood where his lord was waiting on the shore. The fine knights came down to meet him,   with every sign of welcome, until they noticed the boat reeking of blood from the ferryman's wound. Then Hagen had plenty of questions to answer.

King Gunther, when he saw the hot blood swilling about in the boat, quickly said: 'But Hagen, what's happened to the ferryman? It looks as if your bravery has been the death of him.'

Hagen disclaimed responsibility, saying: 'I found the boat by a tangled willow, and untied it. I've seen no sign of any ferryman around today; and I've caused no one any harm either.'

Then Lord Gernot of Burgundy spoke up: 'I'm afraid I foresee the death of many of our friends today. How are we to get across, without sailors to help us? I don't like the look of this at all.'

But Hagen shouted out: 'You youngsters, unload the equipment on to the grass. I seem to remember I was the best ferryman ever seen on the Rhine. I can get you over into Gelpfrat's country, never fear.'

First, they hit the horses to encourage them across the river. They swam well, and not a single one was carried away by the current, although a few drifted some distance as they began to tire.   Since there was no escape from the journey, they brought their gold and equipment down to the boat. Hagen was in charge of the operation, and he succeeded in bringing all these mighty knights to the other bank, and into a strange land.

First he took over the thousand proud knights, and then his own men. But there were still more to come; nine thousand retainers he ferried across to the other shore. A considerable achievement for one day.   When he had got them safely to the other side of the river, the bold warrior remembered the strange story told him by the water-sprites, and the King's chaplain nearly lost his life as a result.   He found the reverend gentleman by the pile of church luggage, with his hand resting on the sacred properties. Not that it helped him much when Hagen saw him; God's * unfortunate priest could not escape his unpleasant fate.

Hagen threw him out of the boat. As he tried to clamber back, the others shouted: 'Grab hold, sir!' Young Giselher was angry, and tried to prevent him coming to any harm.*   And Lord Gernot of Burgundy said: 'What good will the chaplain's death do you, Hagen? If it was anyone but you, I'd make them sorry for it. What have you got against the priest?'

The chaplain meanwhile was struggling desperately to keep afloat, hoping that someone would rescue him. But before they could do anything to help him, Hagen angrily pushed him down again, to everyone's horror.   When the unfortunate cleric saw that no help was forthcoming, he turned for the bank. He was in great difficulty, as he knew nothing of swimming, but God brought him safely across to dry land.   And there the sorry priest stood, shaking the water from his clothes. At this Hagen understood that there was no escape from what the wild water-sprites had foretold, and he thought: 'All these warriors must die.'

When they had unloaded the ship, and carried up all the three Kings' equipment, Hagen smashed the boat to pieces, and scattered it on the water. The brave good knights were astonished at this.

'What did you do that for, brother?' said Dankwart. 'How are we supposed to cross over when we make our return journey, back from the Huns to the Rhine?' Quite soon Hagen was to tell him there would be no return journey,   but for the moment the hero of Tronege said: 'I did it in the hope that any coward we may have brought with us will die ignominiously in the water, if he's frightened enough to try to escape.'

They had an outstanding hero with them, by the name of Volker, who was a good speaker, and said what he thought. As far as the fiddler was concerned, Hagen could do no wrong.   Their horses were ready, and their mules loaded; so far they had suffered no serious loss on their journey, except for the King's chaplain. He had to walk home to the Rhine.

AVENTIURE 26

GELPFRAT IS KILLED BY DANKWART

When they were all assembled on the bank, the King asked: 'Who's going to show us the best way through this country, and prevent us getting lost?' Volker the strong answered: 'I'll take care of that myself.'

'Wait a minute, knights and men,' said Hagen. 'It's only right for friends to stick together, as I'm sure you'll agree. Well, here's some news that will shock you: we shall never get back to Burgundy. I was told this by two water-sprites this morning; we shall never come back. I can only advise you heroes to arm yourselves and take every precaution. We have some powerful enemies here, and we ought to travel warily. I was hoping to find that the wise water-sprites were lying. They said that none of us would come back safely to land, except the chaplain. That's why I was so eager to drown him today.'

The news spread quickly through the troops, and bold heroes turned pale and anxious, as they thought of the cruel death waiting for them on their journey. Who could blame them? The place where they had made the crossing and killed the ferryman was called Mehring; and Hagen said again: 'I have made enemies for us along the route; I don't doubt we shall have some fighting to do. I killed that ferryman this morning, and Gelpfrat and Else will know all about it. Be ready, so that they get a rough reception if they attack us here. I know them; they're too brave to overlook a thing like this. Ride your horses gently, so that no one thinks we're running away.' 'I'll take your advice,' said Giselher the warrior.

'But who's going to guide us through the country?' 'Let Volker do it,' they all answered. 'The brave minstrel knows all the paths and ways.' Almost before the request was made, the bold fiddler was ready armed, with his helmet strapped on. His equipment shone proudly in brilliant colours, and he tied a red favour to his lance. Great suffering awaited him and the three Kings.

Meanwhile Gelpfrat and Else the strong had received the

news of the ferryman's death with displeasure. They sent for their warriors, who set out in answer to the summons immediately,   and before long, as I will tell you, they could be seen riding up, men who had inflicted heavy losses and barbarous wounds in many a bitter battle. Seven hundred or more answered Gelpfrat's call.

Their lords led them as a matter of course, when they rode against their fierce enemies, and if they had been less eager in pursuit of the brave strangers, they might have lost fewer men.   For Hagen of Tronege had foreseen everything. No hero could have taken better care of his friends. He and his men, and Dankwart his brother, had taken over the rearguard. This turned out to be a wise precaution.

The last daylight was gone, and he was afraid of loss or injury to his friends. They carried their shields right through Bavarian territory, and it was not long before the heroes were attacked.

They heard the clatter of hoofs on both sides of the road, and behind them as well. But the Bavarians were too careless in their haste, and brave Dankwart had time to warn his men: 'Fasten your helmets. We're being attacked.'

They were forced to halt and then they saw shields gleaming through the darkness. Hagen broke the silence, and said: 'Who is it chasing us?' And Gelpfrat had to answer.

The Margrave from Bavaria said: 'We're looking for our enemies, and our search has led us here. Someone, I don't know who, killed my ferryman today. He was a hero if ever there was one, and his death was a great loss to me.'

And Hagen of Tronege answered: 'So it was your ferryman, was it? He refused to take me across. I'll take the blame. I killed him. I had no choice. If I hadn't, he would almost certainly have killed me.   I offered him gold and clothing as payment for bringing us over into your land, and this annoyed him so much that he hit me with a great heavy oar. I lost my temper at this,   reached for my sword, and warded off his furious attack, wounding him seriously. That's how the hero was killed. If you want compensation, you can have it.' And so the battle started between these uncompromising men.

'I knew well enough,' said Gelpfrat, 'when I saw Gunther and his household riding past, that Hagen would cause trouble. He's not going to get away with it now. The hero will have to stand hostage for the ferryman's death"

They lowered their spears, ready to thrust; Gelpfrat and

Hagen eager to get at each other; Else and Dankwart proudly galloping to try their skill. And they fought grimly. No heroes ever gave a better account of themselves. In one mighty clash, Hagen found himself deposited behind his horse by Gelpfrat's hand. His harness had broken, and he realized the fight had begun in earnest. The din of splintering lances was all round him as the two companies fought. Then Hagen, who was still on the grass where the thrust had left him, began to recover himself. I doubt if his thoughts of Gelpfrat were very loving.

I can't tell you who held their horses, but Hagen and Gelpfrat were both on the ground now, and they flung themselves at each other. Meanwhile their companions kept the battle going. Grimly as Hagen leapt on Gelpfrat, the noble Margrave hacked a great piece out of his shield, so that the sparks flew, and Gunther's brave vassal very nearly lost his life. He called out to Dankwart: 'Help me, dear brother! I've taken on a hero of heroes here, and it looks as if I shall die at his hands.' Brave Dankwart answered: 'Let me settle it for you.'

And the hero sprang on Gelpfrat, and dealt him a fatal blow with his sharp sword. Else would have liked to avenge him, but he and his followers were forced to withdraw with heavy losses. His brother was killed, and he himself was wounded. A good eighty of his warriors lay dead on the battlefield, and Else had to break off and run before Gunther's men.

As the Bavarians gave way, you could hear the frightful sound of blows following them. The men of Tronege chased after their enemies, and those who preferred to escape punishment were only too eager to get away. But in the middle of the pursuit Dankwart spoke up: 'We should turn back quickly, and carry on our way. Let them gallop off; they're blood-stained enough by now. Come on, we'd better hurry back to our friends.'

When they got back to the scene of the attack Hagen of Tronege said: 'Heroes, check if anyone is missing, or lost in the battle through Gelpfrat's anger.' They had four dead to lament. But their enemies had paid dearly, and a hundred or more Bavarians had been killed. The men of Tronege carried the signs on their soiled and bloody shields. The moon shone fitfully through the clouds, and Hagen said: 'No one tell my lords what we have done here today. Leave them in peace till morning.'

When those who had been fighting caught up with the others,

the troops were beginning to complain of tiredness. 'How much longer do we have to ride?' they said, and brave Dankwart answered: 'There'll be no sleep for us tonight.   You must all keep going till dawn.' Then Volker the bold, who was looking after the rest of the company, sent someone to ask the Marshal: 'Where are we going to stop tonight, for our horses and our dear lords to rest?'

And brave Dankwart answered: 'I can't tell you. But we daren't stop before daybreak. After that, we'll lie down on the grass as soon as we find a place.' The news was not very welcome to most of them.

Their bloody aspect remained undiscovered until the bright sun over the mountains announced the morning, and the King saw they had been fighting. He was angry, and said: 'What's this, friend Hagen? It seems you think nothing of riding in my presence with your mail soaked in blood.* Who was responsible for this?' Hagen answered: 'Else. He attacked us by night.   They fell on us to avenge his ferryman. My brother killed Gelpfrat, and Else escaped under great pressure. He lost a hundred and we lost four dead in the fight.'

I cannot tell you where they lay down to rest. But all the inhabitants of the country round about soon heard how the sons of noble Uote were coming to court, and they were warmly received at Passau when they got there.   Their uncle, Bishop Pilgrim, was overjoyed to see his nephews coming into the land with so many knights, and his delight in serving them was apparent at once.   All along the route they were welcomed by their friends. At Passau there was no room to accommodate them, and they had to cross the river to a stretch of open country where they could set up their pavilions and tents.

They were persuaded to stay there one whole day and night, and given the best of everything. After that, they were expected in Rüdeger's country, where the news of their arrival had spread as quickly as at Passau.   When the travel-weary men had rested, they moved on, and as they came nearer to the country, they found a man asleep on the frontier. Hagen stole his great sword from him.   This same good knight was called Eckewart, and he was terribly downcast at losing his sword with the arrival of the heroes. They had hardly found Rüdeger's frontier well guarded.

'What a shameful thing!' said Eckewart. 'Why did the Burgundians have to make this journey? All my happiness was taken from me when I lost Sifrid. And now, Lord Rüdeger, I have failed you too!'

Hagen could see the noble knight's distress, and he gave him back his sword, together with six golden rings. 'Take those, and trust me as a friend; you're a brave warrior, even if you do go to sleep by yourself on the frontier.' *

'God reward you for your rings,' said Eckewart, 'but I'm still unhappy about your journey to the Huns. You killed Sifrid, and you're hated here. I'd honestly advise you to be on your guard.'

'God will have to protect us then,' said Hagen. 'All that these warriors are worried about now is a place to spend the night. The Kings and their men would like to know if there's anywhere we can stay in this country.

'We've ridden our horses to death on the long journey, and our food has run out,' said warrior Hagen. 'We've no chance of buying any, and we could do with someone to show us hospitality tonight, out of the goodness of his heart.'

And Eckewart answered: 'I can take you to someone who will receive you into his house and treat you as you've never been treated before in any country, if you bold warriors will come and meet Rüdeger.   He lives near the road, and he's the most wonderful host who ever owned a house. His heart is as full of virtue as a may-meadow is with flowers; and he's never happier than when entertaining heroes.'

Then King Gunther said: 'Will you be my messenger then, and ask my dear friend Rüdeger if he will take us in, my family and my men, for my sake? If he does, I shall always be at his service.'

'I shall be glad to be your messenger,' said Eckewart. And with a willing heart he set off on his errand, to tell Rüdeger all he had heard. It would be the most welcome news he had received for a long time.

They saw a warrior rushing towards Bechelaren; Rüdeger himself recognized him, and said: 'There's Eckewart, one of Kriemhilde's men, coming along the road in a great hurry.' He was afraid he might have been attacked by enemies,   and went out in front of the house to meet the messenger, who duly delivered his news to the host and his friends, merely waiting to take off his sword and lay it down.   He said to the Margrave: 'Gunther, Lord of Burgundy, Giselher his brother, and Gernot have sent me. They assure you severally of their service.   Hagen and Volker do the same, with many protestations of loyalty. But that's not all; the King's Marshal asked me to say that the good knights would be grateful for your hospitality.'

Laughing for joy, Rüdeger answered: 'This is welcome news, that the proud Kings are willing to accept my services. I shall certainly not refuse them. I shall be delighted to have them under my roof.'

'Dankwart the Marshal asked me to tell you how many you would have to find room for: sixty great warriors, a thousand good knights, and nine thousand men.' Rüdeger was very happy.

'I'm lucky', said Rüdeger, 'that these proud knights should come as guests to my house. I've had too little opportunity of serving them in the past. My friends and relatives, ride out to meet them.'

Knights and men ran to their horses, in full agreement with their Lord's commands, and all the more eager to offer their services. Lady Gotelinde sat in her room, knowing nothing as yet of what had happened.

AVENTIURE 27

THEY COME TO BECHELAREN

Then the Margrave went to his wife and daughter, and told them the welcome news he had just received: how the Queen's brothers were coming to his house.

'My dear,' said Rüdeger, 'you must give the proud Kings a wonderful welcome when they present themselves with their household. And be sure to give a special greeting to Hagen, Gunther's man. There is one with him called Dankwart, and another called Volker, a most accomplished man. You and my daughter should kiss these six, and you should show the knights affection, with due propriety.'

The ladies willingly gave their promise to do this. They then started looking in their trunks for the gorgeous dresses they intended to wear when they went to meet the knights. All the women had plenty to keep them busy. There were no attempts to improve on nature. They merely wore shining golden bands on their heads to keep their beautiful hair tidy in the wind. (I pass on, in all honesty, what I am told.)

But now we can leave the ladies to these and similar activities, and watch Rüdeger's friends as they rush across the fields to greet the Princes, and welcome them into the Margrave's land. When he saw them approaching him, Rüdeger the bold said joyfully: 'Welcome to my country, my Lords, and welcome to your men! It is a great pleasure to me to see you here.'

The knights bowed in perfect friendship, and he left them in no doubt of his affection for them. Hagen and Volker he singled out with his greeting, as old acquaintances. As he received Dankwart, the brave warrior said: 'Since you've offered to take care of us, who's going to look after all the people we've brought with us?' And the Margrave answered: 'You and all your followers can rest in comfort tonight. I'll put such a watch on everything you've brought with you, horses and equipment as well, that nothing, down to the last spur, will be lost or damaged. Put up the pavilions in the field, you men! I'll make good any loss or damage. Unharness the horses, and let them go free.' He was the first host to do this for them.

The guests were glad to take advantage of this offer. Then the lords rode off, and the men threw themselves down in the grass where they stood. I doubt if they had ever been so comfortable and well-treated on the journey before. The noble Margravine came out of the castle to meet them, with her lovely daughter and beautiful maids at her side, all richly attired, and wearing their bracelets and rings. The Burgundians rode up to them, and dismounted, with the utmost politeness, before this dazzling display of precious stones, while thirty-six beautiful maids, and many other ladies and brave men, came out to offer their affectionate greeting.

The young girl, following her mother, kissed all three Kings, and then saw Hagen standing next to them. Her father told her to kiss Hagen as well, but he was so terrifying to look at that she was not at all keen. All the same, she had to do as she was told. The colour came and went in her cheek as she kissed Dankwart and the minstrel in turn. This last honour to Volker was in recognition of his personal bravery. Then Giselher, the knight from Burgundy, took the young Margravine by the hand; her mother did the same to Gunther the brave, and they both went off happily with the heroes.

Rüdeger accompanied Gernot to a spacious hall, where knights and ladies together took their seats. Then the guests were offered wine, and I doubt if heroes were ever better treated. Rüdeger's daughter was the object of many admiring glances. Her beauty set many a knight day-dreaming, and she was proud to be the centre of attraction.* Not that they were allowed to do anything about it, of course; and in any case there were glimpses of many other ladies and maids to be had. The noble fiddler was full of gratitude to his host.

As was the custom, ladies and knights now separated; tables were put up all over the hall, and the guests were feasted magnificently. The noble Margravine honoured the guests by joining them at table. Her daughter was left with the children, where she belonged, and the guests were sorry they could no longer see her. When everyone had eaten and drunk, the beautiful girl was * brought back into the hall, and a jocular conversation began, in which Volker, a brave and carefree warrior, took a leading part.

The minstrel said aloud, for everyone to hear: 'Mighty

Margrave, God has been kind to you, for he has given you a beautiful wife and a blissful existence.   And if only I were a King,' said the minstrel, 'and wore a crown, I should want, with all my heart, to marry your beautiful daughter. She is fair to look upon, and noble and good as well.'

The Margrave answered: 'Why should a King ever want to marry my daughter? My wife and I are exiles here; beauty by itself won't make any difference to the good girl's position.'

Gernot replied, in his well-bred way: 'If I were allowed to choose a sweetheart for myself, there's no one I would more gladly have than such a woman.' And Hagen said benevolently: 'Well, why doesn't Giselher get married? The Margravine is of such noble family that we should all be pleased to serve her if she came to Burgundy and wore a crown.'

Rüdeger and Gotelinde were very much in favour of the idea; in fact they were overjoyed. And the heroes did eventually arrange that Giselher should marry her, as being an alliance worthy of a King.   Some things are so inevitable that no one can stop them. The girl was brought before them, and they swore to give her to Giselher. He in his turn promised to love the lovely girl.*

They allotted her castles and lands, and the noble King, in company with Gernot, confirmed under oath that she would receive them. Then the Margrave said: 'As I have no castles or lands of my own,   I am greatly indebted to you for these promises. My gift to my daughter will be silver and gold, as much as a hundred pack-mules can carry; may it satisfy and gladden the hearts of the hero's relations.'

Then they were both told to stand in a ring, as the custom was, with many young men happily facing them. Their minds were on the things that young people still think of on these occasions.   When they asked the lovely girl if she would take the knight, she was half reluctant and half eager to accept such a magnificent man. She was embarrassed at the question, like many a girl before her.   Her father Rüdeger advised her to say yes, and accept him. And immediately noble Giselher was there to embrace her with his white hands—although it was little enough she had of him in the event.

Then the Margrave said: 'Noble Kings, I will give you my child to take with you, following the normal custom, as soon as you ride back on your way home to Burgundy.' This they agreed to.

The noise and activity were now cut short; the girl was sent to
her room, and the guests were invited to get some sleep, so that
they would be rested on the next day. After this, they were fed,
under their host's affectionate supervision.   When they had
eaten, they made as if to leave for the land of the Huns, but their
noble host protested: 'I'm not going to allow that. You must
stay here for a little longer; I never had such welcome guests.'

Dankwart answered: 'I'm afraid that's impossible. Where
would you find the food, all the bread and wine, to feed so many
knights tonight?' But the host only said: 'I won't hear of your
going.   My dear Lords, you can't refuse me. Why, I could
give you enough food for a fortnight, you and all the followers
you have brought with you! King Etzel has left me well provided
for.'

And however much they protested, they had to stay there till
the morning of the fourth day, when their host performed feats
of liberality that were rumoured far and wide. He gave his
guests horses and clothing,   for their stay had to come to an
end at last. Rüdeger had no thought of setting limits to his
generosity, and gave his guests whatever they asked for, not
listening to anyone who tried to refuse.*

Their horses were brought, ready saddled, to the gate, and the
stranger knights began to assemble, shield in hand, to ride to
Etzel's land.   Before they left the hall their host showered
them with gifts, confident of his ability to win great honour by
showing generosity—he had even given away his beautiful
daughter, to Giselher.   And to Gunther too, that renowned
hero who never accepted gifts, he gave a suit of armour which the
rich and noble King was honoured to wear. Gunther bent his
head over noble Rüdeger's hand in thanks.   And to Gernot
he gave a trusty sword, which he proudly carried into battle
later. The Margrave's wife looked on approvingly at this gift,
which later cost good Rüdeger his life.

Since the King had accepted, Gotelinde offered her own sweet
gifts to Hagen, as she had every right to do, hoping that he would
not leave without allowing her to make her contribution to the
feast. But he had other ideas.

'Of everything I ever saw', he said, 'there's nothing I would
sooner carry away from here than that shield over there on the
wall. I should like to take that to Etzel's land.'

As the Margravine listened to Hagen speaking, she was
reminded of her past sorrow, and she wept. She thought in her

heart of Nuodung's death, killed by Witege, the cause of so much grief to her.   And she said to the warrior: 'I'll give you the shield. If only to God the man were still alive who carried it once in his hand! He was killed in battle, and left me, unlucky woman, to weep for ever.'

The noble Margravine stood up, took down the shield with her own fair hand and brought it to Hagen. He held it in his hand, greatly honoured by the gift.   The sun never shone on a better shield. Its coloured surface, encrusted with precious stones, was covered by shining silk. The price, if anyone had wanted to buy it, must have been at least a thousand marks.   Hagen handed the shield over to be carried away, and it was Dankwart's turn to be presented. He was given costly clothes by the Margrave's daughter, and wore them proudly among the Huns.   And none of these gifts could have been given or accepted, if it had not been for their host, who was so kind as to make it possible. And yet they were soon to face him as an enemy, and kill him.

Volker the bold then took his fiddle, and standing himself very correctly in front of Gotelinde, he played and sang his own sweet songs to her; this was his way of saying goodbye as he left Bechelaren.   The Margravine ordered a chest to be fetched —and this is how she rewarded him in affectionate gratitude: she took out twelve rings, and fitted them on his hand. 'Take these with you to Etzel's land,   and wear them at court, in remembrance of me. And then, after you've gone, I shall hear how you served me at the feast there.' Her wish was fulfilled with a vengeance.

Then the host said to his guests: 'To make your journey easier, I myself will lead you, and take care that you come to no harm on the road.' And he ordered his mules to be loaded at once.   Rüdeger was accompanied by five hundred men, horses and equipment, and rode off happily to the feast at their head. Not a single one ever saw Bechelaren again.   The host parted from his wife with a loving kiss, and Giselher, in the innocence of his heart, did the same. The fair ladies who were now embraced had nothing but weeping and lamentation to look forward to.   On all sides windows were thrown open as the host and his men went to fetch their horses. They must have known in their hearts, I think, that it would end in misery, for ladies and maids wept together.

The troops too were reluctant to part from the good friends at

Bechelaren they would never see again. All the same, they were in high spirits as they rode down the bank of the Danube, and out into the land of the Huns.

Then Rüdeger, that noble and carefree knight, said to the Burgundians: 'But we must let Etzel know we're coming; the news will be the most welcome he has ever received.'   At once a messenger rode down through Austria, telling everyone he met that the heroes from Worms by the Rhine were on their way. The King's subjects were overjoyed.   At the same time messengers hurried on ahead to announce the arrival of the Nibelungs among the Huns. 'Receive them gladly, my Lady Kriemhilde; your dear brothers have come to honour you!' *

Kriemhilde stood in a window, looking out for her family, as a friend might watch for the arrival of friends. She saw a crowd of men from her own country, and told the King, who laughed for joy.   'My happiness is complete,' said Kriemhilde. 'Here come my family, bringing brand-new shields and glittering breastplates. If anyone wants to earn my gold, let him remember my sorrow, and I shall never desert him.'

AVENTIURE 28

THE BURGUNDIANS ARRIVE AMONGST THE HUNS

When old Hildebrand heard that the Burgundians had arrived, he told his lord, who was sad at the news. All the same, he asked him to welcome the brave and carefree knights. Wolfhart the bold sent for the horses, and Dietrich rode out on to the field to greet them, with many stout warriors. The Burgundians had already packed their lordly tents.

When Hagen of Tronege saw them riding in the distance, he said, very correctly, to his lords: 'You bold knights should stand up, and go to meet them, as they've come to welcome you. It's a household I know very well. They're bold knights from Amelunge, led by Dietrich of Verona. They're proud men; you shouldn't despise any service they offer you.'

Then Dietrich and his men dismounted, as was proper, and went towards the guests, offering an affectionate greeting to the heroes from Burgundy. You will want to hear what Lord Dietrich said when he saw them approaching. He told the sons of Uote how much he regretted their journey, and how surprised he was that Rüdeger hadn't known of the danger and warned them.

'Welcome to my Lords, Gunther and Giselher, Gernot and Hagen; and also to Volker and Dankwart the bold. Didn't you know that Kriemhilde is still bitterly mourning for the hero of Nibelunge?'

'I'm surprised she isn't tired of weeping,' said Hagen. 'It's many years now since he was killed. It's time she turned her affections to the King of the Huns. Sifrid won't come back. He was buried long ago.'

'Sifrid's wounds need not detain us. As long as Kriemhilde lives, she'll be a source of danger,' said the Lord of Verona. 'Saviour of the Nibelungs, take care!'

'Why should I take care?' said the proud King. 'Etzel sent messengers, inviting us to his country. That was enough for me. And besides, my sister Kriemhilde sent us all the news.'

'My advice', said Hagen, 'is that you ask Lord Dietrich and

his good heroes to explain more about this. They should be able
to tell you something of Lady Kriemhilde's intentions.'

And the three mighty Kings, Gunther, Gernot and Dietrich,
went aside for a private conference. 'Well, good and noble knight
of Verona, what do you know of the Queen's intentions?'

And the Lord of Verona answered: 'What else can I tell you?
Every day I hear Etzel's wife weeping and wailing, distracted
with grief, and lamenting to Almighty God the death of Sifrid
the strong.'

'Nothing can alter what we heard,' said brave Volker the
minstrel. 'We must ride on to court, and discover what fate
awaits us bold warriors among the Huns.'

And the brave Burgundians continued on their way to court.
They bore themselves proudly, as was the custom in their
country; many a brave Hun was curious to see what sort of man
this Hagen of Tronege was.   There were certainly plenty of
rumours going round, of how he killed Sifrid of the Netherlands,
Kriemhilde's husband, and the strongest knight that ever was.
This was enough to start them asking questions about Hagen at
court.   No one could deny that the hero was a fine figure of a
man, broad-shouldered, tall and majestic, with grizzled hair and
piercing eyes.

Arrangements were then made for the accommodation of the
Burgundians. Gunther's household were separated from the
knights, on the advice of the Queen, who hated him fiercely.
This meant they would be able to kill the youngsters at their
lodging when the time came.   Dankwart, Hagen's brother,
was in charge of them, and the King, in handing them over, was
careful to ask him to look after them well, and supply them with
all their needs. The hero of Burgundy had the welfare of all his
men at heart.

Kriemhilde the fair came forward with her household, to offer
the Nibelungs her treacherous welcome. She kissed Giselher and
took his hand. Hagen looked on, and tightened his helmet.

'Bold knights are likely to think twice', said Hagen, 'after a
greeting like that. The Kings and their men are not equally
welcome, it seems. We were not wise to come to this feast.'

She answered: 'You're welcome to anyone who's pleased to
see you. Do you expect me to greet you out of friendship? What
have you brought me from Worms by the Rhine that would
make you welcome here?'

'If I'd known that warriors were expected to come bringing

gifts for you', said Hagen, 'I should probably have been able to afford something. If I'd realized that was what you wanted, I could have brought you a present easily enough.'

'You could tell me one thing at least: what have you done with the Nibelung treasure? It was my property after all, as you know very well. You could have brought that, couldn't you?'

'Believe me, my Lady Kriemhilde, it's a long time since I had anything to do with the treasure of the Nibelungs. My lords told me to sink it in the Rhine; and there, I'm afraid, it will stay until the day of judgment.'

The Queen answered: 'Just as I thought. You've brought me nothing of it, although it was mine, and I even enjoyed it once. Can you wonder that I grieve day and night?'

'What the devil do you expect me to bring you?' said Hagen. 'I've enough to carry with my shield and armour, my bright helmet and this sword in my hand. What else do you want?'

At this the Queen cried out to all the knights: 'No weapons are to be taken into the hall! Give them to me, you heroes, and I'll have them put away.' 'That's one thing', said Hagen, 'that will never happen.   You would do me too great an honour, bounteous Princess, by carrying my shield and the rest of my armour to my lodgings. You are, after all, a Queen. My father taught me to behave differently. I prefer to be my own treasurer.' *

'Alas!' said Lady Kriemhilde. 'Why should my brother and Hagen refuse to give up their shields? They must have been warned. If I knew who'd done this, I'd have him put to death.'

But Dietrich answered angrily: 'I was the one who warned the noble and mighty Kings, and brave Hagen their vassal! Go on then, you fiend; aren't you going to punish me for it?'

Etzel's wife was put to shame. In mortal fear of Dietrich, she left him without speaking, only darting looks of hate at her enemy.

The two warriors, Dietrich and Hagen, then shook hands; and the carefree warrior said, with great restraint: 'I honestly wish you'd never come amongst the Huns,   after what we've heard from the Queen.' But Hagen answered: 'We shall find a way out of it.' King Etzel saw the two brave men talking together, and asked: 'I should like to know who that knight is, the one Lord Dietrich is greeting so warmly over there. He looks high-spirited enough; I should say he was a hero of quality, whoever his father was.'

One of Kriemhilde's men answered the King: 'He is a

Troneger by birth, and his father's name was Aldrian. He may look cheerful now, but he's a savage man. I can prove the truth of what I say.'

'I'm not likely to see the savage side of him,' said the King, knowing nothing of the Queen's malice, and how she was to vent it on her family, and cause the death of all the Huns.   'I knew Aldrian well; he was one of my men. He won much praise and renown when he was with me. I made him a knight, and gave him my gold. My faithful wife Helche was very fond of him.   That's why I've known so much about Hagen ever since. He and Walther of Spain, two fine lads, were my hostages once, and grew up to be men at my court. Walther ran off with Hildegunde, but I sent Hagen home again.'

He sat thinking of events long past. He had found again his friend from Tronege, who had served him so well in his youth, and was now, in his old age, to kill off all his friends for him.

AVENTIURE 29

KRIEMHILDE ACCUSES HAGEN, AND HE REFUSES
TO STAND FOR HER

Then the two worthy knights, Hagen of Tronege and Lord
Dietrich, parted; and Gunther's man looked round for a
companion in arms. He did not have far to seek,   for he found
Volker standing with Giselher, and invited the resourceful
fiddler to go with him. He knew from personal experience how
fierce he was, and how excellent and brave a knight in every
respect.

The Burgundian lords were still standing about in the court-
yard where they had been left; but these two were seen to detach
themselves and walk, all alone, right across the court till they
arrived in front of a spacious palace. These extraordinary
warriors were afraid of no one.   They sat themselves down on
a bench outside the house, opposite Kriemhilde's hall. Their
magnificent armour shone, and there were many among the on-
lookers who would have liked to know who they were.   The
Huns stared at the insolent heroes as if they were two wild
animals. But when Etzel's wife saw them through the
window, fair Kriemhilde was once again plunged into
gloom.   It reminded her of her sorrow, and she wept.
Etzel's men could not imagine what had so suddenly upset her,
until she said: 'Hagen is to blame, you good and bold heroes.'

They asked her: 'But how did it happen? Only just now we
saw you happy. No one dare do this to you; give us the word,
and he'll pay for it with his life.'

'Whoever avenges my sorrow will never lose my favour. I
would give him anything he wanted. I beg you, on my knees,'
said the King's wife, 'avenge me on Hagen! Take his life!'

At that, sixty brave men got ready to go and murder Hagen
and the fiddler for Kriemhilde.   But when the Queen saw
how few they were, she said fiercely to the heroes: 'You might
as well give up, as try to stand up to Hagen with such a paltry
force.   Hagen of Tronege is strong and brave enough by him-
self, but the one sitting next to him is much stronger still.

163

Volker the fiddler is a dangerous man. It won't be as easy as you seem to think, when you face those heroes.' More got ready when they heard this: four hundred bold knights in all. The Queen would have stopped at nothing to make Hagen and Volker suffer, and the warriors had an anxious time in store for them. When her followers were armed to her satisfaction, the Queen said: 'Stay here and wait a minute. I will go, like a Queen,* to meet my enemies. And you will hear what I have against him, and what Hagen of Tronege, Gunther's man, has done to me. I know he'll be too proud to deny anything, and after that his fate will be no concern of mine.'

Then the brave minstrel Volker saw the noble Queen coming down the steps from the house, and said to his companion: 'Look, friend Hagen, she's coming this way, the woman who invited us to this country so treacherously. I never saw a Queen look so warlike, or lead so many men with swords in their hands. Could it be, friend Hagen, that her intentions towards you are unfriendly? I think you might take more thought for your honour and your life. By the look of it, I should say they were angry about something. And several of them look so bulky about the chest that I could almost fancy they're wearing shining armour under the silk. I can't think who this is directed against, but it's time we got ready to defend ourselves.'

Then Hagen the brave answered angrily: 'I know well enough that it's all directed at me; that's why they carry their shining swords in their hands. But I could take this lot on, and still ride home to Burgundy. Tell me, friend Volker, do you feel like standing and fighting Kriemhilde's men with me? Tell me you will, for friendship's sake, and I'll stand by you faithfully for the rest of my life.'

'Certainly I'll help you,' said the minstrel. 'If it was the King and all his knights coming for us, I'd never go back an inch on my promise of help as long as I live.'

'God in heaven reward you, noble Volker. They can fight me now if they like. What more do I need, now that you say you'll help me? These knights had better advance cautiously now.'

'But I think we should stand up from this seat,' said the minstrel. 'She is a Queen, after all, and we ought to show her that much respect as she passes. She is a noble woman; it will do us both credit.'

'No, not if you love me,' said Hagen. 'If I moved now, these warriors would think I was afraid. I don't stand up from this seat for any of them.   And it's really more in character for both of us not to do it. Why should I honour a woman who hates me? I'll never do it, as long as I live, and I don't care how much King Etzel's wife resents it.'

And Hagen insolently laid a shining sword across his legs. A bright jewel sparkled from the pommel, greener than grass. Kriemhilde recognized it well enough; it was Sifrid's sword.   Seeing the sword again made her grieve in earnest. Its hilt was gold, the scabbard a sheath of red. It reminded her of her sorrow, and she wept. I imagine that was why brave Hagen did it.

Volker the bold pulled his fiddle-bow nearer to him on the bench. It was huge and long, strong like a sword, keen and broad. And they sat there fearlessly, the two carefree knights.   They were evidently too proud to stand up for anyone, and so the noble Queen came right up in front of them, and greeted them as enemies: 'Well, Lord Hagen, and who sent for you? How can you dare to ride into this country, knowing how you wronged me? If you'd been wiser, you would have stayed at home.'

'Nobody sent for me,' said Hagen. 'A certain three warriors were invited here, and these three warriors happen to be my masters, just as I happen to be their vassal. I don't usually stay behind when they ride to court.'

'Why did you make me hate you then? Why did you kill Sifrid, my dear husband, for whom I shall weep till the end of my days?'

'What's the use of going into it now? I should have thought enough had been said about it already. I'm the same Hagen who killed Sifrid, hero of heroes. He paid the full penalty for Lady Kriemhilde's abuse of fair Brünnhilde.   I don't deny anything, mighty Queen. I'm to blame for everything, all your hurt and all your loss. Anyone who wants to, man or woman, can avenge it now. It's true enough that I've caused you plenty of suffering.'

She said: 'Did you hear that, you knights? He admits that he caused all my suffering. Men of Etzel, his fate is in your hands!' The haughty warriors exchanged glances.

If anyone started a fight now, it looked as if the honours would go to the two friends; they had distinguished themselves in many battles already. The Huns were too frightened to go on with what they had so rashly undertaken.   One of them said:

'Why look at me? I don't feel bound by any promise I made. I'm not going to lose my life for anyone's gold. Etzel's wife is trying to lead us into trouble.'   And another one next to him agreed: 'I feel the same. I wouldn't stand up to that fiddler if I were offered castles of gold. I've seen those piercing eyes of his.   And I know Hagen of old; there's not much anyone can tell me about him. I've seen him in action, a score of times, condemning wives by the hundred to a life of mourning.   Again and again he rode out to battle with Walther of Spain, when they were here with Etzel. And they won great honour for the King. You have to admit that Hagen deserves his reputation.   And the knight was still only a child at that time. Look how grizzled those young lads have become now! Now that he's grown to manhood, he's more dangerous than ever. And on top of that, he's carrying Balmung, which he won by a foul and terrible deed.'   And with these words all idea of fighting was abandoned. The Queen was terribly disappointed, but her heroes made off, preferring to avoid death at the fiddler's hands. You could hardly blame them.

Then the fiddler said: 'Well, we've seen that we have enemies here, as we were warned earlier. We'd better join the Kings at court, in case anyone dares to attack our lords.   It's strange how often a man is too frightened to go on when he sees two friends standing by each other. If he's sensible, he abandons the idea. Many a man has saved his skin by the use of his intelligence.'

'I'll come with you,' said Hagen, and they went to the court-yard, where the splendid knights were being received in great style. Volker the bold said in a loud voice   to his lords: 'How much longer are you going to let yourselves be hemmed in like this? You should present yourselves at court, and find out from the King what his intentions are.' At this the brave good heroes began to pair off.

The Prince of Verona himself took Gunther the mighty of Burgundy by the hand; Irnfrid took Gernot the brave; Rüdeger went with Giselher.

But throughout all the pairing, and the presentation at court, Volker and Hagen were never separated again until they came to their last battle. Theirs was a partnership which robbed many noble ladies of their happiness.

A thousand brave knights followed the Kings to court, as well as the sixty warriors that brave Hagen had brought from his own lands. Hawart and Iring, two outstanding men, were seen walking sociably with the Kings. Dankwart, and Wolfhart, a priceless warrior, were on their best behaviour in front of the others. As the Lord of the Rhine entered the palace, Etzel the mighty sprang up from his seat without hesitation. Never did a King offer a warmer greeting.

'Welcome, Lord Gunther, Lord Gernot and your brother Giselher. I sent you my faithful and willing service at Worms by the Rhine, and all your household are welcome as well. And my wife and I would especially welcome you two warriors, Volker the brave and Hagen, to our country. She has sent you many messengers to the Rhine.'

Hagen of Tronege answered: 'Yes, I've heard them. And if I hadn't come to the Huns because of my lords, I would still have ridden here to honour you.' The noble host took these welcome guests by the hand, and led them to the seat where he himself had been sitting. Then the guests were served with mead and wine in great golden dishes, to show the exiles how welcome they were.

Then King Etzel said: 'Believe me, nothing in the world could have made me happier than to see you heroes in my house. And the Queen's grief will be greatly softened by your arrival. I often wonder if I might have offended you, when I think how many noble guests I entertain here, while you have never come to my country. But the pleasure of seeing you now makes up for everything.'

Rüdeger answered, with quiet cheerfulness: 'It is right that you should be pleased to see them. The loyalty of my wife's family is always to be trusted, and they've brought many splendid warriors to your house.'

The lords had arrived at mighty Etzel's court on midsummer eve. He welcomed them as heroes were never welcomed before, and, when it was time to eat, accompanied them to table. No host ever sat with his guests in grander style. Food and drink were provided in plenty, and they were given everything they asked for, in keeping with their fabulous reputation.

AVENTIURE 30

HAGEN AND VOLKER STAND GUARD

The day was nearly over, and the travel-weary knights began to wonder anxiously when they could go to bed and rest. Hagen broached the subject, and it was soon settled.

Gunther said to his host: 'God be with you; we should like to sleep. Give us your leave, and we'll come back tomorrow morning at your convenience.' The King contentedly took leave of his guests.

As they left, they found themselves jostled on all sides, and Volker the brave said to the Huns: 'What do you mean by crowding in on these knights like this? You'd better stand back, if you don't want to get hurt. I'll hit some of you so hard with this fiddle that your loved ones will grieve, if you have any. Why don't you give way? It might be healthier for you if you did. They call themselves warriors, but I doubt if it means much to some of them.' *

Hagen looked behind him when he heard the fiddler's angry words, and said: 'The brave minstrel is right. You heroes of Kriemhilde had better go off to your lodgings. You're not likely to get anywhere now. Come back in the morning if you want to start anything, and let us poor exiles rest tonight. That's the way heroes have always behaved, in my experience.'

The guests were then conducted into a spacious hall, which they found furnished all over with costly beds, long and wide, all ready for the knights. Lady Kriemhilde was plotting their final downfall. They saw cunningly embroidered quilts from Arras, coverlets of the best Arabian silk, and gorgeous overlays of shining material. Blankets of ermine and black sable were provided for their comfort. Under there they could rest all night till the next day came. Never did a King and his household sleep in greater luxury.

'If only we didn't have to sleep here,' said young Giselher. 'If only we and our friends had never come! I'm afraid my sister will have us all killed, in spite of her friendly invitation.'

'Don't worry,' said warrior Hagen. 'I'll keep watch myself tonight. You can rely on me to protect us till morning. After that, it's every man for himself.'

They all bowed to him in gratitude, and made straight for their beds. It was not long before all these splendid warriors were lying down, and Hagen began to put on his armour.   Volker the warrior fiddler then said: 'I should like to keep watch all night with you, Hagen, if you don't despise the offer.' The hero thanked Volker affectionately.

'God reward you, my dear Volker; through all my troubles, you're the only man I would ever want to have by me when I'm hard pressed. I'll repay you, if I live to.'

Then they put on their shining armour, took up their shields, and posted themselves before the door. There they kept faithful watch over the guests.   Volker the bold left his shield leaning against the wall, and went back inside for his fiddle. Then he served his friends in the way he knew best.   He sat on the stone step at the door, the bravest fiddler the world has ever seen. Thankfully the proud exiles heard the sweet music as it flowed from the strings.   At first it swelled and resounded throughout the house, as he proved his courage and artistry together. Then he fiddled softer and sweeter, and all those anxious men in bed were soothed into sleep.   When he saw that none were left awake, the warrior took up his shield again, and went back outside. There he stood at the door to protect the exiles from Kriemhilde's men.

At about the middle of the night, or it may have been earlier,* Volker caught sight of a helmet shining some way off in the dark, and realized that Kriemhilde's men were plotting harm for the guests.   The fiddler said: 'Friend Hagen, we might as well worry together: I can see armed men in front of the house. Unless I'm mistaken, they're going to attack us.'

'Keep quiet then,' said Hagen, 'and let them come closer. Before they even know we're here, we'll knock some of their helmets out of shape, and send them back to Kriemhilde the worse for wear.'

One of the Hunnish knights suddenly saw that the door was guarded, and said hurriedly: 'We can't do it; I can see the fiddler standing on watch.   He's wearing a shining helmet, clear and hard, strong and impenetrable. And his mail is gleaming like fire. Hagen is beside him. The guests are well protected.'

They turned back at once, and Volker, as he watched them,

said angrily to his companion: 'Let me go over to those knights. I should like to put a few questions to Kriemhilde's men.'

'For my sake, I'd rather you didn't,' said Hagen. 'Once you're over there, the bold knights may easily press you so hard that I shall have to come to your help; and that could mean the death of all my people.   As soon as we were both involved in the fight, two or three of them would be in the house like a flash, and could cause such harm to the sleepers as we'd never finish lamenting.'

And Volker answered: 'But I must let them know I've seen them, at least; so that Kriemhilde's men won't be able to deny the treachery they'd obviously like to commit.'   And he shouted over to them: 'What are you doing fully armed like this, you bold warriors? Are you off on a thieving expedition, you men of Kriemhilde? Why don't you invite me and my friend to join you?'

No one answered, and he grew angry: 'For shame, you miserable cowards!' said the proud hero. 'Were you going to murder us in our beds? Is that the usual way to treat such worthy heroes?'

The Queen was told how her messengers had achieved nothing at all, and was understandably dismayed. She had to find some other way, and she was a desperate woman: good heroes perished before she was finished.

AVENTIURE 31

THEY GO TO CHURCH

'My chain mail's getting cold,' said Volker. 'I don't think the night will last much longer; I can tell from the air that dawn is near.' And they started to wake up the sleeping men. The bright morning streamed into the hall where the guests were, and Hagen went round rousing all the knights, to ask if they wanted to go to Mass in the cathedral. The bells were ringing, as they would in a Christian country. Not that Christians and heathens all sang the same thing, or worshipped in harmony, as now became apparent. Gunther's men did want to go to church, and had already got up.

They had dressed themselves up in their best clothes, and were as fine a sight as was ever seen in any kingdom. But Hagen was not impressed, and said: 'This is the wrong place for that sort of clothes. Most of you should know what's going on here. You want swords in your hand, not roses; tough shining helmets, not fancy hats, now that we know the extent of Kriemhilde's spite. I can tell you, we shall have to fight before the day is out. You want breastplates, not silken shirts; good broad shields instead of costly cloaks. Then you'll be ready to fight if anyone wants to start anything. My dear Lords, my family and my men, be thankful you can go to church and lament your desperate plight to God Almighty. And realize once and for all that we are all soon to die. And remember your sins conscientiously when you stand before God. I warn you, proud knights, you'll never hear another Mass unless God in heaven intervenes.'

And so the princes and their men went to the cathedral. Brave Hagen ordered them to stand still, and keep together in the holy precinct, and said: 'Nobody knows what the Huns are likely to do. Lay your shields at your feet, my friends; and if anyone offers you an unfriendly greeting, pay it back with a mortal wound. That's Hagen's advice. Follow it, and you'll prove yourselves worthy of your reputation.'

Volker and Hagen both went in front of the great cathedral.

Their idea was to make it impossible for the King's wife to avoid a clash with them. They were in an uncompromising mood.   Then the Lord of the land came up with his beautiful wife. The crowd of bold knights with her were richly dressed, and the dust rose high as they rode along.

When mighty Etzel saw the Kings and their men in arms, he said at once: 'Why do I find my friends all ready for battle? If anyone has harmed them, it is an offence against me and my hospitality.   I would readily recompense them in any way they think fit, if anyone has given them cause for sadness or alarm. I should like them to know how much I regret this. Whatever they demand shall be done.'

Hagen answered: 'No one has harmed us. It's my lords' habit to wear armour for the first three days of any feast. If anyone molested us here, we should tell Etzel.'

Hagen's words did not escape Kriemhilde, and she gave him a look of bitter hatred. She knew the customs of her own land well enough from long experience, but she was hardly in a position to disclose them.

If anyone had told Etzel the truth now he would have found a way of preventing what later happened, no matter how strong and determined Kriemhilde's hatred of the Burgundians. But in their obstinate pride, they told him nothing.   There was a great crowd moving along with the Queen, but the two friends refused to give way a hand's breadth. The Huns were put out at having to jostle with the gay heroes.   Etzel's stewards were not pleased either, and might well have done something to anger the two knights; but they dared not, in front of the noble King, and nothing happened beyond a lot of pushing and shoving.

When the service was over, and the worshippers were about to leave, the Huns sprang for their horses. Seven thousand warriors rode at the side of Kriemhilde and her fair maids,   who took up their position in mighty Etzel's window, much to his delight, and settled down to watch the carefree heroes ride against each other. And a dazzling collection of foreign knights they saw ride past them in the courtyard.   Dankwart the Marshal was there with the troops (he had taken charge of his Lord's household), and the bold Nibelungs were saddled and ready.

When the Kings and their men were mounted, Volker the strong urged them on to joust as they used to at home, and the heroes followed his advice with glorious success.   Their heart was in it, after all. The noise of the tournament grew, and the great courtyard was full of men. Etzel and Kriemhilde looked on. Six hundred of Dietrich's warriors came up to join the tournament with the guests, hoping for pleasant recreation with the Burgundians. They would have enjoyed themselves if only Dietrich had allowed them. They were good knights who followed Dietrich, and when he heard what they wanted to do he forbade them to compete with Gunther's men. He was afraid for their safety, and with good reason.

As Dietrich's men of Verona moved off, Rüdeger's men from Bechelaren, five hundred of them with shields at the ready, came riding up to the hall. The Margrave would rather have avoided this, and he wisely went among his troops, saying to the warriors: They could see for themselves how hostile the mood of the Burgundians was, and he would be much happier if they kept out of the tournament. When the carefree heroes had withdrawn in their turn, the Thuringians and Danes, a thousand brave men at least, we are told, took their place. The splinters flew for all to see, as Irnfrid and Hawart rode into the tournament. The Rhinelanders stood proudly waiting for them, and many a splendid shield was pierced through and through in the jousts that followed. And then Bloedelin, with three thousand, arrived. Etzel and Kriemhilde could hardly fail to notice him, as the knights were competing directly in front of them. The Queen, foreseeing trouble for the Burgundians, was especially pleased.

Schrutan and Gibeche, Ramung and Hornboge rode into the fray according to their Hunnish customs, and made for the Burgundian heroes. Lances went flying over the wall of the King's palace, but the only effect of their arrival was to increase the noise. The palace and hall rang with the clash of shields, and Gunther's men covered themselves with glory. Their pleasure was so strenuous that their good horses' trappings were soaked with sweat. The Burgundians matched themselves against the Huns with contemptuous confidence.

And Volker the minstrel, a brave knight, said: 'I think these knights are afraid of us. If they really wanted to pick a quarrel, they couldn't have found a better opportunity than this.' He went on: 'They might as well take our horses off and stable them. We can joust again towards evening, when the time comes. Who knows? The Queen may yet find herself awarding the prize to the Burgundians!'

But then they saw a knight riding up, the dazzling splendour of whose appearance outclassed all the other Huns. He must have had a sweetheart somewhere. At all events he was dressed up like a noble knight's bride.

And Volker said: 'I can't resist this one. This ladies' pet needs a bit of rough treatment. Nothing can save him now. And who cares if it does annoy King Etzel's wife?'

'Don't, for my sake,' said the King hurriedly. 'We shall have all the people here against us if we start anything. It would be much better to let the Huns make the first move.' (King Etzel was still sitting by Kriemhilde.)

'I think I'll take a hand in the tournament,' said Hagen. 'It's just as well we should let these ladies and warriors see how we can joust. Not that we can really expect them to shower any of Gunther's men with honours.' *

Then Volker the bold entered the lists again, to the sorrow of many ladies, and pierced the rich Hun with his spear. Weeping and wailing were let loose.   Meanwhile Hagen with sixty warriors promptly galloped on to the field after the fiddler. (Etzel and Kriemhilde saw everything that happened.)   And the three Kings had no intention of leaving their minstrel unprotected amongst his enemies: a thousand heroes rode up and down with insolent assurance, and no one tried to interfere with them.

When the rich Hun was killed his relations raised their voices in weeping and lament, and all their men asked: 'Who did it?' 'It was Volker, the warlike minstrel,' was the answer.   At once the Margrave's Hunnish friends shouted for their swords and shields, and made as if to kill Volker. (The host rushed down from his window at this point.)

The people were in a great tumult and confusion. The Kings had dismounted in front of the palace, and the Burgundians were pushing their horses into the background. In the midst of this scene appeared King Etzel, to settle the dispute.   He tore the great sword from the hands of one of the Huns' relations who happened to be near, and angrily drove them all back. 'I should be a fine host to these heroes   if I let you kill this minstrel before my eyes!' said the King. 'And it would be an injustice. I saw the joust clearly enough in which he pierced the Hun; it was an accident, and no fault of his.   You must leave my guests in peace.' Then he escorted them, while the horses were led off and stabled by their numerous and willing attendants.

174

Etzel took his friends into the palace, where he was determined
to tolerate no more outbreaks of violence. The tables were set up,
and water was brought round. But the Rhinelanders were sur-
rounded by powerful enemies,   and were slow to sit down.
Kriemhilde was unable to control her anxiety, * and said:
'Prince of Verona, I need your advice, help and sympathy.
Things are going badly with me.'

Hildebrand, that renowned hero, answered her: 'Anyone who
wants to kill the Nibelungs can do it by himself. He won't get
me to help him for all the treasure on earth. And he won't get it
all his own way either. These bold and carefree knights aren't
finished yet.' *

Lord Dietrich added his own polite version to this: 'I
shouldn't press your request, mighty Queen. Your family
have done me no harm, that I should want to attack the bold
knights.   And it does you no credit, most noble Princess,
that you should plot the death of your own family. They have
come to this country in good faith. Sifrid will never be avenged
by Dietrich's hand.'

When she found it impossible to shake Dietrich's loyalty, she
turned to Bloedelin, and promised him the extensive terri-
tories Nuodung had once possessed. He was killed, in due
course, by Dankwart, and had little time to gloat over his
acquisition.   She said: 'You help me then, Lord Bloedelin.
You know that my enemies are here in this house, the men who
killed my dear husband Sifrid. Anyone who helps me to avenge
him will earn my undying gratitude.'

Bloedelin answered: 'You must realize, Lady, that I daren't
commit any hostile action for fear of Etzel. He likes having your
family here, and if I did anything to harm them the King would
never forgive me for it.'

'Don't refuse me, Lord Bloedelin. I'll serve you always. I'll
give you silver and gold, and a beautiful girl, Nuodung's bride.
Think how you'd enjoy making love to her.   And I'll give
you lands and castles, and you'll never want for anything again,
once you own those territories where Nuodung ruled. And what
I promise now, I'll faithfully carry out.'

When Lord Bloedelin heard the extent of the reward she
offered, and also because he was much attracted by the beauty of
the lady mentioned, he could already see himself winning the
lovely woman in battle. The decision cost him his life.   He
said to the Queen: 'Go back inside the hall, and I'll start a fight

going before anyone realizes what's happened. Hagen will have to answer for what he's done. I'll hand him over, bound, to you.'

'Arm yourselves,' said Bloedelin, 'all my men! We are to attack the enemy in their lodgings; King Etzel's wife will have it so. We are to risk our lives heroically in this cause.'

When the Queen had produced a sufficiently warlike mood in Bloedelin, she went to table with King Etzel and his men. Her plan for the guests' destruction was ripening.   Seeing no other way of stirring up conflict, and still nursing her old wound in her heart, she called for Etzel's son to be brought to the table. Could any woman have done a more frightful thing for revenge?   And four of Etzel's men carried the young King Ortlieb to the Prince's table, where Hagen was also sitting. The child was later slaughtered to feed his murderous hate.

When the mighty King caught sight of his son, he said benevolently to his wife's family: 'My friends, you see here the only son of your sister and myself. I hope he may be of use to you.   If he takes after his family, he should be a brave man, great and powerful, strong and fair. If I'm spared a little longer, I shall give him twelve countries, so that young Ortlieb can serve you well.   And so I should like to ask you, my dear friends, to take your sister's son with you when you ride back home to the Rhine. Treat him kindly   and bring him up honourably, until he grows to be a man. If anyone anywhere has wronged you, he'll help you to avenge it as soon as he's big enough.' Kriemhilde his wife listened as he spoke.

'I expect he'd earn the trust of these warriors, if he ever lived to be a man,' said Hagen; 'but the young King looks sickly to me; I doubt if I shall ever be presented to Ortlieb at court.'

The King looked at Hagen in hurt silence. Although the carefree Prince said nothing, he was disturbed and depressed by what he heard. Hagen, evidently, was in no mood to be entertained.*   All the King's princes were offended by what Hagen had said about the child. It was as much as they could do to let it pass. Of course, they knew nothing as yet of what this knight was later to do.

176

AVENTIURE 32

DANKWART KILLS BLOEDELIN

Bloedelin's knights were now ready, and a thousand armed men burst in on Dankwart as he sat at table with the younger knights. The bitterest strife ever known between heroes was about to begin.　As Lord Bloedelin approached the table, Marshal Dankwart rose up eagerly to receive him: 'Welcome to our quarters, Lord Bloedelin, although I must say I'm surprised to see you.'

'Don't bother to greet me,' said Bloedelin. 'I've come to kill you, because of your brother Hagen, who killed Sifrid. You and many other warriors must pay for this here amongst the Huns.'

'Surely not, Lord Bloedelin,' said Dankwart. 'You almost make me think we should never have come on this journey. I was a little child when Sifrid lost his life. I can't see why King Etzel's wife should have anything against me.'

'I don't know what else you want me to say. It was your relations, Gunther and Hagen, who were responsible. So defend yourselves while there's time; nothing can save you now. Your lives are forfeit to Kriemhilde.'

'So nothing will move you?' said Dankwart. 'In that case I take back my entreaties; I was wasting my breath.' And the bold warrior leapt up from the table and drew his great sword, long and keen.　He dealt Bloedelin a savage blow which left his head rolling at his feet. 'There's your marriage gift to Nuodung's bride! See if you can make love to her now!' said Dankwart.

'They can give her to some other man tomorrow. And if he wants a bridal gift like yours, send him to me.' (A loyal Hun had told him what miserable fate the Queen was planning for them.)

When Bloedelin's men saw their lord lying dead, they decided they had taken enough from the guests. With upraised swords, and grim determination, they leapt in front of the young lads. They soon wished they hadn't.　Dankwart gave a great shout to all his followers: 'You can see what's coming, you noble

lads. Defend yourselves while there's time! Our need is
desperate enough, thanks to noble Kriemhilde's kind invitation.'

Those who had no swords reached down and picked up the
long foot-rests in front of the benches. The young Burgundians
were not going to give up without a fight, and there were
plenty of sore heads under those helmets as they swung the
heavy stools.   The luckless youngsters fought with such
fierce determination that they eventually drove the armed men
out of the house. But by then there were five hundred or more
lying dead inside,* and the King's retainers were all red and
dripping with blood.   This dreadful news was received by
Etzel's knights with fierce resentment. They were told that
Bloedelin and his men had been killed by Hagen's brother and
the young boys,   and before the King knew what was
happening two thousand or more Huns in their rage had armed
themselves and sought out the youths. The outcome was
inevitable; not a single member of the household was left alive.

The Huns arrived in front of the building with a huge army,
and little thought of hospitality. The unfortunate lads defended
themselves bravely, but their courage was no use to them. They
were all killed, and the final calamity was not far off.   But
there was one wonderful sight in all this savagery. With nine
thousand retainers and twelve of his knights lying dead, Dank-
wart was seen confronting his enemies alone.   The shouting
had died away, and the clash of arms was silenced. Dankwart the
warrior looked over his shoulder and said: 'Alas for the friends
I have lost! Now I must stand alone among my enemies.'

He was the sole target for a rain of sword-blows, but many a
hero's wife was yet to be bereaved. He lowered his grip, held his
shield high in the air, and set about bathing all the chain mail
he could see in blood.   'This is a sad day for me,' said the
son of Aldrian. 'Stand back, you Hunnish knights, and let me
have some air. Give a battle-weary man a chance to cool down.'
And he advanced with his head held high.

As he jumped out of the house, worn out with fighting,
a fresh set of swords clanged about his helmet. Those
who had not witnessed his miraculous feats now fell on the
Burgundian.   'If only to God I could send a message', said
Dankwart, 'to let my brother Hagen know my desperate
position, surrounded by all these knights. He'd help me to
escape, or die with me.'

Some of the Hunnish knights answered him: 'You'll have to

be your own messenger. As soon as we carry your corpse before your brother he'll know the worst. You've done too much damage here already to King Etzel.'

He said: 'Drop your threats and move back a bit, or I shall have to cover a few more suits of mail with blood. I'll bring my own news to court, and take my grievances to my lords as well.'

He proceeded to make himself so unpopular with Etzel's men that they no longer dared to fight with their swords. Instead, they hurled so many spears into his shield that it became too heavy for him to hold. Now that he had no shield they thought they could overpower him. But he went on inflicting deep wounds through helmet after helmet; scores of brave men fell dying in front of him, and the brave Dankwart covered himself with glory. They came at him from both sides, often only to wish they had held back a bit longer; and he fought his way through his enemies like a wild boar escaping from the dogs to the forest. Greater bravery was never seen. His path was continually bathed in fresh steaming blood. No hero could ever have fought better against his enemies than he did. Proudly Hagen's brother made his way to court.

When the court stewards and cup-bearers heard the clash of swords they dropped the drinks and food they were carrying in their hands. There seemed to be a whole army of enemies waiting for him on the steps. 'What's the matter with you stewards?' said the weary warrior. 'You ought to be looking after your guests, bringing choice food to the lords in there, not trying to stop me tell my news.'

Any that were brave enough to jump down between him and the steps were greeted with such a mighty swing of his sword that they soon found it prudent to stand higher up.* His great bravery had achieved wonders that day.

AVENTIURE 33

THE BURGUNDIANS FIGHT WITH THE HUNS

Brave Dankwart stepped into the doorway, and asked King Etzel's household to stand back. His clothes were soaked in blood, and he carried his mighty sword unsheathed in his hand   He shouted across to one warrior with a loud voice: 'You've been sitting too long, brother Hagen. I call on you, and on God in heaven, in our hour of need: the knights and retainers in our lodgings are dead.'

Hagen shouted back: 'Who did it?' 'Bloedelin and his men. And he's paid for it, I might add. I cut off his head with my own hands.'   'It's not much of a payment', said Hagen, 'when people can say of a warrior that he died fighting against a hero. The fine ladies here won't have much to mourn for.   But tell me, brother Dankwart, where did all this blood come from? You must be suffering from your wounds. If the man who did this to you is still in the country, I'll have his life, if the devil himself doesn't save him.'

'No, I'm not hurt. My clothes are soaked in blood, but from other men's wounds. I've killed a lot today—I couldn't say how many, even if I had to on oath.'

'Then guard the door, brother Dankwart, and don't let a single Hun get out. I have an urgent matter to settle with these knights here. They have murdered innocent men.'

'Well, if I'm to be treasurer,' said the brave man, 'I think I know how to wait on such mighty Kings. I'll look after the steps without disgracing myself.' Kriemhilde's warriors began to get desperate.

And Hagen said: 'I can't think what these Hunnish warriors are grumbling about. Surely they're not sorry to lose the company of that fellow at the door, who just brought the latest court news to the Burgundians?   They've been telling us for a long time how Kriemhilde could never get over her grief. Now let's drink to love and concord, and pay back the King's wine. The young Lord of the Huns can be the first instalment.'   With that the good hero Hagen struck at the child

Ortlieb with his sword; the blood spurted out over his hands, and the child's head fell in the Queen's lap. And now a great and terrible slaughter began among the warriors.   He went on to deal a vicious blow, with both hands, at the child's guardian. His head rolled on the floor, a miserable reward from Hagen for his services.

Then he saw a minstrel in front of Etzel's table, and rushing at him in fury, cut off his right hand as it rested on the fiddle. 'Take that as a reward for the message you brought to Burgundy!'   'Oh, my hand!' cried Wärbel the minstrel. 'What have I done to you, Lord Hagen of Tronege? I came to your country in good faith. How can I play my melodies without my hand?'   But Hagen was not interested in whether he ever fiddled again. He was busy inflicting mortal wounds on Etzel's knights, and he went on to kill most of the people in the house.

Volker the bold jumped up from the table, with his fiddle-bow ringing in his hand. It was a barbarous sort of fiddling that Gunther's minstrel now performed, and it earned him many brave Huns as enemies.   The three proud Kings also jumped up from the tables, hoping to settle the dispute before too much damage was done. But their prudence was powerless to stop Hagen and Volker now that they were roused to fury.   And when the Lord of the Rhine realized that peacemaking was out of the question, he himself inflicted some terrible wounds on his enemies. He was a hero among heroes, and he showed it clearly.

Then strong Gernot joined the battle, and killed many a Hunnish hero. With his sharp sword, a present from Rüdeger, he did great havoc among Etzel's knights.   And the youngest son of Lady Uote leapt into the fray. His sword rang out gloriously on the helmets of Etzel's Hunnish knights. Great feats were performed by brave Giselher's hand.   The Kings and their men all performed great deeds of valour, but Giselher stood out amongst them as he confronted the enemy. He was a good hero, and struck down many men to the bloody floor.

And Etzel's men defended themselves desperately, as the guests' bright swords hacked their way through the King's hall. The air was filled with shouts and groans.   The Huns outside wanted to join their friends inside, but they met with little success at the door. Those inside would have liked to get out, but Dankwart let no one up or down the steps.   As a result,

there developed a furious struggle at the door, with much clash-
ing of sword on helmet. Dankwart's position became desperate,
and his loyal brother took steps to relieve him.   Hagen gave
a great shout to Volker: 'You see my brother standing there,
with Hunnish knights raining blows on his head? Relieve my
brother for me, friend, or we'll never see that warrior again.'

'I'll do that—trust me,' said the minstrel. And he went
fiddling through the palace, his cruel sword ringing in his hands,
earning the gratitude of the Rhenish knights.

Volker the brave said to Dankwart: 'You've had a lot to do
today, and your brother sent me to help you. If you'd like to
take a turn outside, I'll guard the inside.'   Bold Dankwart
took up his position in front of the door, and held the steps
against anyone who came up. While heroes' swords were
resounding out there, Volker of Burgundy was doing the
same thing inside.   The brave fiddler shouted over the heads
of the crowd: 'The hall is nicely sealed off, friend Hagen.
Etzel's door is firmly secured, with a thousand bolts in two
heroes' hands.'

When Hagen saw how well the door was guarded he threw
back his shield, and really settled down to taking revenge for
what had happened. From now on his enemies gave up all hope
of survival.

When the Lord of Verona * saw Hagen the strong breaking all
those helmets, the King of the Amelungs jumped up on a bench,
and said: 'I don't like the wine that Hagen's serving here.'

Their host himself was greatly distressed, as was only to be
expected, when he saw so many friends dying before his eyes.
Even his own life was in great danger, and he sat there anxiously.
What use was his crown to him now?

Kriemhilde the mighty Queen called on Dietrich: 'Help me to
get out of here alive, noble knight of Amelunge, in the name of
all good rulers. If I fall into Hagen's hands, he'll kill me.'

'How can I help you, noble Queen?' said Lord Dietrich. 'I'm
worried enough for my own skin. Gunther's men are so furious
that I couldn't guarantee anyone's safety at the moment.'

'Oh, please! Good and noble knight, show your true quality
today, and help me out of this, or I shall die.' Kriemhilde's fears
were by no means groundless.

'I'll try to help you then. But it's a long time since I've seen
so many good knights in such a raging fury. Can you see the
blood spurting through the helmets as their swords fall?'

Then the great warrior called out with a great voice like a hunting-horn, making the whole castle ring with his power. Dietrich's strength was extraordinary.   Gunther heard him calling, in the thick of the fight, and listened. He said: 'That's Dietrich's voice. Our warriors must have killed one of his men.   I can see him on the table waving his hand. Break off the struggle, my friends and family, and let me see and hear what my men have done to the warrior.'

At King Gunther's request and command, they put up their swords, even in the heat of the battle. It showed the great force of his authority that no one aimed another blow. Then he hurriedly asked the Lord of Verona what was the matter.

'Well, noble Dietrich, what have my friends here done to you? I'm ready. I'll gladly do anything in the way of atonement or recompense. If anyone wronged you, I should feel it as an offence against myself.'

And Lord Dietrich answered: 'No one has done anything to me. Just let me take my followers away from the battle and out of this house. Give me your safe-conduct, and I shall serve you all my life.'

'Why these humble entreaties?' said Wolfhart. 'The fiddler hasn't shut the door so firmly that we can't open it wide enough to get out.' 'Hold your tongue,' said Lord Dietrich. 'You'll gain nothing by talking like that.'

And King Gunther answered: 'You have my permission to leave. Take as many as you like out of the house. But leave my enemies behind. I've suffered too much at their hands, here amongst the Huns.'   When Dietrich heard this he tucked the noble Queen, by now in a state of great anxiety, under his arm. Then he led her and Etzel away, one on either side, and six hundred splendid men followed.

Then the noble Margrave Rüdeger said: 'We should like to know if you're going to let any more of your faithful servants leave the house. Good friends and lasting peace belong together.'

Giselher of Burgundy answered: 'Peace and reconciliation are yours for the asking. You and your men have always been loyal to us, and you can lead your friends away without fear.'

When Lord Rüdeger left the hall, five hundred or more of his friends and followers from Bechelaren went with him; they were later to inflict heavy losses on King Gunther   Then one of the Hunnish knights saw Etzel walking near Dietrich, and thought he could use this to his own advantage. But the fiddler dealt him such a blow that his head was sent rolling at Etzel's feet.

When the Lord of the Huns was out of the house, he turned round and looked at Volker. 'Why did I ever invite these guests? It is a bitter thing to have to see all my knights stretched dead in front of them.   A curse on this feast!' said the proud King. 'There's one man in there, Volker by name, who fights like a wild boar, and yet he's a minstrel. I'm lucky to have escaped from that fiend.   His tunes are grisly to hear, his bowing draws blood. Heroes die to his melodies. I don't know what that minstrel has against us, but I never entertained such a malign guest.'

Now that they had let out all they wanted, a terrible noise rose again in the hall, as the guests took their savage revenge for what had happened. Volker the brave smashed helmets by the score.   The proud King Gunther turned back towards the din, and said: 'Can you hear the tunes, Hagen, that Volker over there is playing on the Huns who make for the door? That's a fine red rosin he's got on his bow!'

'My only regret', said Hagen, 'is that I ever sat higher than that warrior in the hall. We've stood together as equals, and if we ever get home again, we'll stay like that, faithful to each other.   Look, mighty King, how eager Volker is to please you! He enjoys earning your silver and gold. His fiddle-bow cuts through tough steel as he smashes the insignia shining on their helmets.   I never saw a fiddler stand so majestically as that warrior Volker has today. His songs penetrate helmets and shields. He deserves to ride good horses and wear splendid clothes.'

Of all the Huns in the hall, not a single one was still alive. The noise died down; there was no one left to fight. The bold and carefree knights laid down their swords.

AVENTIURE 34

THEY THROW THE DEAD OUT OF THE HALL

While the weary lords sat down, Volker and Hagen went out in front of the hall. The two proud men leant over their shields and exchanged pithy comments.

Then warrior Giselher of Burgundy said: 'I'm afraid you can't rest yet, my friends. You'll have to carry the dead out of the house. We haven't finished fighting yet, and we can't leave them lying under our feet any longer. Before the Huns beat us in battle we shall hack some more of those wounds that do my heart good. I wouldn't miss it for anything,' said Giselher.

'Thank God for such a lord,' said Hagen. 'The advice our young lord has just given us could only come from a true warrior. All you Burgundians can be happy now.'

Then they followed the suggestion, and carried the bodies through the door. Seven thousand corpses they threw out, and left them lying at the bottom of the steps. The families of the dead men raised a pitiful lament. One or two of them were not so seriously wounded, and would have recovered with gentler treatment. They were killed off by the fall, which was an added cause for grief to their friends.

Volker the fiddler said, in high spirits: 'Now I see what they meant when they told me the Huns were no good, and wept like women. Why don't they turn their attention to those wounded bodies instead?'

One Margrave thought he was speaking in good faith, and, seeing one of his relatives lying in the blood, he put his arms round him as if to carry him away. The brave fiddler speared him dead as he bent down. When the others saw this they all fled, cursing the minstrel. But he only picked up a tough sharp spear that one of the Huns had thrown at him and hurled it out across the courtyard, far over the heads of the crowd, showing them they had better look for shelter farther away from the hall. They all feared his fierce courage.

By now there were thousands of men standing in front of the house, and Volker and Hagen proceeded to tell King Etzel what they thought of him. The brave good heroes were storing up more trouble for themselves.   'It might increase your people's confidence * if their lords fought in front of them, as all my lords here do. Their swords are used for hacking helmets, and leave a trail of blood behind.'

Etzel was so brave that he laid hold of his shield. 'Careful now!' said Lady Kriemhilde, 'and offer your knights plenty of gold. If Hagen over there gets through to you, you won't live long.'

The king was so brave that nothing could put him off, a rare thing with such powerful rulers, and they had to hold him back by his shield-straps. Fierce Hagen mocked him again.

'The blood-relationship is very thin', said warrior Hagen, 'that binds Etzel and Sifrid together. He loved Kriemhilde before she ever saw you. Isn't it a paltry thing for a king like you to scheme against me?'

The king's wife was furious that he should dare to abuse her in front of Etzel's men, and she started once more to plot the guests' destruction.

She said: 'Whoever kills Hagen of Tronege and brings his head to my feet can have Etzel's shield full to the brim with gold from me. And on top of that I'll reward him with rich castles and lands.'

'Well, I don't know what they're waiting for,' said the minstrel. 'I've never seen heroes stand about so irresolutely when a reward like that was offered. That's hardly the way to win Etzel's approval.   They sit here and don't scruple to eat the king's bread; and when his need is desperate they leave him in the lurch. They think themselves brave, and yet I can see them standing about, wondering what to do. They ought to be ashamed of themselves.'

AVENTIURE 35

IRING IS KILLED

Then Margrave Iring of Denmark called out: 'I have always striven for honour, and have many achievements to my credit. Bring me my armour! I will face Hagen.'

'I shouldn't do that if I were you,' said Hagen. 'But if you insist, you'd better tell the Hunnish warriors to stand back a bit. If two or three of you made a dash into the hall I should send them back down the steps the worse for wear.'

'You won't put me off like that,' said Iring. 'I've tried things before that were just as dangerous. In any case, I intend to face you alone, with my sword. Your arrogant words won't help you.'

Then the warrior Iring was quickly armed; also Irnfrid of Thuringia, a brave lad, and Hawart the strong, together with a thousand men. They intended to stand by Iring in whatever he undertook. The fiddler saw this great crowd of armed men coming up with Iring, with their stout helmets ready strapped on. Good Volker was a trifle annoyed. 'Look, friend Hagen, can you see Iring over there, who was going to face you alone with his sword? Lying isn't for heroes; it makes a man despicable. He's brought a thousand or more men with him!'

'There's no need to accuse me of lying,' said Hawart's man. 'I'm willing to do what I promised. I shall not go back on my word through fear. However fearsome this Hagen may be, I'll face him alone.'

And Iring went on his knees to his relations and his men, begging them to let him meet the knight alone. They were reluctant, knowing only too well this arrogant Hagen from Burgundy. But he begged so long that he eventually had his way. When his followers saw how determined he was to win glory, they let him go. And then a ferocious struggle began between the two men. Iring of Denmark held his spear high in the air, and covered himself with his shield, like the excellent warrior he was. Then he rushed up to Hagen in front of the hall, and a great noise went up from the warriors. First they hurled their spears right through their stout shields and on to their bright armour, so that the shafts flew high in the air. Then, with fierce courage, they both grabbed for their swords.   Hagen was strong and brave, and Iring struck at him till the house resounded. Palace and towers rang to their blows. But the warrior was unable to make any impression.   He left Hagen unscratched and rushed at the fiddler. He thought he might overcome him with his mighty blows, but Volker, the gentle knight, had little difficulty in defending himself.   Then the fiddler struck out, so that the fastenings on his shield flew up over the rim. Iring decided to leave him in peace; he was a man to avoid. Instead he ran at Gunther.

Gunther and Iring were strong men, but their armour was even stronger, and no bloody wounds resulted from their blows.   So he left Gunther and leaped on Gernot, hacking sparks from his mail. But strong Gernot might easily have killed the brave Iring   if he had not jumped out of the way in time. He certainly had plenty of spirit, and in an instant he had killed four of the Burgundian household. This brought Giselher into a towering rage.

'Before God, Lord Iring,' said the boy, 'you'll have to answer to me for the dead lying at your feet.' And he hurled himself at the Dane, and struck him so hard that he stopped in his tracks   and sank to the bloody ground. They all thought that the good hero had fought his last battle, but in fact he lay unwounded at Giselher's feet.   He was dazed by the impact of Giselher's sword on his helmet, and had lost consciousness. Such was the power of Giselher's arm.

When his head began to clear of the effects of this mighty blow, he thought: 'I'm still alive and unwounded. And I've had my first real taste of Giselher's courage.'   He could hear that there were enemies on either side of him, who would hardly have left him alone if they knew the truth. He could also hear Giselher himself close by, and he began to wonder how he could escape.   Then he sprang up like a madman out of the blood, relying on his speed of movement, and ran out of the house. There he found Hagen again, and belaboured him bravely and furiously.

At this Hagen thought: 'You'll have to die. Unless the devil decides to protect you, you haven't a chance.' All the same, Iring, with his good sword Waske, managed to wound Hagen through his helmet.   But as soon as Hagen felt the wound his sword took on a monstrous life of its own. Hawart's man had to give

way and Hagen pursued him down the steps.   Brave Iring
held his shield over his head, and even if there had been three
times as many steps he would never have had a chance to hit
back. With his helmet scattering sparks in all directions   he
came back safe and sound to his own people. Kriemhilde was
given a report of what he had done in his encounter with Hagen,
and she heaped thanks upon him.

'May God reward you, hero of renown! You have cheered me
in heart and spirit. It is a great comfort to see Hagen's armour
red with blood.' And she herself relieved him affectionately of
his shield.

'I shouldn't thank him too much,' said Hagen. 'If he's a real
warrior, he ought to try again. And if he escapes the next time,
you might call him a brave man. The wound he's given me
won't get you very far.   The only result of this blood you see
on my armour is to whet my appetite for more killing. Iring has
merely succeeded in annoying me at last; the damage he's done
is nothing.'

Meanwhile Iring of Denmark was facing the breeze to cool
himself down. He kept his armour on, but undid his helmet.
Everyone congratulated him on his bravery, and the Margrave's
confidence rose and rose.   And Iring spoke again: 'My
friends, arm me quickly; I intend to try again. Perhaps next time
I shall overcome this insolent man.' His battered shield was
exchanged for a new one   and he was soon fully armed once
more, with a strong spear to show his warlike spirit as he closed
with Hagen. But now a murderous hatred for Iring began to rise
in this savage man.

Hagen was too impatient to wait for him, and charged down
to the foot of the steps, raining spears and sword-blows. He was
in a towering rage, and at another time Iring might have been
able to appreciate his strength, but not now.   They hacked
at each other's shields until the sparks swirled all round them.
Hawart's man was mortally wounded by Hagen's sword, which
passed right through his shield and breastplate. He never
recovered.

When the warrior Iring felt the wound, he lifted his shield up
above the strap of his helmet, thinking that nothing worse could
happen to him. But King Gunther's man had not finished with
him yet.   Hagen found a spear lying at his feet, and hurled it
at the hero from Denmark, so that the shaft was left sticking out
of his head. Warrior Hagen had brought his life to a savage

end.   He fell back amongst the Danes, who tore the spear out
of his head before they took off his helmet. His death was near
and his family could only weep.

Then the Queen came and stood over him, and mourned for
Iring the strong. She wept for his wounds, and her grief was
desperate. And the brave and carefree knight said to her while
his family stood by: 'No more laments, proud woman.
What's the use of weeping now? I must die anyway from my
wounds. Death will end my service to you and Etzel.'   And
he said to the Thuringians and Danes: 'The Queen's gifts and
her shining red gold are not for any of you. If you face Hagen,
death will be your only reward.'

The colour drained from his face, and the mask of death was
on Iring the brave. The Danes were dismayed; but Hawart's
man was dead beyond recovery, and there was nothing left for
them to do but fight.

Irnfrid and Hawart leapt in front of the hall with a thousand
men. With a great and barbarous din they sent a hail of sharp
spears at the Burgundians.   Irnfrid the brave charged at the
minstrel, and was severely damaged for his pains. The noble
fiddler struck the Landgrave through his stout helmet with his
usual ferocity.   Lord Irnfrid answered with a blow that burst
open the fiddler's chain mail, and lit up his breastplate with fire;
but even so the Landgrave fell to the minstrel.   Hawart
clashed with Hagen, and the flailing of the heroes' swords was
a wonderful sight. Hawart's fate was death at the hands of the
Burgundian.

When the Danes and Thuringians saw their lords lying dead,
they started a gruesome struggle in front of the house, until
they reached the door, hacking away at helmets and shields with
great bravery.   'Give way,' said Volker, 'and let them in.
They won't accomplish anything, and we'll soon kill them off
once they're inside. They can earn their Queen's presents by
dying.'

As they rashly penetrated into the hall, their heads sank one
after the other under a hail of vicious blows, and they died.
Gernot and Giselher both fought particularly well.   A
thousand and four went in to this mass of hissing and flashing
swords, and not a single knight came out alive. The Burgundians
certainly performed wonders that day.

At last the noise died down and stillness reigned. All round the
blood from the dead men poured through the drains and along

the gutters. Such was the achievement of the brave Rhine-landers.

But now the Burgundians sat and rested, laying down their swords and shields. The brave minstrel still stood at the door, on the look-out for anyone else who might want a fight. King Etzel and his wife gave themselves up to grief, while maids and ladies did violence to their bodies. It was as if Death had turned against them. And there were still many knights to lose their lives at the hands of these guests.

AVENTIURE 36

THE QUEEN SETS FIRE TO THE HALL

'You can take off your helmets,' said warrior Hagen. 'My comrade and I will look after you; and if Etzel's men decide to have another try, I'll warn my lords as quickly as I can.'

The good knights bared their heads, and took their seats on the bodies of the men they had struck down to the bloody floor. The hospitality shown to the noble guests left much to be desired.   Before evening the King and Queen persuaded the Hunnish knights to try again, and twenty thousand at least assembled in front of them, ready to go in and fight.   A fierce attack was mounted against the guests, and Dankwart the bold left his lords, and leapt in front of the door to engage the enemy. Everyone thought he would be killed, but he arrived there safe and sound.   The battle raged until the darkness made it impossible to continue. And all that long summer day the guests, like the good heroes they were, defended themselves against Etzel's men. And the heap of dead at their feet grew and grew.   And this terrible slaughter took place one midsummer day, when Lady Kriemhilde avenged her suffering on her closest relatives and many others; at the same time putting an end to King Etzel's happiness for ever.

When the daylight had gone, their plight was, if anything, worse. They decided they would rather face a quick death than hopelessly prolong their misery.   And so the proud knights asked for a truce.

The heroes, blood-smeared and blackened by their armour, stepped out of the house. The three proud Kings were at a loss who to turn to in their desperation, and they asked for the King to be brought to them.   Etzel and Kriemhilde both came. You could tell they were in their own country by the way their armies kept growing. Etzel said to the guests: 'Well, what do you want of me? If it's peace you want, I'm afraid that's hardly possible   after the damage you've already done. I shall never forgive you for that as long as I live. Remember my son, and all those friends of mine that you've killed! You'll never get peace and reconciliation from me.'

Gunther answered: 'We were under great provocation. All my retainers had been killed in their lodgings by your heroes. Had I deserved that? I came to you in good faith, believing you were my friend.'

And young Giselher said: 'You men of Etzel who are still alive, what have you got against me? Have I ever done anything to you? I rode into this country as a friend.'

They answered: 'As a result of your friendliness the whole town and country round about is full of misery. We should have been happier if you'd never left Worms by the Rhine. You and your brothers have filled the land with orphans.'

The warrior Gunther angrily said: 'If only you would bring to an end this bitter hostility between us, and come to an agreement, both sides would benefit. Etzel has no justification for treating us like this.'

Then the host said to his guests: 'There is no comparison between your sorrow and mine. This great burden of bereavement and disgrace that you have heaped upon me has made it impossible for any of you to escape alive.'

Then strong Gernot said to the King: 'In that case, in the name of God, have the kindness to kill us wretched exiles outright. Let us out into the open; it would be an honourable act.   Whatever is to happen to us, let it come quickly. You have so many fresh men there: if they aren't too cowardly to face us, we shouldn't last long against them, battle-weary as we are. How much longer must we endure this torment?'

Etzel's knights were on the point of letting them out of the palace, when Kriemhilde heard of it, and was much displeased. She soon put a stop to any thought of a truce for the exiles.   'Oh no, you Hunnish knights, I beg you to think again. If you once let these bloodthirsty men out of the hall, your friends and relations are certain to die.   If the sons of Uote, my noble brothers, were the only ones alive, once they got into the fresh air, and cooled their armour, you'd all be lost. Braver warriors than these were never born.'

Young Giselher said: 'Fair sister, I was a fool to trust you when you invited me across the Rhine to this fate. What have I ever done to the Huns to deserve death at their hands?   I was always loyal to you. I never did you any harm. I rode to court here thinking my noble sister loved me still. If you can find it in you to take pity on us, that's all we ask.'

'Why should I pity you? I don't know what pity is.* Hagen

of Tronege has done me a wrong so great that it can never be put right as long as I live. You must all pay for it,' said Etzel's wife.   'If you'd hand over Hagen by himself as a hostage, I don't say that I wouldn't spare your lives; you're my brothers after all, and children of one mother. I'll discuss it with these heroes who stand about me—after you've come to a settlement.'*

'God in heaven forbid!' said Gernot. 'If there were a thousand here, and all of us your blood-relations, we'd all die sooner than give you one man as a hostage. We'll never do that.'

'We must all die anyway,' said Giselher, 'and no one can stop us fighting bravely.* Well, we're still here, if anyone wants to take us on. I never broke faith with a friend.'

And brave Dankwart spoke (he could hardly have been expected to keep quiet): 'And remember, my brother Hagen's not on his own yet. People who refuse us a truce usually regret it before long. You'll see soon enough what I mean.'

Then the Queen said to the Huns: 'You gallant heroes, close in on the steps and avenge my sorrow. I shall never forget my debt to you if you do; and Hagen's insolence will be aptly rewarded.   Let no one out of the house, and I'll set fire to the four corners of the hall. I'll have revenge for all my sufferings yet.' Etzel's warriors leapt to obey.

They drove those who were still standing outside back into the hall with swords and spears. And in all the noise and confusion the Kings refused to be separated from their men; mutual trust and loyalty bound them together.   Then Etzel's wife gave the order to fire the hall. Fanned by the wind, the whole house was soon burning, and a new ordeal began for the knights inside. No troops can ever have been in more desperate straits.   You could hear their voices inside shouting: 'What a horrible way to die! Better to be killed in battle! God have mercy on us, we shall never get out of here alive! This is a monstrous revenge that the Queen is taking on us.'

And one of them said: 'We shall all die. So much for the King's greeting. This heat and this tormenting thirst will kill me. I can't stand it any longer.'

Hagen of Tronege answered him: 'You noble knights, if any-one is suffering from thirst, drink up some of this blood. In a heat like this, it's better than wine. In any case, it's the best we've got at the moment.'

And one of the knights went to a corpse, knelt down, took off his helmet, and drank the blood as it flowed from the wounds.

It was hardly a drink he'd been used to, but it tasted good to him all the same. 'God reward you, Lord Hagen,' said the weary man, 'for showing me such a drink. I've seldom had better wine served out to me. If I live long enough, I'll remember your kindness.' When the others heard him praising the drink, a lot more followed his example, and each of them was filled with new strength. Many fine ladies paid for this with their friends' lives.

All the time flaming brands kept falling on them, and they warded them off on to the floor with their shields. They were tormented by the heat and the smoke, and suffered such agonies as heroes will never experience again. Then Hagen of Tronege spoke again: 'Stand back against the walls so that the brands don't fall on your helmets, and tread them out in the blood. It's a poor feast the Queen is treating us to.'

They suffered like this all through the night; and when day came it found the brave minstrel and his companion Hagen standing as before in front of the house, and leaning on their shields. They knew that Etzel's people had not finished with them yet. And the fiddler said: 'Let's go inside, so that the Huns think we all died in that ordeal they prepared for us. They'll find us ready for them when the fighting starts.'

Then the boy Giselher said: 'There's a cool breeze springing up: dawn can't be far off. God grant that we live to see better times. I never want to be at another feast like this one of Kriemhilde's.'

And then a different voice was heard: 'Yes, I can see the dawn now. But it won't bring any improvement in our position. So arm yourselves, heroes, and be ready to sell your lives dearly. I don't think it'll be long before we have another visit from King Etzel's wife.'

Their host had half expected that all the guests would be dead from their torment in the fire; but in fact there were still six hundred brave men alive in there, the best warriors a king ever had. The Huns who had been set to watch the guests had seen well enough that they were still alive; in spite of all the loss and suffering inflicted on them, they were still standing, quite unharmed, in the room. Kriemhilde was told that a great number of them had survived, but she refused to believe that anyone could have lived through that torment of fire. 'It's more likely that they're all lying dead.'

The Kings and their men, meanwhile, would still have

welcomed any sign of mercy; but as they found none among the Huns, they got ready to sell their lives dearly. Towards morning they were greeted by a pitiless onslaught, and the heroes' plight was again desperate. The brave and proud knights defended themselves gallantly against the rain of spears that was hurled against them. Etzel's followers were sufficiently aroused to want to earn Kriemhilde's gold; and they now had Etzel's orders to obey as well. Before long many knights would fall dead before them.

There was no end to the promises and gifts that Kriemhilde made. She had shields full of red gold brought out, and distributed it to anyone who cared to take it. Greater reward was never offered to spur men into battle. A huge force of armed knights was drawn up against them, and brave Volker said: 'Well, we're still here. They've taken the King's gold in return for finishing us off, and I never saw heroes advancing more eagerly into battle.'

Then several of the Burgundians called out: 'Come a bit closer, you heroes, and let us finish quickly what we have to do. No one can die before his time.' And in a moment their shields were stuck full of spears. What else is there to say? There must have been twelve hundred men struggling back and forth, while the guests found relief for their fevered minds in the many wounds they inflicted. There was no one to settle their differences, and the blood had to flow. Mortal wounds were taken and calls for help were heard in plenty, until all this proud and mighty King's good men were dead. Great was the suffering of their loved ones when they had gone.

AVENTIURE 37

RÜDEGER IS KILLED

The exiles had done good work by the time the husband of
Gotelinde came to court that morning. And when he saw the
suffering on both sides, faithful Rüdeger was deeply distressed.
'I wish to God I had never been born,' said the knight. 'Can
no one put a stop to this misery? I would bring peace to them if
I could, but the King will do nothing now that he sees his own
losses grow heavier and heavier.'

Then good Rüdeger sent a messenger to Dietrich, to see if
they still had a chance of saving the three proud Kings, and
Dietrich sent back: 'What can I, or anyone, do about it? King
Etzel won't let anyone try for a settlement.'

Now one of the Hunnish knights saw Rüdeger standing with
tears in his eyes (which he had been doing for some time), and
said to the Queen: 'Look how he's standing there, the most
powerful man here, under Etzel! Think of the lands and
people who serve him, and all those castles that the King has
made over to Rüdeger! And he hasn't raised a finger in all this
fighting. I suppose he's not interested in what goes on here,
since he's got all he needs already. But I've heard it said that
he's distinguished for his bravery. If so, these troubles haven't
exactly brought it out.'

Faithful Rüdeger looked miserably at the speaker, and
thought: 'You'll pay for that. You accused me of cowardice, and
publicly, at court.' He clenched his fist and ran at him. He
hit the Hun so hard that he fell dead at his feet, giving Etzel one
more loss to lament.

'So much for you, you glorious coward!' said Rüdeger.
'Haven't I got enough grief and sorrow already? What right
have you to reproach me for not fighting here? I've got as much
reason as anyone to hate the guests, and I would have
thrown everything I had against them, if I hadn't been the one
who brought the knights here. Had you forgotten I was their

escort into my lord's land? That's why I can't fight against
them, wretched exile that I am.'

The proud King Etzel spoke to the Margrave: 'Was this all
the help I could expect from you, noble Rüdeger? Surely we
have enough dead in the country, without you adding to the
number? You should be ashamed of yourself.'

And the noble knight answered: 'He provoked me to it, by
questioning my right to the honour and wealth I received from
your hands. Now he's paid a little for his lies.'

Then the Queen came up, and saw what the hero in his
anger had done to the Hun. Her eyes filled with tears, and she
gave way to unbridled lamentation, saying: 'Have the King and
I deserved this,   that you, noble Rüdeger, should add to our
sorrow? Haven't you always said you would risk honour and life
for us? And all our knights were full of your praise.   Remem-
ber, noble knight, the love you swore to me when you persuaded
me to come to Etzel, saying you would serve me till one of us
died. This wretched woman never needed your support so much
as now.'

'Certainly, noble Lady, I swore to risk honour and life for
you. But I never swore to sell my soul. I was the one who
brought these high-born princes to the feast.'

She said: 'Remember your great loyalty, Rüdeger, your
constancy and the oaths you swore, never to rest until you had
avenged my loss and sorrow,' And the Margrave answered:
'Well, have I ever refused you anything?'

Then mighty Etzel began to implore him, and they both went
on their knees before the man. The loyal Margrave was obviously
distressed, and cried out in his wretchedness:

'Oh, God, why did I live to see this? Now I must deny
all I ever had from God—honour, duty and my knowledge
of what is right! If only death would come to save me from all
this!   Whichever I choose, I am condemned to a mean and
despicable action. And if I choose neither, I earn the reproaches
of both sides. Let Him guide me who gave me life!'

The King and his wife renewed their insistent pleading—
with the result that Rüdeger killed many knights, and lost his
own life as well. Listen, and you will hear what misery he was to
cause.   He knew he could only bring loss and unbearable
suffering on himself. He feared that the whole world
would reject him if he laid hands on one of the Burgundians,
and he would have given anything to refuse the King and

Queen.   Accordingly, the brave man said to Etzel: 'Lord
King, take back all I have in your name; I will renounce my
castles and lands, and go on foot into exile.'

But Etzel answered: 'And who could I turn to then? No, I'll
give you these castles and lands for your own, so that you will
avenge me on my enemies. You shall be made a mighty king,
next to Etzel.'

And Rüdeger said again: 'But how can I do such a thing?
I've taken them into my own house; I've offered them food and
drink in friendship; I've given them presents. How can I want
to destroy them now?   The people here may think I'm
afraid. But you see, I've never refused them my service, these
noble Kings and their men. And now I wish I'd never won their
friendship!   I gave my daughter to warrior Giselher; and for
breeding and honour, loyalty and property, she couldn't have
found a better man in all the world. I never saw such a young
king with so many excellent qualities.'

But Kriemhilde said again: 'Noble Rüdeger, take pity on my
plight, and the King's sorrow; remember that no host ever had
such murderous guests in his house.'

Then the Margrave said to the noble woman: 'Very well then.
Rüdeger's life shall be his payment for the favours you
and my Lord have shown him. I must die; I can put it off no
longer.   I know that one or other of them will kill me before
the day is out, and my castles and lands will revert to you. And
so I commend my wife and children to your mercy, together
with the other poor exiles at Bechelaren.'   'May God
reward you, Rüdeger,' said the King, and he and the Queen
cheered up considerably. 'Your people will be safe in our hands;
but I still have enough faith in my cause to believe you may yet
be spared yourself.'

And thus it was that Rüdeger did, after all, put his life and
soul in the balance. Etzel's wife wept as he said: 'I must do as
I promised you. Alas for my friends, whom I attack with a
heavy heart.'

He walked sadly away from the King, and joining his knights
who were standing close by, he said: 'You are all to arm your-
selves. I'm afraid I must attack the brave Burgundians.'

They ordered their retainers to hurry and bring out their
weapons, helmets and shields—fateful news for the Bur-
gundians when they later heard it.

Rüdeger and five hundred men were now fully armed, and

twelve heroes supported him, eager to win glory in battle. They knew nothing of the death that awaited them.

When Rüdeger came in sight of the Burgundians, with his helmet on his head, and his men carrying their sharp swords and bright shields at the ready, the fiddler was dismayed;   but when young Giselher saw his father-in-law with his helmet strapped on ready for battle, what else could he think but that he came as a friend? The noble King was filled with joy.

'Thank God that we made such friends on our way here,' said warrior Giselher. 'My wife will be our salvation yet; I'm certainly thankful that the marriage took place.'

'I can't see what you're so cheerful about,' said the minstrel. 'When did you see so many heroes with helmets on their heads and swords in their hands on a peaceful errand? No, Rüdeger is coming to earn his castles and lands at our expense!'   Even before the fiddler had finished speaking, noble Rüdeger had arrived before the house. He set his good shield down at his feet, and proceeded, as he must, to deny his friends both service and greeting.

The noble Margrave shouted into the hall: 'Defend yourselves, brave Nibelungs! I might have helped you, but instead I bring you nothing but harm. We were friends once; I must break that bond.'

The hard-pressed Burgundians were shocked at his news. They hardly relished the sight of their friend turning against them, after they had suffered such hardship at the hands of their enemies.

'God forbid', said warrior Gunther, 'that you should deny us the friendship and the great loyalty we had looked forward to! I can't believe you would ever do such a thing.'

'I have no choice,' said the brave man. 'I must fight you because I have given my word. So defend yourselves, brave heroes, if you value your lives. King Etzel's wife has left me no alternative.'

'It's too late to break the bond between us,' said the proud King. 'God will reward you, noble Rüdeger, for the love and loyalty you've shown us—if only you don't turn against us now.

'We should never cease to be grateful, my family and I, for what you have given us, if you let us live. Remember the magnificent gifts you made, noble Rüdeger, when you brought us faithfully into Etzel's land.'

'Oh, how I wish I could heap gifts on you as richly and

willingly as I once hoped! That at least would be something I
could be proud of.'

'Turn back, noble Rüdeger,' said Gernot then. 'No host ever
treated his guests with such loving care as you treated us. We
shall show our gratitude if you let us live.'

'Would to God, noble Gernot, I had died an honourable
death and you were safely back on the Rhine, since I have no
alternative but to fight you. Never were heroes more vilely
treated by their friends.'

'May God reward you then, Lord Rüdeger, for your generous
gifts. It is a pity to see so much goodness perish with your death.
You see this sword in my hand that you gave me out of the good-
ness of your heart?   It has never let me down through all this
strife. Its blade has stretched many a knight dead. It is clean and
true, glorious and good. I doubt if any knight ever made a more
precious gift.   And if you insist on attacking us, and kill any
of my friends who are still left, I shall take your life with your
own sword. But it will be with many regrets, for you, Rüdeger,
and for your wonderful wife.'

'Would to God, Lord Gernot, your wish were already ful-
filled and your friends saved. My wife and daughter could do
worse than turn to you.'

Then the son of fair Uote said: 'Why are you doing this, Lord
Rüdeger? You have no enemies among us. It's a terrible thing
you're contemplating. Do you want to make your fair daughter
a widow so soon?   If you and your knights attack me now,
think what a cruel use you'll be making of those qualities for
which I trust you more than any other man, and for which I
took your daughter as my wife.'

'Remember your loyalty, proud and noble King, if God
preserves you in this fight,' said Rüdeger. 'Don't let the girl
suffer because of me. Let your own goodness guide you, and
treat her well.'

'That would only be right,' said young Giselher. 'But if
my family here should die at your hands, you realize that our
firm friendship to you and your daughter would have to be
broken.'

'Well, God have mercy on us then,' said the brave man, and
they raised their shields ready to move in and attack the guests
in Kriemhilde's hall. But at this moment Hagen shouted down
at them with a great voice: 'Wait a minute, noble Rüdeger.
My lords and I have something more to say. We must speak.

What good will it do Etzel to kill us miserable exiles any-
way?   I'm in great difficulty with this shield that Lady
Gotelinde gave me to carry. I brought it peaceably into Etzel's
land, and now these Huns have hacked it to pieces.   If only
God would give me a shield as stout as the one you have in your
hand, noble Rüdeger! Then I should need no other armour in
the fight.'
'I'd gladly help you with my shield, if Kriemhilde would
allow me to offer it. But take it anyway, Hagen; carry it in your
hand, and may you bring it back to Burgundy at last.'
Their eyes filled with tears when they saw him give up his
shield so willingly. It was the last gift that Rüdeger of Beche-
laren ever made to any warrior.   Even Hagen's unbending
spirit and fierce determination were softened at this gift which
the good knight made so soon before his death. And there were
others who were saddened with him.   'May God reward you,
noble Rüdeger. There'll never be another man like you, to give
so nobly to wretched knights like us. Please God, may your
goodness live for ever.'
'This is sad news indeed,' said Hagen. 'We had enough to
bear in other ways, but to fight with our friends is too much
before God.' And the Margrave answered: 'It is a terrible thing
for me too.   'Well, there is one way I can repay you for your
gift, noble Rüdeger. Whatever these proud knights do to you,
my hand will never touch you in the battle, even if you killed all
the Burgundians one by one.'
Good Rüdeger acknowledged this with a formal bow. And
everyone wept to think that this sorrowful outcome could not be
averted by any man's efforts. The source of all virtues died with
Rüdeger.   Then Volker the minstrel was heard speaking
from the house: 'Since my companion Hagen has offered you
this truce, you can rely on the same treatment from me. You
earned it when we first arrived in this country.   And you can
be my messenger, noble Margrave. These red rings were given
to me by the Margravine, to wear in the festivities here. You can
see them yourself, and be my witness that I didn't fail her.'
'Would to God', said Rüdeger, 'the Margravine could give
you more! I shall be glad to tell my dear wife what you have said
and done, if I ever see her alive again. You can rely on me.'
Having made this promise, Rüdeger raised up his shield,
and without any further hesitation hurled himself in war-
like fashion at the guests, and laid about him savagely with

his sword.   Volker and Hagen both kept away, as they had
promised him, but he found others just as brave standing in the
door, who gave him plenty to think about.

Gunther and Gernot, with murderous intent, let him through,
like true heroes. But Giselher hung back, still uneasy. He had
not yet given up all hope of living, and so he avoided a clash with
Rüdeger.   Then the Margrave's men leapt at their enemies,
following their lord like true warriors. They split open many a
helmet and proud shield with the sharp swords they held in their
hands.   And the weary Burgundians answered with mighty
blows, well aimed and penetrating deep, through the chain mail
to the heart. They performed wonders in that battle.

Now that Rüdeger's followers had come inside, Volker and
Hagen jumped up to join in. They were giving quarter to one
man only, and they brought the blood spurting out of the
helmets in front of them.   The savage din of the swords
resounded in the hall; shield clasps flew from their mountings;
precious stones fell smashed into the blood. No one will ever
fight so fiercely again.   The Lord of Bechelaren went up and
down, facing his man with courage, and showing that day what
a brave and excellent warrior he was.

Gunther and Gernot were standing together killing hero after
hero, while another pair, Giselher and Dankwart, calmly and
resolutely dispatched scores to their graves.

Rüdeger displayed his strength, valour and the quality of his
sword, as he killed heroes in great numbers. But one of the Bur-
gundians was enraged at the sight, and Rüdeger's end drew
near.   It was Gernot the strong who called out to the Mar-
grave: 'Are you going to kill all my men, noble Rüdeger? It's
too much to bear. I can't look on any longer.   It looks as if
your gift will be turned against you, now that you've robbed me
of so many friends. Turn this way, brave and noble knight, and
I'll do my best to show myself worthy of this sword.'

There were more suits of mail to be stained with blood before
the Margrave could get through to him. But then the two men
leapt at each other, eager to win glory, and each was busy, ward-
ing off the other's mighty blows.   Their swords were so
sharp that nothing could withstand them, and Rüdeger struck
Gernot through his tough helmet, so that the blood poured
down. The brave good knight was not slow to return the
compliment.   He raised Rüdeger's gift in his hand and,
mortally wounded as he was, dealt him a blow which cut right

through his good shield, and landed on his neck. This was the death of the husband of fair Gotelinde.

Never was a generous gift so cruelly repaid, as when Gernot and Rüdeger fell dead together, killed by each other's hand. Hagen's rage boiled up at the sight of this terrible loss, and   the hero of Tronege said: 'This is a sad day for us wretched exiles. Our loss in these two is so great that their people and their lands will never recover from it. It must be repaid with the lives of Rüdeger's brave men.'

'Alas for my brother sent to his death here! Is there no end to these dreadful happenings? And I must mourn for noble Rüdeger too. A double grief for a double loss!'

When Giselher saw his brother lying dead the plight of those who were left inside grew desperate indeed. Death stalked wherever Rüdeger's followers could be found, and soon there was not a single one left alive.   Gunther and Giselher, Hagen, Dankwart and Volker, those stout-hearted warriors, went to where the two men lay, and wept bitterly.   'Yes, death is thinning us out,' said the boy Giselher. 'But leave your weeping, and come and cool your armour in the fresh air. We need a break from fighting, and I doubt if God intends to let us live much longer.'

And so they rested again, some sitting, some leaning. Rüdeger's heroes were all dead. The din had subsided. The silence lasted so long that Etzel began to be uneasy.   'What kind of service is this?' said the King's wife. 'This sort of loyalty from Rüdeger will never make our enemies pay the price. He'd rather take them safely back to Burgundy.   What was the use, King Etzel, of giving him all he wanted? Instead of avenging us, the villain is trying to make peace.' But Volker, that gentle knight, answered: 'I'm afraid you're mistaken, most noble Queen. If I dared to call such a high-born lady a liar, I should say you've vilely slandered Rüdeger. If it was peace he and his men were expecting, they didn't find it.   He followed his King's command so faithfully that he and his followers lie dead in here. You, Kriemhilde, had better look round for someone else to command. The hero Rüdeger has served you as far as a man can.   If you don't believe it, we'll show you.' And then, in their heartfelt grief,* they brought out the mutilated hero, so that the King could see him. Etzel's warriors were dismayed as never before.

When they saw the Margrave's corpse carried out, no clerk

could describe or record the contortions into which they were thrown, men and women alike, by their grief.   Etzel's sorrow was so great that the mighty King bellowed like a lion, and wailed with anguish. His wife joined him, and they gave way to uncontrolled lament for the death of good Rüdeger.

AVENTIURE 38

ALL LORD DIETRICH'S MEN ARE KILLED

Then a lamentation was raised on all sides, so great that the palace and towers resounded with the wailing. It reached the ears of one of Dietrich's men, and he hurried back with this startling news to the Prince: 'Listen, my Lord Dietrich! Never in all my life did I experience such a monstrous lamentation as I've just heard. I think King Etzel himself must have come to some harm. How else could they all be in such a state? The King, or Kriemhilde, it must be. One of them has been killed through the fury of these brave guests. Gentle knights are weeping uncontrollably.'

Then the hero of Verona said: 'Don't be too hasty, my friends. Whatever the exiled knights have done, remember how desperate they are, and let them still enjoy the truce I promised them.'

Then brave Wolfhart said: 'I'll go and find out what they've done, my Lord, and let you know the reason for this lament, when I've discovered it.'

But Lord Dietrich said: 'When a man is angry, he's liable to be brash in his speech,* and knights can easily lose their self-control. I'd rather it wasn't you who put the question to them, Wolfhart.' Instead he asked Helpfrich to hurry off and find out from Etzel's men, or from the guests themselves, what had happened. The messenger arrived on a scene of indescribable misery and asked: 'What's happened here?' One of the crowd answered: 'All happiness has been banished from the land of the Huns. Here lies Rüdeger, killed by the Burgundians. And of those he brought with him not one remains alive.' Helpfrich was horrified. He came back weeping to Dietrich, and never had he borne any message so reluctantly.

'What have you found out?' said Dietrich. 'Why are you weeping so bitterly, warrior Helpfrich?' And the noble knight answered: 'What else could I do but lament? the Burgundians have killed good Rüdeger.'

Then the hero of Verona said: 'This cannot be the will of

God. Such a brutal revenge would only please the devil. How could Rüdeger have deserved this from them? Why, I know for a fact that he loves the exiles dearly.'

Wolfhart spoke up: 'If they did kill him, every one of them will pay for it with his life. We could never hold up our heads again if we let this pass, after all that good Rüdeger has done for us.'

The Lord of the Amelungs wanted to know more details, and he sent Hildebrand to the guests to find out their version of what had happened, while he himself waited, sitting anxiously at the window. The battle-bold knight, the old soldier Hildebrand, wanted to approach the guests in a civilized manner, carrying neither shield nor weapon. But he was abused for this by his nephew. Savage Wolfhart said: 'If you go unarmed like that, you're bound to be insulted and sent back ignominiously. If you go armed, they'll treat you with more respect.'

Wisdom gave way to inexperience, and Hildebrand equipped himself accordingly. But before he knew what was happening, all Dietrich's knights were ready armed, sword in hand, much to the hero's dismay. He asked them where they thought they were going. 'We're coming with you. Perhaps if we're there, Hagen of Tronege will think twice before insulting you in his usual style.' When Hildebrand heard this he made no further objection.

Then brave Volker saw Dietrich's men of Verona in arms, sword at their side, and shield in hand; and he said to his Burgundian Lords: 'I can see Dietrich's men in warlike mood; fully armed, with their helmets on their heads. They're coming to attack us. It's beginning to look desperate for us miserable exiles.'

As he was speaking Hildebrand came up, and rested his shield on the ground at his feet. 'Good heroes, what had Rüdeger done to you?' he asked. 'My Lord Dietrich has sent me to find out if it's true, as we're told, that one of you has killed the noble Margrave. If it is, we shall never recover from the blow.'

Hagen of Tronege answered: 'The story is true. I wish, for Rüdeger's sake, that the messenger had deceived you, and he was still alive. Men and women will never cease to mourn his death.'

When they heard this confirmation of Rüdeger's death, the loyal knights lamented; tears poured down their bearded chins. Their loss was great indeed. Then Sigestab, the Duke of

Verona, said: 'This, then, is the end of the peace which Rüdeger
brought us after our suffering. The hope of every exile lies dead,
killed by you heroes.'   And warrior Wolfwin of Amelunge
said: 'If I'd seen my father slain today, my loss could not have
been greater than it is now Rüdeger is dead. And who can
comfort the good Margrave's wife?'   Then warrior Wolfhart
broke out angrily: 'Who is there now to lead the heroes in
battle, as the Margrave did so many times? Alas, noble Rüdeger,
to think that we have lost you like this!'

Wolfbrand and Helpfrich, Helmnot, and all their friends,
wept for his death. Hildebrand, too weighed down with sorrow
to ask any further, merely said: 'Well, you warriors, now do
what my lord sent me for.   Give us Rüdeger from the hall,
dead as he is, and the death of all our happiness. Let us offer
him the loyal and faithful service he always gave to us, and many
others.   We are exiles too, as he was. Why do you keep us
waiting? Let us carry him away, and pay our debt to him after
his death. Far better if we could have done it while he was still
alive.'

Then King Gunther spoke: 'I can think of no nobler thing
than the service a man renders to his dead friend. I call that true
constancy when I see it. You are right to reward him. He has
given you much happiness.'

'How long do we have to go on with these entreaties?' said
warrior Wolfhart. 'Now that you've killed the source of all our
happiness, and we can never enjoy him again, let us carry the
knight away and bury him.'

To this Volker answered: 'No one's going to give him to you.
The warrior's lying in the house where he fell mortally wounded,
into the blood. Go and fetch him yourself; and perform a service
to Rüdeger worthy of the name.'

And brave Wolfhart said: 'God knows, minstrel, you're not
wise to provoke us. You've wronged us enough already. If it
weren't for my lord, you'd find yourself in trouble. We can't do
anything because he won't let us fight.'

Then the fiddler answered: 'That's a coward's way, to do
nothing without permission. I don't call that the attitude of a
real hero.' Hagen was pleased with his friend's speech.

But Wolfhart said: 'Don't be too eager, or I'll make such a
mess of your fiddle-strings that you'll have plenty to tell them
when you get back to the Rhine. Your arrogance is more than an
honourable man can stand.'

To which the fiddler answered: 'If you take the melody out of my strings, I'll wipe the shine off your helmet before I think about riding to Burgundy.' *

At that Wolfhart made as if to spring at him, but his uncle Hildebrand held him back. 'You're mad to let yourself be carried away by childish anger. My lord would never forgive you.'

'Let the lion loose, old soldier, if he's so fierce,' said Volker the warrior. 'But once he comes within reach of me, even if he's killed the whole world single-handed, I'll hit him so hard that he'll never have a chance to tell the tale.'

Wolfhart was in a raging fury at this; he snatched up his shield and rushed off like a savage lion, with his friends hastily following behind.   But even his huge strides, as he ran towards the palace wall, were not long enough to prevent Hildebrand getting to the steps before him. The old man was determined not to let him enter the battle first; and both soon found what they were looking for from the exiles.   The old soldier Hildebrand leapt on Hagen, and their two swords resounded in their hands. They were properly roused, as anyone could see, and the air round their shields glowed fiery red.   But the men of Verona were strong enough to separate them in the confusion of the battle, and Hildebrand at once turned his attention away from Hagen. Then strong Wolfhart ran at brave Volker   and hit the fiddler on his stout helmet, so that his sword-blade sliced right through it to the metal fastenings. The brave minstrel was not slow to pay him back, and he belaboured Wolfhart till the sparks flew.   A fierce hatred burned between them as they struck fire from each other's armour—until warrior Wolfwin came between them. No one but a hero could have done such a thing.

Gunther the knight received the renowned heroes of Amelung with open arms; while Lord Giselher made their shining helmets red and dripping with blood.   Hagen's brother Dankwart was a man of fierce determination. The things he had done to Etzel's knights in the battle so far were now put in the shade, and the son of brave Aldrian fought like a madman.   Ritschart and Gerbart, Helpfrich and Wichart, had been through many hectic battles before this one, and Gunther's men were not allowed to forget it. Wolfbrand was a magnificent figure in the fight.   And old Hildebrand fought like one possessed, while knight after good knight was struck dead by Wolfhart's hand, and lay in the blood. And so the good brave knights took their revenge for Rüdeger's death.   Dietrich's nephew Sigestab fought bravely as he always did, and scores of good helmets were smashed on his enemies' heads. He fought more gloriously in this battle than ever before—   until Volker the strong saw what was happening. The hero was enraged at the stream of blood that flowed from any armour brave Sigestab touched, and he leapt towards him.   Sigestab did not last long once the fiddler brought his artistry to bear on him. He was killed by Volker's sword, and it was old Hildebrand, with his usual bravery, who avenged his death.

'Alas for my dear lord, struck down here by Volker's hand!' said the old soldier. 'This fiddler's days are numbered now.' Hildebrand the brave was more in earnest than ever before.   He dealt Volker a blow that sent the clasps from his helmet and shield flying at the palace wall. And that was the end of strong Volker, the brave minstrel.

Then Dietrich's men hurled themselves into the fight, sending bits of chain mail spinning far and wide, their sword-points flashing high in the air, as they brought a stream of hot blood from every helmet they reached.   For Hagen of Tronege the sight of Volker lying dead was the cruellest of all the losses he had suffered throughout the whole feast. And what a bitter revenge he now took for the hero's death!   'Old Hildebrand's not going to get away with that. He's killed my helper, the best comrade-in-arms I ever had.' And lifting his shield higher, he moved off with his sword flailing.

Helpfrich the strong killed Dankwart; and Gunther and Giselher were dismayed to see him go down. He had sold his life dearly however.   Meanwhile Wolfhart went backwards and forwards, cutting down Gunther's men without pause. Three times he had passed right through the hall and back, and knight after knight had fallen at his hands.   Until at last Giselher called out to him: 'I could have wished for a less savage enemy; but turn towards me, brave and noble knight. I'll help you to finish the slaughter; there must be an end to it soon.'

So Wolfhart turned to confront Giselher, and while they both continued to leave gaping wounds all round them, he fought his way so fiercely towards the King that the blood sprayed up over his head as he trod.   The son of fair Uote received the brave hero savagely, with furious blows, when he arrived. The warrior's strength could not save him. Never was such bravery seen in such a young king.   He hit Wolfhart through his breastplate, and the blood poured out. He wounded Dietrich's man to death; and he was the only knight alive who could have done it.   When brave Wolfhart felt the wound he dropped his shield, raised his sharp sword high in the air and brought it down on Giselher, slicing through helmet and mail.   This blow brought cruel death to both of them, for Dietrich's man died immediately after.* Old Hildebrand saw Wolfhart fall, and I doubt if he was ever as sad again until he died.

All Gunther's and all Dietrich's men had now been killed; and Hildebrand went over to where Wolfhart was lying in the blood. He put his arms round the good brave knight,   and would have carried him out of the house, but he was just too heavy, and he had to leave him lying there. The dying man looked up out of the blood, and saw his uncle trying to help.

And he said, mortally wounded as he was: 'My dear Uncle, this isn't the time to trouble about me. Look out for Hagen; that's more important. He has a savage heart, that man.   And if my nearest and dearest want to lament my death, tell them from me that there's no need to weep. I have fallen gloriously at the hand of a King.   And I've sold my life dearly enough here to bring tears to the eyes of many a good knight's wife. If anyone asks you, tell them I've killed a hundred or more single-handed.'

Then Hagen remembered the minstrel, robbed of his life by brave Hildebrand, and he said to the warrior: 'Now you can pay for some of the suffering you've caused me, and all the gallant knights you've taken from us.'   He rained blows on Hildebrand, and Balmung, the sword he had taken from Sifrid when he killed him, rang out for all to hear. The old man defended himself bravely enough   and brought his own broad sword, which was by no means blunt, down on the hero of Tronege. But he could not damage this man of Gunther's. Then Hagen hit him again, right through his shining breastplate,   and old Hildebrand, feeling the wound, decided he had taken enough damage from Hagen. He threw his shield over his back, and ran away, taking his gaping wound with him.

The only ones left alive out of all the warriors in the hall were Gunther and Hagen. Old Hildebrand, covered with blood, went off to take the terrible news to Dietrich.   He found him still sadly sitting. But the Prince's suffering was not yet complete, and when he saw Hildebrand in his bloody armour, he asked him anxiously what had happened: 'Tell me, old soldier,

why are you so wet with blood? Who did it? Did you fight with
the guests in the house after all? My orders were plain enough;
you were to avoid this.'

And he answered his lord: 'Hagen did it. He gave me these
wounds in the hall as I was trying to get away. I was lucky to
escape from the fiend with my life.'

The Lord of Verona said: 'You got what you deserved, for
breaking the truce I gave them. You heard me promise friend-
ship to those knights. If it wasn't such a shameful thing to do,
I'd have you put to death.'

'Don't be too angry, my Lord Dietrich. My friends and I
have suffered enough already. We wanted to carry Rüdeger's
body away, but King Gunther's men wouldn't allow it.'

'Then Rüdeger is dead? Oh, what a terrible loss! All my
sorrows are nothing compared with this misery. Noble Gotelinde
is my cousin. And what is to happen to the wretched orphans at
Bechelaren?'   Rüdeger's death brought back to Dietrich the
loyalty he had shown, and the misery they had shared, and the
hero gave way to uncontrollable grief: 'Alas for the faithful
helper I have lost. No one can ever replace him.   Do you
know now for certain, old soldier, which knight it was that
killed him?' He answered: 'Gernot the strong did this violent
deed. And he in his turn was killed by Rüdeger.'

'Then tell my men to arm themselves and prepare to follow
me. And have my shining armour brought. I myself will
question these heroes from Burgundy.'

But the old soldier Hildebrand answered: 'Who will come if I
call? All that's left of your army is standing in front of you. I'm
the only one; the others are dead.' Dietrich was shocked at this
news, as he had every reason to be,   for of all his misfortunes
this was the greatest he had yet suffered. He said: 'If all my men
are dead, then God must have forsaken me. Pity poor Dietrich,
who was once a rich, proud and powerful King!   But how
could they *all* die, all my splendid heroes, at the hands of those
battle-weary men? I thought the Burgundians were nearly
finished. But for my evil destiny, death would never have struck
my friends.   So my unhappy fate has come upon me at last!
Well, are any of the guests still alive?' And old soldier Hilde-
brand replied: 'No one, by God, but Hagen alone, and Gunther
the proud King.'

'To think that I've lost you, beloved Wolfhart! I wish
I had never been born! And Sigestab and Wolfwin, and

Wolfbrand as well! Who can help me now to come to my
country of Amelunge?   And Helpfrich the brave, he's dead
as well, you say? And Gerbart and Wichart—my mourning will
never end. Never shall I know happiness again! If only a man
could die of grief!'

AVENTIURE 39

LORD DIETRICH FIGHTS WITH GUNTHER AND HAGEN

Then Lord Dietrich fetched out his own armour, and old Hildebrand helped him to get ready. The great man lamented so violently that the whole house was filled with his voice. But his heroism returned, and he armed himself in grim earnest. He took a stout shield in his hand, and the two left immediately, he and old soldier Hildebrand.

Then Hagen of Tronege said: 'I can see Lord Dietrich coming along. He'll want to fight it out with us after the terrible losses he's suffered here. It looks as if the prize winners will be picked today. And I hope Lord Dietrich of Verona doesn't think he's so strong and fearsome that I shan't dare to face him', said Hagen, 'if he tries to take his revenge on us for what's happened.'

Dietrich and Hildebrand heard what Hagen said, and came right up to the hall, where they found the two knights standing outside, leaning against the wall. Dietrich rested his good shield on the ground. Bowed down with sorrow, Dietrich spoke: 'Why have you, Gunther, a mighty King, turned against an exile like me? Have I done you any wrong? My last consolation has been taken away from me. Killing the hero Rüdeger was too small a calamity for you: now you've robbed me of all my men. Nothing I had done to you was so terrible as to deserve this. Think of yourselves and your own sorrow; the death of your friends and your grim struggle. Doesn't it weigh you down? Then think how I must feel at the death of Rüdeger. No man ever suffered a greater loss in all the world. You didn't consider my grief, or your own. All my happiness lies dead at your hands. Never shall I finish lamenting for my people.'

'Our guilt is not so very great,' said Hagen. 'Your warriors came up to the house armed to the teeth, and in great numbers. I suspect you've been misinformed.'

'What else do you want me to believe? Hildebrand has told

214

me what I know. When my knights from Amelunge asked you to give them Rüdeger's body from the hall, you threw insults down at the brave heroes instead.'

The King of the Rhine answered: 'They said they wanted to carry Rüdeger away, and I withheld my permission more as a gesture against Etzel than against your men. Then Wolfhart became abusive.'

At which the hero of Verona said: 'It doesn't make any difference. Gunther, noble King, remember what you stand for, and make good the wrongs you've done me. Offer me a recompense I can accept.   If you consent to be my prisoner, together with your man, I will make sure, as far as is in my power, that you come to no harm from anyone here among the Huns. You will find me loyal and true.'

'God forbid', said Hagen, 'that two warriors should give themselves up while they're still standing armed and unbeaten in front of you, and still free to come and go without asking their enemies.'

'I should advise you not to refuse,' said Dietrich. 'Both of you, Gunther and Hagen, have given me so much offence and sorrow, that it would be only just for you to make it good.   You can have my faithful assurance, and I'll give you my hand on it, that I'll ride home with you to your own country. I'll give you a safe-conduct, or die in the attempt. And my own great sorrow will be put aside to save you.'

But Hagen said: 'You can give up that idea. A fine story it would make, two brave knights like us surrendering to you without a fight! We don't fit the part. And as far as I can see, you've only got Hildebrand at your side.'

Then old soldier Hildebrand spoke up: 'By God, Hagen, the time will come when you'll be glad to accept a settlement from anyone who's prepared to give it. You'd be well advised to welcome my lord's offer now!'

'You know, old Hildebrand, I think I'd be more likely to accept such an offer even than to run away out of a room as disgracefully as you did out of this one. I'd always thought you weren't afraid to face your enemies.'

Hildebrand answered: 'What right have you to criticize me? Who was it sat on his shield near the Wasgenstein, and watched Walther of Spain killing all his friends? You've done enough discreditable things in your time.'

But Lord Dietrich interrupted: 'I don't like to hear heroes

squabbling like old women. Hildebrand, I forbid you to say any more. I have too much real sorrow to bear in my exile.   Well, warrior Hagen, what was it you bold knights said to each other when you saw me coming, fully armed? Didn't I hear you say you wanted to take me on in single combat?'

'You did, and no one denies it,' said Warrior Hagen. 'I'll try my luck against you, and my blows won't be gentle ones, unless the sword of Nibelung lets me down. Asking both of us to give ourselves up was a good way of making me angry.'

When Dietrich heard the fierce determination in Hagen's voice, he quickly snatched up his shield. Hagen leapt down the steps, and fell on him in a flash, while the good sword of Nibelung clanged on Dietrich's armour.   Lord Dietrich could see well enough that the brave man was in a savage mood, and he was content to defend himself against his wild blows. He knew this gentle knight Hagen of old.   He was also afraid of Balmung, which was no ordinary sword; but by dealing a skilful blow from time to time, he did overcome Hagen in the end. For he opened a great gaping wound eventually,   and thought to himself: 'You're exhausted from long fighting. It would be no honour to kill you now. I'll see if I can overpower you and take you prisoner.' It was a dangerous thing to do.

He dropped his shield, and grasped Hagen with all the strength of his mighty arms. And so the brave man was subdued, much to noble Gunther's dismay.   Then Dietrich bound Hagen, and led him to the noble Queen. The bravest knight that ever carried a sword was given into her hand, and her great sorrow was turned to happiness.   Joyfully the wife of Etzel showed her thanks: 'God save you, body and soul! You've made up for all my misery. I'll never cease to show my gratitude till death prevents me.'

And Lord Dietrich said: 'Let him live, noble Queen. If you give him the opportunity, you'll see how handsomely he atones for all he has done to you. Don't take advantage of him, now he's your prisoner.'

She ordered Hagen to be taken to his dungeon, where he lay in chains, and hidden from sight. And the noble King Gunther called out: 'Where has the hero of Verona gone? He must answer to me for this deed.'

Then Lord Dietrich went towards him. Gunther's courage was renowned, and without waiting any longer, he ran out in front of the hall. A tremendous clashing of swords arose.   Lord

Dietrich may have had a long and glorious career behind him, but Gunther was so mad with rage, and his hatred was so bitter after his terrible loss, that people still say it was a wonder Dietrich survived.   There was plenty of strength and courage on both sides. Palace and towers resounded as they hacked at each other's stout helmets. King Gunther was filled with heroism.   But eventually Dietrich overcame him just the same as Hagen. The blood poured out through his chain mail, set free by the sharp sword in Dietrich's hand. Lord Gunther, for all his weariness, had defended himself very creditably.

He too was bound by Dietrich, although kings should not by rights suffer such indignity; but Dietrich was afraid the King and his man would kill everyone in sight if he let them go free.   Dietrich of Verona took him by the hand, and led him bound before Kriemhilde. Her cares fell from her, to see him brought so low, and she said: 'Welcome, Gunther of Burgundy.'

He answered: 'My dear sister, I might be more thankful if your greeting were more friendly. But I know the hatred you really feel; there's no warmth in your welcome for Hagen and me.'

Then the hero of Verona said: 'Noble Queen, never before were such good knights taken prisoner, as the ones I make over to you now. Proud Lady, let these wretched exiles draw some comfort from my protection.'

She said she would be glad to, and Dietrich wept as he left them. But Etzel's wife went on to take a savage revenge on those matchless heroes. She killed them both.   To spare them nothing, she threw them into separate dungeons, and refused to let them see each other, until the time came to show Hagen her brother's head. She had her full revenge on both of them.

Then she went to Hagen, and addressed him with savage hatred: 'If you give me back what you took from me, you may yet come back to Burgundy alive.'

Fierce Hagen answered: 'Noble Queen, you're wasting your breath. I've sworn never to reveal the treasure to anyone, as long as any of my lords are alive.'

'I'll soon finish that,' said the noble woman, and ordered her brother to be killed. They cut off his head, and she held it by the hair in front of Hagen. The hero of Tronege was sad.

When he saw his lord's head, he said to Kriemhilde in his distress: 'So, you've finished it as you wanted to; and everything has turned out as I thought it would.   Now the noble

King of the Burgundians is dead; and young Giselher, and Lord Gernot. No one knows where the treasure is hidden but God and me. And it'll be safe from you for ever, you fiend.'

She said: 'So this is all you have to offer me in recompense? Then I'll claim Sifrid's sword at least. My sweet husband, for whom I suffered such grief because of you, was wearing it when I saw him for the last time.'

She drew the sword from its sheath (he was powerless to stop her) and resolved to rob the knight of his life. She raised it in her hands, and struck off his head. King Etzel was sad to see it.

'Alas!' said the Prince. 'The best warrior who ever fought or carried a shield is struck down by a woman's hand. It hurts me to see it, although I was his enemy.'

But old Hildebrand said: 'She's not going to get away with it, whatever happens to me afterwards. How could she dare to strike him? He may have given me pain and trouble, but I'll avenge the brave Troneger's death all the same.' Angrily he leapt at Kriemhilde, and swung his heavy sword at the Queen. Then she knew what terror was, as Hildebrand attacked her; but it made no difference, however loud she screamed.

And so the whole ill-fated company were dead, and a noble woman hacked to pieces. Dietrich and Etzel wept for the relatives and men they had lost.

A glorious way of life had died with them, and all the people were wrapped in misery and grief. And so the King's feast ended in sorrow, as happiness always does at the last.

I can't tell you what happened after that, except that knights and ladies and young boys could be seen weeping for the death of their friends.

My story ends here: that was the fate of the Nibelungs.

NOTES

AVENTIURE 1

10, 3. 'Honour' (MHG *êre*) was less restricted in meaning at this time. It included 'reputation, standing and position'.

11. These various functions are not very clearly differentiated. For 'treasurer' (MHG *kameraere*) cf. M-S. Comm. 531, 2. A 'marshal' (MHG *marschalc*) seems to have been a sort of quartermaster. Cf. 1424; 1622.

13. There is an old MHG lyric poem which uses the same image of someone (male or female) training a falcon, only to lose it when the process is complete. The 'training' of Sifrid assumes great importance later on in the NL, where he is used for various predatory expeditions, and finally lost through Kriemhilde's own fault.

AVENTIURE 2

22, 4. Here, as in 26, 3–4, de Boor offers an emasculated translation, apparently on the assumption that sex and Sifrid are incompatible. For further evidence to the contrary, compare Gunther's warning, 655.

43, 3–4. An interesting and ominous preference (see Av. 3), which may also be taken as a flat description of Sifrid's political function.

AVENTIURE 3

59, 2. MHG *selbe zwelfte* usually means '12 including me', but see 64.

59, 3. I have taken MHG *dar* to mean 'thus far'. But cf. de Boor's note.

121, 4. Or: 'My lords haven't done anything to deserve this.' The version offered here, which involves reading MHG *heten* as pret. subj. (instead of pret. indic., de Boor), and puts less strain on *solher*, is as likely on linguistic grounds, and means more.

131, 4. Cf. 224, 4.

136. This speech is a string of *minnesanc* clichés. Cf. also 224, 4.

AVENTIURE 4

181, 2. Here, as in 88, 1, *helfe* can be taken in its usual sense of 'help'. Bartsch gave 'unaccompanied' for *âne alle helfe*, 88, 1, which is an unnecessary but harmless extension of the literal 'unaided'. De Boor applies this suggestion to the present passage (passed over by Bartsch), and discovers in it a comparison between the knightly discipline of the Burgundians and the unruly masses of the Saxons. It seems pointless to introduce a motif which finds no echo elsewhere in the Saxon war episode, especially when an unforced reading makes good sense. Cf. 1778, 4.

209, 3. I have translated de Boor's text, taking *wisser* as pret. subj., although his suggested emendation of *wol* to *niht* would perhaps make better sense.

221, 2–3. De Boor's note is unnecessary embroidery. The text is as bald and non-committal as the translation offered here.

224, 4. The terminology here, and throughout the courtship of Sifrid and Kriemhilde, is part of a convention of courtly love, treated at length in *minnesanc*. It is sickly and stylized. The fact that it is also rather startling so soon after the Saxon blood-bath is usually put down to the poet's own inveterate courtliness, together with that of his audience. From a less prejudiced point of view, the sight of Sifrid the Terrible billing and cooing has an ominous inappropriateness which foreshadows his final expulsion and ritual murder by the court. See GLL. vol. xiv, pp. 265 ff. In any case, the terms chosen in English are intended to cause some indigestion.

246, 4. The word *verklagen* can mean 'to mourn', or 'to stop mourning', depending on the context. In 269, 3 the second meaning only is possible. Here, there may be some doubt. See de Boor's note.

252, 2. Or: 'beds were found . . .'

AVENTIURE 5
287, 4. The phrase *in hôhen zühten* is usually rendered as: 'with high good breeding', or some such formula expressing courtliness (see de Boor's note). But the word *zuht* also has connotations of 'training' and 'punishment'.

296, 4. Literally: 'never before had a hero given such good service to (or: in the hope of winning) a Queen'.

307, 1–2. Or: 'taking part in anything that was suggested'.

310. Gunther's speech is strained and tortuous. Compare Sifrid's natural generosity in stanzas 314–15.

AVENTIURE 6
325, 1–2. The MHG word means 'brand-new' or 'red-hot'. It is not clear who these maidens were, nor whether a particular piece of news or a string of such reports is referred to. The English has been left as ambiguous as possible.

329. Gunther's inflated style is in nice contrast to his actual achievements, and to the answer of Sifrid (330), who in fact has to do all the work. Compare also his use of inept clichés in 334, where the real fate of Sifrid and Kriemhilde adds bitterness to his fatuous well-wishes.

343, 4. The rather pompous use of one's own name is characteristic of Gunther and Kriemhilde (e.g. 355, 4).

386, 2. The archaic nature of the expression *helede maere* is usually commented on. More interesting is the striking discrepancy between such heroic appellations and the ignominious impotence which follows, and which Sifrid must foresee.

AVENTIURE 7
428, 3. The word here and in 416, 1 is *gewant*, which can be used of civil or military articles of dress. It is difficult to render in English ('rig' or 'equipment' are perhaps near), but the ambiguity is functional.

AVENTIURE 8

483. The translation ignores the usual full-stop after *grôz*.

485, 1. The MHG word (here and in 928, 3 and 986, 2) is *wert*, which appears to have meant any stretch of land surrounded, or nearly surrounded, by water or marsh.

496, 4. The *zuht* of this line is the same as that of line 497, 4, and means his 'heavy hand'. It is true that *zühte* often means 'courtly education', but there is nothing courtly about Sifrid at the moment. He has excellent reasons for not killing the dwarf, and this generosity of his is a characteristic which Gunther, who is nothing if not courtly, lacks by comparison. Cf. 315.

511, 4. De Boor's comment is entirely misleading.

515, 2. The expression *underwant* only occurs twice in the NL; here and in 1132, 3. Both actions are high-handed and unpleasant. The translation 'took charge of' is not satisfactory. Perhaps 'collared' would be nearer.

AVENTIURE 9

531, 2. See de Boor's note. I have taken *kameraere* in the sense of 'treasurer' because there are parallels between Hagen's attitude to the Nibelung treasure and his 'protection' of the Burgundians'. He destroys both . See M-S. Comm. 1746,4.

538, 1. It makes better sense to follow Colleville and Tonnelat (taking *niht* as a noun), than to accept Bartsch's rather tortuous *apo koinou*.

574, 4. Bartsch rendered the phrase: *er waere in swachem muote* as 'he would have been a fool'. Colleville and Tonnelat agree. But *muot* does not usually refer to intelligence.

AVENTIURE 10

684, 4. Literally: 'And he certainly gave her what he was fated to give her,'

686, 4. Or: 'The show was on a grand scale.'

AVENTIURE 11

719, 3. The basic sense of *biderbe* is 'respectable, honest, hard-working'

AVENTIURE 12

725, 3. Or: 'that Sifrid rendered her no feudal obligations'. But *dienen* is not necessarily so restricted. It is widely used in erotic contexts, for instance.

AVENTIURE 13

778, 4. Or: 'never did horses carry so many rich clothes'.

779, 1. Literally: 'Many articles of luggage were transported.'

788, 3. 'Boisterous' is an attempt to render MHG *ungefüege*, the basic meaning of which is 'socially unacceptable'.

804, 1–2. Usually dismissed as a pointless episode, merely serving to show the scale of hospitality offered. But cf. 968.

AVENTIURE 14

814, 1. *ungemach*, as de Boor points out, does not refer to the quarrel, but to the knightly commotion preceding it. The ominous undertone remains, however.

821, 3. The word *eigen* ('own') is often used in the sense of 'bondsman, vassal', but its meaning is wider, and includes anything possessed. Cf. 1741, 3.

842, 4. Or: 'to keep faith with you as an intimate friend'. Cf. 1100, 3.

848, 3. Or: 'I will find out', taking *kum* as future.

850, 2. Literally: 'It was good (or trusty) enough', echoing the words of the narrator in stanza 680.

AVENTIURE 16

947, 1. The word is *hergesellen*, recalling Sifrid's annoyance at being done out of a real fight.

969, 3. The line makes better sense if Bartsch's brackets are ignored.

AVENTIURE 19

1119, 4. MHG *truoc* can mean either 'carried' (as translated here) or 'wore'.

1132, 3. Cf. 515, 2.

AVENTIURE 20

1192, 4. I have translated *ze werbenne* as literally as possible, in spite of the rather puzzling note in de Boor's edition.

1201, 4. The MHG is not clear as to who had previously served whom. I have chosen the alternative which seems to make better sense.

1224. The translation offered is rather free.

1250, 3. The word used here and in 1254, 1 is *minnen*, which de Boor glosses as 'marry'. In fact, it includes most sorts of sex-relationship, including marriage, and is roughly co-extensive with NE 'love'.

1266, 4. I have followed Colleville and Tonnelat here, against de Boor's note.

1281, 1. The translation is rather free. Literally: 'Fierce Hagen's power (or violence) seemed too strong to her.'

AVENTIURE 21

1294, 4. Literally: 'turned back from her (i.e. Kriemhilde)'.

1312, 4. The MHG word for 'exile' is *ellende*. It is widely used for 'homeless, wretched, miserable' in contexts where physical exile plays no part. In the NL it is applied to all the strangers (Burgundians, Rüdeger, Dietrich) at Etzel's court. Some of these, like Dietrich, are real exiles; others, like Kriemhilde, appear to have come of their own accord. In any case, they are all far from home, and all to be wretched sooner or later.

AVENTIURE 22

1355. The translation is rather free, but the MHG is clear enough.

1357, 2. Literally: 'on costly upholsterings'.

1358, 3. The MHG word *dâ*, translated 'while', really means 'where' and could even have the force of 'since'.

1362. The whole stanza is translated rather freely.

1379, 4. Literally: 'Helche's household, which the lady had previously had in her care . . .'

AVENTIURE 23

1389, 3. *Die site* can also be taken as plural: 'the customs of the court'. The alternative usage followed here is widespread, and seems more likely as far as the sense is concerned, especially as Herrât's attachment to Helche is offered in explanation of her function as instructress. It is true, however, that *site* is usually masc. in the NL.

AVENTIURE 24

1467-8. The second person plural, which is used throughout these two stanzas, could refer to Gunther alone, especially as he is the only one of the Kings who actually has a wife (1468, 3). Against this can be put: (1) MHG *wîp* does not necessarily mean a wedded wife. (2) By the end of the speech at least the address is plural (*herren*: 'My Lords'). (3) Rumold's response to tragedy is inadequate, inept and generalized. His remarks are not precisely relevant to anything but his own healthy preoccupations.

1492, 4. Literally: 'They could receive it gladly: it was given in good faith.' De Boor translates *mit triuwen* ('in good faith') as: 'in gratitude for the good news'. This strains the MHG, and removes the contrast between Uote's unforced behaviour and that of her sons.

AVENTIURE 25

1510, 2-3. Literally: 'he doesn't know how to tell when his honour is complete (or intact)'.

1575, 4. The MHG *gotes arm* can be used as a compound adjective, meaning 'wretched', rather like the NE 'godforsaken'. I have translated it literally, because its application to a priest would in any case revive something of the original force of 'God'.

1576, 4. The MHG is ambiguous. Either: 'But Hagen was determined to do him harm,' or: 'But Giselher couldn't stop Hagen without a fight.' What is clear is that Giselher is strongly and ineffectually against Hagen's action.

AVENTIURE 26

1625, 1-3. Literally: 'It seems you despise my being with you, when (or where) your armour became (or was) so red with blood.' Depending on the force given to *versmâhen* ('despise') and *wurden* ('became' or 'was'), Gunther can either be complaining that Hagen scorned his help in a fight, or objecting to the whole incident.

1634, 4. The episode is sometimes taken as an exercise in courtly magnanimity towards an adversary. It can also be read as a friendly, if contemptuous, warning to a potential ally.

AVENTIURE 27

1669, 4. Literally: 'and she knew how to deserve (or win) it: she was proud and confident (or assured)'.

1673, 2. Or: 'girls were'. Rüdeger's daughter would not have come back alone, but she is singled out for attention.

1680, 4. The pathetic nature of this meaningless ritual comes out clearly in the original, where hackneyed term follows hackneyed term.

1692, 4. Or: 'he insisted on pleasing everyone'.

1715. It is not clear whether another set of messengers is meant, or whether these are the same singular messenger who rode through Austria in the previous stanza.

AVENTIURE 28

1746, 4. MHG *kameraere*. See note to 531, 2.

AVENTIURE 29

1770, 4. MHG *under krône* ('crowned, wearing my crown'). Attention is usually drawn to the official capacity she intends to assume in order to be formally insulted. But there is also an element of showing off her achievements to her family. Hagen's refusal to stand up (1781–2) is a personal rebuff as well as a public provocation. Compare Volker's readiness to be impressed (1780).

AVENTIURE 30

1821, 4. Literally: 'They are all called warriors, and (or but) do not think and feel the same.'

1837, 1. Or perhaps: 'I doubt if such a thing ever happened before.'

AVENTIURE 31

1888, 4. The MHG is ambiguous. It could also mean: 'Gunther's men are not being praised as they should.'

1899, 2. The MHG is ambiguous. I have followed Colleville and Tonnelat, against de Boor, who reads: 'fear of Kriemhilde's plans oppressed them'.

1900, 4. The MHG is ambiguous. Either: 'they have never been conquered before', or: 'they aren't finished yet'.

1919, 4. *Ze kurzewîle guot* is sometimes taken to mean 'in a mood to joke'. But the usual meaning of *kurzewîle* in the NL is 'entertainment', 'relaxation'. Hagen is here refusing to accept Etzel's friendly and hospitable attempts at entertainment.

AVENTIURE 32

1932, 3. It is not clear whether these five hundred were Huns or Burgundians. Probably Huns, compare stanza 1933.

1950, 3. The MHG *hôher stân* often means 'retreat, give way', but here it can be presumably be taken literally as well, or even as a pun.

AVENTIURE 33

1981, 1. Following de Boor and MS.C. MS.B., which is the basis of de Boor's edition, has *Rîne* ('of the Rhine') instead of *Berne* ('of Verona'). The meaning would be: 'While Gunther was watching Hagen . . .'.

AVENTIURE 34

2020, 1. MHG *trôst* can either mean 'comfort', or by extension 'comforter, protector'. The second is more common in the NL, but the first seems to make better sense here.

AVENTIURE 36

2103, 1. Usually taken to mean that Kriemhilde has no pity in her. But the MHG *ungenâde ich hân* could also mean 'pity was never given me'. I have tried to preserve the ambiguity.

2104, 4. The MHG is ambiguous. It could also mean: 'I will discuss the possibility of an agreement with these heroes'.

AVENTIURE 37

2232, 2. The MHG is ambiguous. It could also mean: 'in order to cause Kriemhilde sorrow'.

AVENTIURE 38

2240, 1–3. The syntax is loose. Another reading would be: 'If an angry man is asked a brash question, there's likely to be trouble.'

2270, 3–4. Literally: 'the shine on your helmet will be made dim by my hand, whatever I do about riding to Burgundy'.

2298, 2. The MHG is ambiguous. It could also mean: 'and all Dietrich's men were now dead', with *mêre* as subject of *lebte*.